THE
BROKEN
WEATHERVANE

I0587852

Award-winning Author
Laura DeNooyer

Scrivenings
PRESS
Quench your thirst for story.
www.ScriveningsPress.com

Published by Scrivenings Press LLC
15 Lucky Lane
Morrilton, Arkansas 72110
https://ScriveningsPress.com

Printed in the United States of America

Paperback ISBN 978-1-64917-496-3

eBook ISBN 978-1-64917-497-0

Editor: Linda Fulkerson

Cover design by Linda Fulkerson - www.bookmarketinggraphics.com

"Laura DeNooyer has once again charmed us in *The Broken Weathervane* with engaging characters, historical authenticity and a sprinkling of literary quotations fitting for the characters and the time period. Mix in family secrets, an understanding of mental illness and a love story or two and DeNooyer has given us another winner!"

—JANE KIRKPATRICK, BESTSELLING AUTHOR
OF *ACROSS THE CRYING SANDS*

"*The Broken Weathervane* surprised me in the best way. It was engaging, heartfelt, and avoided cliches and easy answers. I loved how the characters were complex and authentic. I recommend this story to fans of Amanda Cox and Sara Brunsvold."

—KATIE POWNER, CHRISTY AWARD-WINNING AUTHOR
OF *WHEN THE ROAD COMES AROUND*

"This beautifully written novel follows Leslie Wickersham, a grant writer who has always tried to hide her grandparents' complicated past, until she ends up working for an academic whose research threatens to expose everything—and whose presence in her life becomes impossible to ignore. *The Broken Weathervane* is a bittersweet story about family secrets, reluctant love, and how the past refuses to stay buried."

—SUZANNE WOODS FISHER, BESTSELLING AUTHOR
OF *THE MOONLIGHT SCHOOL*

"DeNooyer crafts a compelling story exploring sensitive issues of mental illness and the desire to protect those we love. Her tender portrayals and raw relationships offer readers a heartfelt story of hope and healing."

—SARAH LOUDIN THOMAS, AWARD-WINNING AUTHOR OF *THESE TANGLED THREADS*

"Laura DeNooyer winds a unique and mesmerizing strand of story DNA, as she entwines captivating characters, complex plot, and compelling literary beauty in *The Broken Weathervane*. While she tackles issues of mental illness trauma in a true way that displays both our innate human frailty and beautiful fullness, DeNooyer writes with grace and depth. Most importantly, the story doesn't fail to culminate in hope and compassion. With her signature style, complicated relationships are explored and the past is unraveled, and DeNooyer drops mentions of other literary works like sweet lemon drops to savor along the way. Readers will relish this enthralling story."

—NAOMI MUSCH, HISTORICAL FICTION AUTHOR AND AWARD FINALIST FOR *SEASON OF MY ENEMY*, *THE ANGEL AND THE SKY PILOT* (COURTING THE COUNTRY PREACHER), AND *MIST O'ER THE VOYAGEUR*

To my dad, who told me the story of how his dad and uncle loved their brother well.

"The highest form of knowledge is empathy, for it requires us to suspend our egos and live in another's world."

— BILL BULLARD, MEMOIRIST

"Educating the mind without educating the heart is no education at all."

— ARISTOTLE

"Empathy is the only human superpower—it can shrink distance, cut through social and power hierarchies, and transcend differences."

— ELIZABETH THOMAS, ACTRESS

"Education is for improving the lives of others and for leaving your community and world better than you found it."

— MARIAN WRIGHT EDELMAN

Chapter One

2015

All washed up at age thirty-five.

The premonition rumbled through Leslie Wickersham like a morose headline announcing her dismal future. Seated in the office of Raymond University's administration building, Leslie Wickersham squinted at the framed quotation above the clock.

Time is too slow for those who wait, too swift for those who fear, too long for those who grieve, too short for those who rejoice, but for those who love, time is eternity.
—*Henry Van Dyke*

Its pithy wisdom churned her stomach. If she weren't awaiting her third interview, she'd snap a picture, post it on Instagram, and ask, "Is time a friend or an enemy?"

Instead, she stared at the clock as if the hands had stopped at the hour of someone's death, like back in the day. Perhaps this moment marked the demise of her career. Tomorrow she might be bagging groceries at Klipton's.

Her phone pinged. Grimacing, she grabbed it from her purse to silence it. One look revealed a text from Vic, her ex. Ugh. She'd blocked him, so he must have a new number. She plunged the silenced phone back into her purse and wiped her sweaty palms.

An attractive man, perhaps early forties, with golden brown, windblown hair swaggered to the counter, a hint of Old Spice wafting. His presence engulfed the room the way a lake sunrise fills both sky and water, silently relishing its own brilliance. A plaid scarf circled his neck. Bronze whiskers framed his square jaw.

His voice affirmed his virtuosity as a lecturer. "Maggie, has anyone approved my proposal yet?"

The gray-haired administration assistant stiffened. "I'm sorry, Dr. Stafford. We're still in the hiring process." She glanced at Leslie. "I'll call when I have news."

Was this the inimitable Gregory Stafford?

Leslie expected to see him, but not so soon. Her muscles tensed. Four years ago, when freelancing, she'd sought him for an interview as the renowned expert on the Buckwalter family. He'd thoroughly rebuffed her email with choice words about the magazine she wrote for. He deemed the publication *as inconsequential as a dog scratching fleas.* But what did Gregory Scott Stafford, PhD, know? That magazine had far more readers than his lofty academic articles did.

Lofty but eloquent. She knew them well, having read several.

Dr. Stafford followed the direction of Maggie's glance and nodded at Leslie. His green eyes briefly lit, but his stiff "How do you do?" left Leslie cold. His attention returned to Maggie.

Déjà vu. Another dismissive gesture.

He pulled a worn calendar from his bag as if he hadn't yet joined the 21st century. "What's the holdup? My grant proposal has a deadline." When he clapped the countertop, Maggie flinched. He strutted out the door.

Leslie exhaled as if Dr. Stafford's judgments had been directed at her.

"Leslie?" The provost appeared from around the corner. His deep voice and wizened face made up for his shorter stature.

Leslie approached him, hand outstretched. "I'm honored to meet you, Provost Martin."

He gave a hearty handshake. "At least you didn't call me Dr. Martens, like the shoes. Unlike our last candidate." He chuckled.

His humor eased her anxiety, but interviews were not her forte. *Inhale, exhale.* Time to ramp up the fake confidence.

In his office, he sat across from her at his desk. "It's good to finally meet you." He scanned her resume. "I'm impressed with your experience as an educator, editor, and grant proposal evaluator. Eighteen out of twenty grants were accepted."

"I was grateful to help those projects receive funds. Each worthy in its own right."

"But the best project in the world won't receive funds without a flawless presentation." He knuckled the desktop. "I once facilitated a board that gave funds to study the mating habits of hummingbirds over one that assessed additional uses of whale oil for machinery and lubricating spacecraft. It boiled down to presentation over practicality."

Leslie smiled. Did practicality matter at universities? "True. That's why I started my own business, helping people put their best foot forward."

He riffled through her application. "Considering all your accolades, what do you perceive is your greatest weakness?"

This question she hated. Her jaw twitched. "Self-criticism, second-guessing myself."

"What do you do then?"

"Call my best friend, then apply creative problem-solving skills." She cited examples.

"Which book should everyone read? Fiction or non-fiction."

This question she loved. She plunged ahead. "*To Kill a Mockingbird*. The hero chooses to fight a losing battle but proceeds because it's the right thing to do. The issues are just as relevant today. And *story* is my preferred method for inspiring someone to empathy and action, whether it's the failing hero, the persecuted African American, or the slighted Boo Radleys."

"Excellent." He checked the resume again. "BA double major in Communications and Secondary Education in Literature. With your teaching background, you'll have no difficulty transitioning from social service projects to scholarly ones." He removed his glasses and wiped the lenses. "How badly do you want this role, Leslie?"

Not the time to admit she was at wits' end finding a suitable job. "My previous positions dovetail perfectly into this one, Dr. Martin. I love this small, historic university in the heart of Avondale." With only 3,000 students, Raymond University was primarily a liberal arts college with recent additions of post-graduate degrees in engineering and business administration. Perhaps humor would calm her thumping heart. "But I wouldn't rob a bank for it."

"I'm glad you're not *that* desperate." He chortled. "You have an impressive online presence via Facebook, Instagram, Pinterest, plus a blog and podcast."

"Yes, sir." Her mind raced. Had he heard her phone ping earlier? Had she inadvertently posted something controversial, degrading, or offensive? Did she post too many baby animal gifs? Oh, dear. Hold on. She was jumping to conclusions. Self-criticism escalating to mental self-flagellation. Case in point.

"Seems folks hang on your every word. Why?"

Swallowing, she straightened. "I want to reduce the stigma of mental illness. After helping Avondale High School obtain a grant for a mental health initiative, I built a platform to create awareness and direct people to community resources."

"In the name of altruism?"

"Getting paid would've been a bonus. My reward was watching attitudes change and students begin therapy. It started while teaching students with depression, OCD, and other ailments. They floundered in the classroom. They were bullied too."

"Ah, the Boo Radleys. Tell me about the grant."

"It involved writing curriculum tied to literature for discussing current treatments and fighting stigma." She mentioned research she'd gathered to convince potential funders of the need, including her survey of thirty schools.

He nodded. "An impressive endeavor."

"My podcast continued the conversation. I interviewed faculty and students from high schools around the country."

"Well done. Raymond University's on the cutting edge, too —of a different sort." Again, he wiped his glasses. "We're combining scholarly research with community interests. Rather than focus on faculty publishing only in scholarly journals that comprise less than point zero zero one percent of the population, the powers that be insist we become more consumer-friendly."

"How?" Wasn't it enough that Raymond University still had an English major while much of academia shut down humanities to focus on STEM?

"The board wants scholarly events to create public interest. Partnering with local organizations. Hosting relevant panel discussions. And using social media to the university's advantage."

Cutting edge or dead end? That would require periodically stepping down from Mt. Olympus. "How do professors feel about it?" Perhaps it was like handing out plebeian doughnuts versus French croissants at a fancy bakery.

"The majority are onboard. Our social media coordinator handles communication, but one man is going for full professor promotion and needs a boost in community outreach. Of which social media is a means." He leaned forward. "This is how you can serve us, Leslie, as a side hustle. You'd be compensated. On top of being the grants officer."

An image of a stodgy, accomplished professor hunched over a smartphone posting Instagram images elicited a smile. Like imagining him in dinosaur pajamas. Perhaps this additional task was the reason the provost wanted to meet her in person. "Would I monitor his social media or teach him how?"

"Both, until skills are mastered. For planning community events, you'll brainstorm together, identifying where his expertise overlaps the common good." He adjusted his glasses. "Your superintendent gave glowing reviews of your classroom performance. I'm guessing you miss the classroom?"

She shuddered inwardly. Was this a veiled attempt to learn why she'd left her previous job? No way would she allude to her burnout due to marital problems. On top of his emotional abuse, Vic had an affair. Leslie left him after one year of marriage. Spiteful, he milked her for every shared penny. Her life spiraled out of control.

What had Vic texted earlier? She'd have to block his new number.

"I miss the student rapport," she replied. "As Instructional Designer, I enjoyed writing the mental health curriculum."

Though another teacher implemented it when she couldn't. "But I was ready for new challenges. While teaching, I'd accumulated enough accounts to freelance in writing grant proposals." And considered supplementing her income by bagging groceries. "I love helping people submit proposals that contribute to community welfare."

Provost Martin explained more about the grants officer role. She'd facilitate proposals of 150 full-time faculty members in all departments, tracking deadlines and submissions for federal and privately funded sources. "Instructors are welcoming someone to spearhead the grant supervision. With your skillset, Leslie, you've much to offer Raymond University. On behalf of President Wilson and myself, I'm delighted to offer you the role of grants officer. And social media overseer for one." He presented a contract.

A real contract—finally! Did the room just brighten from her grin? "Thank you. Which professor will I work with, regarding outreach?"

He clucked his tongue. "The most reluctant one, but he's motivated, just one semester from becoming full professor. Dr. Gregory Stafford."

What? She blinked as if nudged from a dream. Anyone but him. Shame flushed her face from his crisp greeting earlier. And the patronizing way he'd turned down her interview request. Would he remember? Her saving grace was that she'd used her married name then. Leslie Rinaldi. Since they'd only emailed, he wouldn't recognize her.

"Does he know you're hiring me to assist him?" Plebeian doughnuts. Stale ones. Without any chocolate frosting, glaze, or sprinkles.

"He knows he'll have help but doesn't know who'll have the pleasure."

Great. Pleasure was not the word that came to mind. "Any suggestions for warming him up to the idea?"

"That's in your wheelhouse. No doubt you have the savvy for such a task."

She eyed the contract again. No obligation to sign it.

He stood. "Before you go, I'd like to introduce you to Dr. Stafford."

Her heart thunked her rib cage as if seeking an escape. But how could she refuse without resembling a timid dog slinking away?

They donned coats for a brisk January walk. Outside, the provost pointed out campus landmarks. Leslie's head spun.

In Worthington Hall's English Department, they stood at an office doorway. And there he was. Gregory Scott Stafford stepped toward them. His tousled hair, bristly chin, and two parallel ends of a plaid scarf lent an air of avant-garde and youth, despite his forty-plus status. The walls boasted a combination of literature quotes and baseball hats. Milwaukee Brewers pennants cascaded from the ceiling as if celebrating the accomplishments heralded by three framed diplomas—from Duke, Harvard, and Oxford.

Near the bookshelf, looking out of place, hung a rustic metal rooster. Odd.

Provost Martin gestured. "This is Ms. Leslie Wickersham, our top candidate for grants officer, soon to join us, assuming I've been convincing enough." He introduced Dr. Stafford, professor of twentieth-century American literature. "And avid Brewers fan."

The professor's seafoam eyes mesmerized her. He offered his hand. "And in dire need of a grants officer so I can continue following my passion. I saw you earlier. You'll be a welcome addition."

Would he recant once he recalled their email exchange?

Assuming he remembered. Engulfed in his spicy cologne, Leslie reciprocated, her fingers lost in a warm, firm handshake. "A pleasure to meet you, Dr. Stafford. Are you referring to your research on the Linus Fritz Buckwalter family?"

"Ah, you've done your homework. Yes, I hope to follow one more family branch to complete my extensive, certified biography." He'd been working on that biography four years ago. And she knew exactly which branch he referred to.

"When did you start researching the Buckwalters?"

"It's a lifelong dream, ever since reading *The Broken Weathervane* as a teen. I was smitten. Have you read his works?"

"Yes, all twelve novels. He's a fascinating man. I'm guessing you know which aspects of his life experience wound up in his fiction."

"With his tendency to exaggerate, it's hard telling. As good ole Fritz said, 'Hyperbole is wed to one's deepest dreams. The more far-fetched, the more tethered to reality.'"

One of many familiar quips. She gestured toward a photo on the wall, two men shaking hands. "You got to meet him."

The provost intervened. "Good to know you have common ground. That'll aid you both in community outreach and building your social media platform."

"What?" Greg's eyes widened. "I thought Ms. Wickersham would oversee proposals."

"She's multi-faceted."

Greg ran his hand through wavy hair and loped back to the desk. "We'll talk later." He plunked on his chair without another glance.

Chuckling, Provost Martin waved her into the hallway. "You just witnessed resistance to new ideas in action."

"I see my work is cut out for me."

"And for him. Little does he know."

That wasn't all Dr. Greg Stafford didn't know, besides good manners. Her hands fisted. She possessed plenty of Buckwalter information he lacked. Facts he'd likely trade his mother for. But no way would she reveal such coveted intel, even though she craved learning details he alone knew. Could she work with the professor and retain any self-esteem? And if she finally obtained key information, would she be sorry?

Like Moby Dick to Captain Ahab, Dr. Stafford could be her bane.

CHAPTER TWO

L eslie waved to her cousin Max across the restaurant. Good ole reliable Max. Thank goodness for his generosity. Otherwise, she'd never eat out. She'd been swallowing her pride to accept his dinner offers ever since her rough patch four years ago. The rift that kept on giving.

Max sidled over to Leslie's booth. "What's the verdict, cuz?"

"I got the job!"

He offered a high-five as the waitress appeared. "Hey, Maisie." His noting of her name tag prefaced a wink. "What specials do you recommend for a special cousin celebrating a new job?"

Of course, he confirmed Leslie as a cousin. *You flirt.* Yet a small price to pay for free meals. She loved Kipp's Diner for the adorable decor. Max loved it for the adorable waitresses.

Maisie smiled. "I can offer a complimentary dessert." She took orders and left.

Max leaned forward. "Tell me all about it, Les. No surprise you're a shoo-in."

"Besides managing grant proposals, I'm helping with social media."

"What? The antiquated university's going all modern and high-tech?" He spread his fingers like an opening sea anemone and made a sizzling sound. "That's you, Les. Hot stuff. Leading them into the twenty-first century."

She smirked. "We'll see. But if I get Greg Stafford onboard, it'll prove I can work with anybody."

"*The* Greg Stafford? Mr. I-can't-be-bothered-with-trifling-women's-magazines?"

"The very one who blew me off like dandelion fluff."

"The planets are aligned, finally. Hey, this is your chance to pick his brain."

"If he lets me do the picking."

"Isn't that why you applied there?"

"Partially. He's still the best source of Buckwalter intel." She needed details about his interviews with Fritz's heirs for her own project. "Working there gives me opportunities to approach him, but I didn't expect to be hired as the burr in his saddle."

"You'll win him over. You've never run from a challenge."

"At least I won't be begging for a job at Klipton's."

"You'll be in your element, Les. College atmosphere. Closer to the source. More inspiration for finishing your novel."

Leslie sipped water. "Dr. Stafford's got hard-won nuggets he's saving for his Buckwalter biography. He'd sooner go joyriding on Moby Dick than share them with me."

"So, what's your angle?"

"My only leverage is *my* hard-won nuggets. And anything Oma tells me. If she changes her mind."

"How's the novel going?"

"I finished the second draft." Thank goodness for her

critique group. "It's shaping up, but I'm stuck. I'm missing details."

"Ones only Greg knows."

"Okay, I know we've both done it, but don't refer to him as Greg anymore, or I'll accidentally call him that to his face."

Max chuckled. "That I'd like to see."

"Besides, I'd be crazy to mention my historical fiction to him. Me, the peon."

"At least he won't see you as competition."

"Right, that's laughable. Like a slug racing an antelope."

"You're no slug, Les. At least compare yourself to something higher up the food chain."

"Okay, a squirrel."

"Give yourself some credit."

"Okay, a hound dog."

"All right, all right. Did you meet the guy yet?"

"Briefly. He was friendly until Dr. Martin mentioned social media." She drank more water. "He probably only respects women with capital letters after their names, the more the better. I have a BA. Plus, we're both starting with mutual distrust."

"Yours is well grounded." He pressed his thumb and twisted it on the table as if squashing a bug, his usual gesture whenever mentioning her ex. "Any Vic updates?"

"He got a new number and texted me today. I blocked him again."

"What he'd say?"

She winced, not wanting to reveal Vic's threats. "Wishing me well, as usual. Asking about your well-being."

"Yeah, right. In defense of my half of the human race, not all of us men are pond scum."

"You're the exception." Despite harmless flirting with pretty-faced waitresses. "I ended up with the frog anyhow. Not one who turns into a prince." She fingered her teacup. "At least Greg's not pretending to charm me. That was my downfall with Vic." Three years of sweet-talking led to marriage, then being duped. Despite a year of therapy, that nightmare still needled her self-esteem.

"With Greg, what you see is what you get. That's the safe way."

"Look who's talking, Romeo."

He offered a lopsided grin. "I only charm the girls who like the attention. It doesn't go beyond the surface."

Leslie squinted. "If we weren't cousins, I would *not* be hanging out with you, Casanova."

"Tough you can't decide between Romeo or Casanova. And lucky for me, we share bloodlines. Can't imagine life without you, cuz."

She couldn't, either. Besides being childhood friends, he'd stood by her through that treacherous year with Vic.

"Hey, is Greg married?"

She shrugged. "Who cares? I didn't check his ring finger."

"Well, if he goes after pretty faces, I'm wondering how he could resist *yours*." He waggled his eyebrows. "You're blonde and brainy. A package deal."

She cringed at the notion of the older, cocky professor trying to woo her for his own benefit. "You're sweet, Max, but shut up. The main thing is, regarding Greg—I mean, Dr. Stafford—I won't have to deal with deceitful charm."

"No, just the tongue of a snake and the mood of a ravenous bear."

"Preferable to fake charm. Say, are you going to Crestwood with me next Saturday? Your mom says Oma wants to see us." Her grandma had raised her.

"I might be playing pickleball with Susie-Q."

"Who's Susie-Q?" Leslie pouted. "I thought *we* were pickleball partners."

"As always. But Susie is Q for Quality."

Quality flirt? "Whatever." Leslie rolled her eyes. "Why don't you ever date level-headed girls with names like Ruth or Barbara or Edna?"

He quirked an eyebrow. "Edna? Seriously?" He lifted his glass. "Cheers! Congrats again on your new job. Here's to taming the hungry bear."

* * *

That evening, Leslie poised over her laptop. She did finger calisthenics, then prepared to strike keys with reckless abandon. But it was no use.

Stupid novel! Why was she so driven to write it? She popped up so fast the chair rolled back several feet. She stalked to the bookshelf and swiped a framed eight-by-ten photo.

This crazy novel venture was the impetus for seeking Dr. Stafford's expertise. When she'd sought that interview for the article, she figured his potent facts would benefit her novel too. A story about an author she'd long been fascinated by.

Who just happened to be kin.

She blinked at the 1990s photograph from childhood. Leslie sat with Great-uncle Fritz on his front porch in Dillard, Wisconsin. With Max, Leslie soaked in his tall tales, laughing indulgently. Though Fritz's readers were adults, he could spin a child's tale so delightfully giddy, the story threads still wrapped around her years later.

No doubt Greg Stafford would trade his first printing book collection for information she kept safely tucked away from probing eyes.

As a granddaughter of Fritz's brother Edmund, she'd hidden her branch of the family tree at Oma's request. Too much drama—including his few days in jail, captured on microfilm in newspaper archives. Family turmoil prompted Oma's move from Dillard and a surname change to Wickersham after her husband Edmund passed away in the 1950s. But what else happened? To put it in literary terms, Leslie didn't even know the inciting incident.

She held a wedding photo of Klara and Edmund, an enigmatic man her grandma fondly called her soulmate, her Eddie. They had two little girls—one of them Leslie's mom.

She swapped photos and gazed at her mother, whose arm sheltered seven-year-old Leslie. But instead of protecting her, she'd ripped her heart open by walking out. Forever. This was the last picture of them together.

Biting her lip, Leslie traipsed to the dinette. She browsed through mail, mostly junk, only one letter, to her post office box. Return address: Vic Rinaldi. Ugh. Not from the law firm that maneuvered their divorce, but directly from him. Fortunately, he didn't know where she lived.

Earlier, his text said:

Got a new number. Check your mail. Vic

Eight little words written to infuriate her. She just wanted him out of her life, and he knew it.

She slammed the envelope on the tabletop and whirled away. In the tiny kitchen, she put away dishes. *Plunk, plunk, plunk.* How'd they pile so quickly? She hardly cooked. Suppers consisted of anything that fit on a microwave plate.

Leslie never told Vic about her Buckwalter kinship, since Oma didn't trust him and had sworn her to secrecy. But shortly before Leslie vacated their apartment, Vic went through her files in a fit of retaliation and inadvertently discovered the paperwork connecting her to Fritz Buckwalter. He was furious she'd never told him—his cue to double down and take charge.

That was Vic—doing what a narcissist does best. Now she was paying for her previous silence. Literally. She wanted to tell her lawyer about Vic's shenanigans, but her meager income had gone to a year of therapy after the divorce.

Furthermore, living under Edmund's umbrella of shame, she'd never want Greg Stafford to charm her out of intel due to his passion for research. She wouldn't trust his tactics if he knew her heritage.

As inconsequential as a dog scratching fleas. Greg meant the magazine, but it might as well be her. She had no clout, while he thrived as a bigwig among his cronies. Never mind she'd won a short story contest last year, was a finalist in other contests, and published freelance articles. Stafford researched American literary icons and cozied up to contemporary authors with multiple publishing credits. Whereas she was a mouse among elephants.

Did he refuse her because she wasn't a bona fide journalist? Or because he disdained sharing hard-won expertise in a common women's magazine?

Leslie paged through a family album, pictures encapsulating the twentieth century. She and Max danced across later pages in full color.

Every summer, she'd spent two months at her aunt and uncle's home. Aunt Martha and Uncle Russ treated her like a daughter. He'd scoop her to his shoulders for zoo walks and tossing breadcrumbs to the ducks, comforted her for scraped knees, cradled her on his lap for bedtime fairy tales. He'd patiently handled her teen angst as she slogged through middle and high school. He'd tell her she was pretty, and read stories she'd scribbled on notebook paper, applauding her creativity.

Sad was the day he passed away, shortly after she'd graduated with a Bachelor of Arts.

He never would've endorsed Vic Rinaldi. He'd have spied red flags long before she did, though Vic's charm defied all radar.

Fritz and his brothers, August and Edmund, flitted through the album in gray, black, and white while standing on the porch, waiting on customers at Buckwalter Brothers Grocery, posing by their automobiles, or encircled by their wives and children.

Fourteen years ago, Leslie visited Great-uncle Fritz and pried him with questions. While Great-aunt Wilma spoiled her with Fritz's favorite desserts—Bee Sting Cake and Apple Strudel—jovial Fritz expounded on his childhood and the grocery store venture, his detour to literary fame. In his inimitable way, he relayed hilarious town anecdotes, family farm capers, and new novel ideas while chain-smoking cigars and blowing smoke to the clouds.

According to Fritz, they were one big happy family with a thriving business, even after he enjoyed literary success. Reminiscing on how he and Edmund loved wordplay, puns, and riddles, he showed her copies of old newsletters they'd printed in the early 1940s.

But she needed more data. She'd milked Grandma's and Aunt Martha's memories, but Leslie suspected they were holding out. Certain questions still prompted flickers of pain, shrugs, answers as vague as oatmeal, and a change of subject. Moreover, Oma discouraged contact with Fritz's descendants. Leslie's interview requests met dead ends.

Her only recourse was Greg Stafford, who'd met them all. But even he didn't know everything. Oma never afforded him the coveted interview.

Sighing, Leslie replaced the album. Anxiety pricked her.

She got the job contract, but could she earn Greg's respect? If so, he might be receptive to aiding her. That is, if she ever conjured the gumption to tell him about writing historical fiction. With no intention of revealing her family ties, she needed that angle.

Her pet project. Her ticket to sanity, akin to journaling. She planned to integrate Fritz and Edmund as characters while staging events around them. Staying true to their lives, she'd show Fritz's impact amidst his rise to literary fame. Though fictionalized, it was a way to wrestle through the chaos of her roots, to reconcile the past, to deal with family branches that had been lopped off as limbs for kindling—mainly her grandfather's offspring. If Greg Stafford gleaned any of that from his interviews, maybe she'd discover why her cousins continually rebuffed her.

Or why her mother left, without a hint of her father's identity.

But to gain Stafford's help, she needed his respect. To be true to the Buckwalters and understand family dynamics, as long as her grandma remained silent, Leslie needed information he was saving for the biography.

Back at the table, she opened the letter from Vic.

Hey Leslie,
I need another $300 by the 15th. You know the gig.
—Vic

She knew the gig, all right. For six months now. If she failed to send money, he'd call the press—or Greg Stafford. He'd reveal Leslie as Fritz's great-niece, granddaughter of Edmund, divulging a tie her grandmother had worked hard to suppress for over sixty years.

CHAPTER THREE

Seated across from Gregory Scott Stafford's desk, Leslie grasped her notebook of brainstorms, including strategies to win him over to embrace her ideas. She also needed to secure his trust for sharing Buckwalter intel. *The wooing starts now.*

He should have come to her office but refused. At least the view here offered points of interest, whereas her own walls awaited decorating. While he leisurely shuffled student papers at his desk, she surveyed blue and gold baseball paraphernalia alternating with literary quotes. The rustic metal rooster probably once topped a barn roof. Outside the window, stone and brick buildings featured unique diagonal patterns and arched walkways. In a few months, ivy would climb the sides of the oldest structures.

Greg finally looked up, sporting the windswept look with a plaid tan scarf. If he weren't so arrogant, she could be smitten by those seafoam eyes and ruggedly handsome features with enough crinkle lines to prove he smiled. Though no smile emerged now.

"How may I help you, Ms. Wickersham?" He folded his hands and glanced at the clock. "In ten minutes or less."

She'd signed up for fifteen. "Two things, Dr. Stafford. First, thanks for emailing your grant proposal. I have questions."

"Fire away."

She glanced at page one of the printed proposal. "After investigating Dritlein Fellowship's website, I called about recent programs they've funded but hadn't posted on the web. Turns out they've changed their focus."

He pursed his lips as if repulsed by the notion of her knowing something he didn't.

"No doubt you already knew that. This lowers the chances of obtaining funds, so I suggest targeting a different source." She awaited affirmation.

"And your esteemed recommendation is ...?"

Sarcasm already? Her throat tightened. "Experience dictates it's far better to shift direction and check off all the boxes rather than expand the vision in meager hopes of a yes. So, after some online exploration and more calls, I propose we kill two birds with one stone." Why was she out of breath? The room grew stuffy, reflecting his demeanor.

One brow raised. "Which two birds are those, Ms. Wickersham?"

"First, tying your goals to department goals and further melding them to the funder's objectives and application rubric. Secondly, seek community versus scholarship funding, to foster community relevance."

He tapped his chin, setting it up a notch. "You do realize my project is an *academic* endeavor. Or did you not read past page one?"

"There's no doubting the academic merit, Professor. But Provost Martin tells me that future projects must promote community interests." She dared not mention social media yet. One limping step at a time.

"Most local funding lacks the prestige of scholarly funds."

"Like eating plebeian doughnuts rather than French croissants." There! Take that!

He knuckled his desk. "A fitting metaphor. It's like requesting Burger King to fund research on Mark Twain rather than soliciting from the Berkhof Foundation."

"Dr. Stafford, I found three well-suited local foundations." Leslie set a paper on his desk. "This highlights how their vision and assets dovetail with your plans. I'll email you additional information." She barely caught her breath. "Meanwhile"—she pulled out another sheet— "please compare this summary to yours on page two. I experimented with fewer details and less literary jargon. If we appeal to a local foundation, the style must be tailored to the audience." She set it on his desk. "Our mission statement must be obvious, not lost in the—"

"Weeds?" He cocked his head without a glance at the paper.

"Not weeds. Shuffle. Not lost in the shuffle."

"Ah-ha. Because shuffle is much less insulting than weeds."

"No insult intended, Dr. Stafford. I'm also suggesting a different format." She handed him another page, which he ignored. She set it before him. "If you compare this to your page three, you'll notice a lot more breathing space"—unlike this room—"with more white space. Bullet points, headings and subheadings, along with graphs, diagrams, and photos, will add visual appeal over long, rambling paragraphs." *Oh, dear.* That spilled out.

"Rambling?" His brows arched. "Like you're doing now?"

"This is for reaching a different audience, not someone living in an ivory tower."

"Is that all, Ms. Wickersham? Or do you have other insights I failed to glean?'

"One more thought. Regarding the Outcome/Impact section, I'd like to try a little storytelling. My success with grant writing revolves around the emotional appeal, utilizing the five senses, emphasizing the project's impact on the community." *Whew.* Her breath rattled as if she'd just completed a 5K.

Greg leaned forward. "You mentioned two things to discuss. Have we only covered one, or have we taken liberties by rounding up to ten?"

"That was one item, the proposal. My second question is, well, I'd like to see your syllabus. Syllabuses, rather. Or syllabi." Sweat formed on her brow. "Whichever word you prefer."

"Did Provost Martin hire you as an educational consultant too?"

"No, sir. This is to learn more about your personal style and approach in the classroom."

"For what purpose?"

"Familiarity with your content will aid me in seeking out appropriate venues for community events."

He rolled his eyes. "Ms. Wickersham, I regret I have no syllabi to offer you." In the unmistakable tone of *bug off.* "Syllabuses, either." He smirked. "My print copies are gone, but you can pick one up at the dean's office."

"Then may I attend your class?"

"Have you paid tuition?" he snapped. "I prefer not to be observed like an animal at the zoo, but if the dean believes it's necessary, then I'll permit it."

"Thank you. I'll attend as your virtual assistant. Which includes taking advantage of social media for strengthening your platform."

"I have all the platform I need with readers prominent in

their fields. Surely Provost Martin gave you a litany of my scholarly publications."

"He did. He also instructed me to further your reach. To the less scholarly among us."

"Of which you stand first in line."

Leslie bristled, then reined herself in. "May I please have a do-over?"

He winced as if offended by her bourgeois choice of words. As if she'd handed him plebeian doughnuts. "A do-over?"

She groped for a baseball analogy. "Like calling in the pinch hitter. I've obviously approached this all wrong. We're supposed to be on the same side."

"Is that so? I was confused." He blinked, those blue-green eyes like a piece of distant sea, flashing in sunshine. Such beauty seemed wasted on this toad.

"I'm also wondering about your preferred approach on social media, topics to raise, and profile details. And your Buckwalter biography." She squinted at the clock. "But our time is up. Let's meet after you peruse my suggestions." She stood.

He stood, too, surely an attempt to hasten her departure. "I may have a spare ten minutes next week, Tuesday."

Unbelievable! She gritted her teeth. "All right, then." Turning, she noted a plaque above the doorway, a quote by eighteenth-century author Horace Walpole.

Imagination was given to man to compensate him for what he isn't. A sense of humor was provided to console him for what he is.

In his case, a schmuck. Lacking both imagination and humor.

* * *

In her office, Leslie scanned the bare walls. The little window only afforded a parking lot view, but at least it lured pale sunlight, combating January doldrums. Though longing for spring, she was thrilled about a new start here at Raymond U. Its location in the town of Avondale made Wisconsin seem as cozy as her grandmother's afghan.

Despite the damper of Greg Stafford's arrogance, coming to work was a joy. She'd soon decorate her office with lithographs of literary scenes she'd previously hung in her classroom. But no family pictures. Nothing tying her to the Buckwalters.

At her desk, she googled Greg's name. A Wikipedia article carried a short summary with a list of articles and book titles with embedded links to scholarly sites or Amazon. But no website or Facebook page. Clearly the guy didn't want to be online, satisfied to merely occupy the annals of academia.

Well, that would change today. She created his Instagram account with a new email account to verify things. Oh—she forgot to ask which handle he'd prefer, Doctor or Professor. Better go with the more highly esteemed Doctor for now.

Temptation taunted. Instead of typing PhD, she typed in Greg Stafford, Curmudgeon, hashtag Scrooge, hashtag Uriah Heep. No, Uriah Heep was too harsh. So were Mr. Hyde, Captain Hook, and Long John Silver.

Besides, his specialty was American authors. Hashtag Dr. Frankenstein, Captain Ahab, Tom Buchanan, or Rhett Butler.

After reckless fun with nicknames, she deleted them and started over.

Chapter Four

L eslie slipped into the classroom and ducked into the back row. Two minutes to spare, after a morning consumed by assessing timelines, schedules, and funding sources. She prepared to take notes for twentieth century American Literature, hoping to blend in with thirty students and not incite Gregory Stafford's displeasure.

The professor jotted three points on a whiteboard with a question:

What was the influence of Fitzgerald and Hemingway on
Mailer's philosophy and art?

Was this the barebones outline constituting part of his clandestine syllabus? Which she'd requested from the dean's office yesterday. She would pick up a print copy this afternoon.

Too bad he wasn't lecturing on Fritz Buckwalter, akin to F. Scott Fitzgerald's breadth of influence, according to some.

He faced the class, spreading his arms. Immediately

mesmerized, Leslie neglected notetaking. She soaked in words, as smooth as the worn pine on her grandma's rocker. He utilized the platform, walking and gesturing.

Ten minutes later, she jerked to attention. She jotted phrases that caught her ear. Were his lectures always this amazing? She stared at him until his gaze darted her direction. Chin down, she scribbled in her spiral.

Halfway through, he posed questions, Socratic method in full force. He probed student assumptions, pressing them to clarify concepts, to offer reasons and evidence. He challenged their perspectives, drawing out implications, returning question for question. Leslie enjoyed the verbal ping-pong.

Fifty minutes flew by. When students rose to leave, she clipped to the door.

"Ms. Wickersham." The professor's now arid voice carried above the din. She froze. "Please meet me in my office in five minutes."

Nodding, she forced a pleasant glance his way, then bolted out.

Seated across from Greg Stafford five minutes later sadly revived junior high days, getting caught swapping lunches, the teacher glaring. But she hadn't done anything wrong. Why'd he call her in? Why'd she feel like a guilty child?

During his lecture, her admiration for his intelligence and eloquence blossomed. She could complement his strengths by orchestrating events with the community benefiting from his expertise. If only his acuity in common courtesy matched his classroom finesse.

Greg cocked his head. "Dean Meyer wanted me to follow

up with you. I hope you gained enough intel to preclude another visit to my classroom." Whatever charm he exuded in the classroom dissipated.

"I did." Though her appetite was whetted for more of his lectures. "Now I can envision the right venue and angle for a community event, featuring you, Dr. Stafford." Maggie, the administration assistant, had told her, in general, to use Doctor as opposed to Professor when in doubt, unless instructed otherwise. In Maggie's estimation, only the most arrogant and insecure ones insisted upon being called Doctor. The title Professor conveyed an emphasis on knowledge and teaching above research.

He crossed his arms. "What's the pay?"

Seriously? "It depends. Do you want to lecture, facilitate discussions, or run workshops? Do you want to speak on Buckwalter or other authors? All while making your vital knowledge relevant to the average person."

"Relating to the average person is overrated."

Such arrogance! "This is *expanding* your reach, not changing it. Like the heart creating new blood vessels despite blockages." And man, did he have blockages.

"Were you a science teacher?"

"No, I taught high school English and literature. For ten years." Perspiring, she cringed. Despite their common interests, with him, she was surely only two sentences away from ignorance on any given topic.

"By broadening one's audience, one loses effectiveness. You can't please everybody."

"But Instagram followers *choose* to follow you. They'll never benefit if you stay confined to academic circles."

"*Confined* is not the word I'd use. I don't need popularity, Miss Wickersham. Only respect in said academic circles. *That* I already have."

"Raymond University wants both. Frankly, your argument is with Provost Martin, not me." Why'd this room suck the breath out of her? "I don't understand your resistance. Didn't you mutually agree on the criteria for becoming full professor?"

He pouted as if trapped.

Good. "So, do you want your handle to be doctor or professor?"

"Handle?"

"Your name on the Instagram account. What everyone sees." In her notebook, she crossed out *Curmudgeon* and *Hashtag Scrooge.*

"Professor, of course," he said as if she should have known. But she'd expected him to say Doctor.

"What specialty coffees do you drink? Smells like caramel."

He folded his hands on the desk. "I fail to see the relevance."

"For your profile. I'll include your education, certifications, and publications, but it's fun to include nonessentials. Like Caramel Macchiato Latte."

"Congratulations. You guessed it. Now if you don't mind, I must return to work."

"A few more profile questions first. Who's in your family— that is, wife and children—what's your favorite city, and do you have any pets?"

"None, Oxford, none."

No wonder he was cranky. "What's your favorite literary quote?"

He pointed to the Horace Walpole sign above the door.

"I'm making memes—"

"Excuse me? As in the biological concept of cultural transmission?"

"Um, not exactly. Well, sort of. I mean—" What *did* she mean? "Internet memes. Graphics with images and quotes, humorous or provocative. I'm guessing you'd go for provocative."

"What purpose does a meme serve?"

"Look." On her phone, she showed him a history scholar's Instagram page. "This professor uses quotes to get engagement, drawing dozens of comments." She scrolled through, then pocketed the phone. "I'd like a list of your favorite literary quotes with provocative questions relating to contemporary society. We'll promote your books, too, but this is primarily about serving your readers." She paused to catch her breath. "Social media is fickle. It's not property you own."

"Thus, disproving the need. I rest my case."

"No, sir. It's a means to an end. You make initial connections on Instagram, then direct people to spaces you *do* own. Such as your email list, website, and blog."

He rolled his eyes. "Are you ever at a loss for ways to navigate the digital universe?"

"Never." She smiled. "I have many ideas, Professor. Such as 'Motivation Monday,' 'Then and Now,' 'Would You Rather' surveys, and 'Behind The Scenes.' I want to pick your brain, so each post reflects your tastes and interests."

"Then read my books and articles."

"I'd love to read your dissertation on the Buckwalter family. May I?"

"Be my guest." He picked up a Milwaukee Brewers pencil holder and rotated it in his hands as if warming up for a pitch. Hopefully not at her. "Check the college library."

"I will. Please tell me your top five contemporary fiction titles."

"We're playing *Jeopardy* now? Top five for a hundred, please."

"My idea for a weekly post is sharing a one-star Amazon review of a highly esteemed book. People guess the title."

His lips twitched as if resisting a smile. "By highly esteemed, are you referring to its commercial success?"

"Not necessarily. I purposely didn't say popular." Nothing like the word *popular* to spoil the stodgy professor's idea of fun.

"Good. Because my favorite tomes are those with more footnotes than text, from peer-reviewed sources, including ten pages of bibliography and a five-page minimum index."

She grinned. "I doubt that's your only idea of a good time. After all, you're a lover of great literature. Is your favorite novel *The Broken Weathervane?*"

"Bingo." He pulled a red pen from his Milwaukee Brewer pencil holder and poised over a student paper.

She should take his cue but couldn't resist another tactic. "Listen to this one-star review of a classic. 'Just a bunch of people going to each other's houses.' Which novel is that?"

He guffawed. "Must be British or high society New York City. Georgian Era, Victorian Era, or Gilded Age." He lifted his chin. "I'll go with any Jane Austen title."

Leslie raised a fist. "You got it. *Pride and Prejudice.*"

"Just don't tell me this lame reviewer is one of my students."

She laughed and stood. "I'll make another appointment soon."

He stood, too, gentleman that he was. "I have ten minutes next Tuesday."

"That's becoming your customary tagline." Could she tease a smile from him? "Reminds me of Mr. Wimpy on Popeye. 'I'll gladly pay you Tuesday for a hamburger today.'" She grinned. She used to watch old Popeye cartoons with Uncle Russ and Max.

He walked to the door and opened it. "With Dickens, Steinbeck, and Twain at your disposal, you offer me Mr. Wimpy?"

Did she detect a slight edge of a smile? Or a tolerant smirk?

Her face heated from attempts at humor falling flat, but she wouldn't cower. "There's more wisdom in Popeye than meets the eye, Professor. It takes an insightful soul to embrace it." She walked out. Now how stupid was that?

CHAPTER FIVE

Oma met Leslie at the door with a hug. Without betraying her eighty-five years, she appeared frailer than two months ago. A genuine smile illuminated her.

Aunt Martha urged them to the table. Her oversized, peach-colored shirt rippled as she set down a bowl of cubed melons. Short, frosted hair debated between white and gray streaks.

Unfortunately, Max had to work, then play pickleball with Susie-Q.

Leslie picked up a cucumber sandwich. Just like Auntie to prepare items as if for high tea. "Sorry I haven't been here lately. Job searching and starting work consumed me." Plus, sending Vic three hundred dollars monthly dipped into her gasoline budget.

Oma set a napkin on her lap. "Did you find a job you love?" Such was her mantra. Do what you love.

"Yes. And no." Oops—that slipped. "I'm the grants officer at Raymond University."

Aunt Martha offered a petit four. "That deserves an early dessert."

Accepting it, Leslie smiled. "Making up for all those times you forced me to clean my plate before leaving the table."

Oma harrumphed. "There's no compensating for such rigidity. Food conservation rules the day. That's why grandmothers are so popular." To Leslie, she said, "Don't tell your aunt about giving Max ice cream whenever he asked."

Leslie pouted. "Max got more dessert than I did."

"That's because I was playing mother to you," Oma said.

Leslie chuckled. "I'm relishing the college atmosphere."

"That's lovely, dear." Oma nibbled her sandwich.

Aunt Martha quirked an eyebrow—the way Max would—and filled water glasses with a crystal pitcher. "And the downside?"

"Raymond University hopes to be cutting edge regarding community engagement." Leslie explained the social media concept. "However, beyond teaching an old dog new tricks, this offends certain professors' philosophy of scholarship. Fortunately, I only manage one. He's going for full professor and happens to view social media"—*and me*—"as the devil."

Oma smirked, her sweet voice cloaking any derision. "Sounds like the good ole professor isn't as teachable as his star pupils."

"Ironic, huh?" Leslie finished a sandwich bite. "Incidentally, um, it's Greg Stafford."

Oma's hand fluttered to her heart. "That vermin!"

Aunt Martha's mouth formed a wide *O*. "Heavens to Betsy!"

"Vermin, Oma?"

"Perhaps that's harsh." Oma puckered her lips in thought. "He's not fork-tongued. No fangs either. But he has the tenacity of a cockroach."

Visualizing a giant cockroach sitting at Stafford's desk drew a smile. "Don't worry. He has no idea of my family ties. Plus, I'd never want him to cozy up to me just because of my family connection."

Aunt Martha dipped a ladle in the soup. "Good ole Greg. If he only knew how we're on a first-name basis as if he were the neighbor. Ha! But a university job seems too close for comfort. Aren't you concerned he'll discover our branch of the family tree?"

"How? There's no completed family tree online. With Oma's name change, move, and having only daughters, we've put off discovery."

"So far." Aunt Martha shook her head, hair swaying. "Yet Greg still discovered your oma's whereabouts."

"Did he ever say how he found you, Oma?"

"Al Dyer. Al owned the Dillard hardware store forever. He gave Greg my number and post office box and said I was going by a different last name. Fortunately, he didn't know which name. But Greg's trying to wear me down." She raised her hands high, fingers wavering. "Heaven forbid."

"How often does he call?" Leslie asked.

"He sends a letter every two months, inquiring after my well-being and reminding me he's still available for an interview. It's the chance for *my* voice, he says. Honey, I could wallpaper the den with his letters."

"Double layers. That's on top of monthly phone calls." Aunt Martha ladled more soup into Leslie's bowl.

"You've talked to him?"

"I usually let the phone go to—what's it called?" Oma lifted her chin as if reaching for a word. "Voicemail, that's it. But last month I picked up just to give him the thrill of hearing my voice."

"And spurring hope that he's one step closer to that interview?"

"I declined, of course, after a lovely chat about nostalgic downtown Dillard, the weather, and the Brewers' idiosyncrasies." She giggled. "My, he's a charmer."

Leslie balked. "Seriously? Oma, don't fall for it."

Aunt Martha narrowed her eyes. "He's waiting for her to go senile and reveal all."

"Greg wants samples of your opa's writing for his Fritz biography," Oma said. "Both Fritz and Eddie loved writing stories."

"Do you still have Opa's?"

"Somewhere far from the light of day where Greg can't find them."

"May I read them?"

"Eventually."

Aunt Martha passed the sandwich platter. "I don't know who's more stubborn. Your grandmother or Greg Stafford."

"I'm counting on Oma."

Oma leaned forward. "You don't have to worry about me spilling the beans, honey. I'm wearing down and headed to glory soon."

Leslie startled. "Are you ill?"

"Just normal old-age aches and pains. But feeling weaker daily."

Leslie's fork spearing a melon cube plopped on the plate. "Oma, don't talk that way."

"It's my only comfort. And I have something to give you, so you'll never forget me whether you want to or not." Oma pulled a book, *The Broken Weathervane*, from a drawstring bag. "First, here's my original copy of your Great-uncle Fritz's first novel. Signed and dated 1958."

Leslie took the faded book. Brittle pages had yellowed, the

cover was worn, but the binding held firm. *Wouldn't Greg love to see this!* Though he probably had one. She opened the book and read the inscription:

> *Dear Klara,*
> *Consider this tale a tribute to Eddie. His story matters.*
> *Ever your loving brother-in-law,*
> *Linus Fritz Buckwalter*

"A tribute to Eddie?" Leslie frowned. It had been thirteen years since she'd read the novel. "Experts say this story reflects Fritz's childhood. Which character represents Eddie?" Knowing so little about her grandfather's short life, she wasn't sure.

"You'll soon know." Oma pulled out a notebook. "Here's something even more rare. My journal from 1952 to 1958."

Leslie's eyes widened. "You kept a diary?"

"From ages twenty-one to twenty-seven. Starting in our first year of marriage when your opa joined August and Fritz working at Buckwalter Brothers Grocery." Oma fingered her teacup. "I wish I had the weathervane to give you. After it broke, your opa kept the rooster part in the garage, then the bureau drawer. It meant a lot to him, made him feel connected to the farm and his parents. Especially his father whom he felt responsible for."

"What do you mean?" Leslie took the journal. Rare were the moments when Oma spoke freely about her husband and his family.

"You'll read about it. After my dear Eddie passed away, I let Fritz take the weathervane, thinking he'd give it back later. Or donate it to the Buckwalter Archives or a museum. But after Fritz died, his family claimed they couldn't find it. Somebody probably sold it at auction to a collector."

"Did it have personal meaning for you, Oma?"

"Only because it meant so much to Eddie. With or without that rooster, I could tell which way the wind was blowing. Wives and mothers are emotional meteorologists. They see storm clouds over the horizon."

Leslie leaned in. "Which storm clouds, Oma?"

Oma tapped the notebook.

Leslie tenderly riffled through pages, noting the steady cursive of a much younger hand. "This is amazing, definitely a treasure."

Oma nodded. "More amazing than you think. For it contains the *truth*."

"About what?"

"Everything. Every family event that mattered during those years. Things the newspapers didn't even get right."

"Like what?" Aunt Martha asked.

"Things Fritz didn't want to reveal to reporters regarding the business, or later to journalists wanting interviews about his literary success. Plenty the world would love to know but hasn't had opportunity."

"Why didn't you destroy this?" Leslie asked. "To keep it from the wrong hands."

"Because I want it in *your* hands. You deserve to know what really happened during those years. You may share with Max only. I've lived with these secrets for too long." She tented her fingers in slow motion. "I'm too burdened to take them to my grave. Alone."

Leslie glanced at her aunt. "Have you read this?"

"No. I've seen how carrying the burden of truth wreaks havoc on your oma. I prefer ignorance. I don't go digging in all those ghostly places like you do."

Leslie scooted forward. "But Oma, are you expecting me to

read this, then keep everything locked up inside me all my days? Toting the same burden you do?"

"Darling." Oma held up her hands in a stop motion. "I will not bind you to silence. I charge you with deciding how to handle this information. That is, after I'm gone. I can't deal with the fallout."

"Do any documents back up your record of events?"

"Possibly, but you'll know what I write is true, because nobody would ever invent my side of the story."

"Is there something worse than Opa's jail time?" A news article from the *The Lynwood Press* attested to Edmund's thirty-day sentence for a traffic violation and disturbing the peace. But that jail time didn't seem like enough to put them firmly under Edmund's umbrella of shame. There must have been far more chaos. *Hiding in here.* Leslie fingered the journal.

Being Fritz's progeny would be a different story. A better one.

Oma nodded. "Plenty worse. Along with family dysfunction. That's the word they use nowadays, right? Dysfunctional." Oma took Leslie's hand. "Perhaps it explains why your mother ran away."

Leslie blinked. The biggest mystery of her life. Why'd her mother abandon her at age seven, leaving her with Oma?

"How will a 1950s diary explain why Dodie abandoned the family?" Aunt Martha asked.

"You'll know when you read it." Oma sighed as if relinquishing her burden. "Secrets destroy. They creep in like cancer, robbing vitality and strength. Maybe that's why I'm ailing. It's a wonder I haven't died already." She squeezed her granddaughter's hand. "That's why I won't tell you what to do with the truth, Leslie. It's yours to decide."

CHAPTER SIX

March 1952

Not again.

Poised at the cash register, Linus Fritz Buckwalter spotted his younger brother down the soup aisle. Disheveled rather than sporting his usual tidy appearance, Edmund shadowed old Mrs. Winslow—too close for comfort if her widening eyes were any indication.

Fritz punched in the price of Skippy peanut butter, grateful this new-fangled cash register stated correct change. With Eddie's compilation of odd behaviors, he needed reliability, no mental gymnastics required. He called his older brother. "August!"

No answer from the back room where August was taking inventory.

Fritz's attention darted between the register and Eddie's hand on Mrs. Winslow's arm. She swatted him away, but Fritz couldn't discern her words. He pushed the button for the final price. The money drawer zinged open. "That's $16.47, Mrs. Ewald."

Heading a line of four customers, the woman pinned her squealing, squirming two-year-old to the cart's interior and handed Fritz a twenty.

With another glance at Eddie, he scooped out change and inadvertently dropped coins on the counter. Some plinked to the linoleum floor. "So sorry. Hold on." He bent over to retrieve the money. "August!" In his haste, he could barely scrape up the coins.

"Get your hands off me!" Mrs. Winslow shrieked from the soup aisle.

Fritz popped up empty-handed. "Excuse me, ma'am. I'll be right back. August!"

"Coming." August charged from the stockroom.

Fritz dashed to the Campbell's soup display, where red-faced Mrs. Winslow clutched her purse across her chest.

Eddie tugged on the handbag. "Show me your purse, or I'll conduct a citizen's arrest."

Fritz grabbed his brother's arm. "Just a sordid moment, Eddie. Mrs. Winslow's a tried-and-true customer for seven years."

Eddie shook his arm away. "I saw her do it. She slipped three soup cans in her purse, looking up and down the aisle as guilty as a cat in the cream jar."

Alma Winslow, a wiry, white-haired woman, spoke in a rare voice, more mountain lion than mouse. "I've *never* stolen a thing in my life. What's gotten into you, Edmund Buckwalter?" She shook the purse in front of his face. "Only a magician could fit soup cans in here."

Fritz gripped his brother's arm as Eddie's muscles bulged. Why hadn't Eddie shaved this morning?

"Let me go," Eddie snapped. "Don't let her get away with it. The more regular the customer, the more tricks they know."

"Settle down, Eddie." Fritz kept his voice low near his brother's ear. "We'll figure it out. Go in the back and count the Kellogg's products."

Eddie's bristly face reddened. "Somebody has to catch shoplifters." He thrashed to free himself from Fritz's hold. Customers gathered down the aisle, gawking and gasping. His voice escalated. "Those Communists are everywhere, taking what they deem is common property. You're gonna keep losing money. Before you know it, the store's gonna close for good."

Never mind that the store had been thriving for seven years. In the wake of economic growth and post-war production, folks flocked to Buckwalter Brothers Grocery. Despite the Korean War with President Truman's tax increases and price controls, business excelled.

That hardly mattered now. Fritz had to calm his brother before Eddie succumbed to another weekly tantrum. "Mrs. Winslow, I'm sorry for the accusations. Your groceries are on the house. Shop in peace."

Eddie dodged Fritz with as much finesse as Dick Button's triple jump in the Winter Olympics figure skating event. Fritz grabbed Eddie's arm and lugged him toward the stockroom, past the checkout, where August rang up a customer.

Eddie shook his fist. "You can't get away with this, Alma Winslow!"

Fritz pushed Eddie through the doorway and slammed the door behind them. "Get a hold of yourself, Eddie." He blocked the door. What shadow had befallen him? Until three months ago, Fritz considered his twenty-one-year-old brother mature for his age. Eddie had worked here since age sixteen, still tending their parents' farm. Though the store took priority, the brothers had the common bond of stories and aspirations to write a novel.

Eddie paced the room, shaking a fist. "You don't appreciate what I do around here. Folks take advantage of you. And now you're giving her a load of free groceries! Why reward that Communist for shoplifting? Folks'll steal you blind."

"She's no Communist." Patience fizzling, Fritz closed his eyes, gathering gumption. When Eddie was spitting mad, he had no more sense than a gnat. This was the fifth time he'd cornered a supposed suspect, including Miss Klausen, the kind schoolteacher, and Pastor Wiedemeyer, the pious Lutheran minister.

Eddie kicked a crate of produce. "You didn't even open her purse. It's full of Life Savers too!" His voice surely echoed throughout all forty-eight states.

Though his pulse rose, Fritz remained calm. "Look, Eddie. I'm driving you home now. August and I will drop by tonight." It was time to deliver their plan, brewing for weeks.

"No, you need me *here* to catch those thieves."

Fritz withdrew a key from his pocket. "We're heading straight to the Chevy. No stops, no talking to customers." He didn't want to call the police like someone had last time. A threat would produce another outburst.

Eddie's heavy breathing came in spurts, his fists tight. "You can't do this to me."

"I'm just taking you home." Far from customers. "We'll talk tonight."

"You bet we will." Eddie swiped his cap from the stand and plopped it on his head, tugging it over his brow. He stalked out, Fritz trailing. One knowing glance toward August at the cash register was all Fritz needed to convey his intentions.

Unfortunately, driving Eddie home early was a weekly habit.

* * *

In the kitchen, Klara Buckwalter heard commotion on the front steps. She raced to the door and yanked it open. "Eddie! Fritz, what are you doing here? Where's our car?" Eddie stomped inside, his tie loose, hair mussed, his handsome features darkened.

Fritz remained on the porch. "We had an incident. He needs to calm down. August and I will stop by after supper."

Klara sighed. By now, she well knew how to handle her husband's erratic moods. As Fritz drove off, she tended to supper preparations, letting Eddie blow off steam. No amount of talking would help.

An hour later, his stomping turned to brooding. She called him to a dinner of beef rouladen. He slumped into the dining room chair.

She wished she had schnitzel, his favorite, but rouladen would have to do. "What happened at the store, dear?"

"More shoplifters. August and Fritz don't believe me."

She briefly closed her eyes, summoning patience. "How frustrating."

"Don't placate me. You don't believe me either."

"I know you're always truthful, Eddie. That's why I can depend on you. Always." Truthful, but not rational. Lately, he saw and heard things nobody else saw or heard.

His woeful eyes revealed a pathway to his soul. Her intuition revealed the shoplifting incidents as the least of his problems.

She set a hand on his arm. "What's really troubling you?"

He lowered his face into his hands. "It's all my fault. If I'd done what Papa asked that day, he'd still be alive."

She went behind his chair, wrapping her arms around his

chest and crinkled shirt. Did he not take a clean, pressed shirt that morning? "You can't take the blame for his decision."

"If I'd cleaned the gutters and coated the weathervane, he wouldn't have tried it himself. I kept procrastinating."

"You can't keep reliving this. You give yourself too much power. Only God ordains when we live and die."

"I should've obeyed," he murmured. "He was between hired hands, kept asking me for help. I always had excuses, sick and tired of farm grunt work. I wanted to be at the store, but Papa still relied on me."

"But you never intended harm. You always helped. That's just one incident—"

"The one that decided his fate."

She pressed her lips together. What else could she say that hadn't been said? He was forever tormented by that fateful day eight months ago, only two months before their wedding. "Your father loved you. If you could ask him today, he'd never blame you. He'd want you to go on with your life."

"That doesn't change the facts." He removed Klara's arms from around his shoulders and pushed his plate away. "I'm not hungry."

"You'll feel better after a good meal." She kept her voice soothing. "Then tonight, after indulging in fresh apple strudel, we'll read another chapter of *For Whom the Bell Tolls*. Nobody reads with as much feeling as you do." She kissed his cheek, sat, and filled his plate with beef and scalloped potatoes.

He offered a sad smile and took her hand. "You're the best thing that ever happened to me, Klara."

* * *

After supper, Klara placed steaming mugs of coffee and apple strudel before Eddie and his brothers. No Buckwalter gathering existed without the brew, the stronger the better.

Fritz stroked his mustache, a preface to possibly upsetting news. "The grocery business is more competitive, Klara. I'm sure Eddie mentioned it." Eddie talked plenty about work, but she never knew which parts were true. "We've discussed moving the store to a larger building."

"Still downtown?" she asked.

"A few blocks from Main Street. It'll be close enough for downtown business but will entice more customers from the Burgess district. Furthermore, it has a parking lot. With more families driving automobiles now, we can offer free parking."

August swallowed coffee and blinked, as if the strong brew proved too pungent for his tastes. But it surely wasn't the coffee. More likely it was reticence about Eddie. "The larger size requires more employees. Wilma and Irma want to help when the young ones are in school. We invite your help, too, Klara."

"I'd love to." At least until they started their family. Married six months, she hoped to get pregnant soon. "Did you find a building?"

August pulled a paper from his bag. "On Thirty-first and Maple."

"It's regal, robust, and ripe for renovation," Fritz announced with his trademark alliteration.

Eddie stiffened. "You didn't tell me about this."

"We're telling you now," August said. "We just got approval."

Eddie narrowed his eyes. "You put an offer on a building behind my back? I thought we were equal partners."

"Equal, yes," Fritz said.

Eddie speared Fritz's unsaid words: "But partners, no."

Legally, Buckwalter Brothers Grocery consisted of August

and Fritz, seven and five years older than Eddie, respectively. To avoid grueling farm life, they'd saved up to start the grocery business after the war. As a teen in the late 1940s, Eddie stocked shelves part-time when not farming. August and Fritz officially welcomed him as a full-time employee last year.

"Partners, not yet," Fritz added. "We value your contributions, Eddie. But a partner needs more work experience. And time."

"You started as partners at my age." Eddie countered. "Why not me?"

Klara already knew the answer. So did Eddie. He just couldn't accept it. She touched his arm. "Let's hear what they came to say."

His jaw tightened. The muscle underneath his sleeve stiffened.

August pointed to the store diagram. "The first floor has fifteen thousand square feet, quadrupling our current space. We currently have no way to expand the checkout lane or widen aisles to fit multiple carts. But here we'll have double the aisles with plenty of room between them for better traffic flow." He pointed to an end cap. "We can strategically place displays. We're hoping you'll do that for us, Eddie. It's your strong suit."

Eddie pursed his lips.

"We're competing with chain grocery stores now," August continued. "Kroger on the north side, Piggly Wiggly on the south. Being homegrown and family-owned, we can offer just as much and more. But it'll depend on effective advertising, going the extra mile for customers *and* employees."

"With all the newfangled ideas." Fritz waved a forkful of strudel. "We'll install conveyor belts at the checkout, like Henry Ford's assembly line. Other stores are doing it. With the laundromat next door, housewives can get two chores done at once. We'll have employee uniforms, besides aprons." Fritz took a generous bite, then dumped more sugar and cream in his coffee. "We'll offer free samples. Aisles of smiles, with cookies and strudel."

"You want me to do advertising and displays?" Eddie asked.

"Exactly," August said. "With your creative eye, you'll be perfect for that."

"Dazzling displays amongst a dither of discoveries." Fritz scooped up more strudel. "Flaunting fine fare with a flourish."

Klara giggled, hoping Eddie would join the whimsical chorus as he often did.

Eddie was unamused. "How about waiting on customers?"

August cleared his throat. "With your penchant for nonstop ideas, advertising is your best option."

Eddie's eyes flashed. "What happened to me becoming partner? Have you changed your mind?"

"No," August said. "Only the timing changed. We want to come to an agreement."

"What agreement?" Klara asked.

"The agreement that Eddie's tasks entail displays and advertising, and part-time inventory and stocking shelves. With a pay increase."

Eddie bristled. "No waiting on customers?"

Klara firmed her grip on his arm. "Eddie."

August leaned over, elbows on knees. "Frankly, Eddie, we can't have more outbursts like today. Folks are buzzing about it. Weekly profits dropped."

"That's because shoplifters walk out scot-free."

Fritz harrumphed. "Nobody you pegged as a shoplifter was guilty. Miss Klausen wouldn't hurt a flea. Pastor Wiedemeyer is as honest as a grasshopper among chickens. Swiping Campbell's soup cans would never cross Alma Winslow's mind, not even in her dreams. Where are these accusations coming from?"

"I saw it happen, plain as day. Communists surround us. When nobody's watching, they grab merchandise and stuff it in their bags."

"Why would they do that if you're watching in plain sight?"

"They didn't see me. I was shelving cereal, minding my own business. You didn't even check Mrs. Winslow's purse. You trust her measly word over mine."

Fritz stroked his mustache again. "Soup cans would never fit in her purse."

August nodded. "She showed me her purse later. Nothing but money, lipstick, and other woman paraphernalia."

"By then, she'd have taken the cans out," Eddie snapped. "The proof was gone."

"We *did* check bags the previous four times," August said. "This time, Fritz didn't."

"You always stand up for him. You're both against me."

"Listen." Fritz's voice thinned. "Nobody's against you. But these accusations come from nowhere. We can't have customers gossiping, fearful they'll be targeted when they walk into our store. You can't sling around the word Communist."

"Don't you read the papers?" Eddie slammed his fist into his palm. "I'm trying to help, but you won't trust me."

August leaned forward. "What we value most is your knack for creativity. Your innovation will be a big boon to the store. Especially after our move."

"See? That's another thing. You put an offer on a building behind my back. Why didn't you tell me?"

"We've been talking after hours," August said. "The days you left early."

"The days you *made* me leave early."

"For good reason," Fritz huffed. "Frankly, Eddie, it's been

impossible to talk about anything because you fly off the handle. You're—"

August smoothly cut in. "This arrangement just transpired. We were excited to tell you and put you in charge of advertising."

"As long as I don't mingle with customers."

August hesitated. "Right."

Klara rubbed her husband's shoulder. "This is perfect. All those ideas galloping through your head—you'll make them come alive." Her hands danced to her words. "Newspaper advertisements, radio jingles. Dr. Pepper and Mr. Peanut displays. Folks will flock to the store."

"When's the move?" Eddie asked as if still nursing his disgruntled status.

"We'll finalize the purchase this month," August said, "but we need an additional bank loan to renovate. Hopefully by August, we'll have a grand opening."

"You have blueprints?" Eddie asked.

Before Eddie could charge them with making more plans excluding him, August replied, "Only simple sketches like this. With an accepted offer, we'll talk to Nelson Associates about drawing up plans."

"We'd like your input on the floor plan, Eddie," Fritz said. "Considering customer flow and strategic displays. Sketch ideas and we'll pass them along to the architect." He slugged down the last bit of coffee and stood.

August stood, too, offering his hand to Eddie. "Can we count on you?"

Eddie rose, hesitated, then shook his hand. "Yes."

"Wonderful," August said. "By the way, can you please return the store key?"

Eddie's eyes widened. "What for?"

Fritz nudged August. "Never mind."

After Fritz and August left, Klara hugged Eddie. "You'll be marvelous in this role."

His own embrace went limp. "They still don't believe me."

Klara swallowed hard and rested her head against his chest. What do you say to someone who's convinced of a fact that doesn't exist? No, Eddie didn't make things up. He truly believed they happened. That was worse. "Why don't you conjure some magic right now? Write some jingles or work on your novel."

Eddie spent an hour at the dining room table jotting rhymes and sketching. Then he traipsed to his typewriter on the desk. Two hours later, he was still typing. That man had more ideas than ants on an anthill. He'd wooed her with his spirited stories. When he proposed marriage, he crooned a song he'd written just for her.

Klara didn't want to disturb the muse.

CHAPTER SEVEN

2015

Monday morning, Leslie caught up with Gregory Stafford in the hallway, headed toward the English office. This news couldn't wait. "Professor, I found the perfect event for you."

He kept barreling forward. "Does it pay well?"

"That's a secondary issue." She hadn't asked about pay.

"My time is valuable. Please schedule an appointment through Janet."

"We should discuss it *now*. I'll gladly pay you Tuesday for an impromptu visit today." She grinned, shocked by her Popeye satire, which might only invite disdain.

The pull at the corner of his mouth surely denoted mirth. Was she cracking his stoic exterior? "Five minutes only," he said. "Starting now."

Success! No time to waste. She trotted alongside him, matching his long strides. "The public library had a cancellation this Friday. They want to schedule another event in its place. I promised to call them back within an hour." Words spilled out to meet the five-minute deadline. "When I offered your expertise on the Buckwalter legacy, the librarian was thrilled. They'll create new digital fliers, and I'll advertise on your Instagram account." She panted. "Which is coming along quite nicely, by the way."

Gregory abruptly turned a corner. She followed suit, as if attached at the hip.

She struggled to talk as he sped up. A good thing she played pickleball weekly. She stepped in front of him and walked backward, checking behind her. "Which is something else we need to discuss. I want more input on content, frequency, and timing. I'm aiming for—"

She collided with Professor Norma Tomquist, a middle-aged, displaced Southern belle.

"Honey, those eyes in the back of your head need some adjustment." The older woman's sing-songy accent was paramount.

"Oh! I'm so sorry, Professor Tomquist." Leslie's face flushed. "Please excuse me." She side-stepped her.

Greg ambled through the English office doorway and strutted to his office, Leslie at his heels.

She continued. "At least one post per week will be related to an upcoming local event. The other two posts will alternate between food for thought and asking a literary question. I'll need to pick your brain for those." Catching her breath at the door, she added, "Do you like cats?"

He offered a sideways glance. "Excuse me?"

"To indicate whether you prefer kittens or puppies. Posting cute little pet videos is a sure way to gain attention and Facebook followers."

His sour look rivaled curdled milk. "Surely you jest."

She smiled. "Lucky for you, I am. I figured irresistible pet videos are not how you want to brand yourself." Couldn't he appreciate her humor? What would Elizabeth Bennet say in her inimitable manner? Good grief, why was she thinking of *Pride and Prejudice*?

"Are pet videos worth mentioning with only two minutes to spare?" He made no secret of eyeing his wall clock.

"Absolutely. Now any idea going forward will be seen as an improvement." She handed him a paper. "This schedule has ideas for Instagram posts."

"*You're* doing the posting, correct? While I use my time for more worthwhile endeavors?"

"Yes, Professor. Later, I'll show you how it works so you can keep it going."

He rolled his eyes. "Marvelous."

"Are you willing to speak about the Buckwalters on Friday evening? Seven p.m. at the public library to about fifty people?"

"Again, what's the going rate?"

"It's pro bono, professor."

"I don't offer my hard-earned expertise for free."

"Consider this your opportunity to give back to the community." Provost Martin's words, actually. But she didn't want to drag the provost into the discussion the way one sibling bullies another as the favored child. "As a bonus, they're serving *hors d'oeuvres*."

"I've never relied on food to entice people to my lectures."

"Ah, but now they'll have both intellectual and physical nourishment."

"Money they spend on nonessentials could pay the lecturer."

"The provost plans on attending." So much for leaving him out of the equation, but she was at wits' end.

"I suppose I must oblige, then." His lips pressed into an incorrigible line.

* * *

Friday evening, Leslie arrived early at Avondale Public Library to set up. The library's bright, contemporary style contrasted with January's gloom.

Donna, the outreach coordinator, introduced the head librarian, Amanda Dexter—closer to Greg's age—a beautiful, classy woman with ample cleavage and a sensual, husky voice that defied all librarian stereotypes.

Amanda shook Leslie's hand as if her fingers were feathers, then gestured to the *hors d'oeuvres* table. "We've been taking full advantage of our new demo kitchen. I requested crab and avocado toast, bruschetta, skewered beef and mushroom bites, fruit and cheese kabobs, and cream cheese with caramelized onion canapés. Only the best for Dr. Stafford."

Any potential wages embellished this table. "It's lovely."

"As trendsetters, Avondale Public Library has one of the first demo kitchens."

Leslie was put off by Amanda's tone, as if the woman thrived on playing the one-up game. Better save her emotional energy for dealing with Gregory.

Bobbing over to Leslie, Max sported faded jeans and a Milwaukee Bucks T-shirt. "Hey, cuz! It's looking good here, especially those yummy horse-oov-res." Typical goofball Max, never one for pretensions or French words.

"Very funny. This evening, it's *hors d'oeuvres*. Glad you came."

"Wouldn't miss it for the world." He lowered his voice. "Renowned expert on the family. Is he here yet?"

"Shh. No. Should be soon."

The room filled with over fifty people. Leslie, Donna, and Max set up more chairs.

A bustle occurred at the doorway. Gregory—flashing a

broad smile. His plaid scarf and tousled hair were picked over by January's bluster. Four department cronies followed him in, chatting.

Amanda Dexter breezed over and kissed Greg's cheek. He gave her a friendly hug.

Clearly, Gregory Scott Stafford knew how to work a room. And, clearly, he was far too cozy with Amanda Dexter.

Leslie walked toward him and waited as if in line to meet the Prince of Wales. Finally, she found an opening. "Good to see you, Professor. Please help yourself to *hors d'oeuvres.*" *In lieu of your pay. Ha!*

Gregory nodded stiffly, as if his charm had reached an impasse. "Thank you, Ms. Wickersham."

Amanda Dexter swept over again. "Greg, the crab and avocado toasts are to die for." Taking his arm, she led him to the food table. The charm resurged.

Leslie found Max indulging in skewered beef and mushroom bites.

"A bit hifalutin for my tastes, cuz, but it'll do."

"You're loving a free meal for a change."

"Spot on. Do they pay you enough for your insights?"

"Hardly."

Max nodded toward Greg. "Shall I take care of this guy for you?"

She chuckled as they sat.

At the lectern, Donna welcomed everyone. Introducing Greg took three minutes, listing credentials, publications, and awards for research and articles.

He took the stage with a smile. "Thanks, Donna. You might say I write rare books. Ones that anyone *rarely* needs or buys." The audience chuckled.

Did he just crack a joke? Leslie readied her pen and

notebook, excited to learn. What information was he privy to? What had Fritz revealed to him?

Gregory's demeanor resembled his stance in class. "When I survey my students about their initial impressions of Linus Fritz Buckwalter, they surmise that Buckwalter was prolific, verbose, tenacious, and obstinate. By the course's end, they're surprised to discover he was also a businessman and family man, quite humble and generous."

Hmm. Perhaps like Greg himself? With crusty outside layers obscuring the real man?

Face bright, he raked fingers through wavy hair, which overlapped his scarf and black turtleneck. The lectern didn't bind him. He paced and gestured as he spoke.

"I had the good fortune to meet Fritz Buckwalter ten years ago, when I started work on his biography, a continuation of my dissertation. This was a much-coveted interview in the world of literature, for he'd given none since the 1980s."

Max elbowed Leslie, whispering, "How'd Greg convince Fritz to give an interview?"

She shrugged.

Gregory listed Buckwalter relatives he'd interrogated, including Fritz's wife Wilma, four children, twelve grandchildren, his brother August, sister-in-law Irma, two sisters, and various hometown old-timers, including Al Dyer, the hardware store owner who gave Greg her grandmother's phone number and Crestwood post office box number.

Greg summarized Fritz's early years in Dillard. August, Fritz, Edmund, and their two sisters, Gerda and Elise, grew up on a Wisconsin dairy farm in the 1920s, '30s, and '40s, children of Germans who immigrated in 1919, shortly after World War I.

"During the Great War, no German in America had any credibility. Even German names and words were disparaged, whether food, businesses, or buildings. Hamburgers and frankfurters became liberty sandwiches and liberty sausages. Sauerkraut morphed to liberty cabbage. The government changed German town and street names. Frankfort Street, Bismarck Avenue, and other roads in Dillard were renamed for trees, such as Maple Street and Oak Street.

"The U.S. government interned thousands of German citizens between 1940 and 1948. Fortunately, that didn't include the Buckwalter patriarch Frederick. He managed to convince the Feds he was pro-USA, not pro-Nazi.

"Fritz and August couldn't wait to abandon farm work and go into business for themselves. Missing the draft as teens, August and Fritz sought jobs at Ellis Grocery in Dillard, where they were initially refused due to their German heritage. But persistence won. During the war, the owner hired them after school hours and during summers. Afterward, Fritz and August bought him out with money they'd saved for years and their father's financial help. They were advised to abandon their German surname for business. But Fritz was adamant about using it. He said, 'The Buckwalters will rise with the name proudly handed down by our father, or we'll not rise at all.'

"They bought the downtown building, renamed the business Buckwalter Brothers Grocery, and launched their own venture. It was successful from the get-go, no doubt helped by the fact that forty percent of Dillard was comprised of German citizens. Plus, the post-war economy flourished. In 1950 and 1951, August was drafted to serve in the Korean War, so Fritz manned the store with help from Eddie."

Already familiar with these basics, Leslie, anticipated a fascinating talk with Greg unveiling coveted family facts.

CHAPTER EIGHT

Gregory swiveled and trekked across the room. "Fritz Buckwalter's first three books have a distinct tone, while sharing traits with his later works. Yet his award-winning style sets those three apart and are considered his best quality work." Greg nodded to Amanda Dexter, who punched a button. A PowerPoint screen appeared behind him. "What does this list of titles have in common?" The list included *Madame Bovary*; *Catch-22*; *Jane Eyre*; *Frankenstein*; *Cry, the Beloved Country*; and *To Kill a Mockingbird*.

A woman raised her hand. "They're all written by first-time authors?"

"Yes, ma'am. Each is a debut novel. Many are considered that author's best work. In Fritz Buckwalter's case, he always considered himself a wordsmith, even aspiring to publish novels as a child. Later, however, family demands and the grocery business swallowed his time. He had little hope of finishing his first novel, but late nights spent with his typewriter finally paid off, resulting in *The Broken Weathervane*. Barclay Publishing saw the treasure it was and swooped it up." He lifted a hand.

"But only after Fritz received seventeen rejections elsewhere for other titles."

The audience murmured in surprise.

"Barclay published Buckwalter's first three novels within three years. I asked Fritz how he could churn them out so quickly while working full-time. He said late-night creativity was a perfect counterpoint to his crowded days. In fact, he drew upon personal experiences for the novels' anecdotes, which paid off with public and critical acclaim. And big, fat paychecks."

Chuckles rippled across the room. A hand went up. "Did he quit the store to write full-time?"

"Fritz was committed to the family business. The thriving store kept the family in the limelight as the neighborhood heartbeat. Perfect for a man who never shied from attention."

No kidding. Family reunions proved that notion as Uncle Fritz told back-to-back stories like a chain smoker.

"His customers joked about watching their words around Mr. Buckwalter, or some unsuspecting person might find himself as a character in his book. No telling whether it would be as hero, comical sidekick, or villain."

More chuckles surfaced.

"Buckwalter told me he had an idyllic childhood despite challenges of farm life. After reading *The Broken Weathervane* about a Midwestern farm family, being smitten by its beauty and poignancy, I'd always wondered how closely it reflected his childhood. Since he only gave intermittent interviews, I asked him to set the record straight amidst conflicting speculations."

Gregory leaned on the lectern as if honing in on a juicy tidbit, an exclusive secret for this privileged audience to relish. "I'm offering you a prized piece of information reserved for my upcoming biography." He winked at the front row—was it Amanda Dexter? "The five Buckwalter siblings correlate to five children in the novel's Werner family. Three other kids were thrown in for good measure, to complicate the plot. In the book, representing the three brothers, August, Fritz, and Edmund are Erich, Hubert, and Oskar, respectively."

Pacing again, Greg rattled off novel events similar to most heartland rural experiences. He paused at the lectern. "One incident stands out as unique to the Buckwalter experience— the death of the patriarch, Thomas Werner. He falls off a ladder when climbing to repair the weathervane. Oskar in the novel blames himself, since he'd procrastinated doing chores.

"Dillard's town hall records indicate that Frederick Buckwalter actually died in this manner. Fritz told me his brother Edmund, aka Oskar, indeed felt responsible for his father's death."

Leslie nudged Max. "That's in Oma's diary. It haunted him." No wonder Fritz wrote that inscription. *Consider this tale a tribute to Eddie. His story matters.*

Greg lifted a book. "I want to read a favorite passage that hints of the pathos and depth this story embraces. I hope this inspires you to check out the book from your friendly neighborhood library." He winked again at the front row. "How am I doing, ladies? Got to make a library plug, right?"

Folks laughed. Amanda Dexter stood and faced the group. "We have five copies, and the county has fifteen. We also have a book club bag with ten copies. This novel inspires great discussion."

Smiling, Greg held up his hand. "But no rushing to the bookshelves until I've finished my speech." He read, "'The boy's stomach clenched as the metal rooster silhouette sharpened against the resplendent sunset of orange, rosy hues. The noble fowl perched on the barn roof, its arrow pointing south as if it had no doubt. How could he have misjudged the situation? How could prevailing meadow winds that promised hope now render as still as doldrums?"

Melancholy seeped through Leslie. Greg's mellifluous, moving interpretation twisted through her with pangs of longing. She could listen to him all evening.

Greg closed the book. "The weathervane is a metaphor for one of the Werner children. Whichever conclusion you draw, you'll have both allies and opponents. Fritz told me who it refers to, but that revelation remains for the biography."

He shared more incidents. "After World War II, America experienced great economic growth which benefited the store too. Eventually, the grocery moved from downtown Dillard to the outskirts, a fifteen-thousand square foot building with a parking lot. More families owned automobiles, so this was a draw. The store flourished until the fire."

Max faced Leslie. "Fire?" he mouthed.

"It's in the newspapers, 1952," she whispered.

"Fortunately," Greg said, "insurance covered it. The Buckwalters rebuilt and prospered in Dillard for decades. Fritz told me the fire was accidental, probably faulty wiring, though nobody determined its cause. In the novel, however, it's arson. I can't say more without giving spoilers." He offered another wink, then grinned. Oh, so handsome. And winsome.

Max grabbed Leslie's pen and wrote in the margin: *fire in the diaries?*

She wrote *not that far yet.*

Greg continued. "Fritz's second novel, *Small Town, Big Dreams*, spotlights a hardware store rather than a grocery, with the ups and downs of managing a small-town business during wartime when men were drafted, women joined the work force, and factories transformed to churn out military machines. Fritz told me his long-standing friendship with Al Dyer, the hardware store owner, was the basis for understanding all things hardware. That, and some home repair disasters."

The audience chortled.

"Another source of hardware knowledge might be Edmund. Al Dyer told me that he employed Edmund for six weeks, though Edmund still worked at the grocery store."

Leslie wrinkled her brow. Surely Oma's journal would explain it.

Greg tugged on his scarf. "In 1945, at age twenty, Fritz was influenced by George Orwell's *Animal Farm*, impacting his third novel which espouses social commentary on Dillard's town politics. *Trouble Triumphs in Trumbull* was published fifteen years later." He relayed the zany clashes between prominent Dillard citizens regarding policies on everything from alcohol intake to zoning laws.

As he continued another twenty minutes, Leslie scribbled quickly, her eyes fastened to Greg, too late noting she'd crisscrossed lines and run off the page.

He asked for questions.

"Professor Stafford," a man asked, "when will your Buckwalter biography be published?"

"It's at the publisher, but I'm still holding out for another interview with a Buckwalter relative. If that doesn't materialize, the book goes to press in two months."

Leslie mouthed *Oma*. Max winked knowingly.

"With whom?" a woman asked.

"Fritz's sister-in-law Klara. She married Edmund."

Go ahead, tell them how you keep hounding her month after month.

Another man raised his hand. "How do you account for Buckwalter's first three novels standing head and shoulders above the other nine?"

"That's purely a matter for conjecture, but if he'd given up the grocery business, the latter novels might have matched the quality of the first three. The publisher didn't care as long as the money kept rolling in. Fritz remained a popular regional author for thirty years. Frankly, without the grocery, he would've lacked the fodder of experiences that served his novels so well. Fritz is to the Midwest what John Steinbeck is to Bakersfield and Monterey. What Twain is to Hannibal and the Mississippi River."

More questions and answers followed, but no new information for Leslie.

Joining Greg, Donna thanked him profusely. Applause filled the room. He raised a hand, as if soaking it all in.

Amanda Dexter glided to the professor. "Marvelous, Greg, as usual." She slid a hand on his arm and cozied up so close he could hardly avoid her cleavage, but Leslie observed his propriety, removal of his arm, and averting his eyes. Thankfully.

A twinge of jealousy poked her. Not romantic jealousy, but a wish for his respect and warmth. She already admired his scholarly instincts, but his delivery of basic facts with finesse and flair mesmerized her. Facts that could prove mundane in someone else's hands.

She wished he'd grant her a measure of humor and banter too. But not too much charm. *That* she didn't trust.

Max hung around the *hors d'oeuvres* table. While gathering leftover plates, Leslie eyed Greg, waiting for the right moment to say goodnight.

Bits of dialogue drifted over. Professor Chambers clapped him on the back. "Sounds like you're the bee's knees, the cat's meow, and the tiger's stripes. Provost Martin will have to give you an ego-ectomy back at the office Monday." His entourage erupted in laughter.

Donna chimed in. "Next time, I'd love to tie in Fritz Buckwalter's favorite foods."

"That would be bratwursts and sauerkraut," Gregory said.

Leslie stepped over. "With dessert, of course. Bee Sting Cake and Apple Strudel."

The group chuckled as Greg's eyes widened.

Oops—she only knew that tidbit from personal experience. "All hearsay. But Professor Stafford's the expert." She faced him. "Thank you so much for your enlightening talk tonight." *And your lovely reading.* "Have a great weekend."

"Thank you, Ms. Wickersham. Enjoy your weekend too." His voice was stiff. He'd been more jovial with Donna. And far too familiar with Amanda Dexter.

Thankfully, she and Max were headed out for coffee to debrief.

Chapter Nine

Monday morning, Leslie slipped into Gregory's empty office with a caramel latte and left it on his desk with a note.

Thanks for a successful evening at the library. Please enjoy this caramel latte on me. It's necessary due to your Instagram post today.
—*Leslie*

Leslie. Not the abominable *Ms. Wickersham.*

That afternoon, arriving for her two o'clock appointment, she stopped short outside his open door. Voices buzzed inside. Words between him and a female student took shape.

"But I really want to stay in your class, Professor. I'm learning a lot. Next semester, my schedule will be too packed."

"It's your choice, Ms. Reynolds." Greg's voice was kind. "But if you remain, I highly encourage you to get writing help from the tutoring center. Your essays have the biggest impact on your final grade."

"I know. I never knew how hard it was to write about literature."

"Content-wise, you've mastered it. You offer keen insights. For that I commend you." He cited her strong points. "Comparative literature is one thing, but there are basic flaws in your paragraph structure and sentence flow. I'd like to offer you the chance to redo the paper."

The girl's voice wavered. "The tutoring center's booked for three weeks."

"Are they that shorthanded? Inexcusable. Hold on." Following was a clunk and some clicks. "Ted? Professor Greg Stafford here." His tone was amicable. "I need an appointment for three-thirty ... What?" He whispered. "Does two-thirty work, Ms. Reynolds?" Back to regular volume. "I'm sending Samantha Reynolds there at two-thirty. She needs weekly essay instruction ... I hope you can hire some help. Students need your expertise ... All right, then. Goodbye." The phone clanged. "You're all set."

"Thank you, Professor."

"All in a day's work. Now go tackle those paragraphs. And be kind to William Faulkner, will you?" He chuckled. "He's not such a bad guy. With no high school diploma, he still won the Nobel Prize, two National Book Awards, and two Pulitzers."

Samantha whisked around the doorway, smiling. She reminded Leslie of frumpy girls in high school who worked just as hard for grades as they did to fit in with their peers. Leslie was relieved the girl wasn't gorgeous. Duty and compassion ruled the day, regardless of looks or popularity.

Glimpsing this side of the professor warmed her. She knocked on his open door. The clear latte cup still topped his desk, hardly a drop left.

He lifted a file from his cabinet. "How do some students

graduate from high school when they can't write their way out of a paper bag? Answer that and make my day."

"Too many students, too few teachers, too few writing assignments, too little time, and too small a salary."

"Well, that's a tidy summation."

"Did it make your day?"

"I'll let you know by day's end." He cocked his head. "Is finding a caramel latte on my desk going to become a Monday morning ritual?"

She smiled. "Wishful thinking, Professor?"

"That depends. What's the Instagram connection?"

She chuckled. They sat on either side of student papers topping his desk. "Maybe you should check your posts more regularly."

"That would be a first."

Even though she'd emailed him links to his account with a password and pertinent information. "I purchased your latte from Spence's, not a national chain, to be community-minded. Today I posted a picture of the latte with a caption. You already have 275 likes, with dozens of comments. It'll take time to reply to them."

His eyebrows raised. "Reply?"

"If you want engagement."

Words punctuated his paper shuffling. "Ludicrous. Such frivolity," he huffed. "I'm no Taylor Swift wannabe."

"Look." She opened her laptop to his Instagram page and scrolled through posts of memes followed by comments and her replies written as his ghostwriter. She started to close the laptop.

"Hold on." He scrolled back to a previous post.

She reined in a snarky remark. Smug satisfaction settled in as he spouted observations and retorts.

She pointed. "I've established a pattern. It starts with

'Motivation Monday,' using a line from literature as a motivational quote or provocative question. Which you will provide. For Tuesday's 'Then and Now,' another book quote makes a statement about contemporary society and asks followers if they agree or disagree. Wednesday' asks, 'What Are You Reading?' Thursday is 'Would You Rather?' having to do with surveys and choices regarding characters, situations, and favorite titles. Friday is either a 'Fun Fact' or 'Behind the Scenes.' That's where I'm—I mean *you're* sharing a one- or two-star Amazon review of a classic and readers guess the title. Check out this review of *To Kill A Mockingbird*. And their guesses."

Reading it actually produced a chuckle.

Leslie took the laptop and sat across from him. "I'll make graphics, but I need your provocative questions. Some you ask in class to get students thinking. Open-ended, not too novel-specific so as not to alienate followers."

"What if alienating them is exactly what I wish to do?"

"Then speak to Provost Martin about that, not me."

"Fine, then. Let's get on with it." He rattled off several questions that sent Leslie's pen flying over the page.

"Perfect! I can't wait to design memes for these."

"A creative outlet for you?"

"Definitely. I've always enjoyed creating lesson plans and finding new ways to present material."

"Classroom purposes I understand. But all this hoopla about memes"—he twirled a finger in the air—"I fail to grasp."

Leslie notched up the enthusiasm. "It's *fun*, professor. Good plain fun. You're missing out."

He harrumphed. "Your Instagram obsession is over the top, well beyond criteria for full professor."

"Perhaps. But I see you're not ready for so much

merrymaking. Instead, I'll apply your questions myself. For now. What'd you think of Friday's event?"

"Was that your husband with you at the library?"

Leslie startled. He noticed? And why would he care? "No, that's Max, my cousin. I bribed him with food." Never mind Max would have come anyhow just to hear a Buckwalter lecture. Max in his shabby jeans and T-shirt. Max who whisked around the room like a dervish in search of pretty girls. Max who called the appetizers horse-oov-res.

Maybe she shouldn't have admitted Max was her cousin. No, she wouldn't be reduced to embarrassment by the arrogant Gregory Scott Stafford, aka Tom Buchanan from *The Great Gatsby*. In demeanor only. Greg certainly exceeded Tom's intelligence.

"You seem fairly confident about Fritz's dessert habits," he said. "How could you possibly know his favorites?"

She turned coy, attempting humor. "I don't reveal my sources." Which involved her own visits to Fritz and Wilma, plus family reunions.

Greg narrowed his eyes. Mission failed. Humor fell as flat as a German pancake.

"Pretty sure I read somewhere about his sweet tooth," she added hastily. "With a penchant for German food, who wouldn't love Bee Sting Cake and Apple Strudel?" Switch tactics. "What was it like for you, being with Fritz Buckwalter?"

His face brightened. Then he hesitated. "Surely you can imagine, Ms. Wickersham. Meeting such an esteemed author I've idolized since high school."

"Leslie."

"Pardon?"

"Please call me Leslie. After all, I bought you a caramel

latte and made your Instagram posts. That puts us on a first name basis. For me, that is. I'll still call you Professor. Sir."

"You have a point. I'll concede to that, *Leslie*."

Score one for Leslie!

"You may call me Greg, here in the office."

"Thank you, I will ... eventually." At least now if the name *Greg* slipped out here as it easily did with her relatives, he wouldn't balk. "How'd you convince Fritz to give you an interview after so many years of him resisting the press?"

"Because I'm *not* the press. I assured him I wanted to write a bona fide biography that honors him and his legacy. I also assured him of my impeccable research and use of primary documents. I expressed my disappointment in so-called experts who rely on secondhand sources to publish misleading information. I want to do justice to the Buckwalters."

She longed to tell him about her historical fiction project and pick his brain but feared inviting criticism. "With the grocery business, I wonder why Edmund worked for Al Dyer."

"It's a curious thing. Al said Edmund had other jobs around town too. I verified employee records." He rattled off a list of businesses, then winked. "I *always* reveal my sources."

Did he just wink at her? Leslie half smiled. Was this in the diary? Did Greg know about Edmund's shoplifting accusations? "You didn't mention his multiple jobs Friday night."

"No need to disclose a spotty work record. Besides, I need to save some intel for the biography."

Gratefulness bloomed deep within. Though swimming in a deep well of knowledge, Greg wasn't prone to indiscriminately harm a reputation.

He stroked his bristly chin. "'At once he became an enigma. One side or the other of his nature was perfectly comprehensible; but both sides together were bewildering.'"

Leslie tilted her head in question.

"Jack London, from *The Sea Wolf*, 1904. There's more to Edmund than meets the eye. I assumed his side hustles were due to expertise, but records reveal random menial tasks."

"What else have you learned about him?"

He cocked his head. "You've read the novel. Who best represents the broken weathervane metaphor?"

"You're being a teacher, answering a question with a question."

"And your answer?" His eyes glinted with mischief.

"I'd say Oskar, the equivalent of Edmund." Not to mention Fritz's inscription. *Eddie's story.* "How much is true besides his self-imposed guilt for his father's death?"

"Fritz and I discussed this at length." Greg typed on his laptop, then turned the screen to face her. He pointed to a title page file. "It's all right here in my manuscript. The research. Family interviews. Fritz fabricated a plot that takes us up to Oskar's twenty-fifth year, Hubert's thirtieth. Hubert aka Fritz."

"Are you looking for a proofreader, Professor? I come with good references."

He offered a hearty chortle. "No hidden motives there."

"Donna called me about your next lecture. Are you free in six weeks? Mid-March." *And how well do you know Amanda Dexter? How long?*

"Will it pay?"

"It pays in multiple intangible benefits, Professor. What topics would you like to address?"

"I'm saving Buckwalter information for the biography. How about an evening of Mark Twain, another favorite."

"Mine too. I discussed his quotes with my students. 'I have never let my schooling interfere with my education.'"

Greg frowned. "That's wrongly attributed to Twain. It's

been documented that novelist and essayist Grant Allen, his contemporary, said it multiple times before Twain did."

Leslie's cheeks burned, but she'd had it with his superiority. "Perhaps Twain would forgive the misattribution. After all, it's a clever line." She couldn't resist one more stab at the Fritz topic. "Years ago, I read your book *The Annotated Broken Weathervane.* I've always wanted to ask you about a line you wrote that I shared on my blog." She quoted it.

His eyes widened. "Ms. Wickersham, don't ever say that again. That misquote will forever haunt me. You must've gotten that from Wikipedia. Do I even need to share my opinion of that website?"

"No." Within three minutes, he'd bounced from *Leslie* back to *Ms. Wickersham.* Flustered, she felt a flush crawling up her neck. "I'm sorry, Professor. I quoted you correctly on my blog. I'm just not recalling it right." One attempt to connect through shared interests blew away in one fell swoop.

No way would she ever tell him she was researching for a historical fiction project. Her main ploy to ask for his expertise.

"If you read *The Annotated Broken Weathervane,* Ms. Wickersham, you would know that's *not* what I said."

"I failed to memorize the book. I stand corrected. What *did* you say?" *And why are you so huffy about it?* His resemblance to Tom Buchanan heightened by the second.

He raked a hand through his golden-brown hair. "I'll never live this down. People constantly misquote me. Double check your blog." He recited his original line, a difference of three words that barely changed the meaning.

Seriously? She scribbled it in her notebook. Was it so crucial a difference to merit such scorn? She tempered a glare. "If Amanda Dexter misquoted you, would you be as angry? You'd probably laugh it off." *And appreciate her good looks.*

"How about that sweet student Samantha? Would the fangs come out with her?"

Oh, dear, how'd those words spill out? She needed to smooth this over, but without cowering. That's what Nadine, her therapist, would say. She stood. "I'm sorry. I'm out of line." *No more so than you are.* "I'll send you my blog link so you can see for yourself. I assure you my audience is not scholars seeking to ruin your reputation."

He opened his mouth, but she plowed ahead. "I also promise you a caramel latte every Monday morning for the next two months. Not as penance, mind you. Given your fine compassionate nature, you'll no doubt grant forgiveness. The lattes will tie to Instagram posts and bolster Monday morning engagement." She caught her breath. He again opened his mouth, but she continued. "One more complaint and I'll change that to a broccoli-beets-spinach-kale smoothie." She forced a smile and left.

CHAPTER TEN

August 1952

Klara and Eddie sat in the office of Gerald Norman, the bank's loan officer.

Eddie's face was alive with hope. Despite trying and quitting three consecutive jobs August and Fritz found for him the past four months, he'd been writing newspaper advertisements and radio jingles, putting his creativity to good use. The grand opening at the store's new Maple Street location was in two weeks.

His brothers had deemed the automobile parts store, the automated carwash, and Ben Franklin's five and dime—far from customer service—a better fit, but Eddie viewed them as tactics to keep him from the grocery. Each job led to boredom, frustration, and eventual quitting.

Eddie handed Gerald Norman a piece of paper. "I need three hundred dollars to finish ads and displays for the store's grand opening."

Klara's stomach dropped. Three hundred! She thought they were withdrawing a few dollars for errands.

Mr. Norman eyed the paper, blinking hard. "Buckwalter Brothers Grocery already took out a huge loan for the renovation. Why do you need more?"

"It's on that paper. I'm purchasing advertisements in *The Dillard Herald* and six regional newspapers. I'm buying prime radio spots, too, for several weeks."

Klara balked. "What happened to money allotted for advertisements?"

"It's spent."

"There were concessions for an advertising budget in the previous loan." Mr. Norman pulled a file. "It's all right here. An itemized list."

"That money's good through next week. We need funds for six more weeks."

"After opening day, you'll have profits to work with. You can make do for now."

Eddie frowned. "Haven't we made good on every loan here?"

"Of course, Edmund. The Buckwalter name stands untarnished."

"Then what's the problem?"

"Only August and Fritz request loans. Your name isn't on the account."

Klara closed her eyes. This wasn't new information. *Equal, but not partners.*

"Even if it was, Edmund, all three brothers would have to sign the contract."

Eddie's voice went limp. "All three of us?"

Klara set her hand on his arm. "Eddie, let's go home and figure it out."

"What's there to figure? I'm a Buckwalter brother, aren't I?"

"Did you ask August and Fritz about another loan?" she asked.

"I'll take out one myself."

Klara's eyes darted between him and Gerald Norman. "Eddie, we can't—"

"Yes, we can. We'll have it paid off within two months after opening day."

Mr. Norman pulled out another file and riffled through papers. "Hmm. I'm sorry, Edmund, but your personal credit isn't high enough for a loan approval."

"How much is in our savings?" he asked.

"About eight hundred dollars."

"Then I'll withdraw three hundred."

Klara's hand flew to her heart. "No, Eddie. Not our savings. You can't."

"Why not? I'll have it paid off in no time."

"But that's—" Though Mr. Norman knew Eddie's financial habits, Klara didn't want to broach failures in his presence.

"Are you on their side, too, Klara?" Eddie snapped.

"Of course not! I'm always on your side. We all are. There are no *sides*."

Eddie grabbed a blank savings withdrawal slip from the desk. "Then support me in this." He filled out the slip.

"Let's go home and talk first." She sizzled at being blindsided.

"I'm not leaving without the money. I already put a deposit on display materials. They won't let me pick up the goods without the full amount."

"So now we're in debt? I thought we always consulted each other—" She stopped, not wanting to air grievances in front of Mr. Norman.

"So, I owe money. It's for a good cause. Ultimately, supporting *you*." He signed his name on the slip.

Mr. Norman's jaw tightened. "For such a large withdrawal, I'll need both of your signatures. It's a joint account."

Since when did a woman's signature matter at the bank? Was this Mr. Norman's kind way of preventing a foolish withdrawal?

How could Eddie do this again? His financial recklessness always dumped an avalanche of trouble. No wonder August and Fritz didn't want his name on their business account.

Eddie held the slip for her to sign.

Perspiring, she didn't budge. "How do I know you'll replace this money within two months?" He never had before.

"If I don't pay Roscoe's, I can't pick up my order, and I'll lose the two hundred I put down."

"Two hundred?" Her shaking hands covered her face.

Eddie's voice softened. "I'm sorry, Klara. I should've told you. But I was so excited, I forgot." He waved the slip. "Please. Otherwise, we lose the two-hundred-dollar deposit."

Trembling, she signed her name. *This is the last time.*

* * *

The next week, Klara kneeled in the front yard pulling weeds from the flower bed. Such a dazzling array of marigolds, salvia, and petunias. Yet the ordered beauty belied her inner turmoil and household tension. If only she could send her problems away as easily as uprooting weeds.

At four-thirty, Eddie pulled up in the Chevy and hopped out. He startled upon seeing her. "I thought you were at Wilma's."

"I got back an hour ago to start supper." She stood and

brushed dirt off her pants, worn only for gardening. "I thought you were at work." He'd been employed at Dyer's Hardware for three days.

"I'm on break. I need to grab something and head back." He rushed into the house.

Odd. A break at four-thirty when he normally left at five? She wandered to the automobile and peeked inside. The back seat was lined with three boxes of food items, from canned goods to produce. What on earth?

Eddie popped back out and jogged to the auto. "Gotta go!"

She brushed dirt off her hands. "What are you doing with those food boxes?"

"Making deliveries."

"Since when does Buckwalter Brothers make deliveries?"

"Since I came up with the brilliant idea. Generates extra cash."

"That's wonderful." Then why'd he insist on taking out a loan?

"See you tonight, love." He jumped in the seat and started backing up.

She scooted to the open car window on the passenger side. "Wilma didn't mention anything about deliveries. Neither have August or Fritz."

"They're busy. It's perfect for me since I'm in the stockroom every afternoon."

She waved as he drove away. Suspicious, she stalked inside to call Fritz but paused. She'd give Eddie the benefit of the doubt.

* * *

"How'd the deliveries go, dear?"

Eddie took his time chewing on schnitzel. "As fantastic as your cooking, darling." He leaned over and planted a kiss on her cheek.

She warmed at his compliment, always pleased when he enjoyed her culinary efforts. "Where'd you make deliveries?"

Between bites of potato dumplings and red cabbage, he described his rounds to seven houses around town. "I made their day, saving them an inconvenient trip to the grocery store. All those women had little ones whining and toddling around."

An ache poked her chest. Hopefully, she'd soon have little ones around the house too. "How often will you make deliveries?"

"Daily, I hope. As long as orders keep coming."

"I haven't seen any advertising about it."

He dabbled with bits of bacon and onions on the potato dumpling. "Word of mouth."

She scooped a forkful of cabbage. "Whose word of mouth?"

"Mine, as I see folks."

"August and Fritz must be thrilled about a new avenue of income."

Eddie paused, fork dangling. "This is *my* income. I make the deliveries. I get the profit."

"That's your agreement?"

Eddie set down his fork and folded his arms. "It's my own way of being part of Buckwalter Brothers. Please don't bother Fritz and August about it."

"What do you mean? Don't they know?"

Eddie's face tightened. "No."

"But Eddie ..."

He set a finger on her lips. "Please, Klara, don't say anything. It's a good arrangement. Doing this will help me pay off the bank debt sooner."

"You'd need hundreds of daily deliveries for that."

"No, I'm making one hundred percent profit from the sale, too, not just delivery fees."

"What?"

He shoveled more schnitzel into his mouth. "This pork is the best."

"A hundred percent profit? How?" Then it dawned on her. "Are you taking stockroom inventory behind their backs?"

"It's not hurting anyone."

"Yes, is it. You're stealing, Eddie. It hurts the store, but it's hurting you too. Your conscience."

"Look, it benefits everyone. I'll pay my debt back sooner, and customers are thrilled. That's good for store business."

"Not if you're stealing."

"It's only till the loan's paid off."

Klara stood. "No, Eddie. You can't do this. You need to come clean. Call August now."

"I'd rather call Fritz. He's easier to deal with."

"Then call Fritz." She wanted to say *you do it or I will.*

"After this delicious meal."

Now compliments were reduced to flattery for his own purposes. "I lost my appetite." She scooped up platters and plates and swept into the kitchen. She dumped food into Tupperware containers. Nervous energy sparked each move as dishes clattered in the sink.

Eddie followed and stood behind her, sliding arms around her waist. "Don't worry, Klara. Everything's fine."

She bristled. "You don't know that." This wasn't the Eddie she knew, always honest and responsible.

"I want so much for us, Klara. I love you. I want to do right by you, so you don't have to work at the store. So you can stay home and care for babies."

She whirled around. "If you want to do right by me, then call Fritz and tell him the truth. Maybe he'll let you keep the delivery cash, but you can't take inventory behind his back."

He stroked her hair. "Don't worry, love. Fritz will understand."

No, he won't. When would Fritz's patience run out?

CHAPTER ELEVEN

2015

Leslie was determined Gregory would not forever look down on her. Meanwhile, how would she ask him for anything beyond the meager Buckwalter scraps he'd offered?

After a long day, she slapped her book bag on the table and called Max.

"Hey, cuz! What's up?" His perpetually happy greeting eased her soul. "How's good ole Greg treating you?"

"I'm in the doghouse with him."

"Thought you already were when you slammed his world with social media."

"This is worse. I've misquoted him." She relayed the incident.

"Whoa, that'll come back to bite you."

"Yeah, on top of being his virtual assistant."

"Hey, didn't he agree to the community outreach criteria for full professor? Frankly, he's got to get over himself."

"Well, why don't you just tell him that? Ha!" She plopped on the couch and swung her feet to the coffee table. "I still reply to Instagram comments as if I'm Gregory Scott Stafford."

"Now there's an irony. You put your best foot forward ghostwriting for him, while he treats you like chopped liver."

"Double standard, right? I'll let Pastor Woods know I discovered the unforgivable sin. In case he wants to preach on it. No more quandaries." She adopted a sermon-esque tone. "Never misquote a professor."

Max laughed.

"For all of Greg's vinegar, I still need his knowledge of the Buckwalters."

"How will you get the scoop?"

"I've no idea, but I'm not telling him about my family connection, or he'd probably cozy up to me for his own gain."

"Would that be so terrible?" Max chuckled. "Do I detect a little of Mr. Darcy in our dear professor?"

"Seriously? No way!" Leslie examined the phone as if he'd sent an electrical shock. "You can put that insinuation back where it belongs—in the garbage."

"Methinks thou doth protest too much."

"Stop it, Max," she said, before realizing her additional protest could prove his point. She reined herself in. "I want him to respect me for being *me*, for my skills, for working together. *Not* my ancestry. If that's not enough to fret about, there's Oma's diary."

"So maybe you won't need Greg's knowledge after all."

"Yes, I do. He interviewed family members who refused to speak to me. Maybe he knows why."

"Possibly. Did you learn more about Opa in the diary?"

"There's no shortage of family mayhem." She shared Greg's comments about Edmund's multiple jobs and entries about his savings withdrawal and stealthy store deliveries.

"What's the deal with Opa? Unpredictable moods, shoplifting accusations. Sounds like a bully and a pest."

"Yet Oma only speaks kindly of him."

"She's hiding the dirt."

"She loves him, but he can't seem to flourish. As if taunted by demons." It hit her she'd used present tense, as if living in the angst of 1952. "Loved. Couldn't."

"I wonder what it was like for our moms having him as a father, with all his moods."

Leslie pouted. What would it be like to have a father at all? "I hope your mom shares more after I'm done reading the diary." Her voice dropped. "And maybe I'll learn why my mom abandoned me."

Max's tone denoted compassion. "Maybe it's better wondering than knowing for sure."

"Maybe." Melancholy sucked her in. She took a different tack. "At least I had all those wonderful times at your house every summer. Despite your crazy antics."

"Yeah, lucky you, knowing me more as an annoying brother than a cousin."

They reminisced about his mother's cookies and nightly book reading. Board games, bike rides to the river, and campfires with his dad. Max's pranks and mischief.

Afterward, Leslie picked up *The Broken Weathervane* from the end table. She would reread it after finishing the diary, to piece everything together. *Consider this tale a tribute to Eddie. His story matters.* As she flipped through the diary, Oma's smooth cursive penmanship blurred into an unintelligible mass as pages spun. Much like her family.

Each entry into the muddy family waters of 1952 took an emotional toll, limiting her to one per evening—if not overtired. The payoff would surely come with each new revelation. But every night, she first perused and revised grant applications at home, then tackled Greg's social media posts and interaction—something she couldn't justify using daytime hours for.

Why'd she stupidly misquote him? Now she'd never break down his barriers and gain from his knowledge. She'd have to contrive another way.

Suddenly, she knew how. Without him knowing.

At her laptop on the table, she brought up Raymond University's website to check for professors' email addresses. But something caught her eye. An announcement dominated the home page:

Dedication of the new engineering wing, Stafford Hall, in honor of Professor Douglas Alan Stafford, PhD.

Was Douglas any relation to Greg? The photograph showed a distinguished gentleman. The caption said:

Founder, Instructor, and First Director of Raymond University's Engineering Department, 1960-2010.

A blurb followed:

Raymond University would not be what it is today without visionaries and achievers like Douglas Alan Stafford. He put this institution on the map of small private colleges across America with his dedication to pursuing excellence in scholarship and research.

Considering the man's age, stature, and jawline, he could definitely be Greg's father. Was that why Greg ended up at Raymond? She'd ask him, hoping to compensate for her blunder.

Back to business. She'd use her pseudonym Renee Piquette,

a byline for previous freelance articles. A name Greg wouldn't know. She found his university email address. Good. No worries about how Renee could find it.

She created a new Gmail address with her pseudonym and composed her email in a file, trying to utilize a different voice than when emailing Greg as Leslie.

Dear Dr. Stafford,

I've long admired your works about Linus Fritz Buckwalter and am wondering if you'd consider answering some questions. My purpose in seeking your expertise is twofold. As a writer myself and a fan of Buckwalter's novels, I'm writing historical fiction based on his life and want to accurately portray him. As you know, various biographies contain inconsistencies. My own research, including the Dillard Library archives, brought me to an impasse.

My project will in no way compete with your upcoming biography, which I look forward to reading. I wish to make the inimitable character and spirit of Fritz Buckwalter accessible to the general public, ones who prefer learning through story versus scholarly means.

Below is a list of my publishing credits.

Since you did research via original documents and interviews, I'm wondering if you'd allow me to do a fact-check regarding contradictions posed by unofficial biographers. May I send you a list of approximately twenty short-answer questions over the next few weeks, and some follow-ups?

I value your devotion to true scholarship yet want to respect your time. Additionally, I want to do justice to Linus Fritz Buckwalter. Thus, I'd be honored to benefit from your expertise.

Thank you so much for your consideration.
Warm regards,
Renee Piquette

She reread the message ten times, making adjustments. No room for even one error that might cause a shudder.

Maybe she should sleep on it, tweak it later. She putzed around the apartment, reheated last night's burrito, rearranged pillows, watered plants, straightened her desk, proofread again, gritted her teeth, and hit send. She released a huge sigh.

What had she done? Just one more avenue for making a fool of herself. The dishonorable Leslie Wickersham was now inviting criticism for her alter ego, Renee.

Jittery, she made tea, turned on Netflix for *The Odd Couple*, reruns she used to watch with Uncle Russ and Max. Next month, a remake would be airing, but she couldn't imagine any improvement over the 1960s version.

She could use some good laughs right now. She settled on the couch with an afghan and promptly dropped the teacup from her butterfinger hands.

Leslie popped up with a choice word and settled in with another afghan. Only to find she couldn't concentrate on the show.

Thirty minutes passed. Surely Greg had better things to do at nine p.m. than check his university email. But what if he did?

Like querying magazines as a freelancer, it was preferable to be in limbo while awaiting a reply than to receive a big fat no. Yet she couldn't resist checking.

Oh, my! Her inbox displayed his response. Heart pounding, she couldn't look yet. If he refused her, where would she turn?

She pulled a shade, turned down the TV, and carried cups to the sink, living in one last moment of hope before a rejection.

What would his reasons be? Too busy, too beneath him, not partial to historical fiction or unknown authors, and the clincher—doesn't want to make her privy to hard-won facts saved for his official Buckwalter biography.

His refusal to Leslie Rinaldi four years ago still taunted. *As inconsequential as a dog scratching fleas.*

She finally sat at the desk, mouse hovering over the subject line. She closed her eyes. Once she opened it and read the email, the damage would be done. She hit the button and read:

> *Dear Miss Piquette,*
>
> *Thank you for reaching out to me. Your historical fiction project sounds delightful, though I need a few things before I consent to help you.*
>
> *#1) Send a list of sources you've explored in your Buckwalter research*
>
> *#2) Send a synopsis of your novel*
>
> *#3) Send me two samples of your writing: a) one of your published articles and b) a chapter from your novel— only if you don't mind.*
>
> *Please understand my need to vet you prior to offering help. Based on past disappointing experiences, this is the best way to proceed.*
>
> *Gregory Scott Stafford, PhD*
> *English Composition, 20th Century American Literature*
> *Raymond University*

Her hand flew to her fluttering heart. Yes! He'd written her back! Well, he'd written *Renee*. She scanned his words again. Stipulations, actually. Seriously? But no surprise he'd be concerned about scholarship and excellence. At least he'd bit her bait.

She started typing, then paused. Should she wait ten minutes? Or twenty-four hours? She didn't want to seem desperate.

No, she'd reply now, while he seemed responsive.

But what if he didn't like her writing? Leslie was proud of her articles on mental health issues in education. She'd never told him about them, so he'd have no reason to think she was Renee. She'd utilized the pseudonym to protect her school, staff, and students.

With critique partners, she'd revised her novel umpteen times, expecting to revise more with updated material. But what if he didn't like it? She wrote:

> *Dear Dr. Stafford,*
>
> *Thank you so much for a quick response. Attached are the four items you asked for: the list of resources, the magazine article published in Mental Health Solutions, the novel synopsis, and Chapter One—the first scene featuring Fritz Buckwalter.*
>
> *I look forward to hearing from you again.*
>
> *Renee*

She hit send. Would he reply tonight?

She mulled over an image of him at home. What did he normally do? What'd he have for supper? Surely not fast food or TV dinners. Did he cook? No, he probably did takeout.

Then he'd grade papers, listening to classical music. Smiling at students' clever wording, creative imagery, and logical reasoning. Frowning at bad grammar and misspellings, or a thesis statement fraught with sloppy thinking. Despising formulaic, repetitive essays. Laptop nearby, alongside a rich cup of coffee—the kind Fritz loved—he'd check sources to make sure students didn't plagiarize.

Good grief, stop it!

She played her Spotify playlist of 1960s and '70s popular tunes, blasting it loud enough to drown out her nerves. That music was before her time, but Uncle Russ got her hooked on it. Jimmy Buffet's "Changes in Latitude" fit her current state of angst.

Greg probably wouldn't denote her article, synopsis, and chapters as his bedtime reading. But what if he did? What if he loved it? She'd be over the moon.

More likely, he'd find fault, her writing not up to par. Perhaps he'd consider her story trivial, unmoving.

She replied to Instagram comments but couldn't concentrate. So, she scoured the sink, vacuumed the floor, dusted bookshelves. All tasks she hated. Chiming in with Neil Diamond and the Eagles kept her distracted.

Thirty minutes later, she checked her laptop. Another reply!

She hovered over the keyboard, closing her eyes. Just do it. Get it over with. Like waiting for a shot in the doctor's office. The pain was real, sharp, but over in seconds.

But a *no* would be painful for a long time. Nevertheless, she opened the email.

> *Dear Renee,*
>
> *Thank you for sending the attachments as requested. Your magazine article on mental health was excellent, timely, and spot-on, considering the periodical's tone and audience. Your list of resources helps me know what you've learned already. I can already guess at your questions about inconsistencies, especially among so-called biographies not based on original documents.*
>
> *I find your synopsis intriguing, your chapter engaging. Considering my research and having met Fritz Buckwalter*

in his later years, I can honestly say you've captured his personality, painting a vivid image of the young adult Fritz through words. It's as if you'd met him yourself back in the day.

I'd be happy to answer your questions. Due to my pressing schedule, I'll need 48 hours to respond to emails.

Gregory Scott Stafford, PhD

Leslie clasped her hands and reread the email. Wow!

She ramped up the volume of Aretha Franklin's "Respect" and hopped around the room.

As if you'd met him yourself back in the day. Wouldn't he love to know.

CHAPTER TWELVE

August 1952

During the Grand Opening, Klara worked alongside her sisters-in-law, Wilma and Irma, as August and Fritz greeted customers and awarded door prizes to mothers and children. The Buckwalter sisters, Gerda and Elise, handed out free samples of Oreo cookies and Skippy peanut butter on saltine crackers. The bakery counter offered samples of fresh chocolate chip cookies and wheat bread. Amidst the aroma of baking bread, the cacophony twirled around the store in spirited merriment.

Last week, as Klara hovered, Eddie called Fritz to confess the deliveries and stolen merchandise. Fritz was furious but calmed down when Eddie paid him. He didn't tell August. August might never allow Eddie in the store again.

Fritz let Eddie keep merchandise profits, condoning future deliveries as long as he recorded every item. Going forward, Eddie was allowed in the stockroom only with oversight, from five to six daily.

Since picking up materials, Eddie buried himself in advertising preparation every evening for two weeks. He hardly slept, working like a relentless windup toy.

Yet Klara welcomed his enthusiasm—a far cry from last spring when he took a tailspin and slept for weeks, lacking motivation after each failed job attempt arranged by his brothers. She could barely nudge him to the kitchen table, reminding him to bathe or change clothes. The brothers kept asking for his store key, but he insisted he no longer had it.

Today Eddie monitored produce, peanut butter, and candy displays on the endcaps, exhibits that lured customers down each aisle. With 15,000 square feet, they had more merchandise than ever. Peanut butter alone jumped from three brands to seven, including Beech-Nut, Planters, and Swift's—offering a free plastic coaster with each jar, in four colors. Swift's also sold peanut butter in tins or glass tumblers decorated with whimsical *Wizard of Oz* characters.

The renovated grocery featured a blue and white checkerboard tiled floor and wide aisles—over two carts wide—accommodating longer checkout lines. The counter boasted the newest cash registers and conveyor belts, with displays of comic books, gum, trinkets, and candy, appealing to the kiddos and encouraging last-minute impromptu purchases. Windows spotlighted eye-catching stacks of both canned and bakery goods.

All morning, reporters marched in, fired questions, and took pictures galore. Employees wore crisp royal blue aprons. Voices bubbled as women thumped melons, compared prices, and sampled bread. Neighbors chatted. Clowns entertained squealing youngsters. Red and yellow balloons bobbed over the aisles, ribbons trailing in the wake of spinning ceiling fans.

Better yet, no outbursts or meltdowns. The Buckwalter Brothers Grocery was a happy place for all.

Activities wound down by late afternoon. Surely all the *cha-chings* today indicated plenty of profit after months of investment. Maybe Eddie could repay the three hundred dollars to their savings account in a timely manner.

The buzz of business shifted to sharp, punctuated scraps of words from the middle of the store. Yelling, a burst of expletives —Eddie! Then August and Fritz cajoling him to retreat.

Ignoring the checkout line, Klara ran toward the commotion.

"Let me go!" a woman shrieked, clutching her purse. Her eyes darted around as if seeking escape.

"Shoplifter!" Eddie yelled.

August and Fritz pulled a thrashing Eddie down the aisle.

"Klara, go talk to her," August said.

Something crashed, followed by shouts, gasps, and crying children. Soup cans rolled across the floor like cars in a parade. Eddie slashed an end cap. Glass jars of Oz peanut butter catapulted from shelves and shattered. August and Fritz hunkered down.

"I'm calling the police," a customer said. "Where's the phone?"

Women flocked to the door, children in tow, abandoning half-full carts.

Klara addressed the middle-aged shoplifting suspect, still clutching her purse. "I'm so sorry, ma'am. What's your name?"

"I'm Sandra Benson, and I'm never coming back here. I'm from Tremont."

"Please let us make it up to you, Mrs. Benson. Your groceries are on the house. You won't have to"—she swallowed —"see that man again." *The man I love.* "He's gone now."

"He scared me out of my wits. I'm leaving." Yet she froze, as if one misstep might put her face to face with her assailant.

"How about a Pepsi?" Klara plucked one from the

refrigerated section. "Take a six-pack. Whatever fits in the cart. For free."

"Nothing's free in this life," the woman snapped. "I already paid a price for this."

So have I.

Outside, police sirens wailed.

* * *

People flooded from the store as Fritz strong-armed and dragged Eddie toward the stockroom.

August lagged behind, weaving through the crowd. "Calm down, folks. Settle down."

Inside the stockroom, Fritz slammed the door. "What were you thinking? Now the police are involved."

"Good! They'll arrest those shoplifters."

"No, they're here for *you*—disturbing the peace. Harassing customers, upsetting displays."

"You yanked me. That was an accident."

True. Eddie had slipped from Fritz's grasp and fell against the racks, sending everything sprawling.

A policeman burst through the door. "What's going on?"

"Communist shoplifters!" Eddie shouted.

Fritz waved off his brother. "There was confusion, officer. We've got it under control now."

"Then why are folks bumbling like bees out there?" Officer Davies narrowed his eyes at Eddie. "What shoplifters?"

"The woman in the red dress. *Communist* red," Eddie said. "She had twelve peanut butter jars in her purse."

"You counted?" The cop crossed his arms.

"I watched her with my own eyes. All twelve jars."

"Her purse was large enough for twelve?"

"And more. She was headed to the tuna next."

"Take me to the shoplifter," Officer Davies said.

Eddie stepped forward. "Finally."

"Now just a sordid moment." Fritz blocked him. "Any shoplifters are long gone. Eddie, why don't you go to the station with Officer Davies and explain everything? August and I will settle things here." He threw a desperate glance at the policeman.

"All right, let's go," Eddie said. "I should've called the cops long ago." He followed Officer Davies to the squad car.

Fritz sighed, then faced the mayhem. Three officers were still shooing people out. Employees picked up canned goods and swept glass fragments, wiping stray food and puddles.

August grabbed Fritz's arm, huffing in his ear amidst the chaos. "This has got to stop. But if he's arrested, there goes the Buckwalter reputation down the drain."

A young reporter from *The Dillard Herald* snapped photos. Blast it all! The newspaper staff sent reporters earlier when things were peaceful. Did this one straggle in after hearing sirens?

"I'll go to the station shortly," Fritz said. "Let me handle things here."

August went outside.

Fritz walked toward the young man. "You want news? Come with me." He led him to the stockroom. "What's your name?"

"Fred Rickert, sir. I'm new with *The Herald*." He barely looked twenty.

"Nice to meet you. New to Dillard?"

"Yes, I'm from Hooper."

"Weren't you here this morning?"

"Yes, sir. I interviewed folks and took photographs for the Grand Opening write-up in the paper."

"Thanks in advance for that. So, why'd you return?"

"All the action. I heard sirens and came to find the source."

"So, you took pictures of ...?"

"The mess, sir. Knocked-down shelves. Food, cans, jars rolling around. Customers bumping into each other, then scattering. And Mr. Edmund Buckwalter leaving with the police."

"I see. For being new to town, you haven't missed a thing."

"No, sir. It's my first month on the job. But I arrived before any other reporters."

"Apparently, you're the only one." *Thankfully.*

Outside the stockroom, silence settled in. The policemen must have dismissed everyone. Fritz needed to take care of business quickly so he could get to the police station and undo any damage there. Before Eddie caused more.

Fritz peeked around the doorway. August was outside with the dispersing crowd.

Fritz leaned against the desk and gestured to the young man to sit. "Fred, let me clue you in on something about the newspaper business your boss might not tell you. A little something called posterity."

Fred sat. "As in future generations, sir?"

"Exactly. Negative press does nothing but hurt people. Well, you need it sometimes. Such as when a business is cheating people. Or to warn about danger. But sometimes, negative press sets off a domino effect that hurts worse than the initial problem. It's akin to hanging one's dirty laundry for all to see. It haunts year after year. You following me so far?"

"I think so."

Fritz stroked his mustache. "Conversely, some reporters delight in telling the good. Spreading favorable news. Uplifting humanity, see?"

"Yes, sir."

"Which kind of reporter do you aspire to be?"

"I haven't thought about it. I just do what the boss says."

"Yes, you're responsible. I see that. You're the reliable sort. Capture whatever news will interest the people. And people like catastrophes and thrills, do they not?"

Frowning, Fred nodded.

Fritz leaned forward. "Son, today I'm giving you an opportunity to use your reporting powers for good. Come here." He dug a camera from the desk drawer and waved him over. They stepped into the store.

Matilda was replacing a broom. Teenage Butch dumped a dustpan of shattered glass in the wastebasket.

"Thanks for all your efforts today, Matilda and Butch. You're free to go home."

"Goodnight, Mr. Buckwalter," they chorused and left.

Fritz walked down an aisle, stopping at the bakery counter. "We have our own bakers who arrive at four-thirty every morning to make the perfect doughnuts, muffins, and loaves for all the good people of Dillard." He handed Fred the camera. "Go ahead. Take a photograph." He chuckled at Fred's frown. "My camera's much easier to figure out than yours. You'll manage." He gave a quick demo.

Fred snapped a photo of the bakery corner.

"Take as many as you want."

Fred took two more from different angles. "Thanks for letting me use your camera, sir."

Fritz walked him down aisle after aisle, pointing out highlights, from the extra width allowing two carts side by side to multiple varieties of peanut butter to cardboard cutouts of Betty Crocker, Mr. Peanut, Elsie the Cow, and Tony the Tiger with Kellogg's Frosted Flakes—a brand new mascot that year.

Fred snapped picture after picture.

Fritz noted newfangled features of the cash register and hit a button. The drawer zinged open, full of bills and coins.

"Wow!" Fred's eyes popped open. "You made a killing."

"Indeed." Fritz took a handful of bills, counted out two hundred dollars, and put the rest back. He guided Fred to the stockroom and took the camera. "Looks like the film is used up." He removed the film. "Why do you think I mentioned posterity, Fred?"

"Pretty sure it has to do with uplifting humanity, not just today but for the sake of future generations."

"Precisely. You're an intelligent young man. Which is why I'm happy to give you my film to develop, plus two hundred dollars in exchange for the film in your own camera." Fritz held up his film and the twenty-dollar bills.

Fred looked back and forth from his own camera to the bait.

"One more thing I need in exchange," Fritz added. "Your silence on the matter. Not a word to your boss or anyone about your own film, what you saw earlier, or this money. You can pocket this for yourself, not *The Dillard Herald*."

"You're bribing me?"

"I'm giving you a chance to start your career on the right foot. To uplift humanity. To share stories that build rather than destroy."

CHAPTER THIRTEEN

2015

To escape the cold January wind, Leslie jogged from her car to Hudson Hall. But her insides never felt warmer. Gregory Scott Stafford liked her writing! Engaging, he called it. Better yet, he agreed to help her. Help Renee, that is. New information from Greg would fit more puzzle pieces into the portrait of her ancestors' lives.

But *Leslie* was the one who'd misquoted him yesterday. Then stalked out.

Never mind that. Bursting with happiness, she wondered how she'd keep Professor Stafford's *yes* from radiating to everyone around her. Especially to him.

The tall, arched corridor looked different today, surely due to her mood. Cream brick walls, ornate ceiling beams, and tiled floors appeared more regal than yesterday. The nineteenth-century tapestry shimmered more brightly. She wanted to kiss each painting as she strolled by. She greeted passersby with restrained exuberance.

Her enthusiastic greeting surely befuddled the receptionist. "How're you doing this lovely morning, Maggie?" Was it really she, Leslie, sounding like a meadowlark?

"Not as well as *you*, honey."

Leslie whirled into her office, hung up her coat—and stopped short.

On her desk, rising above books and paperwork, was a tall takeout cup and a note. The top oozed with chocolate-streaked creaminess. Leslie read:

> *Leslie,*
> *I'm sorry for my blustering. Your turn now. Enjoy a*
> *cup of bliss on me.—Greg*
> *P.S. If you abhor culinary surprises, be assured it's a*
> *mocha chocolate frappe—from Spence's, of course.*

Leslie held the note close to her chest. How endearing—and the last thing she expected from Gregory Stafford, PhD. *Greg.*

She was making headway. Should she have postponed writing him as Renee?

But the charade had begun. No turning back now.

She sipped the frappe. Heavenly. How'd he know her favorite? And how'd he enter her locked office?

Carrying the drink, she stepped out. "Hey, Maggie." She lifted the cup. "Were you privy to a little clandestine procedure this morning?"

Maggie lowered her voice. "Professor Stafford conned me into it. I have the master key. All he did was set the drink on your desk."

"How'd he pick the flavor?"

"He asked. Since we've rated all of Spence's drinks, I offered a recommendation."

"Perfect." And shocking. "Thanks for your help getting my day off to a good start."

"You didn't need *my* help, Leslie. Your face glowed when you walked in." She raised a curious eyebrow. "Hot date last night?"

"Hardly!" Leslie blushed.

Despite Greg's disdain for spontaneity, Leslie felt compelled to thank him in person. She slipped back into her coat and trekked outside.

In Worthington Hall, she ambled down the corridor and paused. Where had this audacity come from? Was this Leslie or Renee waltzing into Professor Stafford's office without an appointment? Coat over her arm, she knocked on his open door.

He looked up from his desk and smiled. "Come in!"

She stepped forward. "Thank you for the frappe. And the note. You made my day."

He stood. "You're quite welcome. Making your day even at nine a.m. makes me feel like less of a schmuck."

"Look, I blabbered and walked out yesterday without letting you respond. I—"

He swatted the air. "You left me licking my wounds. But you put me in my place without name-calling, spouting expletives, or yelling. I can respect that."

"Just don't get charming on me."

"What?" His brow lifted.

"Mr. Darcy I can handle, not charming." Oh, no. Why had Max put that notion in her head?

He chuckled. "Mr. Darcy, eh?"

A flush crept up her face. "I'm sorry. Oh, my, I'm not insinuating anything ..."

"Except that I'm typecast for Mr. Darcy." Squinting, he crossed his arms and lifted his chin.

Whatever ground she'd gained was surely lost now. But she squared her shoulders. "Let's just say you freely speak your mind."

"If I freely spoke my mind, I'd no longer be employed here. Nor would I have friends."

She laughed and glanced at his bookshelves, beside the rustic rooster that might have once graced a barn roof. "Do you have a first print edition of Buckwalter novels?"

"Bottom row. Take a look."

She hung her coat on a chair and squatted as daintily as possible to rummage through the shelves. Grateful she was wearing slacks instead of a dress.

Greg stepped behind her, reaching for a higher shelf. She sensed his presence inches away. Peripheral vision caught his arm above her head. "I have others of interest," he said. "Such as the signed copy. Hmm. Now, where is that?"

She found Fritz's second novel, *Small Town, Big Dreams*, pulled it out, and turned as she stood. Not realizing how far he'd leaned over her to reach his book, she found herself face to face with him, inches away, engulfed in Old Spice cologne. His essence captured her. She was close enough to touch his plaid scarf, his wavy golden hair, the crinkles around his eyes, dimples hardly noticeable at previous distances. And his eyes, like two pools of glimmering sea.

Oh, my word! Her nerves tingled as she clutched the book, hoping her palms weren't sweating enough to damage it.

Flustered, she stepped back. "Excuse me. I didn't realize you were right behind me." Another flush took hold. Her cheeks burned.

"Excuse *me*. I shouldn't have crowded you." Was that a blush tinging his cheeks? Or a ruggedness she'd never been close enough to notice before?

Oh, dear. "I really should go. Thanks for letting me see your book." She set it on the desk, then picked it up again. "I'll put it away." She turned, stopped by a hand on her wrist. His touch sent a bolt of electricity up her arm.

"Whoa. You didn't even open it yet." He presented *The Broken Weathervane*. "Here's the one with Fritz's inscription."

"I have a meeting at ten."

"It's only nine-oh-five."

"I have fifty-five minutes of prep." She glanced at the clock. "Yes, fifty-five minutes. Exactly." Could he hear her beating heart? She'd lost her breath in here before, when his arrogance sucked air from the room. But this was different. His very presence was, instead, life-*giving*. Boosting her heart rate. Every molecule of her body screamed for attention.

Yet she could hardly catch her breath. "I'll look at it later." She handed him the book. "Here, I don't want to mess up your system." *Stop babbling!* She sounded like a dolt.

"Alphabetical, actually. Rather common." He cocked his head as if amused, then took the book. "I'll spare you the trouble, though."

She left and scooted down the hallway.

Five seconds later, he called from his doorway. "Forgetting something, Leslie?"

She whirled around to find him grinning, holding her coat.

Seriously? Now she truly was a bona fide dolt.

Chapter Fourteen

September 1952

After a long day, Fritz spied mail on the dining room table. The thick manila envelope was not a welcome sight. A rejected manuscript always came back in his self-addressed stamped envelope.

Wilma set out a platter of bratwurst and sauerkraut, always ready to soften the blow with his favorite dish. At this late hour, four-year-old Frieda was already in bed.

He slit the envelope and pulled out his novel manuscript, prefaced by a letter.

> *Dear Mr. Buckwalter,*
> *Though your story holds promise with an enticing plot, the chronology spins out of control. Your male protagonist is lackluster, and your heroine's dialogue is repetitive to the point of abrasive.*
>
> *The good news? The story compelled me through Chapter Seven, but it will require a major overhaul to*

tempt me to further reading. I suggest you devote yourself to such or start from scratch. This novel is not a good fit for Hamlin & Sons. I wish you well as you seek other publishers.

    Sincerely,

    Mr. Ned Hamlin, senior editor

He tossed the papers on the table and stomped across the room.

Wilma went to him. "I'm so sorry, dear. I know how disappointed you are."

"It's just a foolish childhood dream after all."

"Nonsense." She rubbed his shoulders. "You know how subjective editors are. You never thought you'd sell that short story last year. But Duncan loved it."

"But I want to sell a novel."

"You will. You're a fine storyteller."

"The neighbor kids agree. And sweet Frieda. But I want adults to love my stories too."

"They will. Every rejection is one step closer to the right publisher."

With a hug, he planted a kiss on her cheek. "You're my number one, Wilma."

"And you're mine." She bolstered his embrace with a seductive kiss, then pulled back and smoothed his hair. "The whole community loves you. And the store."

"For now. No telling with Eddie's escapades." He'd never told Wilma about bribing the reporter. But fortunately, Fred Rickert bought into his philosophy of using the press to uplift humanity.

Eddie went willingly to the police station that day, especially with the thickening sidewalk crowd, fists in the air, the shouts echoing down Maple Street, shaking leafy branches.

Eddie had relayed in tedious detail the shoplifting incidents from the previous months, how August and Fritz dismissed them. When questioned alone, Fritz explained Eddie's endeavors as well-intentioned but assured the officer he needn't arrest anybody.

Fortunately, Eddie was still employed at Dyer's Hardware, a miracle in itself. He did inventory at the grocery from five to six p.m., then made deliveries.

Wilma led Fritz to the table. "You did the right thing for Eddie, like usual. You're so patient."

"Maybe too patient." He scratched his neck. "We lost customers that first week at the new building. I feared I'd have to talk August out of pressing charges, but he agreed we don't need a family scandal hitting the newspapers."

Fritz hoped the bribe wouldn't come back to haunt him.

They sat. "Customers keep coming. And Eddie seems stable. That's only because you, August, and Klara care so much for him."

"Does it do any good?" Fritz bent over, elbows on the table, head in hands. "We used to be two peas in a pod, Eddie and me. We ran that printing press for the neighborhood gazette. Interviews, poems, weekly installments of the serialized Canton Boys Adventures. Eddie's imagination never quit."

"Neither did yours." Wilma speared bratwursts and delivered them to his plate.

"Our best times were alternating chapters for the Canton Boys series."

"I remember. Every kid on the block saved their nickels for the next paper, just to find out what happened next to Gus and Tom. Even the girls enjoyed reading them."

He smirked. "Until Betty's mom found out. Not appropriate reading for girls, she claimed. Too adventurous."

"Outlandish, actually." Wilma scooped sauerkraut onto

each plate. "Which is why everyone loved them. Which is why you'll eventually find the right publisher."

"That doesn't solve the Eddie problem." He sliced bratwurst.

"But he's been at Dyer's five weeks now."

"The calm before the storm."

"There now, an empty stomach only invites pessimism. Eat, Fritz."

"No." He dropped his fork. "Eddie probably hates it at the hardware store. We both wanted to grow up to be acclaimed novelists. Klara says he still writes whenever he can. He almost finished a novel."

"That's wonderful! Is it any good?"

"I haven't read it yet but hope to."

"I'm sure he could use your encouragement."

"Yes, especially since he can't seem to stick to most tasks longer than five minutes." Fritz sat back. "As a kid, he'd stay focused for hours. He finished projects, always in good spirits. He was the one helping folks, not needing it himself. But now …"

"I know." Wilma poked her carrots. "Klara says his moods change like *this*." She snapped her fingers. "He's acted strangely ever since your father's death."

Fritz pushed sauerkraut across the plate. "He still blames himself."

"I asked Klara if he'd been to a doctor, but that's a touchy subject." Wilma gestured to his food. "Eat, Fritz."

Someone knocked on the front door. Wilma answered it. August streamed into the parlor, where Fritz joined them.

August tossed his coat over the couch. "We need to talk, Fritz."

"Join us for supper," Wilma said.

"No, thanks." August planted himself by a chair. "I don't

want Eddie at the store anymore. Period. Not even for organizing displays, stocking merchandise, or making deliveries."

Fritz's collar tightened. "Now just a sordid minute—"

"No, listen to me. I've been thinking this over since the Grand Opening. At best, Eddie's a financial menace. At worst, he's going to undo the Buckwalter reputation of honesty and dependability we've built for seven years, and Papa for decades before that."

Fritz traced his mustache. "How do you propose kicking him out of the family?"

"I'm not. Just the business."

"Same thing. He won't make the distinction. Give him a chance."

"He sabotages every chance."

"Would you rather he'd been arrested and jailed?"

"Of course not. That would damage the Buckwalter name. But I can't condone his conjuring of shoplifters who wouldn't even take cracker crumbs from an ant on a picnic."

"There's no good way to separate Eddie from the business without breaking his heart," Fritz replied. "Let's bide our time. He's working on a novel. I'll see to it he gets published. With writing success, maybe he'll willingly step out of the grocery business."

"That's a pipe dream. He can't stay focused longer than it takes to eat a Bismarck."

"Not true. He writes for hours on end, from jingles to novels."

"But he wants to be at the store."

"So let him keep the delivery service. That'll keep him *out* of the store." Fortunately, Fritz never told August about the stolen goods.

"But he's still face to face with customers, without oversight. Like a ticking time bomb."

Fritz pointed to his temple. "Something's not right. He can't think straight. He's got so much happening in his head, he jumps all over himself in the process."

"How can you defend him? He knows exactly what he's doing."

Fritz shook his head. "No, he doesn't. Have a heart, August." His voice dropped. "He's not the same since Papa died."

"For good reason!" August's fist slammed his palm as he stalked across the room.

"Don't go there, brother. It wasn't his fault. That could've happened to anyone. Papa shouldn't have gone up on the roof."

"Eddie should've been there for him."

"He always was. He did everything for Dad, cheerful and helpful, giving more than he took. It's just that one time—"

"And his irresponsibility had cataclysmic effects."

"You can't blame him! You're *looking* for reasons to boot him out."

"Open your eyes, Fritz. Have you forgotten Grand Opening Day?"

Fritz stewed, hands fisting. "Look at the positive. Eddie's been at Dyer's Hardware for five weeks. I conceded to getting him hired there against my better judgment. But I refuse to budge anymore. No drastic measures. We're all family, for heaven's sake."

"We'll be a family without a business if we don't fix this," August snapped.

Wilma faced August. "Should Eddie see a doctor? He's still grieving the loss of your father, burdened by guilt, Klara says. The poor dear. He broods one week, can't sleep the next. Moods turn on a dime. He needs help."

August's eyes widened. "What's the doctor going to do for a foul mood and unplanned spontaneity?"

"Wilma has a point." Fritz stroked his mustache. "Eddie's wallowing in grief, and he'll get back on track soon. He needs time."

August harrumphed. "What he needs is more accountability. He can't be trusted with business. We can't afford the fallout."

"We can't kick him out of the business," Fritz said. "He'll be heartbroken.'"

"There are more than broken hearts at stake."

"Not when we're family. If one of us is harmed, we're all harmed."

"That's my point exactly, regarding the store," August said. "If you let him flounder, we're all going down, tails spinning. Unless we take action."

Fritz straightened. "Then I'll go down with him. I'll be my brother's keeper, even if you won't."

While frying bacon and eggs for breakfast, Klara sang and bounced to "Back in Your Own Backyard" with Pattie Page on the radio. But periodic nausea crept up her throat. Her doctor's appointment later this week might confirm pregnancy. She couldn't wait to tell Eddie.

She set out ingredients for black forest cake, Eddie's favorite. She anticipated his delight upon presenting both the cake and the birth announcement tonight after supper.

Eddie strolled into the kitchen, pecked her cheek, and took her into his arms, accompanied by Tony Bennett's "Because of You." Singing between kisses, he drew Klara closer as their bodies swayed together.

She relished the closeness, his bristly chin against her cheek, his lips brushing hers.

"I finished my novel last night," he said.

No wonder he was so frisky this morning. Klara hugged him. "Congratulations! I can't wait to read it. Will Fritz look it over?"

"Of course. No doubt he'll recognize some of the characters."

When the song ended, Klara slid eggs and bacon onto his plate. "It's not incriminating, is it?"

He chuckled, a rare sound lately. "Nothing dangerous." He sat and ate a strip of bacon as if it were a delicacy.

Klara welcomed his humor and enthusiasm after days of doom and gloom.

"I've been thinking, Klara. After I get published, I'll earn enough to take business classes. Isn't that dandy?"

"Yes, but the closest college is sixty miles away in Avondale."

"I'll drive over a couple times a week." He chomped more bacon. "With my degree, August and Fritz will beg me to return to the store."

Klara's jaw tightened. Working at Dyer's Hardware had sunk his spirits. She reveled in his newfound hopefulness, but his brothers would require more than classes for hiring him back full-time. "That's outlandish, driving so far twice a week. So much gas and time wasted."

"Not wasted. Invested." He whisked over with a hug. "No more fretting, darling. We'll have the newest appliances. Our first child will have the best crib and playpen."

"Eddie, I don't need fancy things. I'm content as long as we have each other." *As long as you're stable.* No guarantees, unfortunately.

"Delicious meal, Klara. I'm off to the races." He straightened his bowtie and scooted out the door.

Klara made the cake batter and slid it into the oven, then found Eddie's manuscript on his desk. She settled into the settee and read the first forty pages.

Brilliant! The man turned phrases so clever, Mark Twain would envy the skill. Each character exuded personality. Vibrant descriptions set her firmly in each scene.

Tonight, she'd ask him to read it aloud to her, instead of *East of Eden*.

As the cake cooled, Klara walked two miles to Buckwalter Brothers Grocery for her shift. On the way, she brooded. Eddie wasn't the same man who'd wooed her for three years, ever since high school graduation. Always pleasant and even keeled, he'd send her on scavenger hunts for bouquets and chocolates. He serenaded her with homespun love songs. Hardworking and responsible, he was devoted to tasks no matter how complex. Nowadays, he barely finished taking out the garbage.

At the store, she smiled at toddlers riding in carts. Soon she'd be the one pushing her own child in a cart. She eagerly anticipated Sunday family dinners after church with rough-and-tumble nieces and nephews. Hopefully, she and Eddie would attend more regularly. When he was out of sorts, she had to finagle excuses for their absence.

That afternoon, when she arrived home, the phone rang. "Hello?"

"Klara?" Agitation edged Al Dyer's voice. Eddie's yells thundered in the background. "You need to get down here *now*. Eddie's having an episode. His car's here, but you need to drive him home."

"We only have one car. Can you bring him?"

"I can't leave the store. Shall I call Fritz?"

"No, I'll find a ride."

Klara called her neighbor Harriet, who dropped her off at Dyer's. She bolted inside, bypassed the boy at the counter, and charged into the back room. Eddie pivoted and paced, growling indiscernible words.

Al slammed the door. "I don't know what's wrong, but he can't come back. If I hadn't restrained him, he would have hit somebody."

"He's never violent," Klara said. "What provoked this?"

"I asked him to redo a task."

"I spent three hours on that task!" Eddie shook his fist. "And it wasn't good enough."

"He re-organized everything with no regard for my system."

"I'm the one locating stuff. My method's efficient."

Al turned toward Klara. "Our families go way back, but I'm sorry. This arrangement isn't working. This turned into a high-risk situation with potential harm to my employees."

"Oh, dear." She laid a calming hand on Eddie's arm.

He jumped back as if dealt an electric shock.

Al handed her Eddie's car key and pointed to the door.

"Come on, Eddie." Klara held her voice steady. "Let's go."

Eddie smacked the wall. "This isn't fair."

"I know." She tugged his sleeve.

Somehow, they got Eddie to the car. He tried to grab the key, but she held on.

Riding home, Eddie sputtered like a near-empty gas tank. His old mantra returned. "I'm the one who should've fallen off the ladder ..."

Klara patted his leg. "Don't talk that way."

At home, he clomped into the bedroom and slammed the door.

Klara slumped into a chair and covered her face. Tears flowed. This isn't how she'd envisioned married life. Especially after only a year, and now pregnant.

Yet she loved the Eddie she'd known since childhood. She loved the Eddie she read books with. She loved the glint in his eye when he talked about his own stories. She loved the harmless mischief he hinted at when a brilliant aspiration captivated him.

And he was brilliant. The novel was proof.

Nerves spent, she switched on the radio, greeted by Nat King Cole's "Unforgettable." She whipped cream, shaved chocolate, and sliced the cake into four layers. Then she diced potatoes.

Thirty minutes later, Eddie stepped into the kitchen wearing a fresh collared shirt and slacks, suitcase in hand. He hadn't been that sharply dressed in weeks. "I'll be back later, Klara. I've business to tend to."

"Where?"

"Time to sign up for that college class. I'll get there before the registrar closes."

"How will you pay?"

"With a scholarship."

"You have to fill out paperwork first. You have to apply."

"Got it covered. Don't fret, Klara."

She pointed to a bowl of cherries. "But I'm making your favorite dessert."

"You're such a dear. I'll eat it when I get back. And I'll leave you the car. I'm hitching a ride to the bus station with Chet." He left.

Klara charged to the window and watched him saunter

down the sidewalk. She clasped the drapes as if she could transfer all her worries to the fabric.

* * *

That evening after dark, he wasn't back. She called their neighbor Chet. He'd taken Eddie to the bus depot, no idea of his return.

Klara called Fritz and explained everything. He drove over. Wilma stayed home with sleeping Frieda.

Klara opened the door before Fritz could knock. "I'm so worried. Shouldn't he be back by now?"

His face registered alarm. He took hold of her shoulders. "We'll find him, Klara. But we'll have to wait till morning to search or report him missing."

Klara paced. "Why does he do this? It drives me crazy."

Fritz handed her a small paper bag. "From Wilma. Chamomile tea."

Klara took it, voice fragmented. "Thanks. I'll heat water. Do you want some?"

"I'll take my old standby. Meanwhile, I'm running to the bus depot." He left.

After preparing coffee and tea, Klara went to Eddie's desk in his study, searching for clues. On a chair lay a foot-high newspaper stack. How long had he been saving those? She riffled through them, dated from the past year, and checkered with square cutouts. Some articles had circled headlines—references to the Red Scare, others with no apparent connection.

She took his manuscript to the parlor.

Fritz returned, reporting that Eddie took the afternoon bus to Avondale. "But I'm not driving there now. He told the ticket agent he might get off earlier. We'll have to wait."

Klara bit her lip and pressed her hand to her belly. She handed him the manuscript. "Eddie said he wanted you to read it before sending it to the publisher."

Fritz's eyes lit up. "He finished the novel? Splendid!" He plopped into a chair and read, instantly mesmerized.

Klara brought out coffee, tea, and black forest cake. "What do you think? He's so proud of it."

"It's excellent. Any publisher would be lucky to get it. Listen." He read description, as crisp as an autumn day, then dialogue between two inimitable characters, equally compelling. "May I take it home?"

"Not yet. That's Eddie's decision. Just read it here." Besides, she wanted to read it first.

He read bits and pieces aloud. They reveled in Eddie's talent and cleverness.

Fritz stayed till ten o'clock. Still no Eddie. He invited her to sleep at their house in the extra bedroom, but she declined in case Eddie returned. She wanted to be here for him.

"But he's not here for *you*," Fritz replied.

"Perhaps that's not by choice. I'll stay regardless." Wishing Eddie had been here to enjoy the cake, she gave Fritz half to take home.

Fritz promised to send Wilma to check on her in the morning.

CHAPTER FIFTEEN

2015

"I have a brilliant idea for a Raymond University event." Leslie addressed Dr. Lucas, English department head, in his office. "This will promote youth writing skills along with intergenerational connection and mental health awareness."

"You got me at the word brilliant." Gray-haired Dr. Lucas grinned from his desk. "Especially if you can connect all *those* dots. Proceed."

"The local chapter of Mental Health Initiatives is offering a grant for any program that encourages dialogue on mental health issues. That was my pet project at Avondale High School. When Professor Stafford mentioned the deplorable state of freshmen writing skills, I got to thinking."

"A dangerous prospect, if the gleam in your eye is any indication." His own gleam inspired her to continue.

"I'm recommending a three-week writers' workshop next year for twenty high school juniors. Each student will be paired with a senior citizen to interview for writing a biographical essay, focused on life challenges either overcome or managed. Students also have a mentor from Raymond U's English faculty to offer guidance on essay development and revision. Essays will be published in a booklet and distributed around the community—at the library, senior living facilities, and elsewhere."

"And the mental health part?"

"Senior citizens are selected based on mental health challenges, such as anxiety or depression, or more complicated issues like bipolar disorder, schizophrenia, PTSD, or OCD." She handed him her three-page summary with grant criteria. Normally, her job as grants officer encompassed coordinating everyone else's proposals, but once she caught wind of this one, she dove right in.

He skimmed the pages. "Seems like the perfect way to bridge the gap between the mental health initiatives you inaugurated at the high school and promoting community awareness."

"It would definitely help students before college."

"Does this put you in the role of Instructional Designer?"

"I'd love to, but I envision the curriculum as a collaborative effort among the English professors. That's more incentive for MHI to award the grant."

"When's the deadline for submitting the proposal?"

"April first. We'll be notified in October if we're chosen to receive funds. That gives us two months to prepare the proposal, eight months to prepare the workshop. We can invite local authors to participate as speakers." She rattled off author names. "That's a win-win for Raymond U's community engagement." And for Greg.

"And makes us more likely to get a yes."

"Do you have faculty mentors in mind?" she asked.

"Some instructors prefer waxing eloquent about ambition and conscience in Macbeth rather than guiding student writing. But Greg Stafford's number one for teaching composition."

"Really?" Just the name made her dizzy, recalling her doltish behavior that morning, the face-to-face encounter by the bookshelf, the smell of cologne. "I figured he'd be partial to waxing eloquent." She rummaged through her notebook so he wouldn't notice the blush creeping across her cheeks.

"His composition classes have the best scores. Besides, this will get his head out of the clouds and his feet in the community." Dr. Lucas twirled a pen. "How's his social media venture coming along?"

"His Instagram account has five hundred-ish followers. He'd have more by posting kitten and puppy videos, but he assured me he doesn't want to be branded that way."

Dr. Lucas blasted a laugh. "If you post a cat video, he might finally take notice."

"For the wrong reasons." She jotted Greg's name. "Who else?"

"Professors Norma Tomquist, Rob Louden, and Sheila MacIntyre. They'll nail it. Have Janet schedule a meeting for tomorrow."

* * *

The next day, Leslie sat in the conference room with Dr. Lucas and four professors, feeling like a dandelion among tulips. On paper, her background attested to her strengths. But maintaining confidence since the fallout with Vic four years ago remained a chore.

If only Greg Stafford weren't on the committee. Could she handle being in the same room? Even without Old Spice. Was it the way his eyes crinkled before he laughed? Or the rustic hint of his wavy hair, whiskers, and plaid scarf?

At Dr. Lucas's cue, Leslie shared the workshop vision. Questions rolled in.

"So, students will write narrative essays?" This from Norma Tomquist, the Southern belle, a white-haired woman with a kindly, maternal face.

"Yes," Leslie replied. "Essays as creative non-fiction, since *story* is the best route to empathy, and thinking differently about mental illness. That's the heart of this proposal, considering Mental Health Initiatives' core values and goals."

Greg's hand shot up. "I, for one, affirm the creative non-fiction path. If I see one more basic five-paragraph essay that repeats three points verbatim in the intro, summary, and each paragraph, I will know what hell is like."

Rob Louden clapped without changing his stoic expression. His rigid posture and perfectly combed hair were a foil to Greg's informality. "Let's hear it for counterarguments, ambiguity, cause and effect."

"Complex relationships too." Motherly Norma Tomquist leaned over to Sheila. "With this workshop, maybe students won't need rehab after Greg's—um, Professor Stafford's—classes anymore."

Leslie guessed her own presence here engendered a level of formality they normally shed when among faculty only.

"Maybe *I* won't need rehab after dealing with said students' stagnant papers," Greg huffed. "Redundant five-paragraph essays should be outlawed. Along with one-ply toilet paper."

Sheila MacIntyre sniggered, followed by everyone else. Her mostly turquoise wardrobe, spiky haircut, and hoop earrings made her appear like somebody trying to defy the onset of age forty. "Not to mention bad grammar."

"Which causes undue stress," Greg added. "Eliciting a fight or flight response. There's a study now to prove it."

Rob Louden chuckled. "Now you know why your blood pressure shoots up when reading freshman papers. And how about ridiculous word usage?"

"Right," Greg said. "Ever wonder how someone investigates clams rather than claims? Or why it would be quiet enough to hear a pig drop?" Laughter ensued.

Norma clucked her tongue. "Proofreading's about as scarce as hen's teeth these days." Her voice suffused with Southern inflection. "By the way, Professor Louden, how're those composition classes you inherited? As fine as frog hair split four ways?"

Rob simpered. "You and your southern idioms. Sure, as fine as frog hair."

Greg snorted. "That's his way of saying the crisis continues." More chuckles from all.

Sheila fingered her hoop earring. "Do we want to work with high, medium, or low-level students?"

Greg tapped his pen on the table. "With a three-week course, they need to come with basic skills intact. No time to start from scratch with kids who can't string a sentence together."

"Do we target college-bound students who are average writers?" Sheila asked. "Or skilled writers wanting an additional challenge?"

"Average writers, to give them a boost," Greg said. "Every year, we have an influx of average students who flounder all semester. The tutoring center can't meet the demand."

Sheila nodded. "Let's target dual enrollment students with college as their goal."

"Should guest authors be novelists?" Rob asked. "Presenting on characterization, dialogue, setting, and plot?"

"Absolutely," Norma said. "Any suggestions?"

Rob Louden chimed in with a list of names. "Art Fullerton too. His creative non-fiction raises the bar for humble little Avondale, Wisconsin."

"Does he even have a heartbeat?" Greg asked. "I've heard him speak."

"And bless that little beating heart of his." Norma's southern accent flowed like honey. "He thinks the sun comes up just to hear him crow."

Greg and Rob chortled.

"How about Jen Ryder?" Sheila said. "She's one of my favorite people."

"That's because you only see her once a year, for events." Greg smirked. "Unlike the rest of us schnooks with whom you're forced to work daily. Not you ladies, of course."

Norma chuckled. "There's something to be said for scarcity."

"What's the three-week schedule?" Rob asked. "Four hours daily? Twice weekly? Every morning? Evening sessions complete with campfire songs, roasted marshmallows, and gunny sack races?" Still no change of expression.

Sheila giggled, hoop earrings swaying. "Boy Scout camp or church picnic?"

"First, we set goals and choose activities," Norma said. "Then we determine the time frame."

"We'll need time for pairs of students and senior citizens to interview," Greg said. "Plus, time for students to meet with their respective professors while working on their drafts. More follow-up with the seniors, then more revision. I vouch for forming three or four writers' groups within the twenty students for peer feedback."

"I vote writers' groups plus daily one-on-one time with a professor," Rob said. "Right after gunny sack races."

"Don't partner me with you." Norma guffawed. "Do interviewees need to be senior citizens? Or anybody struggling with mental health problems?"

Leslie spoke up. "Perhaps it's killing multiple birds with the same stone by using older folks. One, they've lived through their issues with more life experience. Two, they have more time on their hands. Three, they have stories they want to tell. Four, it gives opportunity for young people to gain appreciation for the older generation."

"That's in short supply these days." Greg sat back, resting his pen on his bristly cheek, head cocked, eyes bright. Leslie tried to avoid his gaze. What did he think of her participation in a faculty committee meeting? Did he find her as doltish as she felt in his office yesterday?

"Would the booklets be free or sold as a fundraiser for MHI?" Norma asked. "Free makes them more accessible, but people like supporting a good cause too."

"Profit for MHI might tip the scales in our favor for getting the grant," Rob said.

"Sales won't compensate for grant money, but awareness matters," Dr. Lucas added.

"What if the local authors also judge a contest?" Sheila asked. "The top three essays could receive monetary awards, plus accolades from the judging panel."

"Competition might hurt the cause rather than help," Greg said tersely.

Leslie frowned. Where'd that rancor come from?

Dr. Lucas squinted at Greg. "We're in brainstorming mode, so all ideas are welcome."

Greg made a quick recovery. "What about an author panel where students submit questions about the writing life?"

"A panel may interest the general public too," Leslie added. Talk continued as she scribbled suggestions.

Soon, Dr. Lucas stood. "Leslie, please put our ideas into survey form."

"Good luck arriving at a consensus." Greg harrumphed. "It's easier swallowing a piano than getting this group to agree on anything."

The others concurred with their chortling.

Dr. Lucas continued. "Leslie, ask Janet to schedule another meeting. We'll hash this out more." He divvied up tasks regarding curriculum, panel topics, author availability, and senior citizen participants. At the next meeting, they'd choose the principal investigator for writing the proposal.

The instructors chatted as they filed out. In the hallway, Leslie caught up to Greg. "Excuse me, Professor, I heard about the engineering wing being christened, named after Douglas Alan Stafford. Are you related?"

Greg afforded her a tart glance. "You're just now hearing of Raymond U's patron saint?" He rolled his eyes. "The man's my father."

"So, you'll be attending the ceremonies."

"It's a requirement," he huffed.

"Of whom? Your father or the administration?" How'd that slip out?

"Both." He picked up his step and was beyond her in seconds.

"I'm sorry. I misspoke." She hoped he'd turn around, but he didn't. Sounded like sour grapes and family dysfunction rolled into one big sticky mess.

Why'd these awkward moments occur when she only sought camaraderie?

Chapter Sixteen

L eslie knocked on Greg's open door for their appointment. She inhaled, never knowing what to expect.

He looked up from a stack of papers. "Ah, a little diversion from grading formidable student essays." He gestured to the chair.

A mere diversion? Maybe that was his way of being friendly. She sat. "By formidable, do you mean impressive? Or causing fear and dread?"

He laughed. "I wish it were the former. Though they *are* making an impression. An adverse one that may haunt my dreams tonight."

"Ah, yes, the stagnant five-paragraph essays. Good that you'll be helping high schoolers via the summer workshop."

"I hope we get the grant, Leslie. That workshop's an excellent idea, combining many features into one neat package."

Her face heated. Was she glowing? "Thank you, Dr. Stafford." She couldn't call him Greg yet. "I appreciate that."

Surely compliments were harder to wring from him than lemonade from a brick.

He picked up a book, one she'd covertly slipped into his mailbox earlier. "Any idea who gave this to me? With this handsome bookmark sporting a genuine Twain quote? It was in my mailbox. No note or inscription." He held it closer for her inspection. *Hemingway Didn't Say That: The Truth Behind Familiar Quotations.*

"Must be from somebody who knows how passionate you are about not misquoting people. Which could be anybody in this department."

"Hmm. That doesn't narrow it down." He arched his eyebrows, his magnetizing sea glass eyes wreaking havoc with her focus. "Who are you in cahoots with?"

"Nobody." That much she could safely say.

"You know nothing about this?" He wiggled the book as if jarring her memory.

"Nothing of any good use to you."

"Your wording keeps you in the top five on my list of suspicious donors."

"Is that a good place to be or not?"

"Would my answer change yours?" He grinned.

"No promises." She returned his smile with a coy one of her own.

"Well, then, you may have just moved to number one on the list. Now, what brings you here today?"

"First, I'm sorry for my response yesterday regarding the engineering wing. And your father. I was insensitive."

"No, you weren't." He batted the air. "Don't mind me. It's a delicate topic that would disgruntle me even if the Queen of England broached the subject."

How about buxom, flirty Amanda Dexter?

He tightened his jaw. "My father was a better engineering professor than a dad. He had expectations *nobody* could meet."

Leslie tilted her head at the irony. Could anyone meet Greg's expectations? How many times had she failed in his eyes since taking this job? Though her failings fell into the realm of minutia, he blew them out of proportion. "He must have been difficult to live with."

He shifted. "Yes, now what can I do for you?"

"Plenty. But you won't like it."

"Thanks for the warning." He offered an endearing smirk, upturned mouth shifting to his right.

"It's time to start monitoring your own social media."

His voice sharpened. "Did anyone ever tell you that frivolous tasks are the devil's folly?"

Leslie drew back. "What? No. I was taught to embrace every task with fervor, to suffer the mundane for the sake of appreciating the meaningful."

"Then you wouldn't understand." He pushed his chair back, swiveled away, and trekked to his filing cabinet.

Why'd he always riffle through files when she was in his office? Was it a defense mechanism? Avoidant technique? "Try me."

He shuffled through a drawer, then slammed it shut. He leaned against the wall, arms crossed. "I've no use for Instagram. Weak people need it for attention, flawed people need it to feign perfection. Insecure people need it for high numbers in lieu of true relationships. It replaces scholarly endeavors, a trade-off of meat for gravy."

No wonder he was so resistant. "Thank you for sharing that, Professor Stafford. I *do* understand." Despite dismissing all her efforts for his benefit in one fell swoop. "When I taught high school, we were also contracted to monitor kids before and after school. That made me grumpy. After all, I was there to change the world. I wanted to enrich students' lives with Dickens, Brontë, and Hawthorne, not babysit them."

He narrowed his eyes. "You're speaking as if I'm a student."

Then don't act like one! she wanted to yell. "No, I'm speaking as a co-worker." She crossed her arms. "But if you want teacher talk, here it is. It's time to do your own Instagram. No more spoon feeding."

He sat and frowned as if repulsed by a rat she dangled before him. "I thought you'd be managing it longer."

"It's getting difficult to continue in your voice. Sometimes I don't know how you'd respond to comments."

"I suppose I must thank you for making me look good."

"You're welcome, but it's problematic. Case in point, Jason Hendricks of Thornton Enterprises wants to meet you."

"I know nothing about him. Why should I bother?"

"He's been an active follower from the get-go. He's asking questions I can't answer."

"You know my favorite coffee drinks."

Oh, brother. "That I can handle. But he's asking about American literary influences on 1900s society, which I'm somewhat familiar with, but I'm stumped. Now he's asking to meet you in person. He's a journalist in Dennison."

"How do I know he's not a jailbird or a stalker? Tell him to take one of my classes. He's only thirty miles away."

"It would be good for your community image to meet him. He's a journalist, and—"

"Is he writing an article about me?"

"No. But he's active on your Instagram posts. It might lead to an article."

"I've been written up in scholarly periodicals. I'm not seeking commercial recognition in *Popular Mechanics* or *Cosmopolitan*."

"But this will be a plus when the committee reviews your full professor criteria. Being community-minded and all."

Greg sighed. "I want you to vet him first."

"You mean meet with him?"

"No. I'd never ask you to meet with a stranger. Get him on the phone and drill him with questions. Check the web for jail records. Then tell me if he's worthy of my time."

Leslie cringed at his caustic tone. Everyone was beneath him. Another reason to never reveal she was Edmund's granddaughter. Too bad she wasn't Fritz's granddaughter instead. But enough of Greg's arrogance. Instead of faltering, she sent a mental thanks to Nadine, her former therapist, then straightened and held a steady tone. "I doubt he has a jail record. But even if he did, you can't dismiss someone for having been in jail. Things are more complex than black and white." She lowered her voice. "I read about Edmund Buckwalter's arrest. What did newspapers say about his jail time?"

He folded his hands on his desk, as if respectfully delving into the sacred waters of Buckwalter history. "According to *The Lynwood Press*, he was in for disturbing the peace after a traffic violation. He had no money for the fine."

"How'd the family deal with that? They were all in business together."

"The news never made it to *The Dillard Herald*. Fritz wouldn't even speak of it when I interviewed him. He brushed it off like a passing train in the night."

"What did Lynwood's police department records say?"

"He argued with an officer after a traffic violation."

"Did Eddie stay involved with the grocery store?"

"Fritz said he did, but in a limited role, then full-time for a while. Apparently, Fritz and August ran the store as legal partners. Eddie never was, according to documentation."

Leslie nodded. "Do you know why?"

"Fritz indicated the age difference as the primary reason. He and August started the business in 1945 when Eddie was only fifteen." He smiled. "I'm having a little *déjà vu* here. Someone recently emailed similar questions about Edmund. Have you heard of Renee Piquette? She wrote articles on mental health, which seems to be an area of interest to you."

Leslie numbed and looked down, feigning to find another page in her notebook. As Renee, she'd sent questions two nights ago, still awaiting answers, still hoping he'd broach the topic of the rift between the Buchwalter families. If he knew of it. "The name's familiar. How long ago did she publish?" *Just stop talking!*

"Four or five years ago, in *Mental Health Solutions*."

Fearful her face was tomato red, she bumbled with another page, then stood. "I need to go." Her gaze went to the sienna and brown-streaked metal rooster hanging on the wall. "That rooster. I've been wanting to ask. Where'd you get it?"

Greg's face brightened. "It's a Buckwalter original."

"From the weathervane on their barn? Not a facsimile?"

"It better not be a facsimile, considering the cost. When I saw it on eBay, I called John Buckwalter, Fritz's grandson. He verified it was genuine."

Oma had said it was Eddie's family keepsake that Fritz borrowed and never returned. Wouldn't Oma love to see this! But not in Greg Stafford's office. "eBay? You're kidding."

"Nope. I was surprised the family parted with it, or didn't donate it to a museum, but apparently, they wanted the money. So here it is." He gestured toward the relic. "Take a look."

She walked to the rooster, yearning to touch it, wondering how much they sold it for.

"It's not uncommon for collectors of Americana and folk art to accumulate weathervanes, especially since the 1970s.

Anything from roosters to cows to dogs, from cars to airplanes. Some pieces sell for five and six figures."

She stared at him, wide-eyed. "Oh, my."

He chortled. "Worry not. I have my limits. I never surpass four digits."

A thousand, five, nine? Greg must be doing quite well if he could spend disposable income on broken weathervanes. Despite the historic literary value.

Greg quoted, "'The price and value of ice cream go up commensurate with the temperature and the child's volume demanding it.'"

"Another Fritz-ism."

He took it off the wall. "I see you're dying to touch it." He shoved aside desk piles and set it down.

She stroked the rooster's comb and tail feathers, cool and smooth. "Amazing. Inspiration for the book title, the real deal from the Buckwalter barn. So, this broke off the arrow?"

"The tail feathers originally broke off from the body." He turned the rooster over and pointed. "It's repaired now. If it had originally been made in one piece, it would've been stronger. But the tail feathers were made separate and welded onto the body. Then the feet were welded onto the arrow."

"So regular wear and tear causes it to break?"

"Yes, from years of wind and rain or by dropping it from a height." He turned it back over as if porcelain. "A weathervane requires annual maintenance, like paint and WD40 coating to preserve the finish."

"After a while, it probably didn't get repainted. Look at this lovely patina finish." She stroked the wing. "From oxidation and extreme weather, right?"

"Most likely. Originally, it was painted black, then powder-coated with zinc oxide to prevent corrosion. It's steel, not iron."

"What's the difference?"

"Chemistry class is too far gone, eh? Steel is an alloy made from iron and carbon. Iron is robust, but this combo is stronger than iron alone." He lifted the rooster. "Fourteen-gauge steel is best because it's thicker, heavier, and more durable, as compared to sixteen-gauge and larger numbers."

"You're a walking encyclopedia on weathervanes."

"I do have a fondness for them. I was tempted to start collecting them until this one emptied my pockets."

"It's quite a find." Oma would love seeing it. Leslie hadn't been to the Buckwalter farm in years, since doing research. "Are the arrow and directional signals still on the barn?"

"Possibly. It was kept for posterity, beside a newer weathervane installed by the current owners."

"But the arrow does no good without the rooster."

"Right. Rooster tails are the perfect shape for catching wind." He set the rooster down. "One glance at a weathervane could save money and lives for farmers and mariners wary of storms."

Leslie stroked the wing feathers again. "My oma always said that wives and moms are emotional meteorologists. They see storm clouds over the horizon."

"A wise woman." He cocked his head toward her. "Was your grandmother thinking of weathervanes?"

"Probably." *This very one.* "I wonder how it broke." And how'd her grandfather get the way he was? What happened to cause such odd, erratic behavior? How long was he gone after losing his job at the hardware store and waltzing off to register for college?

In light of the Grand Opening disaster and Fritz's bribe and cover-up, how far would a person go to protect a loved one? Or the family's reputation?

Reading Oma's journal raised Leslie's intrigue while exhausting her at the same time. One entry per night was all she could handle, considering the emotional toll of each episode. Not to mention the late hours she kept due to her new job.

Greg picked up the rooster. "It's a mystery."

"Just like nobody knows why one person gets ill and another one doesn't. Broken people and weathervanes can still point to stormy weather. Or a broken moral compass."

He looked at her with—was it amusement? Appreciation? Admiration, even? "I daresay you've spoken a deep truth that will take some cogitation on my part to digest. Perhaps a step beyond Fritz Buckwalter's metaphor." He paused. She relished his acknowledgement of her depth. "Hey, I just remembered you wanted to see my first printing book." He went to the shelf. "I've got two. This one has Fritz's inscription." He handed it over.

She opened the book with its crisp pages to the inscription with her great-uncle's distinctive handwriting. "'Dear Dr. Stafford, Bountiful blessings on your bona fide Buckwalter biography. May your readers understand there's no substitute for the truth. Respectfully, Linus Fritz Buckwalter.'"

She looked up. "Love the alliteration. So typical. But wow, he was fully depending on you to convey the truth about his life and put to rest any false, competing voices. Ones that have been bothering you all along."

"They bothered him too."

"But he never explained why Edmund held various jobs or what precipitated his jail time?"

"He glossed over such things. He shared light-hearted anecdotes from over the decades, related to his family, the store, and his stories. Tales he never shared elsewhere, except in disguise in the novels."

"Exclusive material, then. But some of the nitty-gritty stuff has been lost forever?" Except in Oma's diary.

He smirked. "Digging for dirt on Fritz Buckwalter?"

"I'm just curious about his reality, especially since hearing your lecture and learning more about Edmund." And reading Oma's journal entries. A pang of guilt poked her. Fritz only told Greg what he wanted him to know. The fun times. The happy times. Community events. Anecdotes that made the family look good.

Oma's diary revealed things she'd wanted *nobody* to know. The truth.

She closed the book. "What a treasure for you. Along with the weathervane."

"Indeed." He eyed her intently. "I have the distinct sense you're itching to say something." She pursed her lips. "You're familiar with his works. You've gleaned insights."

Was he saying he respected her emotional and literary intelligence? Which golden nugget did he expect to fall from her mouth? Could she deliver? "I'm taking a risk here, Professor, but I sense there's far more to Fritz's life story than what he shared. Surely there was more to him than a string of pleasant anecdotes."

"No doubt he was a complex, astute person, given the nature of his novels."

"Right. So how do you deal with the partial picture he gave you?"

"I cross-reference it with my documentation and other family and townsfolk interviews."

"Did anybody ever talk more about Edmund?"

"Not much more than what I shared at the library. Of course, many from his generation have passed on." He squinted at her. "You keep asking about Edmund."

Her heart beat faster as if he could read her mind. "I have a thing for underdogs. Seems he had his share of struggles. Starting with self-imposed guilt for his father's death."

"I wish I knew more about that."

"What did family members and townsfolk say about him?"

"He and Fritz both had effervescent personalities. They were closer than bark on a tree and would do anything for each other."

"Any idiosyncrasies?" Like accusing supposed shoplifters?

"Some old-timers hinted at trouble but remained as vague as a shadow. It's as if they feared the earth would swallow them whole if they said anything."

"Even after five-plus decades?"

"Well, there are still plenty of Buckwalters in Dillard."

"How did Fritz's kids or grandkids speak about Edmund?"

"Fritz's kids recall Edmund fondly. Especially Fritz's daughter Frieda. He was a fun-loving uncle who doted on them."

What about the Opening Day? Fritz's bribe? Why were family reunions so tense during Leslie's childhood and adolescence? Why'd Oma always leave early?

She opened her mouth to speak but nothing came out.

He briefly touched her shoulder. "You've given me food for thought, Leslie."

His fingers sent a zing down her arm. She didn't want to move. Did her gaze at his face convey the tenderness she felt for him? That sparkle in his eye, that twitch in his cheek—was it tenderness for her or respect for a co-worker?

What was she thinking? She was way out of his league. No doctorate, no parents. She was divorced, had wrestled with depression.

She glanced at the clock. "I appreciate your time, Professor. I'll vet this Jason Hendricks and get back to you."

She left, his touch still tingling. Donning her coat, she brushed through the English office and swept down the hallway. She burst into the courtyard, welcoming the cold air.

They'd shared a tender moment, bonding ever so slightly, perhaps not unlike two pieces of steel welded together at one point. A connection, but without promise of permanence.

That look in his eye ... magnetic. Her heartbeat quickened. But no. She couldn't get pulled in. That surely wasn't his intention. *Guard your heart.*

Did he suspect she was Renee? He had no reason to, other than posing a similar question. She'd tell him eventually, especially since she planned on publishing her historical fiction.

She should never have written to him as Renee. But perhaps her charade was justified. Not to mention his own. He seemed perfectly fine letting her masquerade as him on Instagram. If he got angry about her alter ego, she could point out his own inconsistency.

Mostly, she saddened from hiding information. Knowledge he deserved to know, yet she wasn't prepared to share.

Knowledge that would change their relationship. And betray her grandmother.

CHAPTER SEVENTEEN

L eslie arrived at Kipp's Diner for Friday lunch. Three days ago, she'd called Jason Hendricks, as Greg requested. The business call evolved into a delightful thirty-minute dialogue and Jason's invitation to lunch. By then, she was eager to accept—nothing to do with business.

After four years healing from Vic's poison and surviving a gloomy cloud, she finally felt the freedom to date. She would still be sprawled in a ditch like roadkill without her therapist's help in finding courage to trust and take risks again.

She dismissed her flash of feelings for Greg as a mere crush. Their mutual interest in the Buckwalters was hardly enough to cement a bond. How old was he anyhow? Forty-something?

Prior to calling Jason, she'd learned online he had a master's in journalism, was employed twelve years at Dennison's newspaper, freelanced for a magazine, relished American literature, served on two community boards, and attended a community church. In his mid-thirties, like her, he was active on Facebook, Instagram, and Twitter. He was also unmarried and handsome. According to Google, he'd never been in jail.

Jason stood, smiled, and waved as she crossed the room. "It's so good to meet you in person, Leslie."

He was more handsome than his Facebook profile picture, with jet black hair and dreamy, lidded eyes that belied his energetic demeanor. "Thanks for driving to Avondale. I love this place."

"It's definitely got charm, but it's more about the people you're with." He took her coat and pulled out her chair. Outside through the window, snowflakes swirled. But inside, warmth caressed her senses.

"Thank you." Such excellent manners. Uncle Russ would approve. He'd always treated Leslie, Aunt Martha, and his daughters the way he expected their future dates to treat them. But dark images of the horrible year with Vic set her on edge. Vic had charmed her too. Was Leslie just a means to Jason's end of meeting Greg? Again, she needed to guard her heart.

Over the menu, Jason said, "You had your chance to screen me. Is it my turn now?"

"Is that why we're here?"

"Let's call it getting to know you." He winked.

"That's fair." Though she didn't want to be under scrutiny.

"So, you've only been at the university a few weeks?"

"Yep, I'm a newbie, but it's a great fit." Except for doing social media for the stubborn, unteachable one. "As grants officer, I work with all the professors, not just Dr. Stafford."

He followed up with questions. When she turned the focus on him, he'd shift it back to her. His interest seemed genuine. But she'd been fooled before.

Fortunately, he didn't ask more about Greg. She feared slipping that she was his ghostwriter. Surely that little detail would plummet Jason's hero worship and could leak to the social media world.

When she mentioned the summer writers workshop grant,

he perked up. "I'd love to cover that story. We need more programs to address the lack of writing quality in college-bound students. It's a noose around the country's neck."

Odd for him to express interest in publicity. Professors often complained that local newspapers never covered such university events. Hadn't for years. Not newsworthy.

The waitress stopped by for their orders.

Jason chuckled. "Sorry. We haven't even cracked open the menus. Being with this enchanting woman made me forget all about the food."

Leslie blushed. *Don't get roped in.*

They ordered. The next half hour was a pleasant blend of delicious food and discourse. Leslie reveled in conversation with Jason that was so much more comfortable than being with Greg. While Greg was like a tough steak, being with Jason was akin to eating ice cream.

Jason took his last bite of hamburger. "I'm curious why a lovely lady like you isn't already snatched up by someone."

She fingered her water glass. "To be honest, I'm still reeling from a messy divorce four years ago. I'm taking it slowly."

"I understand." His eyes softened. "I'm sorry for what you went through." But he didn't quote Jack London or Buckwalter as Greg might. "Don't feel pressured. If I'm too nosy, just tell me."

"I appreciate that." He seemed like a fine catch himself. "Any particular reason why *you're* still single?"

He wiped his mouth with a napkin. "I've chosen work and travel over marriage because the two didn't seem compatible. Came close to popping the question but backed off. I'm ready for more now."

Leslie squeezed lemon into her tea. "I'll let Dr. Stafford know I'm recommending that you meet him in person."

Jason's eyes widened. "That's great. Thank you. So glad I

passed muster in your eyes. Incidentally, I heard about the upcoming dedication of Raymond's new engineering wing in honor of Dr. Doug Stafford. Any relation to Gregory Stafford?"

"A father-son dynamic duo."

"Really? I'd love to do an article on that. I'll ask Dr. Stafford about it during our appointment."

"Um, no. I recommend not bringing that up."

"Why not?" He frowned.

"I vetted you for a chance to meet him and talk about literary influences on culture, not interview him for an article."

"I just want a quote or two about his father."

"Again, I strongly suggest not."

"What's the big deal?"

Why'd he keep pressing? "The big deal is that goes beyond your purpose for meeting him. He doesn't care for publicity." Among plebeians, anyhow.

"Of course not. Absolutely not." He shook his head vigorously. A little too much. Did Jason have ulterior motives?

They left with an agreement that she'd meet him for dinner next week.

Chapter Eighteen

September 1952

K lara looked out the dark window as she did nightly. Still no Eddie, seven days since he left. She closed the curtains, as sadly as if closing out her husband.

She rubbed her abdomen. Besides weariness and nausea, one doctor visit confirmed her pregnancy—three months along, baby due in March. But Eddie had no idea.

Two years ago, after their engagement, she loved watching him with his nephews and nieces. They'd ride him piggyback at the zoo. At home they played hide-and-seek, then snuggle for story time. Oh, the stories! He spun yarns, the longer the better. Kids hung on his every word. Like Fritz that way.

He couldn't wait to be a dad. Talking about it made his eyes sparkle. He'd say he couldn't wait to make babies with her. She'd blush and gently push him away, unable to admit she anticipated that day too. Days with their own home and yard, flowers bordering the sidewalk. A kitchen burgeoning with aromas of schnitzel, fresh garden produce, and apple streusel cake. A sweet, humble house becoming a home with handmade pillow coverings, lace doilies, and long, luxurious books, with picture books for the children. Fairy tales and fantasies. Nights of cuddling under the bedcovers, endless lovemaking ...

But fourteen months ago—two months before their wedding—disaster struck. He spent more time at the grocery store with August and Fritz. His father hadn't sold the farm yet, still depending on Eddie to manage it.

Frederick Buckwalter, the patriarch, understood why no heirs wanted to inherit the acreage, but expected Eddie's help until the right buyer appeared. Eddie ran himself ragged tending cows, pigs, and goats, checking wheat and alfalfa fields. He'd race through farm duties to get to the store faster.

In July, preoccupied when his father asked him to clean the house gutters and re-coat the weathervane, Eddie kept putting it off. After a week, unsteady Frederick tackled the tasks himself. He climbed onto the barn roof and unfastened the weathervane. On his way down the ladder, he fell. The weathervane dropped and broke. Eddie found his father hours later and delivered the news to his ailing mother. She died three months later of pneumonia. Without Frederick, surely Hilda lost her will to live.

Thus began Eddie's periodic dark moods. He'd brood, reliving the scenario. Repeatedly. No matter how much Klara tried to convince him it wasn't his fault, he couldn't forgive himself. Nothing soothed. *I should have fallen off that ladder, not Papa.*

She folded laundry, a neat stack. Lately, Eddie rarely combed his hair and wore ratty shirts as if in style. The only benefit of his week-long absence was discarding three threadbare shirts without him objecting. On the radio, Jo Stafford crooned her love ballad, "You Belong to Me." How fitting to hear a song reminding the lover that no matter where he traipsed across the world—whether ocean, jungle, or pyramids—he belonged to her.

Reading *Of Mice and Men*, she barely focused. Eddie loved this story. He embraced the gut-wrenching drama of Lennie and George, his protector, and the notion that truly understanding someone can only lead to kindness, never hatred. If Eddie were here, he'd read in his dramatic voice. But tonight, she couldn't stomach such an anguished tale. Was Eddie like simple Lennie? Poor Lennie, always accidentally harming things he only wanted to touch.

His reading of *Animal Farm* employed different voices for each animal, relishing the novel as parable. But that tale was depressing too.

Three days ago, she'd finally given Eddie's manuscript to Fritz. He'd have valid thoughts and edits. Punctuation and spelling weren't Eddie's strong suit.

While she dozed on the settee, a muffled engine startled her awake. The clock chimed ten. She popped up and peered out the window but didn't recognize the automobile. Hers was in the garage.

A man exited the car. Klara ducked behind the drapes. His silhouette closed in—her husband holding a suitcase.

She ran to the kitchen, flicked on the switch, and flung the door open. "Eddie!"

He stepped from the shadows. In the kitchen light, his face reflected a grin. He dropped his bag and hugged her as casually as if he'd only been gone an hour. "My darling Klara."

"Eddie, I've been so worried. Where've you been?" Relief to see him in one piece trumped anger. But aggravation and sleeplessness tinged her tone. "Why didn't you call? What were you doing? I've been tormented for days."

"I had the most wonderful time. Too bad you couldn't come."

"I could've if we'd planned it together. I've been *working* at the store." Somebody in this family had to work consistently.

He swept inside the room as if entering a dance floor and removed his hat. "I've been to more places in the past seven days than we've been in a year. All for securing our future." He flung his hat toward the hatrack and missed. "I visited the college, but I was too late to sign up for this semester. So, I took the bus to Chicago to talk to a publisher about my novel."

"Did you have an appointment?"

"No, it was an impromptu visit. Unfortunately, he couldn't promise anything without me first mailing the entire manuscript."

Exasperated, she reined in her sputtering voice. "A phone call could have saved you time, trouble, gasoline, and money. Did you meet the publisher?"

"I met his secretary. Mr. Paulson wasn't available."

"You can't barge in on people like that." She scuttled around the room, gesturing wildly. "All of this you do while I'm sitting alone at home, wondering where you are? Eddie, we can't live this way. You walked out of here with no regard for me at all." *Or our baby.* She needed to tell him. But he'd spoiled a potentially sweet moment.

"Everything I do, I do for *us.*"

"Really?" She pivoted and set her arms on her hips. "Whose car is that?"

"Ours."

"We already have a car!"

"Now we have two. One for work, and one for your grocery shopping and attending parties with tea and crumpets."

"I don't go to tea parties. Or eat crumpets. I *work* at the store, remember?"

"Well, now you can have all the tea and crumpets you want. Don't let anyone ever say ole Eddie didn't take care of his darling wife. You deserve the best, sweetheart." He leaned in for a kiss.

Her hand became a barricade. "Where'd you get money for a second car?"

"That's the beauty of it. I bought something for the sake of luxury for a change."

"We can't afford luxury."

"We will when I sell my novel."

"That's down the road. Fritz is reading it now. How'd you purchase an automobile?" Especially after draining their savings. He hadn't repaid it all yet.

He pointed to his most handsome smile. "With this, Klara. Nothing but this and the Buckwalter name, tried and true."

"You bought on credit?" The only good Buckwalter names were Fritz and August's. How far from town did he go to find someone who knew the name without Eddie's reputation marring it? "Where?"

"Glencoe." Fifty miles away. "I got off the bus and strolled to the dealership. Picked this right off the lot, last year's Ford sedan. It's a beauty, with the new Fordomatic Drive that does all the gear shifting. An automatic transmission! And double-seal king-size brakes for safer stops in any weather—"

"When do you pay them?"

"I have six months, monthly payments. It's all arranged. Darling, now you can go grocery shopping whenever you please, no waiting for me to get home, no driving me to work."

"How much does it cost?"

"It's a used vehicle, so I got a great deal. Under a thousand bucks."

"Oh, Eddie." She turned away, but he grabbed her arm and twirled her back to him. "Kiss me, Klara."

With her cheek pressed against his, lavender aroma filled her nostrils. A scent she never wore, never even owned. She blinked. His collar was smeared with red. She touched it. "Lipstick?"

He brushed his collar as if flicking off a fly.

"Why's there lipstick on your collar? Why do you smell like lavender?"

"It's nothing, dear. I ... I was at Melson's Department Store in the women's section, finding a gift for you."

"You tried on lipstick and perfume?"

"Of course not!"

She held the tip of her red finger up to his face. "Where'd this come from?"

"Oh ... it-it must have been that waitress at the Hilton—"

"You ate at the Hilton? In Milwaukee? The prices are outrageous!"

"And worth every penny."

"What happened with the waitress?"

"Nothing, nothing, she's a sweet, little thing. She was just overwhelmed that I gave her such a large tip. She's saving for university. I wanted to encourage her."

"How big of a tip?"

"Fifty dollars. I wrote her a check."

"Fifty dollars!" Trembling, Klara drew into herself, arms crossed. She circled the room, muttering.

"It'll pay for her books at college."

"What? That's why she kissed you?"

"Kissed me? Ah, yes ..." He patted his cheek. "I'd better unpack." He picked up the suitcase.

She trailed him into the bedroom. "I thought you went to sign up for classes or find a new job, coming back that same day. Instead, you return seven days later, poorer, having wasted your money on hifalutin food and a car we don't need."

He opened his suitcase on the bed and dug through

clothing, throwing some in the hamper. "Nothing is wasted, my dear. Everything was for a good cause."

"What good cause? Your belly and your convenience? A rejection at the college *and* the publisher?"

He tossed another shirt into the hamper, followed by a pair of women's panties which landed on the floor. They weren't Klara's.

Klara charged toward the hamper. She picked up the panties by the waistband. More lavender fragrance wafted over her. "What's this?"

"I, uh, bought you some lingerie."

"No, you didn't. You would've given this as a gift, not thrown it out of your suitcase."

"I don't know how it got in here."

"You're lying! You keep changing your story."

"Honestly, I don't know."

"Were you drinking?"

"Just a little wine."

"Enough to lose all your senses and sleep with another woman?" Shaking, she covered her face. Her voice rose. "How *could* you, Edmund Buckwalter? How could you be unfaithful?"

He touched her shoulder. "You're overreacting—"

She shrugged off his hand. "Don't ever touch me again!" she screamed. "Have you lost all your senses?" Her arms whirled as she circled the room. "Wining and dining. It's one thing to buy an automobile with money we don't have, but another woman? How *could* you?" She sank into the bed and dissipated into wailing.

He sat beside her, slipping his arm around her. "Klara, I love you more than anything. Please—"

She squeezed out of his embrace and traipsed to the living room, erupting into convulsive sobs. Pain twisted her insides.

How could she ever trust him again? How could she forgive? Something was wrong with him. Something wasn't normal.

Eddie followed her into the living room, tears wetting his cheeks. He fell to his knees and went prostrate. "I'm sorry, Klara. I was wrong. I don't know what overcame me. It's like ... I can't help it. I'm overwhelmed by emotions that tell me to do what feels good in the moment. I'm sorry, I'm sorry. Please forgive me." Now he was wailing too.

It shook her to the core. "I need time. I can't trust you right now." She should kick him out. But she couldn't. He'd already been gone a week, worrying her sick.

She retrieved a pillow and blanket from the bedroom and threw them on the couch. "You're sleeping here tonight." She returned to the bedroom and slammed the door.

Tomorrow, she'd tell him about the baby.

* * *

Fritz pulled paper from the typewriter, wadded it, and threw it in the wastebasket. Over six months, he'd only written four chapters—twenty-eight pages. Double that amount ended up in the garbage. He glanced at the clock. Eleven p.m. He'd been sitting here three hours, since Frieda fell asleep.

Wilma massaged his shoulders. "Fritz, dear, just go to bed. Get a fresh start tomorrow."

"It won't do any good. All I can think about is Eddie. Dad-blast it all! Where'd he go? He's driving us all crazy."

"I know," she murmured. "Poor Klara."

"She's been through the wringer." He rolled another piece of paper into the typewriter.

"Did you finish editing Eddie's manuscript?"

"Almost. It's quite good. He's truly gifted."

A knock sounded on the front door.

"Who in the world?" Fear etched Wilma's voice.

Fritz went to the front window and peeked out. "Klara!"

Wilma threw open the door and practically had to catch Klara as she stumbled inside.

"Eddie's back."

"Thank God." Fritz sighed.

Klara's words squeezed out between breathless cries. "He got back an hour ago ... He wasted a week doing stupid things ... tried to register for college ..."

Wilma guided her to the couch and took her coat.

"He went to a publisher with no appointment ... bought a car ..."

"What?" Fritz sat across from the women. "Bought a car?"

"On credit. Now we're in debt." She covered her face and bent over. "He slept with another woman ... and I haven't even told him I'm pregnant!"

Wilma held her close. "Oh, my dear Klara."

Fritz paced. "How can this be?"

Klara's sobs filled the room, then muffled to whimpers. It was a wonder Frieda hadn't woken up.

Wilma patted Klara's arm. "There, there now. You're having a baby! I'm happy for you. Have you been feeling well?"

"My nausea subsided, but nothing is well. I was thrilled, but Eddie spoiled it."

Fritz's jaw tightened. Eddie stole her joy. "Maybe this pregnancy is just the thing to settle him down."

Klara jumped off the couch. "You think a baby's going to solve his problems? There's something wrong with him. He's not the man I married. He's not the boy I grew up with. It's like a demon overtook him. He doesn't understand what he does or why."

Wilma glanced at Fritz. "Maybe he needs professional help."

Klara's voice rose. "Maybe he needs his brothers treating him like brothers!"

Fritz startled. Now her anger was directed at him? "Klara, we've done everything in our power to help Eddie. We've found him employment five times."

"Employment everywhere but Buckwalter Brothers Grocery. What he wants most in the world is to be part of the family business. He wants equal treatment, fair pay—"

"We've always paid him fairly."

"But you won't even let him walk in the store until after hours. You won't be legally yoked to him."

Fritz walked over and braced her shoulders. "Listen, Klara. I'd love nothing better than to include Eddie as an equal partner." Unlike August. But she needn't know that. "That was the original plan. But something changed. He's done more harm than good for our business."

"How can you say that? He wrote all those advertisements and radio jingles. He designed displays, even bought advertising from his own budget. He drummed up thousands of customers the first month at the new place. He brings in more money by making deliveries."

"All those come at a cost, Klara. You know. The so-called shoplifters. Even the deliveries started out behind my back, with Eddie keeping profits." A fact he'd hidden from August. "He's not always thinking of the store or the family's well-being."

"But he's trying. He wants to." Klara eyed him potently. "He just wants to be part of what you and August have. He's family, for heaven's sake. Family!" She pulled away, and his arms dropped.

He'd never seen her so hysterical. She'd always thanked them for their interventions and job searches, never blaming him for Eddie's bad choices.

After calming, Klara wiped her face. "I'm sorry, Fritz. I'm grateful for all you've done for Eddie, for me. I don't know what we'd do without you." She wrung her hands. "I know you have to think of the store. You've gone beyond the call of duty, seeking compromises." She twirled and planted herself before Fritz. "I love him the best I can, but it's not enough. There's something wrong. He needs help we can't give him."

They all sat again. Fritz took his sister-in-law's hand. "We'll always be here for him, for you, Klara. We're not going anywhere."

"But what next?" Klara bit her lip.

"First, this weekend I'll go with Eddie to return that car to the dealership, whether he likes it or not. Then I'll take him clothes shopping. He looks more bedraggled weekly. I'll be on the lookout for another job opportunity. He can't live off the dream of selling his manuscripts yet. He's an excellent novelist, but that dream takes time." He winced. Time that Fritz didn't have either, to pursue his own dreams. Time sucked by Eddie.

"Will you help him, Fritz? I mean, beyond editing. You can give guidance on how to approach a publisher."

"Of course, Klara. I'll do anything to see him successful." If Eddie made his living writing novels, he wouldn't be begging for more store hours and causing mayhem there. "One more thing. I'll talk to him about seeing a doctor, a psychiatrist if necessary."

CHAPTER NINETEEN

2015

L eslie reread the note from Maggie: *Please see Dr. Stafford at 2:00 p.m. today. High priority.* What? He never asked to see her. Was it about approving Jason Hendricks? No time to ponder now. She faced numerous appointments and a pile of grant proposals begging to be read.

At noon, Dr. Veronica Schmidt, a chemistry professor, came to her office. After dissecting proposals for science equipment, Leslie had other questions. "A lot of excitement in the engineering department with the dedication of the new wing."

"I'm thrilled." Veronica gave a clap that made her bracelet tremble. "Score one more for science, despite it being engineering versus chemistry." Leslie envisioned the jewelry dropping into a flask of chemicals, sizzling and disintegrating. "Douglas Stafford was to the engineering department what Elvis was to rock and roll."

Leslie laughed. "What was he like?" She might glean more about Greg.

"Doug was all business. Not a thing was out of place, from T-squares to gears to calculators. His methods were impeccable. He made Raymond U cutting-edge by first utilizing CAD software and other technology. He also brought in more grant money than any other department during his last twenty years. That's mainly due to his robotics research, bringing much attention to Raymond U. Which brought in more students and researchers."

"Did you know him personally?" Leslie asked.

"Yes, he was here fifty years before retiring five years ago." Veronica pursed her lips. "The truth is, Doug deserves the namesake. He really is Raymond University's Elvis. But he was caustic and critical. Everyone walked on eggshells around him. You had to earn respect, but if you made a mistake, watch out."

Like Greg. "Sounds tough."

"Being in chemistry, I didn't work with him personally, but a crony of mine did. He was harsh with the men but turned on the charm with the ladies. With colleagues, not students. Raymond U's best kept secret."

"He was married, right?"

"Until his wife passed away ten years ago. She was either a saint or a dimwit, tolerating so many shenanigans. She should've left him."

"And his children?"

"You've probably surmised that our own Professor Greg Stafford is his son. Doug had two sons, Adam and Gregory. Adam was the apple of his eye and studied engineering here. He's a researcher for Peterson Corporation."

"And Gregory?"

"Not a science guy by any stretch. He had spectacular

ideas of his own, but they never measured up to the big guy's standards. Unfortunately, Doug had no use for literature or anything Greg valued."

"That's odd in a liberal arts college where all education matters."

"But the bottom line for Douglas was engineering. He's brilliant and innovative but only saw the world one way."

"That must've taken its toll on his sons."

"I think Greg gave up trying to please his father. He went to Duke for history and literature, a double slap in Daddy's face. Bah, humbug." She giggled at her Scrooge literary reference. "Between travels and jobs, Greg earned two master's degrees, at Duke and Harvard, then earned a doctorate at Oxford. He got tenured here."

"What about his mom?"

"She was a sweet lady, encouraging her sons, but no amount of positive reinforcement from one parent compensates for rejection from another."

Or having no parent. Well, the few memories of her mother were nothing to savor. Then she'd walked out for good.

Veronica patted Leslie's hand. "This conversation hit a nerve."

"Just thinking. I'm sad for him." Which was true.

"You needn't worry about him, dear. I think he's come to peace, though it stings from time to time. Like this hoopla about the engineering wing. But when that blows over, the dust will settle. The good thing is, Greg's nothing like his father."

"He can be prickly when things don't meet his criteria of excellence." *Or when you misquote him.*

"Look, I've known both Doug and Greg, and Greg's *not* a chip off the old block. Yes, he has high expectations, but he doesn't trifle with the ladies. He's an asset to Raymond U in scholarship and integrity. He has solid friendships, loyal as a puppy dog. He even goes to church, for heaven's sake! He's a good man, all the way through."

The words relieved the heaviness in Leslie's heart. "Was he ever married?" Oh, brother! Why'd she ask that?

"He had a couple serious relationships but never tied the knot. My guess is, enduring his parents' marriage was scary enough to thwart him." Veronica glanced at her watch. "I need to go, dear. This was just between us."

At two p.m., Leslie paused in the hallway outside Greg's open door.

He was on the phone. "What do you mean, those tacos make Zorito Burrito look like Taco Bell? Them's fightin' words, cowboy ... A guy moves away and forgets his roots." He laughed. "No more tacos to die for ... All right then. See you later."

He was in a good mood, fortunately. How long would it take for Leslie to inadvertently spark his anger? She had a knack for it. Good she had a date with Jason to look forward to.

She peered around the door. "Quite the turn of events, *you* asking *me* here."

Frowning, Greg pointed to his email on the computer screen. "You approved this Jason Hendricks before we even discussed it?"

"You told me to vet him, and I did. I went the extra mile and met him in person."

He looked up. "You met the guy? Why? That wasn't safe."

"I vetted him on the phone, *then* we met. Why do you care?"

"Why'd you need to meet if you'd already vetted him on the phone? Was it a date?"

"I hadn't made my final decision yet." No way would she admit it was a date. "I think you'll enjoy meeting him."

"So, you met with someone who's using you to get to me."

Seriously? Like he'd do if he knew her grandpa was a Buckwalter! "He's not using me."

"Meeting him has skewed your objectivity."

Leslie's blood boiled. Her superior or not, she couldn't let him talk to her that way. "How dare you assume that. I was doing my job."

"By going on a date with an accomplished, good-looking fellow."

"How do you know he's good-looking?"

He turned the laptop screen her way to reveal a headshot of Jason.

"Did you look up his jail record, too? He doesn't have one, if that's your concern."

"I know."

"Then what're you upset about? Are you grumbly about meeting with a journalist? Or because I went on a *date?*" Oops! That slipped. "Which, by the way, is none of your business."

"Rogue journalists who want to meet me are definitely my business."

Leslie set her hands on her hips. "Do you assume everyone under forty is rogue?"

Greg finally stood, as if remembering his manners. "I'm sorry."

She shook her head. "For what, exactly?" She needed to hear it.

"Jumping to conclusions. For speaking my mind as if your personal life is my business. But I truly was concerned about your safety. Too many buzzards, scamps, and degenerates in the world posing as angels."

"Buzzards?"

"Yes, like Lieutenant George Wickham, your Mr. Darcy nemesis. I told you right off the bat to *call* Jason, not meet with him."

Touched, Leslie scaled back her anger. "I appreciate your concern. And I accept your apology."

He offered his endearing smirk. "Figured I'd take the high road."

"Is that a one-time offer only?" She smiled.

He laughed. "Hopefully not." He rattled through papers. "If only we had TAs to hand off these quizzes to. Too much grading. Too many committee meetings. Now ... there it is." He pulled one out and threw her a glance. "Do you play pickleball?"

She startled. "Yes. Why?"

"Are you any good?"

"Depends on who you compare me to."

He eyed her, head cocked. "In your own estimation."

She lifted her chin and crossed her arms. "I've been known to give opponents a run for their money. Been playing eight years, weekly, year-round."

"Are you free tonight?"

What? "For pickleball?"

"Yes. I play Tuesday evenings with my usual foursome but just found out my partner can't make it. I've contacted thirteen people, and nobody's available on such short notice."

"So, I'd be your desperation partner. Number fourteen. At least it's not thirteen."

"Superstitious?"

"When I have reason to be."

He grinned. "Are you game?"

Maybe this was her chance to prove she could be a friend. As equals. Well, probably not equals on the court. Or it could be a chance to make a fool of herself. She narrowed her eyes. "That depends. How good are *you*?"

"My opponents fear me. I've been playing four years. Almost weekly."

"I could've used this hobby to your advantage on your Instagram account if you'd mentioned it."

He dropped papers into the filing cabinet drawer. "I suppose that throws off the *Feng shui* of your social media universe."

"Precisely. I'm glad you understand. I'll play on one condition. Afterward, we stop at Pop's Root Beer Stand, so people can see you supporting local businesses. It'll make a great Instagram post." She was quick to add, "Without mentioning me, of course."

He rolled his eyes, which she'd expected. But she didn't anticipate his next words. "How about Zorito Burrito instead? It's home grown, too, featuring tacos to die for. Not those measly ones my buddy in Albuquerque promotes."

"Seems to me the Southwest could lay claim to the country's best tacos."

"Don't get me started. No judgment till you've tried it."

"You've got a deal."

"It's a hole in the wall. Definitely no *Feng shui* going on there."

"Maybe that's because it's Mexican, not Chinese." She inhaled deeply and let it go. "I'm confused. How'd this meeting get from anger to a pickleball invitation? Should I be flattered or worried?" Was he jealous she'd been out with Jason? No, that couldn't be.

He chuckled. "You've nothing to worry about. Let's just have fun. And kindly note it's not my habit to spend time with someone out of desperation."

"Good, but I'm not sure you answered my question."

"I've quite forgotten the question. Shall I pick you up at five?"

Was this a date or not? Play it safe. "No, thanks, Professor. I'll meet you there."

"Calling me professor on the court is off limits." He winked. At his suggestion, they exchanged cell phone numbers.

CHAPTER TWENTY

N ow Leslie truly had good reason to question her sanity. Why'd she say yes to Dr. Gregory Scott Stafford's invitation to play pickleball?

Why'd he ask *her*? When the notion of his possible attraction to her glimmered, she took a reality check: she was number fourteen. Most likely, he didn't want to miss his game.

She chided herself for entertaining the thought of him liking her. Despite almost swooning in his office once, dating him could only lead to disaster—personally and professionally. If he was smooth-talking, she'd dismiss him as a playboy. Been there, done that—with that snake Vic. Her trust of charm dwindled to zilch. At least with Greg, she knew what she was getting. As Max said, what you see is what you get.

Surely Jason was more her type. Definitely more stable mood-wise. With no eggshells to sidestep.

Fortunately, she was too busy today to fret about the evening.

* * *

After debating which athletic outfit to wear, Leslie picked the magenta V-neck T-shirt and black shorts, under a warm hoodie and fleece jogging pants for defying February winds. She drove to Avondale Sports Complex to meet Greg on Court Four.

He immediately welcomed her—a far cry from the library event. His teal shirt spotlighted sea-green eyes. Golden, wavy hair still had the flyaway look, complementing his whiskers. His shorts revealed strong, toned legs. She felt weak-kneed.

He introduced her to Bill and Carla, probably closer to Greg's forty-plus years. "This is Leslie Wickersham, willing to play with this old curmudgeon in a pinch."

Number fourteen, actually. "Nice meeting you." Leslie shook their hands.

Bill laughed. "If you're old, Greg, then I'm ancient." To Leslie, he said, "Thanks for your sacrifice in playing with Greg here. The game must go on. Even if Amanda can't make it a priority."

"Amanda?" Leslie said.

"Amanda Dexter, aka Avondale's librarian," Carla said. "Greg's partner."

No wonder Greg was so friendly with her. Was Amanda's pickleball attire as revealing as her low-necked dress was? Were they dating? Why'd Leslie care?

"Playing with these two guys is a comedy of errors," Carla said.

Leslie smiled. "I'm up for the challenge." *Maybe.* She might easily tip over right now if someone touched her.

They played doubles for two hours, Leslie doing her best so Greg wouldn't lament his inviting her. As a pair, they seemed evenly matched to Bill and Carla.

He played hard, injecting humorous quips. He offered "nice job," or "good hit," or "that'll show 'em" after her best shots. But how'd she compare to Amanda?

When the 1980s hit, "Jump," blasted from the speakers, Greg and Bill played their paddles like guitars, rivaling Eddie Van Halen's antics. Yes, the good professor bobbed, lunged, and jumped on the pickleball court as if on stage.

What you see is what you get. And she liked what she saw.

Carla shrugged. "See what I mean? Comedy of errors."

* * *

Greg was right. Zorito Burrito was a hole in the wall. Hopefully, the food would compensate for the lack of ambiance. At the counter, Leslie ordered tacos and pulled out her wallet.

Greg nudged her. "Nope. My treat." He added his order and stuck his twenty-dollar bill out farther. She extended hers, but he more than matched it. The cashier glanced back and forth between their bills and finally took Greg's.

"Good choice, young man," Greg said. "Always pay for the girl."

Did he always pay for Amanda Dexter? Did they go out? "Thank you, but that wasn't necessary." After all, they *weren't* on a date.

"Yes, it was. I respect your right to vote, hold office, earn equal pay, and all that rigmarole, but there's a place in the world for chivalry, severely lacking in our culture."

Did he learn that from his father? "Okay, then, Sir Gregory. Zorito Burrito is as good a place for chivalry if there ever was one."

"Glad you agree."

It wasn't hard to agree as he stood there in his teal shirt with alluring wind-blown hair.

At a corner booth, she took out her phone. "Let's get this out of the way. Smile!"

Greg held up a tortilla chip. His dazzling grin held through his words: "Blasted social media, the bane of educated society."

She snapped the shot. "Any ideas for a literary-themed caption instead?"

He offered absurd suggestions, which she vetoed before settling on one. Was he enjoying the banter as much as she was? Maybe he'd resigned himself to his fate.

The server delivered their meal. Tacos were tough to eat with dignity. She took dainty bites and used plenty of napkins.

Curious about his education, travels, and father, she asked a general question to see how he'd fill in the blanks. "So, what was your pathway to becoming an English professor?"

He scooped guacamole on his taco. "I fell in love with books at age two. Upped my game from Dr. Seuss in first grade, devouring chapter books. Read as many classics as I could get my hands on in high school."

"And discovered Fritz Buckwalter?"

"Yes, and read his first seven books. I read the rest in college at Duke. I double majored in literature and history."

"You needed some North Carolina sunshine?"

He grimaced. "Mainly breathing space. I had to pursue my own thing in my own way rather than do the expected."

"Which was ..."

"Study engineering like my brother. A more viable career than literature."

"But *you've* made a career of it." Leslie refolded her tortilla.

"That took me down a circumvented route that included two master's degrees, several research projects, writing, and publishing. I spent four years at Oxford earning my doctorate."

"Pursuing American literature?"

"Can't escape my roots, I guess." He smirked. "I moved back here to research Buckwalter for finishing up my dissertation. While helping my mom and conducting interviews in Dillard, I started the tenure track, teaching at RU. Achieved that five years ago."

"When did you decide to go for full professor?"

"Last year. My publishing history and teaching qualifications are through the roof, but the committee and I agreed upon three additional criteria. Supposedly, I hadn't served on enough committees. So, I had to choose—committees or community engagement."

She smiled. "Community engagement, the lesser of two evils."

"Yup. They also wanted to chisel through my social media resistance to ramp up the engagement and drag me into the twenty-first century."

"And the third thing?"

"The Buckwalter biography, as the touchstone of my publishing career. Grable Press accepted it months ago. We're in the third round of edits." Grable Press was top-notch, espousing numerous bestsellers. "But enough about me. Where do you hail from, Leslie?"

Great. A direct question. She couldn't lie but could avoid details. She offered a sly smile. "Didn't you vet me to see if I was legit?"

"No time to vet. You popped into my office one day unannounced. That was the first I knew you were the grants officer."

"And the new social media liaison in the bargain."

"Ha! You're definitely more than I bargained for."

"I hope someday you'll mean that as a compliment."

"No promises. So, are you from around here?"

"I'm from a little town up north." Where Fritz's sister-in-law Klara moved when she left Dillard. "I went from UW-Milwaukee to teaching at Avondale High School for ten years.

Then I started my own business developing grant proposals. Those two experiences dovetailed perfectly into my current employment here."

"You taught literature, right?"

"English composition. American and Brit lit."

"Yet you still quote Popeye."

"I'm good for much more than Popeye." She adopted a dramatic tone and brought her wrist to her forehead. "'It is a far, far better thing that I do, than I have ever done; it is a far, far better rest that I go to than I have ever known.'"

He chortled. "Hope you're not referring to monitoring my Instagram account as the far, far better thing." His mouth curved up into one of his smirky expressions.

She laughed.

"Do you miss teaching?"

"Sometimes. I enjoyed classroom discussions and helping students improve writing. I loved bringing literature to life and was disappointed I couldn't implement a curriculum I'd written."

"What was it?"

"After watching students suffer from mental illness, I wrote a curriculum as part of a mental health initiative, for which we got a grant. Prior to that, I offered a literature class with a mental health theme. It evoked discussion of mental illness through literary characters, like Septimius in *Mrs. Dalloway*, Lady Macbeth, Mr. Rochester's wife, and Nicole Diver in *Tender is the Night*. We read *I Never Promised You a Rose Garden*." About a teenage girl with schizophrenia. "Students could earn literature or psychology credit."

"Clever. But why didn't you implement the other curriculum? Wasn't that part of the grant criteria?"

"Another teacher implemented it. She still uses it."

He cocked his head. "What prevented you?"

How much should she say? He might not appreciate emotional transparency. Yet that was the curriculum goal, right? At least she'd never been to jail. He drew the line there.

She straightened. If her issues made him look down on her, so be it. "I left the school at year's end because of severe depression. I could hardly function."

"Ah ... thus the interest in mental health initiatives."

"Yes, I could relate, floundering so much I couldn't teach. Irony at its best. The curriculum was mainly about starting a dialogue, to reduce the stigma of mental illness, and encourage kids and parents to get necessary help. Direct them to effective resources."

"A noble cause. I hope it catches on at other schools. Too bad you weren't able to see it in action." He eyed her intently. "It appears you've come out of your black hole."

"I'm doing much better now." She swallowed. "Since my divorce."

His eyebrows raised. "Divorce?"

In the morning, would she be sorry for revealing anything personal? Sitting here nibbling on tacos, magnetized by his eyes, relishing his listening ear, his thoughtful questions ... she *must* resist the attraction. She was aiming for friendship, that's all.

She crossed her arms on the table. "Since I promote open dialogue about mental health, I'll share a bit." Maybe he'd open up too. "I married five years ago after dating a guy for three years. He was kind and charming. I was head over heels in love. But our one-year marriage was a disaster. He turned out to be a narcissist, which I didn't see coming. It was awful. He constantly manipulated, gaslighted, blamed me for everything. He had an affair. I sank into deep depression. I couldn't function at school and left."

She fiddled with her straw, noting his reaction. A gentle frown wrinkled his forehead. "Now I see the red flags. I don't believe in divorce, but I had to get out. My therapist and meds helped my exit, but Vic was just as ruthless during the divorce." *And still is.* She avoided using Vic's last name, Rinaldi, in case Greg would remember Leslie Rinaldi's email four years ago. She brushed away a tear.

He shook his head. "'There is, I believe, in every disposition a tendency to some particular evil—a natural defect, which not even the best education can overcome.'"

She blinked in surprise. "You're quoting Mr. Darcy?"

"It seems to fit." His calm tone merged to disgust. "I'd like to kick that bloodsucker into the middle of the next galaxy."

She drew back. "Mr. Darcy?"

"No." He chuckled. "Your ex."

She offered a weak smile. "I wish you could have. But with all my talk of empathy for the mentally ill, maybe I should have more empathy for him in his emotional blindness."

He swatted the air. "Come on. You were a victim. You needed boundaries more than you needed a bleeding heart."

She *still* needed boundaries, with Vic's monthly extortion. But if she stood up to him, he'd call the press—or Greg—about her Buckwalter connection. If she contacted her lawyer, Vic would somehow make things worse. She sighed. "I suppose. Anyhow, I was reeling for a long time. But my therapist was a lifeline." She crumpled her napkin. "I've learned to practice what I preach about mental health and not hide in the shadows. But I'm ready to change the subject now." She smiled.

"Now I understand why you prefer the Mr. Darcy type."

She felt herself blush. Was he hinting at her taking a liking to him? Hopefully not.

"What's your hometown?"

Rats! She'd had enough transparency for one evening. "Crestwood."

"Is your family still there?"

Here we go, the family questions. "Yes."

"And family entails ...? That is, besides your cousin who enjoyed *hors d'oeuvres* at the library."

He'd noticed Max's wolfish habits? "Mainly my aunt and grandma."

"Everyone else moved away?"

He was treading too close. "That's everybody."

His face registered confusion, but he didn't prod.

"Actually, my grandmother raised me." *The lady you want to interview.*

"Oh."

"My mother left when I was seven. I never knew my father."

"I'm terribly sorry."

She blinked back tears. After twenty-eight years since her mother left, shouldn't she be over it?

Greg's voice lowered. "'Heaven knows we need never be ashamed of our tears, for they are rain upon the blinding dust of earth, overlying our hard hearts.'"

Touched, Leslie brightened at the familiar *Great Expectations* line. "Thank you."

"I don't know what's worse. An angry, hypocritical father, or one you never knew."

"Either one is abandonment."

"Did your father even know about you?"

"I have no idea." Another tear slid down her cheek. She wiped it with her sleeve. "I'm sorry."

"No apologies. I shouldn't have pushed."

"You weren't pushing. It's okay." His sensitivity was both surprising and appreciated. With his interviewing experience, he surely knew how to lasso the nitty-gritty without putting someone on the defensive. She swallowed some water.

"Do you realize Klara Buckwalter lives in Crestwood?" he asked. "Though she goes by a different name now."

Choking on her water fizzled into an awkward cough. "Really? What's the name?"

"Apparently, it's Crestwood's best-kept secret."

Fortunately, he didn't know it was Wickersham. Leslie's anonymity would be over. *Change the subject!* "That committee meeting sure bulldozed my notions of stuffy professor stereotypes."

He chuckled. "I hope you weren't too shocked."

"I was, but I survived." She picked up her purse. "I still have to peruse some proposals tonight."

"But first, how do you rate the tacos?"

"If I don't say ten out of ten, I might be chastised."

He wiggled his pointer finger as if summoning her. "Honesty now ..."

"A solid nine point five."

He feigned astonishment. "What's with the missing half point?"

"See? You can't bear it."

He laughed and pulled out his cell phone. "Allow me to take a selfie of us—*not* for social media." He scooted beside her with a black velvet painting behind them and held up the camera. "Say Zorito Burrito *es numero uno.*"

Back at home, guilt buckled in as she stared at the most recent email from Gregory Scott Stafford. To Renee Piquette. Sent at four-thirty, shortly before meeting at five. Did he suspect she was Renee? Was he testing to see if he got a reply while playing pickleball?

She copied and pasted three new answers into her file, then wrote a brief thank you.

But she didn't hit send. She should stop these exchanges, reveal Renee's identity.

Tonight was the first step toward a comfortable friendship with Greg, without him knowing her as Renee. Now she felt like a fraud. At best a sneak. Double-tongued. Dishonest.

Yet she'd had good reason to contact him as Renee, right? He wasn't receptive to just plain Leslie in her role at Raymond.

But now that he was more approachable, she should tell him before things got out of hand. A two-week charade was better than an interminable one.

Or maybe not. Her confession might mark the end of their friendship. The day after it started. Yet who was he to judge? He seemed fine with her ghostwriting as him on Instagram.

Later in bed, Leslie ruminated as the queen of "I should've said …" She often chewed on the day's activities, rehashing moldy conversations.

Was it too soon to confess her mental health struggles? Had she said too much about her marriage? And why'd she mention her non-existent parents? Well, he'd kept asking. Images of her mother swirled, with an empty space for her father, inviting more tears.

She'd wanted to ask more about his life—particularly his family, his childhood, his father, Amanda Dexter, and other women.

Stop! Why'd she need to know about any women?

After all, she only wanted a friendship built on respect. Now they'd launched one. Which, hopefully, would serve them well as they worked together.

As long as she didn't have to answer direct questions she'd be tempted to lie about.

Reading another journal entry would hardly keep her mind off Greg, since he was the one hoping for more Buckwalter revelations. It was late as she settled in to read. But wading through the heaviness bit by bit was the best she could do for now.

CHAPTER TWENTY-ONE

September 1952

F ritz punched the last numbers on the cash register and set down the peanut butter jar. "Twenty-two dollars and fifty cents, Mrs. Trimberg." He hit the button. *Ca-ching!* He gave change for her bills. "Have a good evening and say hi to Joe for me."

"I certainly will, Mr. Buckwalter."

Fritz pushed her toddler's nose as if it were a button on the cash register. "Ca-ching!"

The boy laughed. "I want money."

"You're the cash register, so *you* must have the money."

The boy fished through his pockets. "I don't have anything." He presented a sour face.

Fritz handed him a sucker. "Now you do."

The front doorbell tinkled. Eddie. What was he doing here early? And why was half of his shirt untucked and pants wrinkled? He looked untidier every day.

It was bad enough when Klara came last night, crying and

inconsolable, blaming Fritz and August for Eddie's shenanigans. If she only knew all the times August would've booted Eddie to the moon if Fritz hadn't intervened. Wilma had insisted that Klara stay overnight in the spare room.

Eddie ducked around the corner. Fritz asked Matilda to take over the register. He found Eddie in the soup aisle and sniffed a foul odor. Had Eddie bathed recently? "What are you doing here so early?" *And what were you thinking, gallivanting around the county?*

Eddie pivoted to face him. "Fritz! You sure know how to scare a guy."

"Look who's talking. Let's head to the stockroom."

"I will at five. I'm doing security."

"We *have* security. Now get moving."

Eddie lowered his voice. "Shh! I've got my eye on two suspicious customers."

"We've talked about this, Eddie." Fritz took his arm.

Eddie shook it loose. "I came early to offer my services for free."

There was nothing free about his services, taking their toll in stress, tension headaches, and angry customers. "Eddie, please. Head to the back."

"Mr. Buckwalter, I have to leave," Matilda called from the cash register.

"Coming!" Fritz replied. "Eddie, don't cause a scene. Just go on in back. *Now.*"

Eddie sighed and drifted down the aisle, his slower gait as sloppy as his appearance.

Fritz buzzed to the customer line and replaced Matilda. Fearful that Eddie might apprehend a potential shoplifter, he cringed every time he heard an unusual noise or raised voice. But the next thirty minutes passed without incident.

After the Closed sign was hung and the door locked, Eddie

charged from the stockroom. "You can't keep doing this to me. Those Communists can't get away with it!"

"Eddie, we had an agreement," August said. "You work in the stockroom. You're welcome here at five, not a minute before."

"You think I'm poison to the customers."

"Not poison, but an annoyance," August replied.

Fritz drew up to Eddie, face to face. "Do you realize what you put Klara through the past seven days? She's a wreck from all her worry. We all are. Then you show up with a brand-new car and a full belly, surrounded by perfume and lipstick—"

Eddie's eyes widened. "She told you?"

"Yes. She's devastated." He grabbed his brother's shirt. "How could you be unfaithful? There's no excuse, not with a sweet, loving woman like Klara." Eddie pushed him away.

August stepped between them. "Stop it, both of you."

Eddie returned to the stockroom. "I'll get started."

"No." August followed him. "You need help."

Eddie heaved a box onto a shelf. "What do you mean?"

"You need professional help. A doctor. Maybe a psychiatrist."

"What? I don't need any psycho shrink."

"Yes, you do. I know someone you can see. From our church."

"I don't need to see anybody. I feel great. I've never felt better in my life."

"Maybe physically," August said. "But there's ... something wrong."

Eddie's eyes flashed. "You're saying I'm fit for the loony bin?"

"No," Fritz interjected. "We want you to see a psychiatrist, get evaluated. Get help."

Eddie picked up box after box and plopped each one down. "Help with what?"

August turned Fritz around and lowered his voice. "This is going to escalate. We've got to get him home first."

"Are we really going to let him loose on Klara?"

August went to Eddie. "Do you have the store key? I need it back."

"Why?" Eddie snarled. "So you can keep me out? You guys are always conspiring against me. They even talk about it on the radio now. Every night at ten."

"What?" August and Fritz said in unison, exchanging confused glances.

"Don't play innocent with me." Eddie jammed a finger into Fritz's chest. "You're doing a radio talk show without me. The way you do everything else. You just want me out of the picture."

Fritz racked his brain to jog a memory, but the only radio gig was an advertisement all three brothers did two months ago. "What radio show?"

Eddie pulled another box down and dropped it on a stack. "Don't pretend you don't know. There are newspaper articles, too, all in code. You're trying to run me out of town."

Fritz's muscles tightened. "Now just a sordid moment—"

"Why are these boxes out of order?" Eddie plopped another one down. Glass rattled. "You shuffle them around just so I have something harmless to do, without giving me any real responsibility. I already organized these last week."

"Last week you were out of town," Fritz snapped. "Now, where's the store key?"

"I don't have it."

"Did you lose it?"

"I wouldn't lose something so important."

"We need to go." August clapped his hat to his head. "Come on. We're dropping by your place, Eddie."

"What for? Klara's still fixing dinner."

"You're lucky she still wants to feed you," August said.

Fritz gave August the evil eye. "We're dropping by to pick up the key."

"I don't have your lousy key."

"We'll look for it."

Eddie let loose with several expletives. "You think I'm gonna break in and rob you? Go ahead and search my house for the blasted key. Then you'll miss tonight's radio show, which is fine with me."

"There's no radio show, Eddie," Fritz said.

August squeezed Fritz's shoulder. "Drop the subject. Let's go. I'm locking up."

"I can't leave this mess." Eddie gestured over the pile of boxes. "I'm just getting started."

That's what I'm afraid of. Fritz grimaced. No stopping him now.

August grabbed the phone from the desk and dialed. "Klara? We're dropping by with Eddie if that's okay. Call Wilma and Irma to let them know Fritz and I will be late for supper."

Fritz switched off the lights in the storeroom.

In the dark, windowless room, Eddie stomped to the door. "I'll get the other lights."

"I'll check them later," Fritz said.

Somehow, August got Eddie's car keys and drove him home in the new automobile.

Fritz followed. He'd drive August back later to pick up his Chevy.

* * *

"You're gonna be sorry for this!" In the living room, Eddie shook his fist.

Klara stamped her foot. "Stop it, Eddie! They're just trying to help." Despite her accusations flung at Fritz last night, she knew how much his brothers loved him. But how much more patience did they have?

"How are they helping?" Eddie pulled Klara into the kitchen and set his hands on her shoulders. Klara gently pushed him away and stepped back. Since learning about his unfaithfulness, she didn't want him touching her.

He lowered his voice. "They go around town gossiping about us. They find every excuse to exclude me at the store. They won't listen to sound advice, so what happens? Shoplifters overrun the grocery. And now August and Fritz tell the whole town every night on WKCC about their plans to thwart us. They make up lies about me, about you."

"That's nonsense."

His face earnest, he grabbed her arm. "Listen, Klara. I'm telling the truth. They write about us in the papers. It's all in code. They want to run us out of town. They should be going after Communists, not us."

She pulled from his grasp, though it pained her to back away. No matter how deluded he was, she trusted his sincerity. "Is that why you circle and cut out articles?"

"Yes. I have proof. It's been happening for months."

Something was desperately wrong. Why couldn't he listen to his well-meaning brothers? He twisted everything out of proportion. He saw things that weren't there, heard radio shows that didn't exist.

Klara left the kitchen. In the parlor, August and Fritz conferred in whispers. "You can leave." She stepped closer, lowering her voice. "After a good meal, he'll be in a better state of mind for me to broach the subject." She swallowed. "Regarding psychiatric help. It's better if I speak to him first."

"Are you sure, Klara?" August asked. "We'll stay as long as you need us."

"Your families need you too. Just go. He has to calm down."

Eddie stepped through the parlor doorway. "Don't talk to them, Klara. They'll suck you in. They just want to talk behind my back."

She opened the front door. "They're leaving. Wash up for dinner, Eddie." He traipsed to the bathroom.

Fritz buttoned his coat. "On Saturday, I'll drive the new automobile back to the dealership. I already called to explain."

August dangled the new Ford automobile keys before them. "Meanwhile, we'll hang onto these. Pretend you don't know where they are. Which will be true, since you won't know whose pocket they're going in."

"I don't know what I'd do without you two." She gave each a hug. They left.

Eddie joined her. "You're the best thing that ever happened to me, Klara."

Was she? Then why'd he abandon her for a week? Why'd he have a one-night stand? If only one. She tensed, anticipating a rough evening. "Let's eat."

* * *

At ten o'clock, Fritz sat up in bed, unable to sleep. Wilma rolled over, breathing steadily. Such a good woman, putting up with his long store hours, with the complication of Eddie and absent hours from home while she cared for sweet Frieda.

Fritz slinked across the bedroom to the study, then sat at the desk with his typewriter. He should dust it first. The thing never got used. When did he have time to write his novel? He'd stopped and started for months now, constantly interrupted by store demands. And Eddie.

Would there ever be a month of normalcy, where he could enjoy pleasant evenings at home without worrying about his brother? Where he could play games with Frieda, talk with Wilma, then write?

He'd chosen three publishers where Eddie could submit his manuscript after editing. His brother had fine talent. And far more energy and time at night to put it to use.

He slid a new piece of paper into the roller. Chapter five. He should reread what he wrote the last time, which was when? Two months ago, now? At least he had four chapters under his belt. Four in twelve months. Deplorable.

He read pages to get his bearings. The muse stirred. Finally. He typed for an hour, adrenaline surging.

Until it hit him. He'd never gone back to the store to turn off the lights. They usually kept one on to deter burglars. But they'd left all the lights on in the main room.

He sighed. He really should check. Otherwise, the night cops would assume something was askew. He quickly dressed, grabbed his key ring and flashlight.

* * *

Klara lay in bed, her throat dry. After Eddie's perpetual brooding and condemnation of psychiatry, sleep evaded her. He'd turned on the radio at ten to big band music, then reported the talk show sabotaging him, sabotaging the store. Was he hearing voices?

He'd mentioned something about checking store lights. When she reminded him he didn't have the key, he settled on the couch to sleep.

Did their Chevy just go down the driveway? August and

Fritz had only taken keys to the Ford. She peered out the window. The automobile backed into the street.

Eddie wasn't on the couch. The pillow and blanket twisted into a tousled mess. Maybe he went to the store. But if he no longer had the key, then where? Should she call Fritz?

No, she couldn't call Fritz for everything. He was surely wearing out.

The clock said eleven oh five. She'd never get to sleep. All this stress surely impacted the baby. Which, in waiting for the perfect moment, she hadn't even told Eddie yet.

She turned on the radio in search of soothing music to woo her to sleep. Perry Como's "If" wafted over her. She sighed, recalling tender late-night moments with her husband—the one she used to know only months ago.

But when Patti Page crooned "Tennessee Waltz." Klara snapped off the radio.

It was a song she and Eddie often slow danced to, never bothered by the mournful lyrics about losing one's lover to someone else. Now she couldn't bear it.

CHAPTER TWENTY-TWO

2015

L eslie folded her napkin and set it on the tablecloth. "That was the best Chicken Cacciatore."

Jason smiled, ever so appealing in his collared shirt and tie. He reached for her hand. "And I have the best of company."

Could he look any more handsome? Despite a missing button and wrinkled sleeves. But he had to come right from work. At least during two hours of conversation, he never mentioned Greg or the upcoming dedication. Their meeting was scheduled for Friday.

His eyes gleamed. "Shall we keep the mojo going with a walk along the river? It's mild for February." Through the window, lamplights glowed in the darkness like fireflies.

Minutes later, they strolled the boardwalk. She let him hold her hand after four years of no men. Not for lack of suitors, but for healing. Four years of self-protection to avoid another charming skunk like Vic.

But Jason's charm was different. And he was nothing like Greg. No prickly moods or being number fourteen in line for pickleball, which could hardly be considered a date by anyone's standards. Jason said all the right things without going over the top, like Vic had. With Jason, the glacial wall of her heart started melting. She deserved a pleasant time with a good man.

Jason stopped at the bridge railing, taking her hands. Gazing at her, he leaned in for a kiss.

She froze. "Um ... I'm not quite ready."

He straightened. His mild scowl shifted to a subtle smile. "I'm sorry. I misread the cues."

Had she given cues? Yes. She hardly broke eye contact with him all evening. "I'm sorry. It's not you. I've enjoyed every minute together, but it takes time." He nodded. "Which sounds lame, since I've had four years. But this is my first real date since my divorce."

"Hopefully this crossroads has a yellow light, not a red one."

"It's definitely yellow. Thank you for understanding."

"I'm sure kissing you will be worth waiting for."

She smiled, and almost kissed him on the spot.

*　*　*

Late Friday afternoon, Greg texted Leslie to stop by his office before leaving. He must want to tell her about his meeting with Jason. She walked over.

At his filing cabinet, riffling through papers, he glanced her way. "Take a seat." He spoke like a principal addressing a wayward student.

Catching her breath, she sat. "Is something wrong, Professor?" Back to his official title. She always had difficulty breathing in his office—either from his arrogance or his appeal when he wasn't arrogant. He huffed. Had he discovered Renee Piquette's true identity? "Your demeanor's pretty rigid for someone who does an impressive Eddie Van Halen air guitar."

His mouth was a grim line.

She swallowed. "I wasted a good joke."

"What'd you tell Jason Hendricks about my relationship with my father?"

"Nothing. Why?"

He plopped files onto his desk. "He noted the irony of Doug Stafford's vital influence on this campus as opposed to his family life."

Muscles tensing, she racked her brain for previous dialogues. "Professor, I never said anything personal about you to him, or to anyone."

"Did you discuss my father or the engineering wing?"

It came back in bits and pieces. "He asked about the upcoming dedication, if Douglas Stafford was related to you. All I said was 'A father-son dynamic duo.'"

"Dynamic duo. Now we are Batman and Robin?"

"Apparently, that was my inept way of vaguely answering a direct question."

"Apparently, Jason felt free to quote your dynamic duo line here in my office. Then he asked what it was like growing up in my father's shadow."

Leslie stood. "I told him to not mention the engineering wing or your father. He was only seeing you to discuss literature, per his original intention."

He narrowed his eyes. "His direction went well beyond such intentions."

She hated being on the defensive. Under his glare, the air was suctioned from the room. "I vetted him as you asked. He passed the test. No ulterior motives were evident."

"How can you possibly be objective if you're dating him?"

His words rankled her. "That's none of your business. I did what you asked. Do you want me to talk to him, or have you sufficiently put him in his place?" In which case, she'd hear about it tonight.

"Say nothing. I took care of it."

Oh, no. "How?"

"You needn't worry. That scamp won't be bothering me again."

Leslie stepped closer to his desk. "What are you afraid of, Professor?"

"I don't trust journalists. And this one seems bent on digging for family dirt."

She tilted her head. "What else is going on?"

He startled, then gestured at the chair. They both sat. "I've been jaded by journalists and non-scholars who write about my favorite topics."

"I'm not following."

"Pseudo-scholars constantly take information from my hard-earned research and interviews, put it in their own slipshod articles and books, and never credit me."

"You probably wouldn't want your name associated with it."

"Good point, but the principle remains. They steal my research and misuse it."

"Do you call them out?"

"Yes, but there's no purpose in throwing lawsuits around." He shook his head. "No matter how much due diligence I give a project, other folks will misconstrue facts, using secondary and unreliable sources."

"That's why I like getting my history lessons by reading historical fiction." She smiled, hoping to soften the moment. "Artistic license saves the day."

"Then you and Renee Piquette would get along fine."

She froze. "Renee? Oh yeah ..."

"She's writing that historical fiction about Fritz Buckwalter."

"Did you make her sign a contract so she'll credit you for all your help?"

"I like believing she'll do that in good faith."

Her face warmed. Was this a trap? Did he suspect she was Renee? "Maybe you're no cynic after all. You still have faith in the human race."

"Very little. But I do have great respect for the Buckwalter relatives I've met. Fritz, his wife and siblings, four children, twelve grandchildren. I'm fortunate they let me into their lives by granting interviews. Ten years ago, the two daughters showed me around the former Buckwalter farm. They verified much of what Fritz shared with me earlier."

He stared at the rustic rooster on the wall. "I suspect there's a deeper meaning of that weathervane as a metaphor in *The Broken Weathervane*. One I haven't quite grasped."

One that Leslie was only beginning to, considering Eddie's troubles.

"I've pondered it since your commentary on wives and mothers being emotional meteorologists." He eyed her keenly. "What do *you* think, Leslie?"

"I've been brooding over it."

He lifted an eyebrow. "Must be that melancholy streak you have."

"Aren't all lovers of literature subject to melancholy?"

He nodded. "It's a requirement. Especially for the novelist."

Leslie shifted and quoted a line she believed fit Greg, regarding people who used his work without crediting him. "'Every man has his secret sorrows which the world knows not; and often times we call a man cold when he is only sad.'"

Greg cocked his head. "Lovely rendition of Longfellow. It hit me right here." He put a fist to his heart and smiled.

Did she really have power to move his emotions? The thought made her dizzy.

He rolled a pen in his fingers. "I've had to forgive plenty of folks in my day, after years of holding grudges. Fortunately, God still grins, despite my inadequacies."

"Glad you got to that point. Forgiving, that is."

"It's not just the lack of credit that bothers me. After studying the Buckwalter family for years, I feel like I know them. I disdain those who take my information for their own purposes, mixing up facts without regard for truth."

"That would make me angry too." Little did he know. What would Greg do if he knew she was a Buckwalter? Or if he became privy to everything in Oma's diary? All the family drama Fritz concealed—would it end up in Greg's book, upon which full professorship hinged?

"The fabrications floating around out there demean those who opened their lives to me, trusting that I'd capture the true Buckwalter experience."

Which is possibly far from the truth. Oma's perspective on Edmund changed everything. An ache tugged her. Greg worked so hard to seek the truth, but he'd only caught one viewpoint—from Fritz's progeny. Half the story. If Fritz kept Eddie's escapades from the newspapers, did he remain silent with his family too?

"The biography will likely go to press without the last interview I wanted. Klara Buckwalter refuses to give me one, no matter how much I sweet talk her."

"I can't imagine you sweet-talking anyone."

His brows raised. "True. That's not my style."

Nope. Mr. Darcy through and through. To a point. "How'd you find her? And when's the last time you contacted her?"

"I call her monthly. Three years ago, an old Dillard connection gave me her Crestwood post office box number and phone number. No street address, or I could've Googled it. I sent letters and left voice messages. Two months ago, she finally picked up the phone, quite upset I'd found her. She confirmed she'd been a Buckwalter but refused to share her current surname. Since the 1960s, actually. I asked if she'd be willing to share samples of Edmund's writing to use for the biography. She refused that too."

"That'd be fascinating to read."

"Absolutely. I also wanted her to flesh out the family tree. According to Fritz, Edmund and Klara had two daughters, but I've found nothing beyond that. Nothing in census records. Her name change definitely guarded her privacy."

Leslie's face warmed. "Another Jackie Kennedy."

"Or she's hiding a secret." Greg frowned, lips twitching. "After several blatant refusals, we chatted amiably. I wanted her thoughts on Fritz and Edmund, but she declined anything beyond small talk. The big revelation of the day was discovering she's a Brewers fan."

Yup, Oma loved baseball. "Any clues about possible secrets? Family tensions? Bad blood?" And why family reunions were so formidable?

"Only that it's possibly related to tight-lipped old-timers. And connected to Edmund's odd jobs around town."

"What'd she say about Edmund's stories?"

"She implied she still had them, from childhood and after marriage."

"I wonder what he wrote. Historical fiction? Fantasy, sci-fi?"

"Fritz showed me some humorous adventure stories they co-wrote as kids. He mentioned Edmund's later writing was serious and poignant, laced with humor. He had a keen wit."

Leslie recalled a favorite quote. "'More passion is destroyed at the breakfast table than in a time warp.'" Greg cocked his head. "Janet Burroway. From her book *Writing Fiction*."

"Is writing fiction something you aspire to?"

Again, her face heated. No way would she disclose her writing endeavors, identical to Renee Piquette's. "When I taught literature, I had students consider writing from the author's perspective. I'd assign exercises in character development or rewriting a scene from a different point of view, in a different voice."

Greg chuckled. "Excellent. And I'll take down-home stories over melodrama any day."

"Me too. But how disappointing to not get the interview. Or writing samples."

"That dead end is worse than finding out students write papers based on nothing but CliffsNotes. Fortunately, Grable Press took the official biography without Klara's interview. Which is good, since becoming a full professor depends on its publication."

"Is everything on track for that?"

"Yes, thanks to you." He offered that endearing smirk. "I can check off the community connection and social media boxes, assuming I soon monitor my own account."

"My work's definitely cut out for me."

He chortled. "Surely just being in my office is work enough for you."

"You're very perceptive." She narrowed her eyes before granting a smile of her own. "Speaking of community connection, Donna at the library says they're considering *The Broken Weathervane* as the book selection this fall for Avondale Reads. They want you to speak again. You could tie in the biography, hot off the press by then."

"If I don't hold out for Klara's interview."

She stood to go. "Then I'll tell Donna yes?"

"Wait." He held up a hand. "I'm in a quandary. I need to ask you to not see Jason again."

Her mouth dropped open. "What? You're crossing into my personal life."

"For good reason. Just for a few weeks."

"Why? Did you discover he did jail time?"

"No. Clean record."

"What's this about? Him rankling your feathers?"

He folded his hands on the desk. "Can I trust my words will not leave this room?"

Her heart sped up. "That depends. What's the risk?"

He eyed her intently. "Jason told me something of magnitude I don't want shared yet. And I don't want him to use you again to get to me."

"He didn't. He was a perfect gentleman."

Greg arched an eyebrow. "That means nothing when someone woos, wheedles, and wangles to get his way."

"But Professor—"

"Leslie." He raised a pointer finger. "He claims to be a Buckwalter relative."

"What?" She balked. *Oh, my word. Hold on ...* Greg didn't know of her familial ties. "I thought you'd met all the descendants."

"Fritz's and August's. Jason says he's an unknown descendant of Edmund."

She plunked against the chair back, resisting the urge to fan herself as heat crept up her neck. She knew all of Edmund's progeny: herself, her mom, plus Aunt Martha and her kids and grandkids. *Don't act like it matters. Breathe in, breathe out.* "Well, that could certainly change things. How is he related?"

"He says his grandmother had a brief affair with Edmund back in 1952."

Her stomach clamped. Oma's journal entries swept through her brain at a dizzying pace. *Oh, dear.* Was this from that week of cavorting? Did Oma know he'd gotten someone pregnant? She'd be devastated. Or maybe she wrote about it in later entries.

She held her voice steady. "That would be scandalous then. Did Jason do DNA testing?" Good thing she'd never done one of those commercial tests. Fortunately, her name wouldn't show up. Nor would a test prove his relationship to Edmund unless her mother, Aunt Martha, or cousins had taken it.

"He hasn't. I told him to not contact me again until he gets the test, assuming one of Edmund's progenies has taken one. He insists he always knew the connection but kept it under wraps."

"He told only you?"

"Supposedly. That's the real reason he wanted to meet with me. He caught wind of the biography and deemed it time to go public with his family ties. He wants to be acknowledged as part of the Buckwalter crew. He'd been silent for the sake of legitimate descendants."

Leslie gulped, her hands numbing. "How many family members know?"

"His sister, parents, and unmarried grandmother. She was a waitress in Milwaukee."

Images of Eddie sharpened in her brain. The night he came home with lipstick on his collar, smelling like lavender, with an announcement that he'd given a waitress a fifty-dollar tip for textbooks. If she got pregnant in 1952, so much for her further education.

She blinked, trying to stay present though her stomach was sinking and her mind filling with another era.

"Leslie, you don't look well."

She shook her head as if snapping out of her fog. "I'm okay.

What if his DNA test proves the bloodlines?" And to think she almost kissed the guy. She fumbled her laptop, then caught it before it slipped off her lap. "It'll be a terrible heartache for Klara Buckwalter to learn about the adultery. The pregnancy. If she doesn't already know."

"No doubt. I'd want to ask her about it, face to face, and would respect her privacy if she didn't want it to go public."

"Really? You don't see Eddie's affair as public domain? That was seventy years ago."

"But his family is still alive. That makes all the difference." He tapped a pen on the desk. "Frankly, unless there's a more vital connection to Fritz's life, information like this might only warrant a paragraph or two."

Ugh. Thank goodness for that, but it sounded so cut and dried. Devastating family news tucked into a chapter as an afterthought. *Oh, by the way ...*

Greg shoved a pile of student papers. "I'm not taking Jason seriously until he gets a DNA test."

"Why would he make up a whopper like that? It's more prestigious to claim Fritz as an ancestor." Her gesture looped the air. Her laptop slid again. She caught it. "Is there some inheritance he hopes to gain?"

"Not that I know of."

"How do you know Jason won't tell someone else?"

"I don't. But do you understand why I prefer you don't see him for now? I don't mean to meddle, but I don't trust him."

She tipped her chin up. "How do I know it's *me* you don't trust?"

He eyed her intently. "If I didn't trust you, I wouldn't have shared that bombshell."

If you only knew. Guilt poked her for withholding information. Not to mention the Renee charade. She was hardly worthy of his trust.

Plus, if Jason was Edmund's grandson, their dating relationship was over. Finished. Kaput.

"You look pale."

Leslie touched her cooled cheek. "Nothing a little frappe can't cure." She stood, weak-kneed.

He followed suit. "I'm walking you out."

"I won't faint." She managed a weak smile, pulled on her coat, picked up her bag.

"I'm not taking any chances." He grabbed his own coat, then gripped her elbow and walked alongside her to the parking lot. "Can I drive you home? I'll pick up your car later."

"No, no, I'll be fine."

"If it's rest you need, stay off that blasted social media."

CHAPTER TWENTY-THREE

September 1952

Fritz parked in the grocery store lot and squinted across the block. Was that Eddie's car in the street shadows, on the lamplight's periphery? Odd. He'd check after addressing the lights. Everything inside the building appeared dark. Hmm. He was sure he'd left the main light on—not the usual nightlights.

While here, he'd also pick up the storeroom mess left over from the argument with Eddie. He looked for Ron, the usual cop on beat, to tell him not to be alarmed by lights switching. But he didn't see him.

Fritz entered through the back door. The store was pitch black. He turned on the flashlight to head to the corner switches.

He stopped and sniffed. Smoke! Where was that coming from? He jogged toward the back. A crackling noise rankled his nerves. Fire?

At the stockroom door, he hesitated before touching the

knob. Smoke slipped through the crack under the door. Should he even risk opening it and spreading fire? Or was it small enough to douse with a bucket of water?

Every minute mattered. If he ran outside, he might save himself, but how would he call for help? The phone was in the stockroom. Or he'd find Ron.

He grabbed a hunk of his coat to twist the knob open.

Whoosh! Smoke billowed out and blew him back. Tongues of fire jeered and danced. Coughing, he charged outside through the back door.

Across the parking lot, a lone figure darted to the only car, parked outside the lamppost light. Its silhouette matched Eddie's form. The Chevy engine rumbled to life. The car jerked and sped down the street.

What was Eddie doing here? Maybe he'd come to check on the lights too. Fritz almost yelled his name, but instead ran around the building to Maple Street and found the cop. "Fire at Buckwalters'!"

Ron charged to his car and called in the emergency. Minutes later, firetrucks zoomed down the street. But it was too late.

The blaze filled and swallowed the store interior, leaving nothing but a shell. Fritz watched from across the street, numb on the sidewalk as if viewing a nightmare.

Ron took Fritz aside and offered condolences. "What brought you down here tonight?"

"Earlier, I left the store in a rush and came back to turn on the nightlights."

"What time did you arrive?"

"Eleven." Seemed like hours ago.

"Was anyone else here?"

"No, only me." No way would he incriminate Eddie. At least he hadn't shouted his name.

"Are you sure?"

"Yes. There's no reason for anyone to be here this time of night."

"Does the store meet code regulations for avoiding fire hazards?"

"Absolutely. We've only been at this location six weeks. It passed inspection before we opened, and again two weeks ago. We're vigilant about safety."

"Sometimes things get overlooked, Fritz. Does anyone smoke in the store?"

"Never. Only at home."

Ron set his hand on Fritz's shoulder. "I know you're in shock now. We'll revisit this tomorrow, after the fire marshals conduct a search."

* * *

At midnight, someone pounded on the front door.

Jolted from sleep, Klara grabbed her robe and stumbled from the bedroom. Eddie stirred on the couch. Why'd the room smell like smoke? More like campfire than cigarette. She squinted through the window, the porch light revealing her brother-in-law resembling a wild man—hair unkempt, face red, eyes wide as if he'd seen a bear.

She swung the door open. "Fritz! What's wrong?" She switched on a lamp.

"Where's Eddie?" Fritz made a beeline for the couch and shook his brother's shoulder. "Get up! *Now!*"

Sleepy-eyed Eddie startled, then lifted himself to his elbows. "Can't you let a man sleep? It's middle of the night."

"Where were you an hour ago?"

"On this couch."

"Then why'd I see your car in the street near the store parking lot?"

Klara picked up Eddie's discarded shirt from a heap on the floor. The acrid aroma reeked. "What happened?"

"The store burned down," Fritz said.

Eddie shot off the couch. "What?" Klara covered her mouth with a gasp.

Fritz stepped toward him. "What were you doing there?"

"Nothing!"

He turned to Klara. "Did Eddie go anywhere in the past hour?"

Eddie raised an arm. "Don't drag her into this. You don't believe me?"

"I saw your car there," Fritz said. "You can't lie your way out of this."

Klara's eyes darted from brother to brother.

Fritz faced Eddie. "The fire marshals are investigating. They'll get to the bottom of this. Tell me the truth before they haul you away."

Klara's voice trembled. "You can't let them do that."

"What happened at the store?" Fritz panted. "Klara, was Eddie gone around eleven tonight?"

Eddie gave her a brazen look that could have stopped a raging bull in its tracks.

"How dare you put Eddie on trial and ask me to testify against him!"

"Be grateful it's *me* doing the asking. Before he gets charged with arson."

"Arson!" Klara held the smoky shirt to her chest.

Fritz yanked the shirt from her grasp. "Smoke!"

"Of course," Eddie said. "I had a cigarette."

"At the store?"

"No. In the backyard."

Klara's voice rattled. "He smokes every night."

"What were you doing at the store tonight?" Fritz asked.

"I don't have the key, remember?"

"No?" Fritz yanked smoky pants from the clothing heap. Metal clattered. He withdrew a ring of five keys from a pocket. "Then where'd this store key come from?"

"Eddie!" Klara said. "You said you didn't have it anymore."

"I forgot."

Fritz shoved the key in his face. "Why'd you go to the store?"

"To check on the lights."

"That wasn't your responsibility," Fritz said.

"Right. Nothing is." Eddie's hands fisted. He pounded the end table. Klara jumped. "You and August are fine and dandy without me. You don't trust me." He stamped around the room. "You talk to the whole town about me on the radio. You let shoplifters run rampant. Then you say *I'm* the problem. Me!"

"So, you burn the store down?"

"See? You're accusing me again." His voice escalated. "Why would I burn down the Buckwalter Brothers Grocery, when *I'm* a Buckwalter? Or have you disowned me completely?"

Fritz charged at Eddie and pinned him to the wall. "Did you start the fire?"

"It was an accident! I threw my cigarette in the wastebasket. Maybe it wasn't completely extinguished."

"Oh, Eddie ..." Klara buried her face in her hands.

"If you left, then why are your clothes smoky?"

"I threw it in, then picked up boxes. I reorganized shelves." Eddie's voice was strained, frantic. "When the fire started, I fetched a pail from the broom closet and got water. But one measly pail of water didn't help. I closed the door and left, figuring the fire would contain itself."

Fritz released Eddie roughly. Eddie clunked against the wall. "What're we supposed to do? It'll take months to rebuild. Months! We've lost our merchandise, our renovations."

Eddie spat the words. "Insurance will cover it."

"If it was accidental, why'd you run off so fast without reporting it? A cop was right there." Fritz shook the smoky shirt. "Why'd you lie about being there?"

"I knew you'd blame me. I saw you run out of the store and knew you'd call the firemen. I had to get out." He lifted his arms in a mock gesture. "But don't worry. The Buckwalter Brothers will rise again. With or without me."

"That was *your* choice, Eddie. You sabotaged yourself, like usual. I can't do a thing about it when the cops come to get you. You rise or fall on your own this time. I've had it."

"So have I." Eddie stomped to the kitchen. "I always rise and fall on my own."

Moments later, he stumbled through the doorway, a knife blade at his wrist. "I'll make it easy for you. I'm done with everything." With one swift motion, blood spilled from his vein.

Klara screamed. Fritz charged to the phone and called an ambulance.

She grabbed the smoky shirt and ran to Eddie. Fumbling, she tried to grab his wrist.

Eddie yanked his arm back. "Don't touch me, Klara. You're about to be rescued from all my failures." He slit his other wrist. More blood flowed. "*I* should have fallen off that ladder, not Papa ..."

"Stop it!" She bumped his arm. The knife flew, skidding across the floor. Fritz grasped Eddie's upper arms to hold him still. Klara scrambled to tie the sleeve around his wrist. She took the pillowcase from the couch, dumped out the pillow, and wrapped the other flailing wrist as blood splattered.

Moments later, a siren wailed as an ambulance pulled up.

* * *

The next afternoon, after the inspection, Fritz sat in the fire marshal's office wringing his hands. The marshal had already interviewed August.

Fritz had been awake over thirty hours. He'd accompanied Eddie and Klara to the hospital and stayed all morning while Eddie was treated and sedated. Wilma dropped Frieda off at Irma's so she could sit with Klara at Eddie's bedside.

The adrenaline was slowing down. The marshal's talking droned in his ears.

Reginald Mason scanned the fire report again. His deep-set eyes nearly disappeared in his puffy face and bearded chin. "Nearest I can tell, the fire started in the stockroom, possibly the wastebasket. A combination of combustible materials along with a cigar or cigarette that wasn't disposed of properly. One that wasn't extinguished."

"Nobody smokes in our store. We forbid it."

Reginald grunted. "Nobody's allowed in after hours, either, but somebody was."

"A cigarette can smolder for hours without detection, right? Someone could have smoked during store hours. We close at five. The fire wasn't detected until eleven."

"You said you were there yesterday until five-fifteen. You and your brothers left then?"

"Yes."

"If someone was smoking while you were there, you would've smelled it. Is there a chance you left the store unlocked when you left?"

Fritz frowned. "I know I locked it. But we left without turning off the lights."

"What was so pressing that you forgot the lights?"

Fritz hardly wanted to explain Eddie's fit after another

shoplifting hallucination. "A lot on our minds, Mr. Mason. As usual."

"When you remembered the lights later, did you suspect you'd left the store unlocked?"

"No. We've never left the store unlocked."

"That you know of," Reginald huffed.

"I'm sure of it."

"Who else has a key besides you?"

"August. But he was home in bed."

"Nobody else has a key?"

"No." That was true. Fritz now had Eddie's key. As of midnight.

"What about Edmund?"

"Eddie doesn't have a key." As long as Mr. Mason spoke in present tense, Fritz wasn't lying.

"Why not? Isn't he one of the Buckwalter Brothers?"

"Legally, only August and I are. Eddie was only fifteen when we started the store."

"I see. Then I'll need to question Edmund."

"Good luck with that. He's in the hospital. He got severely ill last night." Images of Eddie cutting his wrists and bleeding out haunted him. Then the ambulance crew charging in ...

"Sorry to hear that. I still need to talk to him, though. I'll clear it with the hospital staff."

"He's in much pain and distress. You'll need to wait several days." Eddie's mental state was none of Reginald Mason's business.

The fire marshal raised a brow. "This has nothing to do with smoke inhalation?"

"Absolutely not."

The man sat back, voice gravelly. "Fires don't start themselves, Mr. Buckwalter. My crew didn't see any electrical problems. Nor was anything out of place in the bakery area and ovens, the opposite side of the store from the stockroom. Everything points to the stockroom."

"Seems that way. But then we're back to square one."

Reginald Mason's gruffness cut to the quick. "Some folks get the notion to burn down their own business for insurance money."

"Why would I do that? The store was brand new." His voice escalated. "We just renovated the building according to our own designs. It opened after months of hard work. Business was booming. Insurance fraud was the last thing on my mind."

Mr. Mason leaned forward, an imposing figure, elbows on the desk. "Why have you never made Edmund one of the Buckwalter Brothers? On paper, that is. Business-wise."

No way would Fritz open that can of worms with non-family members. "We've been so preoccupied with moving and day-to-day business, we had no time for additional paperwork."

"How does Edmund feel about that?"

"He likes being part of the business."

"Yet he doesn't have the benefit on paper. Does he get paid well for his labors here?"

"Definitely. He took charge of advertising and inventory."

"On top of other jobs around town. Odd scenario, looking in from the outside."

"What's your point?" Fritz snapped.

Mr. Mason honed in on Fritz, narrow eyes heated. "Does Eddie have motive to harm you or the store?"

Fritz chuckled. "Eddie's as good-hearted as they come. He only wants good for the store." Thus, the obsession with pseudo-shoplifters.

Mr. Mason harrumphed. "Are you sure nobody was smoking in the store yesterday?"

Fritz leaned forward, elbows on his knees, trying to match

Reginald's bulk with his own intensity. "Yes, I'm positive." Eddie needed serious help, not jail time.

"You're absolutely sure Eddie wasn't at the store after hours last night?"

"How could I see in the dark?" Fritz's arms flailed. "With fire blazing, it was impossible to know anything for sure except that my business was burning to a crisp."

CHAPTER TWENTY-FOUR

2015

Leslie held up her phone across the desk from Greg. "Your post went viral!"

"Why do you look so happy?" He grunted. "Sounds akin to a contagious disease."

She laughed. "No, going viral can be a good thing. And controversial posts are popular."

He squinted at the Instagram post through reading glasses. "Did I stir up controversy?" He read the open-ended question aloud.

"Scroll down. Comments galore. Over six hundred followers await your words with bated breath."

He whistled. "What's this reference to a survey?"

"Last week I surveyed your followers about literary cultural references, which led to this week's question. People are connecting stories to current events in Avondale and nationally."

He continued scrolling. "Questions about coffee drinks? Asiago bagels?"

"Yeah, social media inadvertently invites a bit of assumed familiarity. Some folks care more about your eating habits than literary influences."

He harrumphed. "Do they want to know my sheet thread count too?"

She chuckled. "Some ask how you enjoyed your morning latte."

He peered over his glasses. "You haven't asked about my recent latte experiences."

"I wouldn't trouble you with such minutia, Professor." She smiled. "I assume you thoroughly enjoy each one. Especially when I see your empty cup afterward."

"Thanks for sparing me the minutia."

"Look." She pulled a chair to the side of the desk and opened her laptop. "Monday's posts are called 'Monday Morning Brew.' Coffee and thoughts brewing together. I've made memes with provocative quotes from authors or literature, past and present. Each post has at least five hashtags. Some weeks—"

"Whoa, hold on. Explain hashtags."

"They're a way to label and categorize each post. Hashtags send the posts to people interested in those topics. Asking questions ensures more engagement. Tuesdays are 'Then & Now.' I choose a book quote, put it in today's context, and ask if they agree or disagree. Wednesday is 'What Are You Reading?' Everyone loves sharing their current titles. Thursday is 'Would You Rather?' I give short surveys or choices between characters to meet, settings to visit, situations to experience. And Friday is 'Fun Facts' in the form of a 'Did You Know' question or 'Behind the Scenes' in an author's life."

Fidgeting, he nodded as if placating her.

"Twice monthly I promote one of your books. Influencers warn to not self-promote more than once every ten posts. It's all about serving your followers. Look, I made this aesthetic video of images related to your title, including lines from endorsements. I'm pleased with how it captures your book's tone." She veered to the video. The music of Mozart's "Sonata in C" played in the background. "What do you think, Professor?"

"How do you measure sales generated from this?"

"You can't. But it's not about the sales. It's—"

"About serving the community." He rolled his eyes. "When do you find time for all this ... posting?" He spat it out with the force of a curse word.

"I spend three hours a month planning and preparing photos, quotes, and graphics, post daily, and reply to comments every evening."

"Monday through Friday?"

"Yes. Later, you can reduce frequency. Posting daily gave us a jump-start."

"Weekly might be palatable." He scrolled on her screen, commenting with intermittent smiles. "Good question ... Clever ... Outlandish ... What is he thinking?" After they bantered over several comments, he pointed to one. "Your responses seem to reflect my own."

She grinned. "Thank you, Professor. That's what ghostwriting is. I work hard to capture your voice, the biggest challenge of all. Which is the perfect segue. I'm in a quandary about how to reply to some of them. Time for you to learn something new."

He dropped his pen as if playing hot potato. "Oh, no. I'm not ready to play this game."

"Look, I did the hard part by getting it going. You already have an enthusiastic following. Just post one new question, at least weekly. And reply to comments. Maybe an hour a week. We'll brainstorm together."

He gestured as if snapping a whip. "Do you realize what I can do with one hour? I can grade five student essays. Deliver a lecture. Outline three lectures. Write a chapter for my book. Or edit two chapters. Consult fellow scholars about future projects. Formulate the plan for my next grant proposal. And you want me to stare at a screen and read absurdities?"

"Some comments are extremely thoughtful. You just read some." She lifted her chin. "Complex answers. Not just five-paragraph-essay mentality." He huffed. "These folks will want to hear your lectures, buy your books, or attend Raymond U. That's the purpose. Engagement. Community. Bolster the school's involvement and reputation."

"Isn't that what social media coordinators are for? We have a department for that."

She narrowed her eyes. "Isn't this part of the criteria that you and the promotion committee devised *together*?

"Touché." He sighed. "But can we dwindle it down to once weekly?"

"Soon. It's still gaining traction."

"How have you managed to capture my voice?"

"By osmosis. I've been reading your dissertation and other works."

He removed his glasses. "Have you now?"

"I've got a list of questions. Especially about the dissertation."

"More questions about Edmund, I presume?" He winked. "Considering your preoccupation with underdogs."

"I'm curious about Fritz, too, lest you think I'm slighting him. I'm wondering about their father's death, how that impacted Edmund. Them."

"I address that more in the biography. I gleaned some

details but can't speak to long-term emotional impact." He eyed the weathervane. "Fritz mentioned the loss of their father was keenly felt due to Frederick's strength, encouragement, and affection." Greg went to the window. "I can't comprehend that kind of loss. Sometimes I fear what my father's death will feel like."

His poignancy and openness struck her. "Is he ill?"

"Not that I know of."

Having no parents, she could only draw upon imagination and friends' experiences. And losing Uncle Russ. "It's probably equally painful to lose a close, loving parent as it is to lose a cold, distant one. With the former, you grieve the loss of goodness and hold tight to pleasant memories. With the latter, you can only grieve what could have been but was never captured."

He blinked as if deeply moved.

"I'm sorry for how it's been with your father."

"Thank you. I've done all I can to bridge the gap, but he remains who he is. Which is a big fish in a small pond, longing to be big fish in a big pond. He compensated by taking out his discontent on all the other fish. Especially his family."

She nodded, not wanting to break the spell of his transparency. Why was he sharing such a raw wound with her? She stayed riveted to his distraught face. His eyes went from window to rooster and back.

"One reason I got my undergrad elsewhere was to get out from under his spell here. But I also wanted to try becoming a big fish in a big pond."

"That's why you went to Duke?"

"Yes. I fared quite well there. Harvard and Oxford, too, but nothing changed."

"Meaning?"

"My father envied my success. He never rose above the

competition when he was at University of Michigan. But here I was, with measly literature and history degrees—in his mind—finding much acclaim in publishing, lecturing, and being sought after. His criticism rose to new heights."

"Why couldn't he rejoice in your successes?"

"Because he's the center of his own universe."

Would he mention his father's affairs? And other things Veronica told her?

"Why didn't you stay in Oxford after finishing your research here?"

"My mother got ill. I wanted to be closer. She had cancer and passed away two years later. I tended to her while my father found reasons to be away."

"Being there for her is something you'll never regret."

"Absolutely."

"Did you hope to win your father's approval by coming to Raymond?"

He cocked his head her way. Had she overstepped? "That's bold of you, but I opened that door. By then, I'd given up hopes of pleasing him but wanted to return for my mom. I came to Raymond to obtain tenure. With or without his approval." He stepped to his desk. "Enough of that melancholy. My apologies for being insensitive to your own plight, without parents to grieve."

Her heart lifted at his kindness. "There's plenty to grieve, believe me. But thank you." Ready to change the subject, she pointed to her phone. "So, what's next?"

"I'll bite the bullet and we'll begin Instagram lessons *now*. Ten minutes a day for the next week, for starters. Do you have time in your schedule?"

She smiled. "I'll make the time."

Chapter Twenty-Five

The auditorium buzzed with Raymond University faculty and staff, select Avondale citizens, and reporters. Chairs lined the stage, featuring honored guests. Leslie craned her neck to find Greg. She finally spotted him in the front row with cronies, then sat near the back.

The college president, Dr. Wilson, offered a long, formal greeting, then continued. "Tonight, we celebrate the dedication of the new engineering wing in honor of its deserved namesake, Dr. Douglas Alan Stafford, professor emeritus, on our faculty for fifty years." He gestured toward the tall, thin man who stood and bowed. The audience applauded. Did Greg?

What was it like having a father admired from afar, with a dark underside at home?

"I'd like to acknowledge Dr. Stafford's two sons. Adam graduated cum laude in engineering in 1990 and has since carried the torch of his father's legacy at Peterson Corporation. Professor Gregory Stafford earned two master's degrees at Duke and Harvard, his doctorate at Oxford, then obtained tenure here. He proliferates the Stafford verve and tenacity by serving on our English faculty." He gestured toward Adam on stage and Greg in the front row. They stood to more applause.

A litany of Adam's accolades included the promotion of robotics as a mentor of young students in STEM programs, FIRST LEGO League, FIRST Tech Challenge, and FIRST Robotics Competition. Adam went to the lectern. "Thank you, Dr. Wilson. With great pleasure, I honor my father, who paved the way for engineering at Raymond. He also paved the way at home, and it all started with Legos." Chuckles rippled across the audience.

"That was before FIRST LEGO League began in 1998. Our father had us building skyscrapers in the dining room, requiring Mother to serve dinner on TV trays in the den."

More chuckles.

During his fifteen-minute talk, he mentioned his father's influence at home as if Legos were all kids needed for a well-adjusted childhood. "Our father did everything possible to urge us to follow in his footsteps. When my brother's interests shifted from Legos to Robert Louis Stevenson, my father lured him back by convincing him to build Treasure Island out of Legos."

The audience chortled. Leslie guessed that Greg didn't.

After Adam shared more anecdotes about his father mentoring him through college and beyond, two professors relayed Dr. Douglas Stafford's fifty years of accomplishments at Raymond. Finally, Dr. Stafford, showing all of his eighty years, shuffled to the lectern and grasped both sides amidst a standing ovation. News reporters aimed cameras. Lights flashed.

Distracted by lights, Leslie's eyes darted over the auditorium. *Oh, no!* A few feet away in the aisle, Jason Hendricks snapped pictures. Uncharacteristically, his collared shirt was rumpled, his cuffs unbuttoned. She tensed. What was he doing here? He'd never mentioned coming. Greg better not see him.

Jason, who claimed to be an Edmund Buckwalter descendent. What did he really know? If he said something that helped Greg connect the dots, could she be found out?

Doug Stafford still seemed a force to be reckoned with. His slightly bent stature hardly undercut his height. With the microphone's help, his voice boomed as if in a cavern. For ten minutes, he thanked numerous people, cited favorite Raymond memories, and acknowledged Adam, not Gregory. Why? Because only Adam pursued the same passion?

Afterward, people proceeded to the Dickerson Room for a dessert reception. Leslie sidled to the table for a plate of finger food, watching for Jason.

People filed in. When Greg entered, a camera flash lit his face. He stepped back in surprise, then tried to duck and re-enter from a different angle, stuck facing the cameraman.

Leslie headed over and stopped six feet away as Greg addressed Jason.

Greg was brusque. "Hendricks, you've no business being here."

Jason seemed undaunted. "Any comments on tonight's program, Dr. Stafford?"

"No comment." Greg stepped away.

Jason blocked him. "Any idea why your father didn't acknowledge you?"

Leslie fumed. How dare he! How could charming Jason suddenly adopt the manners of a bull? And his shoes were scuffed up, of all things.

Was this her fault for insisting Greg meet Jason? She'd trusted Jason too soon, falling for a charmer. Her usual deplorable mode of operation.

Greg's jaw tightened. "No comment, just a

recommendation. A brood of vipers meets across the street at Fargo's Bar and Grill. That's more your style." He pivoted but Jason blocked his path as if playing basketball.

Leslie swept over to Greg. With Jason behind her, she cheerily met Greg's surprised expression. "Dr. Stafford, I want to hand deliver these delicious cheesecake tortes. I recommend the fruit punch too." She handed him the plate and slipped her hand through his arm to guide him away. She'd deal with Jason shortly.

Greg acquiesced, following her lead. "Sniffing out trouble, are you?"

"I'm saving you from a scene and some bad press."

"I knew I could count on you to save the day." He smirked, but his eyes offered sweetness, sending a shiver down her spine. Why'd he have that effect on her? "I fight my own battles, you know."

"That's what I'm afraid of. You probably want to punch the guy's lights out."

"And you're talking me down from the ledge?"

"Hopefully." She tightened her grasp of his arm. "I had no idea Jason would show up."

"Never mind him. He's a blip on the radar. Incidentally, the tortes were a good ploy."

"Enjoy them. I'll see you later."

He kept her hand locked in the crook of his elbow. "I'm game for your good company. If you can tolerate hobnobbing with a pack of nettlesome professors."

She grinned, probably looking like a Barrel of Monkeys figure. "First, I need to greet somebody. I'll be right back."

She found Jason across the room, taking a photo of Dr. Doug Stafford and his son Adam. She touched his arm before he could snap another picture. "What are you doing here?"

He fumbled his camera. "Leslie! Nice seeing you. I should have escorted you here."

Hadn't he seen her earlier? "Looks like you're here on business." She crossed her arms. "After I told you Greg Stafford wants nothing to do with the press."

"I'm not the press. This is freelance for a magazine."

"Regardless, I distinctly told you the parameters. What's going on?"

"I have work obligations, Leslie." He lowered his camera. "Would you like to go out for coffee?"

"You've got to be kidding."

Jason feigned an innocent puppy dog. Or rather, the sad, reprimanded pup after chewing slippers. "That coffee shop—"

"Sorry, Jason. Pretty sure I'll have a headache after this reception." Starting now. "Shall I put your camera away?" She reached for it.

He slipped the camera into the bag. "I got my pictures. I'd love to take you out."

Unbelievable! But maybe he could enlighten her about his supposed connection to the Buckwalter family. "All right, then. I'll meet you at nine at Kipp's Diner." She pivoted away.

Greg stood in a circle of professors. She stepped beside him. The profs chatted as if family dysfunction hadn't been aired on stage and aggressive camera lights hadn't flashed.

"At least you know what a hashtag is," Professor Rob Louden said to Dr. Lucas. "Unlike Professor Stafford here. Ignorant and proud of it."

"I'll have you know times are a-changing," Greg said. "Leslie's giving me lessons."

She sensed his sour mood while doing his best to maintain a happy face.

Norma Tomquist hooted. "Well, bless your ignorant little heart. You finally succumbed?"

Greg relayed a funny instance of posting a grammatical error he couldn't fix till hours later when Leslie showed up. Another time he'd inadvertently posted a puppy image he couldn't remove.

"I'll bet you lost five hundred followers over the bad grammar," Sheila MacIntyre said.

"But gained them all back with the puppy," Rob added.

Laughter rippled through the group.

Norma turned to Leslie. "My hat's off to you, honey, trying to bring the good professor into the twenty-first century."

"Thanks." Leslie smiled.

Greg's eyes glinted, despite weariness the grievous evening etched in his face. He excused himself and moseyed over to his father as Dr. Douglas Stafford headed out the door. Leslie watched the stiff interchange and shake of hands—probably the bare minimum Greg could offer. She didn't hear their brief dialogue.

Though smitten with guilt for insisting Greg meet Jason, and more guilt for plans to meet Jason afterward, she headed Greg's way. "Goodnight, Professor. I hope you're doing alright."

"Thank you for your dutiful hovering." When she gaped, he smiled. "I'm just glad the evening's nearly over. Excuse me, Leslie, but I need to greet more colleagues. I'll see you Monday." He tapped her forearm and walked away.

She held her arm where he'd touched her.

CHAPTER TWENTY-SIX

As the reception dwindled, Leslie left, glancing over her shoulder to avoid Greg. He couldn't dictate her social life. And she never promised she wouldn't see Jason. But she didn't want Greg to assume she'd betray him. In fact, she planned on giving Jason the what-for.

At Kipp's Diner, Leslie slid into Jason's booth.

His face brightened. "Thanks for coming, despite being miffed."

She steadied her voice, needing his trust. "I thought you'd be hands-off regarding the wing dedication. Instead, you show up doing a photoshoot."

"Ah ... what did Dr. Stafford tell you about our meeting Friday?"

"Look. Gr—Dr. Stafford's my superior and doesn't relay his business to me. Even if he did, that's confidential."

He clasped his hands on the table. "I get it. The loyalty runs deep."

The waitress stopped by. He ordered Coke, and Leslie ordered tea.

Jason leaned forward. "Have you ever considered your trust might be misplaced?"

"No." She squinted at him. Was Jason really a Buckwalter? His oval face and high cheekbones resembled the mid-twenties Edmund from her photo album.

He displayed his phone screen. "This is Gregory Scott Stafford's secret website."

"What? He doesn't—" She almost said Greg didn't even know how to manage a Facebook page, let alone rig a website.

"Check this out." Jason scrolled and directed her to various pages. "It's all part of his secret plan, but I'm on to him."

You're nuts! "What're you talking about? This site is about the Flintstones. Fred, Wilma, and the gang."

"It's all in code." Jason pointed out images and phrases, reinterpreting each in terms of a plot against the literary world.

She took note of the website URL to examine later. "Jason, this seems far-fetched. That's not how he operates. Even if he did, how's he hurting the literary world?"

"This is serious, Leslie. Too many people blow this off despite dire consequences. The main thing is, Gregory Stafford is a traitor."

"Like Benedict Arnold? Against the government?"

"No. A traitor to Raymond University. A traitor to the Buckwalter family that he claims to highly esteem and know everything about."

"How?"

"I gave him key Buckwalter information, but he dismissed it. Yet he's claiming his book is the bona fide Fritz Buckwalter biography. There's nothing authentic about it."

Leslie shivered. "What information?"

He lowered his voice. "You promise you won't say a word to him or anyone else?"

"I can keep confidences, Jason, as long as the stakes aren't too high."

He crossed his arms. "You just gave yourself an out."

"If circumstances call for it." She eyed him potently, willing him to divulge.

His gaze circled the room. "I'm a Buckwalter descendent, but the professor doesn't believe me."

How could she show surprise without revealing how it impacted her personally? She gaped. "Seriously? You're an unknown limb on the family tree? Where do you fit in?"

"Fritz Buckwalter was my great-uncle. His brother Edmund was my grandfather."

"Edmund had two daughters, Martha and Dolores." That was generally known. "Is one of them your mother?" Her mother could've had more children.

"No. Eddie had an affair and conceived my father, Sam Hendricks. His mom—my grandmother—was Bertha Hendricks. She worked in Milwaukee to earn money for college, then got pregnant. By him. She abandoned college plans and waitressed her whole life while raising my dad."

"So only you, your dad, and grandmother know about your parentage? Grand parentage."

"My mom and sister do too."

"Is your grandmother still alive?"

"No, she passed away five years ago."

"Have you had a DNA test?"

"No. I don't need a test to know the truth."

For her grandmother's sake, she didn't want to encourage a DNA test. "Why is it so important for the truth to come out now?"

"I've been hiding under this rock for decades. Dr. Stafford is publishing the biography, and I want to be recognized as

Fritz Buckwalter's great-nephew. He's an American literary icon."

"What do you know about your grandfather?"

"Nothing. My grandmother only knew him for one evening. Then he disappeared."

"She never contacted him about the pregnancy? Or asked for support?"

"No. She knew he was married because of his wedding ring. She blamed herself for what happened, not just him. She didn't know how to find him, didn't even know what town he lived in. Years later, when Fritz became famous, she put two and two together. But Grandma never wanted to interfere with his married life."

"Except that one night she didn't mind." Her tone was terse.

He drew back. "Whoa. I said she was sorry."

"I'm sorry. I ... never mind. Your grandma probably didn't know Edmund had passed away by the time she learned about his relationship to Fritz."

"How do *you* know?"

"I was a literature teacher and read about the Buckwalters. I'm guessing you want to know your Buckwalter cousins."

"Definitely. Not just Edmund's progeny, but those of Fritz, August, and the sisters too."

How much longer could she sit here pretending she was far removed from the circumstances? "I'm sure Dr. Stafford didn't have to remind you of the sensitivity of this situation. If your claim is true, the shock will send ripples throughout the family."

"First, there's no *if*. It's absolutely true. Secondly, the sensitive nature is what kept me from saying anything until now. It's why I only told *him*."

"But you're telling me now."

"Figured I should come clean since we're dating."

Not anymore. If he was telling the truth, they were second cousins.

"I appreciate your sharing." But she wasn't ready to reveal anything. "Seems you're trying to pit me against Dr. Stafford."

"I want you aligned with the truth. If that pits you against him, so be it."

"I'm in a quandary. You're telling me one thing, but without proof. And you're blaming the professor for not trusting *you*? Do you realize what would happen if he believed anybody who walked into his office making outlandish claims? He writes nothing without documentation."

"I get it, but he completely dismissed me." Jason waved his hand with a flourish. "I also wanted to ask him what he knows about Edmund, since he was my grandfather."

She could hardly admit Jason was currently facing the Edmund Buckwalter expert. Besides her grandmother. "Of course. I'm sorry you never knew him." Sort of.

"I'm afraid Dr. Stafford's too big for his own britches."

"What?"

Jason scrolled on his phone again. "This website. These clues." He cited another list of coded mumbo jumbo as if Greg hailed from another planet and was planning an invasion.

Numbness crept over her, words of Eddie accusing his brothers. *You talk about me to the whole town on the radio. You let shoplifters run rampant. Then you say* I'm *the problem. Me!*

Was Jason truly a descendent with a similar problem? What was Edmund's issue anyhow? She needed to read more diary entries.

She gestured to the phone. "Anybody can devise a plot based on code language."

Jason frowned, then softened. "Leslie, I'm telling you this

for your own good. I'm concerned about you working for Dr. Stafford. Be watchful so he doesn't hoodwink you."

They write about us in the papers. It's all in code ... They want to run us out of town ... They make up lies about me, about you.

Beads of perspiration covered her forehead. She wiped her brow with quaking fingers. "Is this so-called conspiracy the reason you spoke so candidly to Dr. Stafford after the wing dedication?" Beyond candid. It was rude and uncalled for.

"I was asking questions the public wants to know."

"It was inappropriate. Mean-spirited, even."

"Look, Dr. Stafford gets away with too much already. He needs to come clean."

"Then ask him about his plan to overtake the world. Instead, you kick him in the gut regarding his father."

"His father's embarrassed about his son's involvement in the syndicate of underground activities. No wonder he doesn't want to be publicly associated with him."

"If you want Gr—Dr. Stafford to believe you and include you in the book, why are you attacking him?"

"Because he *doesn't* believe me."

"He never believes anything without proof. He's a researcher."

"That's another thing. He does shabby research. I've read his works."

Hadn't Greg just told her about others who *borrowed* his findings without crediting him, twisting his words as part of their own shoddy investigations? "Maybe you've only read *about* his work. So-called experts who quoted him."

"Why are you sticking up for him?"

"He's my superior, and I tend to give the benefit of the doubt."

"But not to me."

Is this how her grandmother felt when dealing with Edmund's delusions? "I haven't known you as long, Jason. I've read Dr. Stafford's works for years, including footnotes and sources. What you're claiming seems outside the box."

"Bizarre. Outrageous."

She pursed her lips. "It's too late to wade through all of this tonight." She stood and took out money to cover her tea and a tip.

Jason stood, too. "No, it's my treat."

"This isn't a date. I came to discuss what happened at the dedication." She set money on the table and left.

CHAPTER TWENTY-SEVEN

September 1952

A t Eddie's hospital bedside, Klara squeezed his hand, his wrists bound in cloth strips. He'd been sleeping since the doctor sedated him hours ago.

She closed her eyes, tears brimming. *How long, Lord?* How long would Eddie be tormented? What could she possibly do to help him that she wasn't already doing?

Her other hand rested on her abdomen. In six months, she would bring a babe into the world. A baby born to a floundering father, a fearful, confused mother. What kind of home could she create for a newborn under such circumstances?

This wasn't how she envisioned pregnancy or motherhood.

She couldn't shake yesterday's image from her head. Her once cheerful, winsome husband scowling, eyes expanding like a rabid dog, face distorted, lunging in the kitchen doorway, knife in hand, blood flowing from his wrists.

At least the ambulance whisking him away brought him to

a place of reckoning. Maybe here at the hospital, they'd find answers.

Fritz shuffled into the room and sat. "Good, he's still sleeping. We need to talk. I've done everything possible to keep his conduct out of the newspapers and keep him out of jail, but we can't hide him forever." He stroked his mustache. "Eddie needs psychiatric help."

"Dr. Mainard gathered that, based on the wrist-slitting."

"Maybe Eddie needs help for an extended period of time."

Klara drew back. "You mean an asylum?"

"A mental institution, they're called now. Mental hospital. If that's what it takes."

Her hand went from her abdomen to her throat, where words stuck.

"Klara." Fritz touched her forearm. "I want what's best for him. Apparently, just loving him isn't enough. He needs help we can't offer. Dr. Mainard mentioned moving him to another location."

She blinked, fighting tears. Her eyes were red enough. "Meaning an asylum?"

"Mental hospital. I don't know how long. But he needs treatment sooner than later."

She stroked Eddie's cheek. His whiskered face came into focus through her tears. "He must agree to go."

"He might not ever agree, Klara. He sees things nobody else does. He misses things everyone else knows. He might not see the need for help. We'll have to join forces and see that he gets it, whether he's onboard or not."

Her voice wavered. "How can I do that to him?"

Fritz's face stirred with compassion. "A better question is how could you *not*? You might think you're sending him into the fire, but frankly, I see it as sending him *away* from the fire."

An apt choice of words, metaphor or not. Unfortunately.

"But whatever torments him, he takes with him, wherever he goes."

"We'll have to trust the psychiatrists will know what to do." Fritz tousled Eddie's hair. His words choked. "I want to see my brother return. The Eddie I know and love."

* * *

Eddie nibbled on crackers while the nurse and Klara hovered. His sadness lingered as he eased back on pillows. Then Fritz and the nurse left.

Klara took his hand. "Eddie ... I'm pregnant."

He scooted up a few inches. "What?"

"You're going to be a father."

His smile spread like butter melting over toast. "A father! Oh, Klara." He leaned over to kiss her cheek. "When I get out of here, I'll paint the extra room. I'll make a cradle. I'll make you put your feet up every night so I can rub them." He patted her stomach with its slight bulge. "Does he keep you up at night kicking?"

She giggled. "Not yet."

"When will he be born? Or she?"

Klara swallowed. "In six months. March."

He frowned. "You're only telling me now?"

She hardly wanted to bring up all the reasons for her silence, clouding the moment with his infidelity and recklessness. "It was recently confirmed."

His eyes carried the promise of a sparkle. "Ah. I'll build a swing set. Then a treehouse. I can't wait to rock him in the rocking chair, tell him all about Paul Bunyan and Pecos Bill."

"Or Slue-foot Sue, if it's a girl."

He turned on his side and gazed at her. "You're the best thing that's ever happened to me, Klara. And now a baby!" He caressed her cheek. "How're you feeling? Any morning sickness?"

"I'm doing better now. I'm so glad to see *you* happy."

"Why wouldn't I be? This is wonderful news."

"And you'll be a wonderful father. But Eddie, considering the past few months, after talking to the doctor, I think it might be best for you to go ... to a mental hospital for help. With treatment, things will go better for you, for me, for our little one."

"You want me to go to a loony bin? With a bunch of crazies?"

"No, a psychiatric hospital. We can't bring a child into our home with all the chaos."

He plopped back on his pillow, stared at the ceiling.

She stroked his forehead, then wove her fingers through his hair. "Please understand."

A long moment passed before he rolled back toward her. "I do. I want to be a good husband, a good father. I'll do whatever it takes. As long as I can take my typewriter."

* * *

Klara and Fritz stepped inside Carlton Mental Hospital. He set the heavy case on the ground. A week ago, Eddie arrived after a three-day hospital stay. The closest institution was private, not state-owned—an hour drive from Dillard. Fritz said not to worry about finances. He'd cover it.

She and Fritz were allowed weekly visits. This was the first. A nurse ushered them down a corridor, eyeing Fritz's case suspiciously.

Klara's steps slowed, her breath jagged, occasionally winded from pregnancy. "Dr. Branson said we could keep

Eddie's typewriter in the closet, and they'd bring it to the dayroom when he wants it, under surveillance."

The nurse rolled her eyes. "One more thing to monitor."

"I'd think you'd welcome it," Klara snapped. "If it helps a patient find purpose and keeps him happily occupied, what harm is there?"

"Have *you* ever worked in this place?"

How'd this woman get a job here? With the compassion of a rhino.

In his office, after greetings, Dr. Branson sat at his desk. "Aside from the intake interview, three psychiatrists have observed Edmund to narrow down a diagnosis. There's an overlap of symptoms from manic-depressive illness, also referred to as manic depression, and paranoid schizophrenia."

Klara's breath caught. "Meaning what? How do you know which one?"

"We'll monitor him closely to discern. Both conditions have similar symptoms, such as high and low moods, delusions, sometimes hallucinations. In manic depression, one experiences bouts of heavy sadness. The lack of interest in life, speaking in a dull, flat tone, with inability to follow through characterizes depression as well as the negative traits of schizophrenia. Delusions and hallucinations are more pronounced with schizophrenia, including complete breaks from reality, such as being convinced people are trying to harm him. He might also exhibit disorganized speech and catatonic behavior."

Stop talking! She grasped the armrests. How much more could she take?

"The common disruption of thoughts and speech and talking in circles is typical of schizophrenia. However, mania has similar patterns, with rapid speech and racing thoughts.

We'll observe his distractibility during conversations and tasks."
He explained that hallucinations could involve any of the
senses. Tactile ones could feel like insects on the skin.

"Eddie believes there's a radio show every night with
messages about his brothers trying to keep him out of the
business," Klara murmured.

"Typical of both schizophrenia and manic depression.
Delusions include believing someone's pursuing you, or
thinking you have a supernatural power. Some believe a
celebrity loves them, or that his wife is cheating. Grandiose
delusions cause patients to believe they're famous, like Mark
Twain reincarnated, or that they can fly. He could believe
thoughts are planted in his head by others or being transmitted
elsewhere. Conspiracies run rampant. Sometimes personal
hygiene takes a back seat to everything."

Dr. Branson checked his clipboard. "Schizophrenia is
known for hallucinations. Paranoid schizophrenia is most
common. Besides irrationality and bizarre notions, paranoia
assumes others are watching and planning harm. We had a
woman here who was convinced Martians lived in her
neighborhood, trying to poison her through tap water. One man
believed an automobile billboard contained special messages
for him."

Klara trembled. "Eddie finds such messages in the
newspapers."

"Are schizophrenics violent?" Fritz asked.

"Rarely. But a situation due to delusions could lead to
violence. The primary feature is a mental splitting of thought,
impacting the process between thoughts and actions."

"What's a manic episode?" Fritz asked.

"A patient with manic depression vacillates between
euphoria and melancholy. During mania, he experiences

extreme well-being with irrationality and delusional thinking, and exhibits risky behavior such as heavy spending, drinking, or sexuality without regard for consequences. During depression, he falls prey to listlessness, lack of motivation, and suicidal notions."

"Eddie experiences all of that." Klara's head was spinning.

"Hearing non-existent, conspiratorial radio programs and witnessing non-existent shoplifting episodes could be due to paranoid schizophrenia. It accompanies confused thinking and trouble concentrating."

Klara stretched her fingers just to feel them. Was she dreaming? "I don't understand. Eddie wasn't always this way. When we were growing up, when we courted, he was lively, sociable, and cheerful. It's only been eight months."

"As is often the case. These conditions are no respecter of persons, Mrs. Buckwalter. They often manifest themselves in men your husband's age, late teens or early twenties. In women, too, in late twenties or early thirties."

"What causes it?"

"Some say there's a genetic predisposition. Others claim environmental causes."

"Genetic?" Klara's hand went to her abdomen. "Could our child have it?"

He hesitated. "There's a six times greater chance of developing it if a parent has it. But please don't jump the gun, Mrs. Buckwalter. You have enough concerns for today."

"What about environmental causes?" Fritz asked.

"For those who are predisposed, a personal trauma can trigger symptoms. Did Eddie experience any trauma in the years before exhibiting unusual behaviors?"

Klara looked at Fritz. "Your father. Oh, dear ..."

Fritz took over. "My father died fourteen months ago.

When Eddie procrastinated chores, my aging father climbed to the barn roof, then fell. Eddie blames himself. Still."

"We keep saying it's not his fault," Klara added. "But guilt eats him away."

"I'm sorry to hear that. And sorry for your loss." Dr. Branson frowned. "It's possible such a trauma triggered his mental state."

Klara sniffled. "Is it treatable?"

"Various treatments have worked on subjects—"

"You mean people?" Fritz couldn't keep the edge from his voice.

"People, yes," Dr. Branson replied as if clueless about his offense. "Experimental drugs, such as the antipsychotic chlorpromazine, called CPZ, calm a patient. European and American researchers are learning more about its efficacy and safety as we speak. Until lately, most people with schizophrenia spent their lives institutionalized. We have better practices now."

Quavering, Klara nudged out the words. "Such as ..."

"Besides insulin coma therapy, methanol shock, electroconvulsive therapy—"

Klara's hands flew to her chest. "That's horrible. Remedies worse than the sickness."

"We also utilize cognitive behavioral therapy, talking through all aspects of the patient's experience. Part of the trouble is getting the subject—uh, patient—to accept that he has a diagnosis. They don't see things clearly."

"How do you convince someone who's delusional?" Klara bit her lip.

Fritz tapped her arm. "Eddie's in the right place to get help."

"Definitely." The doctor glanced at the clipboard. "We do a

thorough exam to rule out medical conditions with similar symptoms. There's also an experimental drug called lithium for manic depression that has met some success, but with no clinical studies to back up claims. Lithium can reduce the recurrence of manic episodes."

"With side effects?" Fritz asked.

"Some people experience emotional numbing, disconnection from their feelings. It can also result in tremors, lethargy, and a general loss of interest in life."

"How is that helpful?" Klara snapped.

"Mrs. Buckwalter, we'll do all we can to pinpoint the diagnosis and prescribe proper treatment."

"Trading one set of evils for another."

"But someone on medication can return home and live comfortably as opposed to remaining in the hospital for life."

"So, Eddie will return home soon?" she asked.

"That's my goal for all patients, Mrs. Buckwalter. But I can't make promises. We'll need weeks of surveillance."

"Weeks?"

Fritz patted her hand. "Klara, the break will do you good. It'll be calm at home, good for you and the baby. Eddie's in good hands here."

"The best." Dr. Branson said. "I'll observe him three more weeks before making a definitive diagnosis."

"Will medication end the delusions?" Klara asked.

"Possibly, but neither lithium nor CPZ are officially approved by the Food and Drug Administration. They're experimental, so we must apply for either one. Meanwhile, we'll rely on other therapies. Mrs. Buckwalter, you look shellshocked."

"I am." Words of diagnoses and treatments caved in on her.

"I see you brought the typewriter. He'll need to use it where we can monitor him, in our dayroom. Leave it here and go see your husband. We'll explain everything to him next week."

A nurse led them. Trudging unsteadily down the corridor, Klara's eyes stayed front and center, avoiding stares or odd comments from lingering patients. In the sparse dayroom, two dozen patients meandered or draped over chairs, some at tables.

Eddie popped up from a chair and smiled. "Klara!"

She swooped over and hugged him, Fritz lagging to give Klara preference. "Oh, my dear Eddie." Her fingers slid over his wrists, bumpy with scabs, but no bandages.

He gave her a deep, longing kiss. She didn't care if people watched. "Oh, Klara, my love. Are you taking me home?"

She held his shoulders. "Not yet. They're going to help you here. I just spoke to the doctor. He's a good man."

"Dr. Branson? Did he say when I can leave?"

"No, he'll observe you a few weeks."

"Weeks?" He was aghast. "I need to go home and work."

"Eddie, he says they've helped many patients. He needs to observe you. Then he'll offer treatment." She took his hand. "It's for our baby. You agreed."

Sighing, he cupped her cheek. "I hope you're taking good care of our little one." He patted her stomach and kissed her again.

Clearly the doctor's work loomed heavy—first, convincing Eddie he had a problem. "I brought your typewriter. Whenever you want it, ask them to bring it here."

Eyes shining, his handsome grin returned.

Fritz walked over and embraced him. "Eddie, you're looking as scrappy as ever."

"Same for you, brother."

Klara requested the typewriter from an attendant. Minutes later, he set it on a table.

Eddie opened the case to find the typewriter topped by a

stack of fresh paper. He lifted the sheets high, as if displaying a prize. "Wonderful, beautiful paper! I can't wait to start writing again. He slipped a sheet into the roller. "When I'm done with this story, Fritz, will you critique it?"

"You don't even have to ask."

Chapter Twenty-Eight

October 1952 — three weeks later

F ritz faced Carlton Mental Hospital with trepidation. On the grounds, past high wire fences and locked gates, patients and attendants ambled to outbuildings—the craft shop, gymnasium, and greenhouse. The surrounding acres nurtured farmland that patients cared for. If it wasn't post-harvest, Eddie might enjoy outdoor time reminiscent of their childhood farm. But now the land lay fallow. Stark branches released their leaves, turning desert brown, dead underfoot.

Beyond the gate, he squinted at faces full of angst, fear, anger, or placidity. Most ignored him. One woman leered. Another scowled. He shivered and pulled his coat tighter against the October winds. Staring at the huge, bland box of a building before him underscored the oncoming of winter, overlapping his fears for Eddie in this wretched, dismal place.

Inside, Fritz inquired at the front desk. "I have an appointment with my brother Edmund Buckwalter." Nearby, a middle-aged man and a teenage girl snarled. From upstairs, a scream echoed. Nobody blinked or responded. Were such screams expected behavior? Poor Eddie, subject to this environment a month now, where bizarre practices and peculiarities were reduced to normal.

The woman at the desk shooed the man and teenager away. "You're not allowed here. Go back to the dayroom." They shuffled off with choice words. Fritz winced. She peered at her calendar. "Mr. Fritz Buckwalter? Edmund moved upstairs to Ward D." Where the worst cases went.

"What happened? He was in Ward B."

"He got into a fist fight—"

"He doesn't do fisticuffs. He yells."

"He was out of control. They moved him to Ward D to calm him with a cold sheet pack."

"What?"

"A form of hydrotherapy."

"How cold is it?"

"Ice cold. The colder the sheets, the better the outcome," the woman replied nonchalantly.

"That's inhumane. And how does locking him in Ward D help?"

"We have a staff with expertise. The doctor will explain."

"What provoked him?" Another hallucination?

"If I could keep track of every fight, squabble, and provocation, I'd be working in the White House instead of this dump." She picked up the phone. "Please send Edmund Buckwalter to the dayroom in Ward B. He has a visitor." She looked at Fritz. "Don't fret. Ward D isn't a death sentence. After he cools down in a few days, he'll return to Ward B."

"Cools down? You mean freezes to death from cold sheets?"

Another yell pierced the air, perhaps from the stairwell. A groan followed.

The woman at the desk paid no mind. "Head on over. He'll arrive shortly."

Fritz shuffled down the corridor, guilt pinching. Though appalled by Eddie's surroundings, Fritz relished the peaceful reprieve in Dillard. No time for wallowing in the store's destruction. August and Fritz obtained insurance money and sought bids for rebuilding Buckwalter Brothers Grocery. Without interruptions from Eddie's buffoonery and crises.

Renovation would take months. Meanwhile, they rented space on Cherry Street to sell newly acquired merchandise. Klara helped, wanting to donate hours to compensate for damages. Health insurance didn't cover mental health hospitalization, but Fritz assured Klara that he'd supply everything they couldn't afford. Wilma invited her for supper often.

With a clearer head and restful sleep, Fritz finally had time and energy to type his novel—convincing himself Eddie was getting the best treatment. But today, he doubted it.

Fritz hung his coat on a chair and paced. Some patients sat at tables with pumpkin centerpieces, writing or drawing with crayons, attendants hovering. As potential weapons for self-harm, pens and pencils were forbidden. Other patients lounged on padded chairs, reading novels or magazines. A group huddled in the corner. Four attendants made rounds. Two men and a woman took turns smoking cigarettes, heavily supervised.

Minutes later, Eddie appeared. His face lit as he waved. "Fritz!"

Fritz shook his hand. "You doing okay?"

"Depends on how you define okay." They sat.

"Heard through the grapevine you're in Ward D. What happened?"

Eddie reddened. "I'm not proud of it, but I had to let him know how awful it was."

"Who? What?"

"A guy named Milton. I turn my back for one minute, and he swipes my manuscript and hides it. I was frantic. I looked everywhere. Over two hundred fifty pages written in three weeks, the best I've written yet. And the only copy."

Fritz's heart raced. The worst disaster for a writer. No way to replace such a floodgate of creativity. "Did you find it?" That seemed more important than whatever happened to Milton.

"It took two days. Two days of torture, I'm telling you. I was practically pulling my hair out. I pleaded with everyone to help me find it. There are only so many hiding places since most of the building is off-limits to patients. Can't go outside your ward."

"How'd you find it?"

"First, they had to restrain me because I started pummeling him. They dragged me to Ward D and shoved me into a wet sheet pack."

"I heard. What's that like?"

"They wrap you up with cold, icy sheets and restrain you in bed. You lie there about four hours. It calms you down."

Alarm lanced Fritz's voice. "Because you're apparently freezing to death." How common was that treatment? He shuddered.

"They said if my behavior improves, I'll go back to Ward B. Meanwhile, they put Milton in isolation, with only crackers and water, until he revealed the hiding place. He finally gave in."

"Where was it?"

"Behind water pipes in the back corner of the upstairs bathroom. But some of the pages had cigarette holes. Not to burn them, but obliterating some words."

Fritz's knuckles itched to punch this Milton himself. "How'd he get a hold of cigarettes?"

Eddie lowered his voice. "It's not hard if you keep your eyes open. Just watch the wastebaskets near the nurse's station after they dispose of them."

Fritz cringed, envisioning the smoldering cigarette that led to fire and Eddie's meltdown. "Where's the manuscript now?"

"Under lock and key at the nurse's station. I retyped the burned pages."

"I can take it home for safekeeping."

A thirty-ish brown-haired man limped over and kicked Eddie's chair. "Don't start typing now. Makes too much racket."

"Mind your own business, Leonard," Eddie said.

Leonard jerked a thumb Eddie's way, addressing Fritz. "This guy thinks he's God's gift to the literary world. He gets his own typewriter and drives us all crazy."

A woman chuckled. "We're already crazy. He drives us batty, that's what he does."

"Same thing, Peggy," the man said.

Still seated, Eddie gritted his teeth and turned away.

"Do you go to the craft shop?" Fritz asked.

"Yeah, I've done silk screening and block printing. Got more ideas for store advertisements. They have clay, fabric, watercolors, and collage materials. I go whenever I'm not typing. Sometimes they won't let me type till late afternoon, when it thins out, so as not to bother folks with the noise."

"Cuts down on arguments. Do you work outside?"

"I milk Molly the cow. There's a dairy on the premises."

"Like the good ole days on the farm, eh?"

Eddie narrowed his eyes. "I should've fallen off that ladder, not Papa ..." The event sparking his downward spiral.

"It wasn't your fault, Eddie. Can I see the manuscript?"

Eddie dashed to an attendant. Upon his return, the brothers chatted about routines, rules, food, bedtime rituals—

like standing in line for a sedative—and cognitive behavioral therapy.

Leonard and Peggy wandered over, interrupting. Eddie's jaw tightened while answering Fritz's questions. It seemed to require great effort to stay on track.

The attendant reappeared with the manuscript.

Fritz read the first three pages, then looked up. "This is superb. I'm already hooked. Your protagonist jumps off the page. I'm already worried about what happens next." A twinge of jealousy soured his stomach. What a gift his brother had! With time to let it flourish—three weeks on the typewriter. But how absurd was it to envy Eddie in the mental hospital with all the time in the world to create stories?

Eddie's eyes lit. "Superb? Really? That means a lot coming from you."

"How far are you?"

"You're holding the entire manuscript. Beginning, middle, end."

"Written at the speed of lightning."

Eddie offered a sheepish grin. "It's got a misspelling or two. You'll proofread, right?"

"You're lucky I don't charge for catching wayward words." Which averaged three per paragraph. But Eddie's witty quips, beautiful turns of a phrase, clever plots, and intriguing characters more than compensated for errors.

"Nip those mistakes in the bud."

Apparently, those buds already opened. The corrected page would be covered in red marks like a student essay. "Want suggestions on characterization, scenes, and plot?"

"Of course. You have the best ideas. Then I need help finding a publisher."

Fritz smirked. "My vast wealth of knowledge and vital professional connections are at your disposal."

"How's *your* novel going?" Eddie leaned back, hands behind his head.

Normally, this would be salt in the wound. "Perpetuating my usual claptrap and codswallop, horsefeathers and hogwash. I haven't yet mastered lightning speed, though. I sent my first manuscript out five times now. Haven't heard back yet. Maybe the fifth publisher is the charm. Second manuscript's underway, so I plunk on the typewriter nightly." He guffawed. "My primary success is keeping my typewriter from getting dusty."

"What's taking them so long to notice your genius?" Eddie grinned.

Fritz stroked his mustache. "Great question."

"Sure you don't mind reading mine? It takes time away from yours."

"Your success is mine." Eddie's writing success could provide an income for doing something fulfilling and meaningful while pursuing his passion. Minimizing public occasions for emotional eruptions. Eddie needed to thrive this way. Or was that reaching too high?

"When you're done, I'll retype it."

By the time Fritz finished in a week or so, Eddie would be on medication. How would that impact him? Dr. Branson had reported Eddie's range of moody displays. Without work stress, outbursts were less frequent. Despite the stolen manuscript fiasco.

Leonard circled around to Eddie. "That'll be the day—you, a famous author."

Fritz opened his mouth, unsure about protocol for telling a patient to scat. Why'd they keep riling Eddie?

Peggy grabbed the manuscript and tossed several sheets in the air. As papers sailed back to earth, Leonard grabbed one.

"Coming in for a landing. Put those dreams where they belong."

Eddie jumped up and punched Leonard in the face.

"Yow!" Leonard reeled backward, hand covering a bloody nose.

Fritz lunged. "No, Eddie!" He pulled his brother back, Eddie's strength compounded by his temper. He thrashed in Fritz's arms, then broke loose, aiming for Leonard.

Peggy tossed pages like a child throwing confetti.

Eddie yelled, reminiscent of store episodes. Phrases were garbled and senseless, snatches of rage toward Leonard. "They should throw you off the radio!" To Fritz, he explained, "It's a conspiracy. Leonard and Peggy are incognito. They're really Marlon Brando and Elizabeth Taylor out to get me."

Fritz grimaced. Even if Eddie were stable, who could endure Leonard and Peggy's provocations?

Three attendants swooped over. In a cacophony of bedlam, one manhandled Eddie. One calmly steered Leonard away. The other latched onto Peggy.

Fritz stewed, fists tightening as if winding up for the punch.

The attendant clasping Eddie's arm shouted a jumble of accusations at Eddie, concluding with, "You're going right back to Ward D like you deserve."

Shaking, Fritz got in the attendant's face. "Now just a wretched, sordid minute. These two ding-a-lings have been yanking his chain since I got here. You've gotta do something!"

"Eddie's out of control. Look who has the bloody nose."

"Because that nitwit Leonard can't keep his big mouth shut. He needs a muzzle." Did Fritz really just say that here at the mental hospital? He was ready to smack Leonard and Peggy. The attendant, too, for good measure. How dare they insinuate Eddie was the only culprit?

"When you've earned a spot on the hospital board, I'll take your suggestion under consideration," the attendant spouted.

Papers fluttered over. One grazed Fritz's head.

Clenching his teeth, Fritz swiped it, then got on his hands and knees to gather the rest before anyone else could. Good thing the pages were numbered.

Another attendant addressed Fritz. "Sir, it's best you leave now. Your brother's headed up to Ward D."

"For more cold sheet therapy?" Fritz inadvertently shivered.

"Most likely. At minimum."

"You can't treat my brother this way. This wasn't his fault."

The attendant smirked. "*Now* look who's deluded."

Near the doorway, Eddie yelled and twisted in the attendant's grasp. Fritz watched him disappear from view, shouts echoing in the hallway.

Clutching the papers, Fritz headed to the front desk. His stomach lurched, nerves shot. He'd make sure the doctor knew who instigated the trouble. Maybe he'd find Eddie a different place—if such a thing existed.

Last month, Eddie had received a draft notice for joining the Korean War efforts but was dismissed from duty for medical reasons. Was living here any better? Mental illness brought its own kind of warfare.

CHAPTER TWENTY-NINE

2015

Leslie closed her laptop, her gaze sweeping the table of professors. "That's all. I'll be submitting the grant proposal tomorrow."

Rob Louden nodded. "Well done, comrades. This workshop will give prospective Raymond U students an enjoyable challenge with a taste of college expectations."

Greg snorted. "At least they'll be assured we don't eat children for breakfast."

Leslie winced. Not far from her assumptions about him six weeks ago.

Norma Tomquist, ever the Southern belle, smiled primly. "Well, bless your heart, Greg." Recently, Leslie had noted the switch to informal addresses in her presence. "Nobody ever thought Rob, Sheila, and I ate children for breakfast." They chuckled as Norma patted Leslie's hand. "You've done a lovely job with this project, honey. And managed to hold your head high among the rabble rousers."

"Rein in your sweet Southern charm, Norma," Greg said. "My blood sugar's going through the roof."

Laughing, Sheila MacIntyre shook her head, hoop earrings twinkling. "That's better than bringing out your fangs and claws, Greg. Now, Leslie, can you give me Ben Porter's phone number? I'll call him about which senior citizen residents he recommends."

Leslie dug her silenced phone from her bag and swiped to open it. The page opened to Instagram. Her heart skipped a beat.

Before her blinked a recent post by Jason Hendricks: *Greg Stafford: Chip off the Old Block? NOT.* The post had over 3000 likes and multiple shares.

Looked like she'd be doing damage control.

Perspiration gathered in every possible spot. With Greg in her periphery, her eyes remained glued to the phone, aimed as far from him as possible. "Um, what did you need?"

"Ben Porter's number," Sheila said.

Norma touched Leslie's arm. "Honey, what's wrong? You look like someone just died."

Definitely prophetic. She'd be dead the minute Greg caught wind of this. Fangs, claws, and all. She swallowed. She must call Jason, demand that he delete this immediately.

She managed to relay Ben Porter's number, voice steady. *Don't panic.* She stuffed her phone and laptop in the bag and trotted toward the door.

Greg was instantly beside her. "What's going on? Are you all right?"

"I have an appointment." To give Jason a piece of her mind. She brushed past him and headed across the courtyard, coat flapping over her arm. She was too hot to put it on.

In her office, she shut the door and examined the viral Instagram post.

She threw a hand to her forehead. How? Why? That idiot Jason! Greg hadn't wanted publicity, good or bad, especially related to the new wing. Nothing in this post insinuated good.

The link took her to an online article: "Greg Stafford: Chip off the Old Block? NOT." She skimmed it as tension squeezed every muscle. The article recapped the engineering wing dedication, speculating why only one of Douglas Stafford's sons spoke, why Greg apparently avoided the spotlight. It capsulized Douglas's college history as compared to his sons' career paths, concluding that the older brother definitely fell from the same tree, while the younger brother followed his own questionable path of wilted flora. Not to mention three quotes by Greg that were surely misquotes or taken out of context.

Several paragraphs harped on Greg's shoddy research tactics, claiming he wasn't the presumed Buckwalter expert. One photograph was Greg shaking hands with his father after the dedication, both men frowning. Like a sensational *National Enquirer* story.

There was no mention of Jason's Buckwalter lineage, thankfully. No secret coded Flintstone websites or literary conspiracies. Whew!

Unfortunately, the piece was well written. Intelligent. With citations. Making it believable to the average critic. Was Jason delusional or just plain mean-spirited?

Another claw of guilt dug into Leslie for withholding her own lineage from Greg. But she'd never discredit him.

Light-headed, Leslie clung to the desk and guided herself into the chair. She breathed deeply, then called Jason. No answer. She tried three more times. Nothing.

She texted: *Call me immediately. Emergency.*

Full of adrenaline, she jumped up, circled the desk, and pounded a fist on the filing cabinet. How could this happen?

Why'd Jason do such a despicable thing? Was this retaliation for Greg dismissing his claim to be a Buckwalter?

Leslie called Thornton Enterprises, Jason's employer. Both Jason and his boss were out, so Leslie left her number with the receptionist. "Have them both call immediately unless they want a lawsuit. Today's article must come down."

She checked Instagram likes, shares, and comments growing by the minute. Even if Jason took down the post, too many people had seen it by now. It was only a matter of time—perhaps minutes—before Greg caught wind of it.

She must tell him herself and beg for mercy. The damage was done. She felt responsible for insisting that Greg meet Jason.

Once again, she'd been duped. Lured by Jason's charm, then betrayed. She should've insisted he not write one word or post one photo. Assuming it would have done any good.

More deep breathing. *Be strong. Be humble.* And, as if sending a telepathic message to Greg, *Be kind.*

Her phone pinged. A text from Jason:

> Blame yourself. You chose to side with
> Stafford against me. Don't bother texting
> back. I'm out of here.

Blood drained from her face. She called him. No answer.

She'd have to confess to Greg that she'd met with Jason last week, even after Greg asked her not to. He'd surely view her actions as a betrayal.

She texted Greg.

> May I drop by? Crucial.

Ten seconds later, he replied:

> I already had my latte today.

Great, he was in a good mood. She tapped her reply:

Other business.

Come on over, but no time to rewrite my part
of the proposal.

Barely conscious, she traipsed to Worthington Hall, to his door. He looked up and smiled.

Her heart would have fluttered if not for dour news. She briefly relished his cheery face one last time before he'd become privy to Jason's libel. And—if he blamed her—the last time he'd ever grant her such a warm smile.

Self-talk pervaded. *Be strong. Be humble. Be truthful. Don't faint. Don't panic.*

He closed a file drawer and carried papers to the desk. "I'd say 'good to see you' but I'm not sure it would be reciprocated. What's up?"

She swallowed. *Get it over with.* "I'm so sorry, Professor, but Jason Hendricks posted an Instagram message that went viral. It's linked to his online article posted this morning."

He looked wary. "You're telling me because ..."

She winced. "You're the subject of the post and article."

"I never signed off on anything."

"I know." She could hardly breathe. "The article's about the wing dedication, father and son comparisons."

Greg's face reddened. His fist pounded his hand as a cuss word spilled out. "Excuse my French." He paced.

Just one expletive with a fist-in-hand was a relief compared to her expectations. "I'm so sorry. I already tried to call Jason and Thornton Enterprises. I'm waiting for his call. I'm demanding that the article come down."

He whirled about the office. "Blast it all! Another reporter rips someone to shreds." He rummaged through papers at his desk. "Where are my notes? I wrote down everything we talked about. Where's the article so I know what I'm dealing with?"

Leslie showed him the Instagram post.

Frowning, he bit his lip. "A contagious disease would be preferable to *this* kind of viral."

Trembling, she clicked the button that went to the article and handed him her phone. She wished the corner of his office had sand to bury her head in. As he read, his cheeks deepened from cherry to scarlet as if ready to explode. Her fingers tightened into fists.

He handed her the phone without so much as a glance. Mumbling, he stamped across the office, opened and closed a file drawer, opened a second one and perused folders. "I knew it. I never should've trusted him, never should've agreed to meet him. Blast it all. Blast Instagram. Blast Twitter. Blast Facebook." He plopped files on the floor since the desk was full. "Where are my notes? I never remember what I file them under."

"Try rogue." The word slipped out. Leslie stiffened in case comic relief wasn't welcome.

"See? I told you so." But no smile. "Rogue, whippersnapper, weasel, scheming schmuck, conniving cretan, sleazy slime ball, lousy lout."

Any other day, she'd join the alliteration. How could he think alliteratively when angry?

"That odious opportunist. Unbelievable." He smacked his desk and riffled through more papers, mumbling a slew of words. Of course, he was furious with her. He couldn't even afford her a glance. "I never gave that dirtbag permission to write about me, much less quote me. *Mis*-quote, actually. Several times. Without context. He calls himself a reporter? It's a travesty."

She blinked to keep tears at bay. *Don't cry.* "I'm sure you have plenty of other choice words too." For her.

"The article wouldn't carry as much weight if he hadn't written it so well. Making his ludicrous claims about my inadequacies and inferior research methods all the more believable."

"Dr. Stafford, I'm so sorry I insisted on Jason meeting you. I mistakenly trusted him. This is all my fault. I'll do whatever I can to get the article down." She faltered, hardly able to keep her voice steady. "Please forgive me." *Don't cry.* She sank into a chair before her knees could give out. Jason's text haunted her. *Blame yourself. You chose to side with Stafford against me.* But Greg would assume she'd aligned with Jason. Numbness crept in.

Was there any truth to Jason's ludicrous accusations about Greg? No, there couldn't be.

He finally looked at her. She kept blinking, his now confused expression shifting focus as his eyes riveted to hers. "Ah ..." His face softened. "You've nothing to apologize for."

"Yes, I do. It's completely my fault."

"Is your byline on the article?"

"No."

"Did you give him permission to write about me?"

"Absolutely not."

"Then it's not your fault. Stay here while I make a call."

"I already tried."

"This is between Slimeball and me."

She stood. "Then I should go now."

"Please stay." He gestured to the chair. She sat. "What's Thornton Enterprises' number? And his boss's name?"

Leslie read them off her phone.

Greg called and asked for the boss, then waited. When he spoke again, his demeanor was calm and cool. "Dr. Greg

Stafford here, Raymond University. I have two requests. First, if you don't want a libel lawsuit, take down the online article about me immediately. Secondly, have its author Jason Hendricks call me within three minutes."

He recited his number. "No more discussion. Dealing with your staff at Dysfunction Central is trouble enough. I've been misquoted and misrepresented more times in that article than in the past twenty years. Furthermore, even if the piece were a glowing report on my character, Hendricks had no permission to publish it.

"Watch your email for my formal letter of complaint ... I expect Jason to call me right after you pull the article down ... I wish you better luck in taking the high road with future publishing endeavors."

He plopped the phone on his desk. "Keep an eye on the post while I find my notes."

Leslie kept tabs on her phone, periodically refreshing the page. She wanted to go home and cry in her pillow. For a month.

Three minutes later, Greg's phone rang.

"Dr. Greg Stafford here ... Thanks for calling so quickly, Jason." Though stern, his voice returned to calm and collected. "Three things. Your feature article about me is coming down faster than Vesuvius erupted. Secondly, kindly remove your viral Instagram post about me, or you'll see consequences more monumental than Vesuvius. Thirdly, what kind of weasel writes tripe as a substitute for responsible journalism and even worse, *uses* a class act lady like Leslie Wickersham to get to me? You don't deserve her or anyone of her caliber ... Stop babbling since I'm not listening anyhow."

Was Jason trying to claim his article was Leslie's fault?

Greg continued. "I'm emailing your boss the details of your

misquotes and how you took advantage of my very capable and worthy assistant. Farewell."

Class act lady of high caliber? Capable and worthy? That's how he viewed her? Somebody had better pin her to the ground before she floated away. She gripped the edge of her chair. "Thank you, Dr. Stafford."

"Greg. At least call me Greg." He re-engaged with his paper stack. "I thought we were already on a first name basis. Besides, I hold Jason fully culpable. He's a snake charmer."

"And I'm a sucker. Again." Her voice tripped. "I should never have trusted him."

"Come on now." He batted the air dismissively. "No beating yourself up. He's very good at what he does, unfortunately."

"But this hurt more than just me. It hurt *you*."

He pulled his chair over and sat almost knee to knee, eyeing her intently. His spicy cologne filled her. His whiskers, laugh lines, his sea foam eyes. "You've made your contrition quite clear, so not another word about it. Frankly, I'm more concerned that he hurt *you*."

She tilted her head. Really? "But he didn't portray you accurately. He exposed the rivalry with your father. He decimated your reputation as a researcher."

"The ratfink could have likened me to Atticus Finch or Sherlock Holmes, but it still wouldn't matter. He was dead wrong to write the article, never mind the libel."

"But hundreds have seen the posts."

"Proving you can never keep a good social media mogul down. But that's my problem, not yours."

"How can you dismiss this so easily?"

He leaned forward, elbows on his knees. If he got any closer, she might jump out of her skin from the thrill. Why'd he have that effect on her? "I've told you about non-scholars who take so-called research into their own hands or borrow my own hard-earned tidbits without crediting me. It's the way of the world. I focus on my own scholarship, not their shoddy techniques."

"But this is different. Jason attacked your *character*."

Greg set a warm, comforting hand on hers, spreading a tingle up her arm. "Worse, he took advantage of *your* good character to do so."

Despite his kindness, shame washed over her. How could she have been so naive? The story of her life with men. She sniffled. "Um. I need to tell you something." His brows arched. "Jason is blaming me for his writing the article."

"That's convoluted."

"Maybe not. You asked me not to meet with him again, but I did. Right after the wing dedication." He drew back several inches. "But it wasn't a date," she quickly added.

He frowned. "Why'd you meet?"

Should she divulge all? At least confess to being a Buckwalter? "I ... I was furious at him for showing up, for photographing you, and saying such rude things. It was uncalled for."

"So, you went to bat for me."

"Yes, and he told me about his supposed Buckwalter connection. I didn't let on I knew."

His brows arched. "He told *you*? Why?"

"He was trying to pit me against you, since you didn't believe him. He ranted about your shabby research and said he knew more than you did about Edmund's line."

As did she. Should she tell him Edmund was her grandfather? And Jason's outlandish notions of Greg's literary conspiracy? But considering Edmund's hardships, she couldn't yet tell Greg about the crazy website and plot to overthrow the literary world. "Please understand. I didn't reveal anything you told me. In fact, I stood up for you. I said your research was impeccable. That you're fastidious about resources. All of that."

Greg uttered a low chuckle, as if amused. "Then I owe you a debt of gratitude for believing in me. But listen. I fight my own battles and would never send you into the trenches for my sake." His voice lowered. "Not to mention, he manipulated you. Now he's blaming you for his own anger and actions. That's dead wrong. Don't go down that road again, Leslie."

Face warming, she looked at her lap. How could she be such a dunce? Similar to getting sucked into Vic's ongoing emotional chaos.

He squeezed her hand, his voice soothing. "If you'll allow it, I'll see to it that this never happens to you again. With anyone."

How would he make sure of that? She looked up, heating from his touch on her fingers, warmed by his graciousness.

How would he respond to learning she was Edmund's granddaughter? He deserved to know, but she couldn't take that step yet. Without finishing the diary, transparency would feel like betraying her grandmother.

But was Leslie making this all about herself? How she didn't want Greg to view her differently with knowledge of her roots? "Greg ... I ..."

"What is it?"

"Nothing." *Don't spill the beans now.* Not while feeling trapped.

Not while he was holding her hand and his heat radiated up her arm. Not while his presence stifled her air flow.

He dropped her hand and stood. "From now on, he-who-shall-not-be-named shall henceforth be known as Buzzard Breath."

She could only manage a half smile. Jason was culpable, but there was also something seriously wrong with him. And that was nothing to smile about.

Chapter Thirty

March 1953—five months later

K lara stood behind Eddie as he typed. She massaged his shoulders as her very pregnant belly pressed against the back of the chair. Outside in the darkness, March winds tickled the windowpanes. Inside, over the past three months since he got home at Christmastime, whirlwinds stirred less often, patches of cloudy weather mixed with sunshine through his calmer demeanor marked by intermittent restlessness, irrationality, and disembodied voices.

He'd been on lithium, the experimental drug for manic depression, and calm enough to handle full-time work at Buckwalter Brothers Grocery—shelving, doing inventory, making deliveries, even waiting on customers at the makeshift store till February, then at the rebuilt Maple Street site. At home, he was writing his third novel.

He stood and cupped her cheeks. "I should be massaging *your* shoulders." He settled her on his chair, pushed a stool over, and lifted her feet. "You're soon to be a mother, and the good doc says to rest."

She smirked. "Then you'll take over cooking tomorrow?"

"The only thing I can make is a mess."

She laughed. "But you could manage pouring cereal."

"Sure. I can sprinkle cinnamon sugar on toast without much trouble." He turned on the radio. Nat King Cole's warm tenor voice called forth "Mona Lisa."

Such a melancholy song. Considering dreams that died at Klara's doorstep, Nat could have sung those lyrics to her. But she shook off negative thoughts to relish sweet moments of past weeks that generated hope.

She savored the banter, his fingers kneading her skin—moments few and far between. It seemed Eddie always walked a tightrope. Though his mood was calmer overall, when he vacillated between euphoria and gloom, from giddiness to agitation, she feared one false step could send him plunging down.

When the song ended, Eddie put a record album on the Victrola in the parlor: Nat King Cole's *Penthouse Serenade*. He took Klara to the couch, swung her legs across its length, propped her with pillows. Behind her on a chair, he continued the massage, humming and musing aloud. "If we have a boy, I'll build him a five-room treehouse. We'll chase monkeys at the zoo. If we have girl, I'll fill her room with fairy tales and buy her princess dresses. Boy or girl, we'll read stories together nightly."

"I can't wait to see you as a father, Eddie." Klara lifted her face for a kiss.

* * *

At midnight in restless sleep, Klara woke in a puddle of

amniotic fluid. Labor began. Eddie called the doctor and drove her to the hospital. Soon she delivered a healthy baby girl.

After the doctor summoned him, Eddie sat in Klara's hospital room, gingerly holding a soft, pink, blanket-wrapped bundle. He stroked her cheeks, her hair, her tiny fingers, cooing, singing "Daisy." Tears wet his eyes. "My little sweetheart, Martha Jean." He composed lullaby lyrics, adding new verses to "Hush, Little Baby."

Klara watched them together, a magical, tender moment as images of labor pains dissolved, along with dissipating flashbacks of Eddie's episodes. This moment she'd treasure forever. Eddie, a father, in love with her, in love with their daughter. Both love at first sight.

Perhaps being a father would enable his recovery.

* * *

May 1953

Tending to baby Martha took more energy and stole more sleep than she'd imagined, but Klara was ripe for the challenge. She'd longed for this day. Even when laying Martha in her cradle, Klara could hardly pull herself away, gently rocking, touching her angelic cheek, singing to accompany the infant's dreams.

Eddie rose to the occasion. Since the babe's birth two months prior, he'd come home from work whistling. He'd cuddle Martha in the rocking chair, nestle together on the couch, or hoist her up and down to shrieks of delight.

Klara cherished nursing times, more intimate with the baby these past weeks than with Eddie. But one evening as Martha slept, Eddie guided Klara to bed and orchestrated an evening of lovemaking like never before. In his arms, Klara savored sweetness, sensuality, and solace in equal amounts.

Had they turned a corner? Would they be a normal family now? Despite glitches, perhaps medication and weekly psychotherapy were all Eddie needed to be of sound mind, meet his responsibilities, and remain stable. *May it be so, dear Lord.*

* * *

After supper, Fritz, Wilma, and Frieda stopped by Eddie and Klara's house to drop off the third draft of Eddie's second novel. Since receiving it at the mental hospital, Fritz assessed it twice between revisions. Now he'd completed proofreading.

While the women and Frieda cooed over Baby Martha, Eddie scanned pages and thanked Fritz profusely. "Are you game for one more? I just finished my third."

Fritz threw up his hands, nearly spilling coffee. "No rest for the weary."

Klara swayed with the baby. When Eddie came home from Carlton five months ago, he groomed and dressed better, speech more organized and fluid. He seemed calmer, more content. Initially, she wondered if lithium had stolen his passion, but the past month of late-night writing proved that theory wrong.

Eddie retrieved a thick manila envelope from his study. "Here you go. Consider that you always get first whack at seeing a masterpiece. All your time invested is a small tradeoff."

"You're lucky you're right," Fritz said.

"My turn." Pregnant Wilma took Martha and sat on the couch. Five-year-old Frieda scooted next to her, enthralled with the infant's fingers. Wilma was due in four months.

Talk ensued about store activities, town gossip, and church events.

"You're attending next week's church potluck and talent show, right?" Wilma asked.

"Maybe." Klara passed a plate of hazelnut cookies. "Is *Roy Rogers* on that night? My dear husband has adopted a new pastime."

"Look who's talking, my dear, with your fondness for *I Love Lucy*." Eddie slurped from a coffee cup. "Now we save money by plopping on the couch with the television set and call it a date."

"We're hardly saving money considering the cost of electricity." Not to mention, when Eddie couldn't sleep, he'd turn on the TV instead of reading or writing. But he'd been so thrilled to surprise her with it last month, after five months of full-time work.

Wilma cooed at the baby. "It's a fine thing to have such entertainment at our beck and call, especially on a rainy day or a blustery night. I loved hearing *Our Miss Brooks* on the radio and enjoy watching it even more."

Fritz snatched another cookie. "I'm partial to Jack Benny and Red Skelton myself."

After Fritz and his family left, Eddie took Martha and read the picture book *Many Moons* by James Thurber. Two-month-old Martha kept grabbing pages.

"Good to see she loves books already." Klara snuggled next to him.

"Despite eating the pages." He set down the book. "Time for storytelling hour." He launched into the most animated, exquisite version of Cinderella that Klara had ever heard. As he gestured for the fairy godmother's wand and called forth tendrils of magic, Martha's tiny hands met his fingertips. Their eyes stayed riveted to each other as if lost in their own world.

That night, Klara slipped into bed exhausted. She curled up next to Eddie, her hand splayed against his chest as it steadily went up and down with each breath. As steady as she hoped their future would be.

* * *

Three days later, Eddie was late for supper. The phone rang early evening.

Klara grabbed it. "Hello, Eddie?"

"No, ma'am, but I'm calling about Edmund Buckwalter. Is this his wife?"

"Yes, this is Klara Buckwalter."

"Ma'am, this is Sergeant Fields from Lynwood. Your husband was arrested for a traffic violation and disturbing the peace. He used his one phone call to contact his brother Fritz, but I wanted to notify you that he'll be here in the Lynwood jail for thirty days."

"Thirty days!" Her heart raced. "Can't he get out on bail?"

"No, he needs to stay here. Says he can't afford the fine."

"Doesn't he get a trial first?"

"We're not about to let him back on the streets right now."

"No ... this can't be." He'd been doing so well. "May I talk to him?"

"That's against protocol, ma'am, but you can come during visiting hours." He rattled off days and times with instructions.

She hung up and buried her face in her hands. How could this be? He'd miss his little Martha, but Klara couldn't stomach the notion of taking her babe to the jailhouse.

At least he was in Lynwood, not Dillard where everyone would find out.

She needed to call Fritz, then Eddie's doctor, once knew the full story. But first she went to Martha on her blanket, kicking and rattling a toy, smiling in blessed oblivion.

Klara drew her close, taking comfort in her baby girl's

warmth, the smell of talcum powder. "Don't worry, honey bunch. Your papa's gonna be okay. I promise."

She prayed it was a promise she could keep.

CHAPTER THIRTY-ONE

May 1953

Fritz made the half-hour trip to Lynwood in fifteen minutes, watching for police cars more than the speedometer. How'd Eddie end up in jail? His two-minute phone call revealed little. Fritz had to ensure this didn't hit the newspapers. After gaining momentum, a publicized setback would prove a huge roadblock to Eddie's recovery.

Stewing, Fritz committed several traffic violations himself. At the jailhouse, he charged in, then slowed to catch his breath. *Calm down, or they'll take you for the fool.*

Upon introducing himself to Officer Snodgrass, he asked, "How much is bail?"

"No bail, Mr. Buckwalter. He pays his debt to society here and now."

Fritz withdrew his checkbook. "What's the fine?"

"He's paying time, not money. He didn't have money for the fine."

"I'll pay it, and he'll pay me back. How much?"

"I don't know what planet you're from, Mr. Buckwalter, but that's not how it works around here."

From a desk, a guy with a pencil on his ear snickered. "Probably from the same planet those Martians came from."

Nerves pulsing, Fritz stroked his mustache. "What happened?"

"We don't discuss offenses with random strangers who come in off the street," Officer Snodgrass said.

Fritz jerked a finger toward the jail on the other side of the wall. "That's my brother there. He'll tell me what happened, but I figured to get your perspective first."

Pencil Guy snorted. "Tell him. He'll see the write-up in tomorrow's paper anyhow."

"Some blasted reporter caught wind of this?" Fritz asked.

"Yeah, *The Lynwood Press*. It'll hit the papers by six a.m."

Fritz smacked a fist on the counter. "No!"

Officer Snodgrass frowned. "That's out of our jurisdiction, Mr. Buckwalter. But here's the report." He shuffled papers. "First, he ignored the stop sign at the Curry Street intersection, nearly colliding with the car that had the right of way. The policeman wrote a ticket, but your brother got out of his car and carried on about helicopters hovering over Lynwood, preparing to swoop in and take him away. Said it was all over the radio stations. Saw it on television too."

Blast the television! Another blessing turned curse. Sounded like last year's delusions when Eddie claimed the radio show featured August and Fritz scheming behind his back.

"He alleges there were aliens, little green men, crossed wires, all kinds of strange communications. The guy wouldn't shut up. He even accused Officer Dentin of being a simpleton since he obviously wasn't comprehending the gravity of such impending doom."

Great. At least Eddie hadn't assaulted the officer.

Pencil Guy chimed in. "Even if we discharged him, he's sure to disturb the peace again. He got everyone on the sidewalk worked into a lather."

Fritz raked fingers through his hair. Hadn't the medication been working? "May I see my brother, please?"

"Visiting hours ain't till tomorrow," Pencil Guy said.

"Look, I drove from Dillard. May I please see him, since I'm here already?"

The men exchanged a glance which included at least one eye roll and a sigh.

Officer Snodgrass picked up a key. "All right, ten minutes. That's it. In the cell. I'll be right in the hallway." He led Fritz to the cell and opened the door. Fritz blinked through the dim light, hoping for a clearer, brighter view to discern Eddie's expression.

Eddie sat on a cot, staring vacantly.

"Eddie." Fritz stepped inside and grasped his shoulder. "Are you okay?"

Eddie looked up as if offended. "Would *you* be?" He gestured across the cell. "This is what happens when nobody believes you. You do somebody a favor, they try to shut you up. But this isn't gonna stop aliens and FBI investigators."

"Which aliens?" Better to play along than argue.

Eddie replied with a disjointed explanation about investigators announcing alien warnings over the car radio while he made deliveries in Lynwood.

Fritz sat beside him on the cot. "Eddie, are these the same people you heard when you thought August and I were on the radio plotting behind your back?"

Eddie's eyes widened. "Did you come in here just to contradict me? Why would I make that up?"

"The thing is, nobody else hears it. Not the cops, not Klara, not Wilma, and those two ladies listen to the radio a lot."

"They don't listen to the right stations."

This was going nowhere fast. "Eddie, things have been so much calmer since you got back from Carlton. So, what happened today?"

"What do you mean *happened*?"

Fritz eyed him closely. "Are you still taking your medication?"

Eddie balked. "I don't need that stuff anymore. I've been doing fine. But that has nothing to do with news on the radio. Are you taking their side over mine?"

"This isn't about sides, Eddie. This is about discerning the truth."

"I *told* you the truth, and you're calling me a liar? We both grew up with the same parents who didn't tolerate the smallest white lie. Why would I start lying now?"

"I don't think you're lying. It's just ..."

"Just what?"

"When did you stop taking your medication? Did the psychiatrist tell you to quit?" Supposedly, stopping lithium required a gradual lowering of doses, not quitting all at once.

"A month ago."

Did Eddie have an accurate feel for the passage of time? "Shortly after Martha was born?"

"Yeah."

"How long have you been hearing men talk about aliens on the radio?"

"Months. Since I got home from Carlton and could finally listen to the radio again."

"But you haven't mentioned it till today."

"I knew you wouldn't believe me. I finally had to tell the

cops. They're the ones who should be paying the most attention."

"Why'd you stop your medication?"

"They're trying to poison me. I've known it from the beginning, even at Carlton, but they watched my every move, so I had to take it."

"Didn't you feel better taking it?"

"Not unless you call bland and listless better. It felt like the life getting sucked out of me."

"I thought you were doing swell. You wrote a whole other novel, for heaven's sake."

"Yeah, but it's not as good. I didn't feel the muse like before. I felt like a damp rag. Every time I took that pill, I felt the poison enter my bloodstream, slowly sucking me dry. It's as if they want me to feel nothing. The sadness is gone, but so is the joy."

"Did you just stop cold turkey?"

"Yeah. I felt unsteady a few days, but it got better."

"Does Klara know?"

"I don't want to bother Klara with all my problems."

Seriously? *No, you just* cause *her problems.* This lack of medication caused another one.

Eddie lowered his voice. "Hey, are you getting me out of here? I'm ready."

Fritz swallowed. "I'll see what I can do."

Snodgrass cleared his throat from the aisle. "Time's up."

Fritz squeezed Eddie's shoulder and walked back to the front counter. He leaned over, elbows planted on the counter. "Listen. I'm here to tell you that putting a guy like Eddie in jail is not going to help him or the community. He has some problems—"

"I'll say." Another snort, this time from Snodgrass.

Fritz hesitated then plunged ahead. "He suffers delusions,

and he's under a psychiatrist's care. He needs help, and sitting here in jail only escalates the problem. Please let me take him home. I'll contact his doctor first thing tomorrow. He'll know what to do."

"You're barking up the wrong tree, Mister," Snodgrass said. "You'll have to talk to the police chief, but good luck with that after the tongue-lashing your brother gave the officer."

After asking around, Fritz couldn't locate the chief. He'd have to wait till tomorrow to contact Eddie's doctor. In the dusk, he stormed to the newspaper office, *The Lynwood Press*. Interior lights revealed two male silhouettes. He banged on the locked door.

"We're closed, man." A silhouette pointed to the clock.

"Please let me in." Fritz raised his voice. "It's about a story for tomorrow's paper."

The door opened. A wiry, gray-haired man frowned. "What's up?"

Fritz stepped in and closed the door. "You have a story about Edmund Buckwalter?"

"Yeah, a good one too." The second guy stood and smirked. This middle-aged, black-vested man bore no resemblance to naive Fred Rickert from *The Dillard Tribune*. These fellows were seasoned, surely not bribable. "What a looney tune!"

Fritz kept a growl from leaving his throat. "That man happens to be my brother. As a newspaper columnist, you, sir, could strive for a less biased choice of words."

The older man, Stan Bishop, according to his desk nameplate, punched his colleague in the arm. "Like I've been telling you, Ned."

"I'm here to ask that you not run that story in the paper," Fritz said.

"Look, Mr. Buckwalter," Stan replied, "it's not every day we get to write about someone who hears Martians and talks about invasions. This gets our readers excited. It'll wake everyone up. Sleepy ole Lynwood will be more alive than ever."

Fritz drew himself up straight before Stan. "Now just a sordid moment. It's obvious my brother has mental problems. Why do you wish to exploit him? I'm asking you to back down. He'll be getting help, and publicizing his behavior does more damage than good."

Ned guffawed. "Should've thought of that before spouting off about little green men."

"Anything that happens in public is considered public domain," Stan said.

Dare he offer to write them a check for not publishing the article? No, he wouldn't get away with it this time. These men would talk—or worse, report the bribe in the paper. That would harm Fritz's reputation and the whole Buckwalter grocery empire, trickling to the family.

One more try. "I understand why you'd jump at such a story, but I'm asking you to consider the harm it causes to someone under psychiatric care, to his wife as well. These anecdotes are not kind, nor do they uplift humanity."

"Eddie Buckwalter wasn't exactly uplifting humanity, either," Ned said.

"All I can do is plead for mercy. He's already going through a rough time. A news article like this will make it worse."

"That's not really our department," Stan said.

Ned chuckled. "Yeah, try the looney bin."

"Is compassion out of your department?" Fritz traipsed out, furious. Perhaps he could take solace knowing the article would be in *The Lynwood Press*, not *The Dillard Tribune*. But it wouldn't take long for news to spread.

* * *

At home that evening, tucked in his office while Wilma read to Frieda, Fritz called Dillard police officer Ron Gresham. "Hey, Ron? I need a favor."

"Name it. I owe you. I don't know what I would've done if you, August, Wilma, and Klara hadn't been so generous with food and cooking when Gracie was sick."

"That's what needs to happen when the good Lord blesses me with a thriving grocery store. We were happy to help, Ron. I don't consider you owe me a dime, but I'm in need of your services." He cleared his throat. With a glance over his shoulder, he lowered his voice. "Eddie's in a bad way and I'm getting him help. Meanwhile, I can't let his hard times become the stuff of newspapers and idle gossip. Do you have connections to the Lynwood police force?"

"Sure do. Blood relation, in fact."

"I thought so, according to my recollection. Hmm. Well, I hate asking ..."

"Spit it out, Fritz. You've always been a straight shooter."

"But I don't want you in a pickle with your relative. Or the law."

"Go on."

"I need something expunged from police records."

Chapter Thirty-Two

June 1953—a month later

D r. Branson scanned his clipboard. "We've determined that Edmund has paranoid schizophrenia, also called dementia praecox."

Fritz grasped Klara's wrist, as much to soothe himself as her. After taking Eddie back to Carlton Mental Hospital following ten days—versus thirty—in jail, Fritz expected more prescription medication, not a new diagnosis. "What does that mean?"

Dr. Branson explained it months ago, but Fritz had discarded his words soon after the doctors diagnosed Eddie with manic depression instead. "It's a common form of schizophrenia that manifests itself with paranoia. A primary symptom is his conviction that people are constantly sabotaging him. That includes voices he hears on radio and television, plotting behind his back, but he hears voices with or without a radio."

"This time it was the car radio," Fritz said. At least *The*

Lynwood Press article reported only two charges—the traffic violation and disturbing the peace—and didn't mention Eddie's delusions. Good thing Stan and Ned didn't succumb to sensationalism.

Fortunately, Officer Ron Gresham confirmed all allusions to aliens were erased from police records.

Klara tilted her head. "He doesn't have manic depression?"

"He has both conditions. They overlap symptoms, particularly moodiness, delusions, and irrationality. He still presents as manic depressive, but the degree of his paranoia and hallucinations takes us into the realm of schizophrenia."

"Both?" Klara paled even more. "What do you recommend?"

"Experimental medication for schizophrenia called chlorpromazine, CPZ for short, is more effective than basic tranquilizers, reducing delusions and hallucinations. Research proves it to be a viable alternative to electroshock therapy and other drastic measures."

Fritz shuddered. "And the side effects?"

"Several have been reported, including dizziness, trouble with balance, a shuffling walk, restlessness, tremors, and sedating effects." At Klara's widening eyes, he quickly added, "No patient experiences everything. They're bothersome but preferred over hallucinations."

"Always a tradeoff," Klara murmured.

"Due to the experimental nature of CPZ, I'll have to keep Edmund here under surveillance for three months to see how he adapts."

"Again?" Klara's hands shook.

"For the good of all, Mrs. Buckwalter. We must monitor his symptoms daily. We'll also meet with him three times weekly for intense cognitive behavioral therapy."

"What about lithium?" Fritz asked.

"Lithium prevents mood extremes. It helped but didn't address the hallucinations, which worsened. Furthermore, I'll only administer one drug at a time."

"Have you told Eddie yet?"

"I'd like you to join us this afternoon when I tell him. It won't be easy. Nobody likes to be told he's delusional."

Fritz stroked his mustache. "If this medication doesn't work, are there alternatives?"

"Temporary treatments such as hydrotherapy with cold sheets—"

"I know," Fritz snapped. "Abominable!"

"It calms patients during an episode. We conduct those regardless of medication."

"Eddie was certain the lithium masqueraded as poison," Fritz said, "which is why he stopped using it at home."

"We'll make sure he swallows the pill while he's here. After that, I'm confident he'll want to continue its use at home."

Fritz winced. Klara would have to watch Eddie like a toddler. At least she needn't worry about finances. As before, since no insurance covered mental health, Fritz promised to pay expenses that store insurance didn't cover.

September 1953—three months later

Eddie jiggled Martha on his knee. "This is the way the ponies ride, *clip-clop, clip-clop.*"

Klara smiled from the kitchen doorway, watching them in the parlor. Though Eddie had only been home a week after three months at Carlton, his little girl responded with delight to his every gesture. He was making up for lost time.

The CPZ was doing its job. The doctor deemed Eddie fit

for life in the community. Voices no longer haunted. He no longer mentioned aliens or non-existent radio shows. Maybe now, finally, they'd be a normal family. And just in time. Klara set a hand on her stomach. In six months, little Martha would have a sibling. And Wilma was due any day. What a thrill to have cousins close by, especially since her own siblings' families lived hours away.

* * *

March 1954—6 months later

At the cash register, Fritz couldn't keep from smiling. At the endcap next to his peanut butter display, Eddie couldn't keep quiet. But it was hullabaloo Fritz welcomed.

"Carl Tischbein!" Eddie thrust a cigar toward the man. "We had a girl yesterday! The most beautiful baby in the world." He held up a Polaroid photo.

Carl pocketed the cigar. "Well done, Eddie. Congratulations! What's her name?"

"Dolores, officially. But we call her Dodie." Eddie sighed contentedly. "Sweet little Dodie. She's already queen of the household."

Carl chuckled. "Queen indeed. Diapers, nighttime feedings, crying at all hours."

"Music to my ears." Eddie danced a jig on the spot. "I have visions of playing horsey, twirling on the merry-go-round, swinging with monkeys at the zoo." He lifted a Swift's Oz peanut butter tin decorated with *Wizard of Oz* characters. "And having picnics at the park, walking the Yellow Brick Road, and eating peanut butter and jelly sandwiches." This drew grins from customers in the checkout line.

A woman rounded the corner.

"Mrs. Collins!" Eddie handed her a cigar. "Here, it's on me. My little daughter Dodie was born yesterday. Isn't she beautiful?" He pointed out the picture.

Mrs. Collins took the cigar with a smile. "Congratulations, Mr. Buckwalter. Two precious girls, you lucky man. I can't promise I'll smoke this, but my husband will certainly enjoy it."

"Oh, excuse me," Eddie said. "I have something better for the ladies." He pulled a pink carnation from a full vase Fritz had purchased for him that morning. "Here you go, ma'am."

Sniffing, she accepted the flower. "Thank you. Much better smelling than a cigar, in my opinion. Fitting for a darling little girl."

"Darling, all right. I have two princesses. Princess Martha and Princess Dodie. Dodie's going to grow up loving fairy tales like her sister. I'll build them a castle instead of a treehouse."

"Perhaps a castle treehouse," Mrs. Collins said.

"Perfect! I'll start developing blueprints today."

She laughed. "Then I expect them to invite me for a spot of tea. My best wishes for you and dear Klara."

* * *

Klara cradled her newborn, Dodie, on her lap. Martha had just turned one. Despite the extra work of changing and washing diapers and chasing a crawler around the house with a newborn on her hip, Klara couldn't be happier.

Eddie's medication remained effective. He seemed stable, calm, happy—even if a bit bland. Periodically, she worried he might go off the medication in efforts to reclaim his previous pep and creative inspirations. But considering August and Fritz kept him busy at the store even when customers roamed, she dismissed that concern. He finally had what he wanted—a full-time place between his brothers at Buckwalter

Grocery. Besides shelving merchandise and arranging displays, he ran the cash register. Klara cheerfully stayed home with her girls.

Fortunately, Fritz had been graciously covering medical bills beyond their reach. She thanked God that Eddie could work instead of accumulating debt.

Fritz and Wilma had a son six months prior, with another baby on the way. With August and Irma's three and the Buckwalter sisters' kids, the clan thrived. Klara was grateful to join forces with her own growing family. On Sundays, everyone gathered at a Buckwalter home for a festive Sunday dinner after church. For too long, Klara had avoided them, drumming up excuses with Eddie's odd behaviors. But now Sunday was a day they looked forward to.

* * *

1954 - 1957

Optimism flooded Klara. In 1953, President Eisenhower saw to the end of the Korean War. Racial segregation in public schools was declared unconstitutional by the United States Supreme Court, guaranteeing equal protection. With vaccinations for children, worries about polio might soon be over. She wished for a vaccination to eliminate schizophrenia, but medication kept Eddie's symptoms at bay.

As Martha and Dodie grew, each day was a joy. Even spilled milk, scraped knees, and periodic tantrums were welcomed as normal life. Best of all was watching Eddie play and read with the girls. Depending on the season, he'd push them on the swing, give horsey and piggyback rides, play hide and seek, run through the sprinkler, rake and jump in leaf piles, or build snowmen together as if reliving his own childhood.

They even had princess tea parties while drinking his favorite peach lemonade.

Seemed like every week, Eddie bought a new record album. He'd play it loudly and dance with the girls. One minute he'd mimic Louis Armstrong playing trumpet. The next minute he was Harry Belafonte chanting the Jamaican "Banana Boat"—all three competing to see who could hold the Day-O note the longest. He'd croon like Pat Boone, then direct a jazz orchestra with as much finesse as Dizzy Gillespie. When "Que Sera, Sera" became a hit, he rivaled Doris Day with a falsetto voice and exaggerated sways, singing to his girls. He danced to polka bands when *The Lawrence Welk Show* joined their weekly television repertoire. After seeing Elvis on *The Ed Sullivan Show*, he'd bounce around singing "Hound Dog." The girls hopped, danced, and giggled along. Though Elvis seemed a bit risqué for Klara's tastes, she enjoyed the father-daughters ensemble.

Every evening, Eddie and Klara took turns reading Dr. Seuss, *Babar the Elephant*, *Curious George*, Madeline books, and *Journey Cake, Ho!* But when Eddie put on his storytelling hat—a turquoise, green, and gold jester's hat—no telling when the fun would stop. Rivaling Fritz's monkeyshines, fun inhabited the realm of fairy tales and tall tales. Eddie spun new adventures for Paul Bunyan, Pecos Bill, Cinderella, and the Bremen Town Musicians. Characters populated each other's stories while Martha giggled and Dodie squealed. The best were tales from his childhood, growing up on the farm.

After the girls went to bed, Eddie read to Klara. If he was too exhausted, they'd watch Danny Thomas's *Make Room for Daddy* on television. When Eddie started watching baseball on TV, Klara joined him. A shared interest developed for the Saturday *Game of the Week*, All-star games, and the World Series in autumn.

Despite improvements, Eddie eventually lacked energy for his own writing. He lost motivation to publish his manuscripts. He told Fritz to not bother submitting them. Meanwhile, Fritz had more time to write and submit his own, but to no avail.

Was Eddie's creative spark gone? Perhaps it was fulfilling enough to thrive amidst the Buckwalter Brothers Grocery and pour his heartfelt stories into his daughters.

But his weariness worsened monthly. He sank into listlessness and apathy. His coordination flagged. He'd trip on the rug, stumble into furniture. Fritz reluctantly reported that Eddie was clumsier at the store, dropping and breaking things, getting so frustrated that Fritz took minutes to calm him down.

Emotionless, Eddie watched television late at night instead of reading. On Saturdays, despite the family rule, he'd turn on TV, forgetting household chores. Games like Uncle Wiggily, Chutes and Ladders, and Candy Land, previously a delight with the girls, now irritated him.

Klara scheduled his doctor appointment, but it was a one-month wait.

* * *

April 1957

Three-year-old Dodie climbed into her father's lap. Sitting cross-legged, she faced him. Her fingers traced his lips as she giggled. "You look like a fish, Papa."

Klara crocheted nearby, frowning. Dodie laughed at his antics, but they were no longer funny. For months, Eddie had no control over facial expressions. One minute he'd blink rapidly, the next minute he'd be chewing—without the gum. He'd grimace instead of smile, at inappropriate times. He'd smack his lips, puff out his cheeks, make fish lips, stick out his tongue, then probe his tongue throughout his mouth. His coordination waned. He'd drop things or trip over nothing. Fortunately, the doctor appointment was tomorrow.

"Papa, push me in the swing," four-year-old Martha called from the doorway. Eddie had built a swing set for the girls the previous summer, with two swings, a slide, and monkey bar rungs.

"Let's go." Eddie picked up Dodie by the waist as she squealed. They headed outdoors in jackets.

On the swing, Dodie pumped her little legs to no avail. Eddie lifted her swing and sent her sailing forward. He pushed both girls in turn. Klara smiled from the doorway.

As Martha went higher, Eddie stepped back to accommodate. In doing so, he stumbled backward and fell. Klara charged forward.

Avoiding Martha's swinging feet on her way back, Eddie lay prostrate and rolled over.

"Papa!" Martha screeched. "Are you okay?"

"Yup!" He got up, dusted himself off, and flashed a grin to Klara. "Don't mind me. It goes with the territory." Another grimace immediately replaced the smile. The fake gum chewing resumed. What was happening? Why was he so much clumsier than last month?

Minutes later, the girls slowed down and slid off the swings.

Dodie lifted her arms. "Papa, I want to go on the monkey bars. Pick me up!"

"Say please, little girl, and Papa will do whatever you want."

Yes, he would. He'd go to the moon and back for her.

"Please, Papa."

He grasped her waist and hoisted her up. She grabbed the metal bar. "Hold me tight!"

"Gotcha, sweetie pie." He kept his hands around her torso as she seized one bar after another. The next bar, then the next.

"This is hard. I'm done." Dodie let go.

Like many times before, Klara expected Eddie to keep hold of Dodie and slowly bring her down. But the next few seconds unfolded so quickly, she wasn't sure what happened. Eddie couldn't coordinate his limbs to keep her within his grasp. He lost his footing. She dropped to the ground, bumping her head. He stumbled over her, landing on his forearms beside her.

Klara flew across the yard and picked up crying Dodie. Next to her, Martha burst into tears. When Eddie didn't get up, Klara bent over him. "Eddie? Are you alright?"

Eddie rolled over on his back. More gum chewing and rapid blinking. "I'm okay ..."

"What happened?"

"I don't know. I ... Is Dodie all right?" He slowly sat up.

Klara stroked Dodie's hair. "A head bump and a bit of fright."

"Come here, baby girl." He spread his arms. Dodie nuzzled her face in his chest. He wrapped his arms around her. "I'm sorry, Dodie. Maybe a big elephant got in the way." She giggled.

Thankfully, no serious harm came to either of them. Hopefully, the doctor would provide answers tomorrow.

CHAPTER THIRTY-THREE

2015

L eslie finished skimming Greg's grant proposal draft for his next project and closed her laptop. "I'll proofread this tomorrow. How easy will it be to switch gears after immersion in Buckwalter history for so long?"

"I've plenty of time to switch gears." He leisurely leaned back in his chair, hands behind his head. He'd never looked so relaxed in her presence. He rolled his eyes. "Now, on to my next Instagram lesson."

Leslie scooted forward. "First, Professor Stafford, your casual posture is not conducive for learning to take place."

He straightened over the desk. "Will this do?" he huffed.

She raised her brows. "Secondly, I must address your attitude of only wanting to accomplish the bare minimum required for this task. What if your student asked that question?"

"I'd soundly box his ears."

Leslie lifted her chin, enjoying the game. "Well, since I'm in no position to box your ears soundly, I'll have to resort to other measures. Meanwhile, mind your posture in order to avoid a crook in the neck, achy shoulders, vertebrae disorders, and headaches. And limit your screen time due to blue light exposure."

"Ten minutes daily should hardly cause such suffering."

"Ah, but as you take charge of your account, you might find yourself addicted."

He blasted a hearty laugh. She relished the sound.

"Have you considered starting your own website and email newsletter?"

He harrumphed. "You're joking."

"No, it's far better to have a website presence and a list you own yourself."

"I'm barely contending with the dragon of Instagram. The less time spent on the World Wide Web, the better."

"I predict you'll become so enamored of social media, you'll change your worldview."

Greg chuckled as the phone rang. "Hey, Janet, what's up? Fred Rickert?" He scribbled a note on his pad. "In 1952? Wow, okay ... How'd he hear of me? ... Amazing ... If it's easier for him, I'll go to Dillard myself ... Okay, I'll call him." He jotted a number. "Thanks." He ended the call. "Now there's a stroke of good fortune."

"Another interview for your book?" Hmm, Fred Rickert sounded familiar.

"Yes, a reporter from *The Dillard Tribune* in 1952. I thought I'd covered my bases there, but this fellow wasn't employed long. He heard of my research and has behind-the-scenes intel. Supposedly."

Leslie numbed. Fred Rickert—the reporter Fritz bribed? Greg wouldn't be happy to find such a chink in Fritz's armor.

The tale didn't fare well for Eddie's reputation either. "Really? Let me know how it goes. If you feel inclined to share."

"Then you'll have no incentive to buy the book." He winked.

After ten minutes of Instagram monitoring, he said, "On to better pastimes. How about more pickleball tonight?"

She restrained her eagerness and narrowed her eyes. "Am I number fourteen?"

Greg shuffled through student papers. "I promise, you're not." His mumbling got lost in the crackling of paper.

"What?"

He looked up, appearing nonchalant. "You're number one. Hashtag first choice."

She laughed. "Now you're speaking in hashtags. I knew you'd catch on." Was she really number one? "Amanda Dexter can't make it?"

"Nope. She canceled this afternoon."

"Well, I do have my stipulations. First, I expect another Eddie Van Halen impression."

"That can be arranged." His green eyes twinkled.

"Secondly, I'd like to try for another Instagram picture afterward at a local establishment. Maybe Pop's Root Beer Stand. We can just pick up root beers and head out."

"How about Ribollita's? I'm always ravenous after pickleball."

She reined in her grin before it grew too wide. "Deal."

Saving her appetite for dinner after pickleball, Leslie washed and rinsed last night's supper dishes and set them in the rack. She'd avoid her usual fare, alternating between cheese and crackers or a loaded baked potato. A periodic casserole spiced up the menu and saved her from three nights of snack food, cooking, or lamenting her limited cooking skills.

Which hardly mattered lately. She had little appetite after reading diary entries. What was happening to her grandfather? First the delusions, then medication and a few good years. But now what? She longed to know more but needed a break from two months of vicariously living her grandmother's heartaches.

On the couch, she checked email. Another message from Greg to Renee Piquette!

But excitement dimmed as if a worm slithered through her gut. How long could she keep up a charade initiated as the only way to secure his aid? Now she considered him a friend. And friends didn't hide behind a false identity.

Greg still had no qualms deceiving the public with Leslie as his ghostwriter, like many celebrities did. But that was different. She had to tell him the truth. But when?

His words came to mind. *I'll see to it this never happens to you again.* So protective, like Uncle Russ or Max. How could Greg make such a promise? Was he planning to be her personal bodyguard and monitor her daily activities to ward off all future foes and suspects?

He obviously spoke in hyperbole. A kind and noble gesture, nonetheless.

She pressed her hand to her chest. Even now, his previous nearness increased her heart rate. He'd scooted the chair so close, took her hand. He gazed at her from his handsome face crinkling with laugh lines. His voice lowered to the seductive level of FM radio voices. His spicy cologne ... she inhaled, certain of the tantalizing aroma nearby.

Stop it! I'm out of his league. She went to the table with her laptop—a better place for Renee Piquette to think clearly and compose an effective email to the good professor. She read:

Renee,

Answers to your latest questions are below.

You're fortunate to have visited Dillard and the library room housing the Buckwalter archives. But how'd you know about the house's layout? That's not common knowledge. It's not mentioned in any nook or cranny connected to the family tree (pardon the mixed metaphor), including scads of family interviews from three generations.

What had she done? She scanned her previous email to find the damaging evidence: a brief mention of the dining room's proximity to a study regarding Fritz's writing habits. It was 1950s information from the diary. Her visits to Fritz and Wilma were at a different house, decades later.

Her hands flew to her cheeks. She should come clean about her relationship to Fritz. But no. Not yet. That would change everything between them.

Perhaps it was time to admit the mysterious Renee was just plain Leslie. In person, though, not in a cowardly email. That still wouldn't explain why she knew details about the house. But she couldn't yet tell him about Klara's diary.

She paced the room stewing about how to respond without more deception.

Finally, she replied:

Dear Dr. Stafford,

Thanks again for your help. Disregard the house question. My source escapes me. Perhaps my vivid imagination filled in the blanks for me. Such is the nature of historical fiction authors.

Renee

She justified stating the source escaped her because she didn't remember which diary page she'd read it on.

But lying by omission was just as deplorable. She must find the courage to confess, and hoped her aggravation didn't overshadow their pickleball game.

CHAPTER THIRTY-FOUR

April 1957

Doctor Branson at Carlton Mental Hospital faced Eddie and Klara. "The things you're experiencing, Edmund, are long-term side effects of the drug chlorpromazine, typical of patients using it for three or four years. That's the risk of taking experimental drugs."

"Then why didn't you take him off it?" Klara snapped.

"This is the first time you're reporting these symptoms."

Guilt twisted her, though the odd tics and clumsiness only occurred the past three months.

Eddie grimaced between gum chewing and lip smacking. "If I go off the drug, will the side effects go away?" But the drug was the only reason her family enjoyed any normalcy. No hallucinations for three years.

"Going off the drug won't diminish side effects." Dr. Branson frowned, as if the worst was yet to come. "I'm sorry, but CPZ causes permanent neurological brain damage."

Klara's eyes widened. "Irreversible?" Eddie would forever

smack his lips, make fish lips, puff his cheeks, and stumble across the house as a health hazard to his own children?

"Unfortunately. The condition of tardive dyskinesia presents as facial tics, repetitive and involuntary movements. Stress makes it worse. The reason you're feeling so fatigued, Edmund, is due to continual muscle contractions. You also have tardive dystonia, affecting the lower limbs. That explains the clumsiness and jerkiness in your arms and legs."

A rock hit Klara's gut. Eddie's face paled as he continuously blinked, then made sucking noises. *No, Lord, this can't be.*

"Some patients with dystonia need crutches—"

"No!" Klara covered her ears. He was barely twenty-seven, and now crutches? With all the odd, awkward facial tics and clumsiness, August and Fritz would surely change their minds about Eddie's role at the store.

Any semblance of calm and needing to be strong for Eddie dissipated. "So, putting him on CPZ bought three good years, but now he'll pay for it the rest of his life?"

"Would you prefer never having those three years, Mrs. Buckwalter?"

Eddie tapped her hand. "Klara, these years mean everything to me. As a husband, father, and brother. Please don't regret them."

"But at what price?"

"Cling to those memories," the doctor said. "But now we must decide our next steps. May I explain your options?"

Klara fretfully fished a tissue from her purse. Eddie nodded and clutched her other hand. She must advocate as best she could.

"First, it's not an option to continue the CPZ. That will only worsen symptoms. Going off CPZ will allow hallucinations to return. So, I'm recommending either insulin coma therapy, Matrazol shock therapy, or electroconvulsive therapy, known as ECT." He explained. Each option induced a seizure or temporary coma over many weeks. The first two involved injections. With ECT, the brain, under anesthesia, was stimulated by a small current of electricity from a machine through two electrodes on the scalp. "The small electric currents trigger a seizure which changes the brain chemistry. Over time, this eliminates delusions and hallucinations."

"What are ECT's side effects?" Eddie asked between chewing motions.

"The anesthesia might cause short term nausea, headache, or fatigue. The effects of ECT may be similar to lithium, feeling bland and lacking motivation."

"A lack of drive, energy, and creativity?" Klara pressed.

"Possibly. Some patients have memory disturbances."

"Another tradeoff." Klara tightened her grasp on Eddie's hand. "There's nothing to make him better without robbing his spirit, joy, and inspiration?"

"You may be overstating the case, Mrs. Buckwalter."

"No, I'm not. That's what lithium did. No wonder he took himself off—"

"Lithium was the wrong drug for him," Doctor Branson stated empathically.

Klara's arms flew up. "Because you failed to diagnose him right the first time! Then—"

Eddie grabbed her hand back. "Klara."

"I watched you slip away before, Eddie. I can't bear watching it again." She berated herself for letting grief and aggravation carry her away. "I'm sorry, Eddie."

* * *

July 1957—three months later

After Eddie completed two months of twice weekly outpatient electroconvulsive therapy—financed by Fritz—Klara hoped his neurological symptoms would somehow disappear while keeping hallucinations at bay. But no such luck. Worse, Eddie seemed like a shell of himself with delayed reactions—his monotone, bland expressions, and demeanor devoid of joy. He still had no gumption to write and didn't care if the first three novels were ever published. He painstakingly started retyping the first one, then quit. After prodding and cajoling him got nowhere, she retyped it herself. Once, in a downward spiral, when he mentioned burning them, she hid the manuscripts for safekeeping.

Monthly, he sank into more listlessness. He forgot store tasks and plans with Klara and the girls. He couldn't recall bedtime stories or childhood ventures, nor the girls' favorite books, toys, or teddy bear names. Television replaced books.

Eddie had no capacity to complete ordinary chores. When August and Fritz reluctantly shortened his hours, Eddie seemed apathetic. With Eddie's reduced income, Klara picked up shifts. At least Fritz still paid for Eddie's doctor visits.

* * *

After supper, Klara joined Eddie on the couch. Martha hopped between them as Dodie scooted into her father's lap. He seemed oblivious, staring into space. Klara nudged him. He wrapped his arms around Dodie whose little hand patted his cheek. A moving cheek due to his probing tongue. He blinked multiple times.

Martha handed Klara *Curious George Rides a Bike*. Eddie used to read with gestures and vocal antics in full force. Same for Dr. Seuss's *If I Ran the Circus*. But not anymore.

Reading, Klara's voice tripped as sadness caught in her throat. *Cry later*, she told herself.

Dodie chose *Madeline and the Bad Hat*, then Mother Goose rhymes. Martha chose *Many Moons* and told Dodie to request *Harold and the Purple Crayon*.

"No. I want Cinderella. Papa, tell it like you used to." Her chubby arms reached his puffy cheeks.

Eddie opened his mouth, then clammed it shut. He tried again. Words emerged in monotone. "Once ... upon a time ..." He grimaced. "I don't remember how it goes."

"Papa, you're scaring me." Dodie drew her legs up and buried her face in her knees.

Klara took the Cinderella book. No sense drawing out Eddie's pain, or his apathetic expressions alternating with frowns. "I'll read, Dodie. It won't be as good as your father tells it, but he's not feeling well." This seemed worse than his previous shenanigans at the store.

ECT proved to be another robber of her husband's best qualities.

Dodie threw a glance at her father. "Are you mad at me, Papa?"

"No, Dodie ... of course not."

"Then why are you always so annoyed?" She pouted.

"I'm not annoyed ... Not at you."

Dodie climbed off his lap and sat on the other side of her mother.

Klara's heart sank. Surely Eddie's did too. "Well, Dodie. You just did me a favor. *I'm* going to sit with your father." She moved into Eddie's lap, throwing her arms around him. "I love you, darling. I want our girls to remember this moment." She kissed him on the mouth.

But for only a second. He started smacking his lips, then sucked like a fish.

Klara held his cheeks. "You're the most loving husband and father, and I love you with all my heart." She kissed each cheek, then his nose. "Our girls will never forget how you tell Cinderella, Slue-foot Sue, or The Frog Prince. Or your skylarking with Fritz, apple picking at the neighbors."

"Tell us again, Papa!" Martha said. "Tell us how Uncle Fritz got you in trouble."

Eddie's brow creased. "You mean when we got home late ... during a storm?"

"No, silly Papa!" Dodie giggled. "Apple picking."

Klara swallowed hard. Dodie mistook his confusion for teasing.

"Apples ..." A smile lit his face before succumbing to another grimace.

"Girls, when your papa gets better, he'll tell you those stories again. But maybe we can tell *him* a story?" Klara moved off his lap and squeezed between him and Martha.

Martha's hand shot up. "I've got one." She started her version of "The Gingerbread Boy."

Halfway through, Dodie interrupted. "Hey, my turn. Next, the Gingerbread Boy sees an elephant." Her contribution echoed Eddie's renditions, the girls' ideas in full bloom.

Martha chanted the cumulative refrain, ending with, "'You can't catch me, I'm the Gingerbread Man.' He kept running down the road, until he ran into—your turn, Papa."

Eddie startled as if he'd been daydreaming. "What?"

Klara squeezed his hand. "Your turn. Pick an animal or a person."

He frowned. "A rake."

Dodie laughed. "Rakes can't eat a Gingerbread Man."

Eddie popped off the couch and screamed. "Stop it, Dodie! Stop laughing at everything." He stomped across the room.

Dodie burst into tears. Cowering, she climbed onto Klara's lap. Martha sat wide-eyed, lips quivering.

Klara didn't know who to attend to first. Poor Dodie had no idea why her father yelled at her—week after week. Yet poor Eddie remained a victim himself.

It took an hour to soothe them both.

* * *

That night in bed, Klara cozied up to Eddie, arm across his chest. At least sleep brought him respite from the involuntary movements that exhausted him by noon. Sleep also brought respite from the agony of all he'd lost.

Wisps of moonlight revealed him staring at the ceiling, between blinks.

"What're you thinking about, dear?" she asked.

"Nothing."

"Martha has your gift for storytelling. Isn't she remarkable?"

A faint smile touched his lips. "Yes. They both are. So much more than I deserve."

"What do you mean?" She scooted up on her elbows to see his face better.

His tongue outlined his lips, then poked inside his cheeks. "I'm running ragged, Klara. I'm weary every night, just from puckering like a fish all day long. I have to rely on that crutch, and my own daughter's frightened just looking at me."

"They know you're ill, Eddie. They know it's the medication."

"It doesn't change how little I can do for them."

"They know you love them. Their whole world revolves around you. I've never seen such Daddy's girls. Especially Dodie."

"Then why'd she abandon me to sit by you? I scared her, that's why."

"That meant nothing. She's only three."

He shook his head. "It meant ... everything."

Klara combed fingers through his hair, across his forehead, down his cheek. "You're reading too much into one little action. Little kids are fickle."

Eddie sat up in bed, then paused as if to get his bearings. "Check the bottom drawer."

Klara switched on the lamplight, opened the bureau drawer, rummaged through shirts. Her fingers jabbed into something hard. "This?" She pulled out the metal rooster from the Buckwalter barn weathervane. "What's this doing here? I thought it was in the garage." The only relic he had from his family farm.

He grimaced. "I wanted it closer."

Sitting beside him on the bed, she handed it to him. His jerky hand rubbed rooster wings and tail feathers. He turned it over, cheeks puffing. "You know why this broke?"

"Why?" She sensed his need to retell the forlorn tale. Why couldn't he remember Cinderella instead of this morbid six-year-old memory?

"Look." He turned it over. His tongue poked his inner cheek. "It should've been made as one piece. This was soldered together, as separate parts. Papa wanted me to fetch the weathervane from the barn roof for repainting the rooster black and add another powder coating. We had to take the whole thing down. But ... I kept procrastinating ..." A tear escaped his eye. "So, Papa went on the roof himself. When he fell, he dropped it. It thunked on the ground into two pieces."

"I know." His self-imposed guilt spiraled through her to form a lump in her chest.

He made chewing motions. "The tail feathers were

separately made, too. But the rooster held together. The arrow and directionals fell off."

"You put up a new weathervane, right?"

"Yes, made as one solid piece. I kept the old arrow up there, for nostalgia's sake. And I kept this. It reminds me of Papa. Our farm, my childhood." Lips smacking, he gazed at the steel poultry, stroked its comb, its feet, its chest. "This ole rooster saved us many a time from an approaching storm. We knew what to do when it pointed toward stormy weather. We'd gather animals to the barn. We moved their food and water supply, then headed to the cellar." His jaw went back and forth, lips puckered. "But it's broken. It won't do what's it made to do. No more use for it." Another tear trickled down his cheek.

She rubbed his back. "But it's just as loved, right? Despite being broken." She tipped his chin her way, till face to face. "Whether someone's broken or not, love isn't bound up in the things you can do, whether or not you can fulfill your purpose. Love is about *knowing* you, all that you were, are, and will be, and still wanting you."

CHAPTER THIRTY-FIVE

2015

Leslie should never have read another entry from Oma's diary before playing pickleball with Greg. She was hardly in the mood now. Paranoid schizophrenia. The symptoms, the treatments, the side effects—all devastating. Those terrible hallucinations. Is that what Jason had? Was he truly a Buckwalter? Was Edmund's mental illness genetic?

Oh, my. Could she get it too?

Her breath caught. Don't jump to conclusions. Do an internet search. Then again, maybe not. She wasn't ready. But if Jason were related, he would eventually need to know about Edmund's illness.

* * *

After two hours of pickleball, including Eddie Van Halen impersonations, Greg asked Leslie, "Would you settle for steak instead of Ribollita's?"

"Settle for? Isn't steak the ultimate?" But she couldn't spend the money. Considering how Vic extricated from her monthly.

"My treat." His gaze stirred a flutter in her heart.

Was this a date? She didn't dare ask. Were university employees even allowed to date each other? It didn't matter. Dating him was out of the question. She had to distract him from the flush overtaking her. "We should go Dutch." She bit her lip.

His voice turned husky, even more alluring. "If you're game, please allow me to indulge in some chivalry."

She agreed. It sure beat leftover spaghetti pie.

They drove to their respective homes to shower and dress. What should she wear? What fit the steakhouse without being flirtatious? What would make him be proud to be with her? She finally chose black pants and a lacy, amber, scoop-neck blouse that emphasized her brown eyes.

This isn't a date, she kept reminding herself. Just friends. Any attraction she felt was chalked up to a schoolgirl crush. Ridiculous.

When he pulled up, she met him in the parking lot. They drove to The Captain's.

At their table, he took her coat and offered an appreciative smile. "You're defying the mid-week doldrums."

"So are you." His blue and rust plaid scarf set off freshly washed wavy, golden-brown hair, overlapping his blue collared shirt, rivaling those green eyes.

After ordering, they chatted light-heartedly till their steaks arrived.

Leslie sliced her meat. "I'm wondering something. How was it for you during the wing dedication?"

"Par for the course. I grew up hearing accolades about my father that didn't fit his home demeanor. Allow me to interpret his speech with a play-by-play of that night. First, the Legos. Adam referenced my dad introducing us to Legos to ignite our imaginations and future careers. But we never had free rein. Instead of encouraging our ideas, he built projects alongside us, far surpassing anything we were capable of. Instead of letting us work out problems, he jumped in and fixed things. Everything you're not supposed to do with students, he did with us."

"Killing the fun."

"Replacing fun with criticism, comparisons, and stress. Another thing, Professor Richardson mentioned my dad mentoring students, his guidance boosting their professions. In contrast, he was never home. His self-esteem came from his job. At home, he read science journals. He'd work with Adam, the promising one who walked in his footsteps. But he had no use for a son who read *Huckleberry Finn* and wrote poetry."

"You wrote poetry?"

"Nothing to brag about. But my mom liked it." His mouth tilted into that endearing smirk before he took another bite.

"What was your mom like?" Leslie recalled Veronica's comments about his mom never standing up for herself. Yet Greg loved her enough to move back to Avondale when she was ill.

"She was a lovely woman, inside and out, but too long silent while my father gallivanted around with travels and ... other women." Disgust tainted his tone.

"Oh. I'm sorry."

"In the spirit of Fritz Buckwalter's alliteration, he's a reprehensible reprobate. A sleazy skunk."

Leslie balked at the revulsion roiling through his words. "I can't imagine."

"I think you can." He cocked his head. "Please excuse my trash talk at the dinner table. Anyhow, Mom tried to make up for everything my dad lacked. She read to us, introduced me to all kinds of books. She did all the motherly things, drove us to ball practice, guitar lessons, debate club, anything we signed up for. But she couldn't combat my dad's dismissiveness, criticism, or, later, his affairs. The elephant in the room. Elephants, plural."

Leslie frowned. Vic's unfaithfulness gripped her, but she focused on Greg, studying his careworn face. "Again, I'm sorry."

He mentioned other accolades, re-interpreting them through his formative experience.

"That's a sad, lonely childhood."

"I've come to terms with it."

"How?"

He inspected an onion ring. "With professional help, twelve years ago, when I returned to Avondale to help Mom. Moving here put me back in the line of fire. Teaching toward tenure on my dad's turf still wasn't good enough for him." He offered a wry smile. "The world can thank me for not pursuing engineering. I'm about as mechanical as the Three Stooges."

She smiled, not just at his humor, but letting down his guard. He trusted her with his pain, much deeper than the cocky professor she first met. He understood mental health issues firsthand. If she hadn't had therapy herself, she'd still be in the doldrums. "Why do you think your father was so demeaning?"

"A therapist helped me see my dad's inability to accept me wasn't a problem with me, but a problem with him. He's got deep-seated issues he never dealt with and never will."

"Must be hard to not take his actions personally."

"You got that right. When I think I'm over it, new incidents still ruffle my feathers."

"Like the wing dedication." His openness offered a glimpse of his inner strength.

"Exactly. I've been in a foul mood since the new wing name was announced in October. I fell prey to kick-the-dog syndrome, channeling my anger into the abominable social media requirement." He eyed her squarely. "I'm very sorry you've taken the brunt of my petulance."

His humility warmed her. "I understand. I appreciate your sharing difficult things."

"I no longer want his conditional respect based on achievements. Whether I make full professor or not."

"Any reason why you wouldn't?"

"Not since you've grounded me in community outreach and all things Instagram." He grinned. "Grable Press just finished final edits. The biography should be released mid-April. But if Klara Buckwalter grants me an interview, which I'm still holding out for, I'll have to make modifications, based on her perspective."

"They'll let you do that?"

"If it happens in the next three weeks. Assuming her outlook doesn't change everything else." He grunted.

Leslie nodded and stirred her soup. "Any luck closing in on Klara?"

"No. I still send her friendly notes and call monthly. I fear she runs the other way when my number appears on the screen."

She kept stirring her soup, steam rising into her already hot face. "What happens if her perspective *does* change everything?"

"That involves an entire rewrite and missing my publishing deadline. Which impacts achieving full professor." He fiddled with another onion ring as if he found it fascinating.

"Any consequences of that other than disappointment?" Denied tenure meant dismissal.

"It's not like tenure. I'd stay here, despite any embarrassment. Everyone knows what I'm reaching for."

The pit in her stomach widened. Could she help him achieve his biography goal without hurting her family? What was she willing to risk? Should she ask Oma to grant Greg an interview? Though it would be painful for Oma to talk about Edmund, it would reveal more of Fritz's devotion to his ailing brother.

Part of her yearned to tell him Klara was her grandmother, that she'd convince her to give Greg an interview, considering he'd worked so hard on this project.

But once you tell people you're a Buckwalter, you're stuck with people knowing the truth, no turning back. Like getting tenure. Once you're in, you're in. But tenure was a good thing, bringing respect, admiration, safety, security. In contrast, people knowing her heritage was a liability. Even more so, knowing her grandfather's formidable history.

Her diary readings confirmed why nobody talked about Edmund's condition in the 1950s. But why was her grandmother still secretive now? Out of respect, though, Leslie would keep silent till she finished the diary.

Though she feared Greg knowing, her family tree shouldn't conflict with his professional interests. Her self-preservation shouldn't trump his goals. Should it?

She must first tell him about Renee. But not now. He was opening up.

"It's your turn." For thirty minutes, he peppered her with questions about the mental health curriculum implementation at Avondale High and her transition to Raymond. Then, "How's your grandmother doing?"

What? Leslie reminded herself he didn't know Oma's

identity. "She's declining. Old age is catching up." Along with secrets.

"Do you see her often?"

"Max and I aim for monthly, but it's been a while." Gas budget depleted by Vic's demands. "My aunt lives with her, so she's well cared for." And when she passes, so do all her Buckwalter memories. "Did you call Fred Rickert, the reporter?"

Greg eyed her at an angle. "I'm done talking shop. We're talking about you."

She swallowed. This had everything to do with her. "You know Fritz is one of my favorite authors."

"Very well then. But don't dish this out. It's for the book." He winked. "I called Fred Rickert, in his eighties. He told me something I'd never heard."

Leslie leaned forward, all ears.

Greg stabbed his steak and sliced. "He claims Fritz bribed him to stay quiet about a fiasco his brother Edmund caused during the store's grand opening."

"Seriously?" Guilt needled her for already knowing the tale, producing another pang for pretending like she didn't.

"Edmund accused customers of shoplifting and created a scene when his brothers intervened. He upset displays, scaring folks off. Some called the police. Eddie went to the station for questioning. Fred Rickert, the reporter present, took pictures of the mess, but Fritz gave him a pep talk about using journalism to uplift humanity, not air dirty laundry. Fritz gave Fred his own film and two hundred bucks in exchange for Fred's incriminating film. And his silence."

Cutting steak, Leslie whistled. "Quite the windfall. Not just the money, but a big scoop for you."

"Absolutely. No wonder Fritz never told me that story. It brings his veracity into question." Greg took a bite of steak.

Leslie sampled her baked potato. "I wonder how often he did that?"

"Even if I knew, it's just hearsay."

Hearsay including hallucinations wiped from Lynwood's police record, Eddie burning down the store, and his time at Carlton. Plus, anything else she hadn't read yet.

Leslie bit her tongue, tempted to share Oma's diary. *No!* Oma gave her free rein, but Leslie didn't yet know the story's conclusion. Sharing family mayhem too soon seemed like a betrayal of privacy.

But what of Greg's biography and reputation as the Buckwalter expert?

He cut more steak. "Hard telling if Edmund's issues were due to a hot temper or a loose screw."

Leslie winced. *Loose screw.* That was her grandfather he spoke of. "There's a different way to frame that."

"You're right. I apologize. Guess I'll never be a contender for Mr. Sensitivity."

Nope. Mr. Darcy through and through. "Let's just say ... maybe Edmund struggled with mental health issues. Did Fred Rickert say more about shoplifters?"

"What do you mean?" He twisted a chunk of meat into the *au jus.*

"If Eddie created a scene, were the customers really shoplifting? Or was he delusional?"

"Fred couldn't say. He heard conflicting testimonies, then reported nothing due to the bribe. But the whole debacle makes me wonder what else was happening. I'm craving Klara's perspective. What didn't Fritz want to reveal?" Greg wiped his chin with his napkin. "Speaking of chaos, I've never been one to beat around the bush, so here goes. Brace yourself. Does your narcissistic ex-husband still give you grief?"

Leslie stiffened. "Excuse me?"

"Sounds like a yes."

"You can't jump to conclusions. Why are you asking such a personal question?"

"First, because of Jason's antics, manipulating and blaming you. Secondly, you weren't convincing enough when you said you couldn't imagine living with a sleazy skunk. Thirdly, my father has similar traits and never let my mother have the upper hand."

"But I'm divorced. Your parents stayed together."

"My mom tried to leave. Twice, to protect us kids. But he guilted her into staying, even after we grew up. She wasn't strong enough to stand against him. If she had, he still would've made her life miserable."

That was Vic. That's how he retaliated for her leaving him, more recently keeping her bound by blackmailing. But she couldn't tell Greg. Not just to avoid humiliation, but for what Vic threatened to share with the world.

"You're about as pale as that dinner plate, which says a lot."

She opened her mouth, but no words went forth.

"Leslie." His voice lowered, calm but firm. "I don't know what he's doing, but you can't let him get away with it. What can I do to help?"

Part of her longed for his assistance—the part that was falling for him. "How could you possibly help me?"

"I can't answer that unless you tell me what's happening." His intensity kept her eyes riveted to his, until she couldn't bear it. She dropped her gaze to the table. Though touched by his protectiveness, she couldn't tell him anything without revealing her Buckwalter connection.

But Max could help. Time to tell Max about Vic's threats.

"I know it's hard to hear, Leslie, but please listen. People like Jason and Vic don't change. Their tactics hold you hostage. I don't want you sucked into that."

Leslie looked up. "I'm finished with Jason, so don't worry."

"Fine and dandy, but that was short term with low stakes. I'm more worried about Vic."

"*You're* worried? Why?"

"Because I don't want to see you hurt or manipulated."

Tears burned behind her eyes. *Don't cry!* She bit her lip, heart melting. "Thank you. Maybe you *should* be in the running for Mr. Sensitivity."

He swatted the air. "Bah! I need that award as much as I need pigs in my bathtub. But I'm serious, Leslie. It's impossible to reason with a narcissist. Trying to grasp their own twisted reasoning will give you an aneurysm. You need to get out from under his thumb. If you want help, just say the word."

His kindness wreaked havoc with her humiliation as a victim, her shame, mixed with anger for his assumptions—however true they were.

Uncle Russ always said to never settle for a guy who didn't protect her and make her well-being his utmost priority. He'd modeled it himself and would surely approve of Greg—though somehow Vic had fooled her.

But why was she so drawn to Greg? Tonight, his compassion and affection emanated, but could he fall for her the way she was for him? Especially without having as many capital letters after her name.

And still, she hadn't confessed to being Renee Piquette. Surely, he'd feel betrayed and regret every kind word he'd offered.

His steps toward friendship engulfed her in warmth. Yet how fair was it to withhold all she knew about the Buckwalters when he was about to publish the official biography? He could become full professor without her information, but once he published the book, it would be too late to reveal the truth. Even if she wanted to.

She didn't deserve protecting. Her silence and the Jason catastrophe proved it. Greg shouldn't see her as a damsel in distress. She'd fallen in her own hole. She'd climb out herself.

Leslie lifted her chin, squared her jaw. No longer would Vic take advantage of her. No longer would she succumb to his blackmailing. She didn't need Greg's assistance.

"Thank you, Greg, but I'm fine. I'll let you know if I need anything."

CHAPTER THIRTY-SIX

July 1957

E ddie ate his last bite of oatmeal. "I want the weathervane on top of the garage."

Klara carried his bowl to the sink. "That's a lovely idea, but how will it work with the arrow broken off? Don't you need a cupola?" She didn't want him climbing a ladder either. Not with his lack of coordination.

He licked his lips, poked inside his cheeks with his tongue. "We'll solder the rooster to a new arrow. After the cupola's installed, Fritz'll put it up."

"Nice to have the rooster up where he belongs." She rinsed the bowl. "The girls will grow up seeing the same sight you saw on the farm as a boy."

He smiled as preface to an involuntary grimace. "Minus the barn, cows, and pigs."

Klara laughed and yelled out the back door. "Martha! Dodie!"

"How long will you be gone?" Eddie asked.

"A couple hours. The fabric store, the yarn shop, then Buckwalters' for groceries. There's a sale on ham." She worked most days since Eddie's ECT, always noting the town's best sales. "And the pond to feed the ducks. Shall I pick up anything? Like a cupola?" She smiled.

Martha and Dodie breezed through the doorway. Martha wiped her brow. "It's hot! Can we go to the ice cream parlor?"

"You know the plan." Klara winked. "Ice cream is for good girls who don't complain while shopping."

"*I'm* not complaining." Dodie lifted her chin as if to prove she was above reproach.

Klara faced Eddie. "Want to come along?"

Eddie blinked repeatedly. "You ladies have a good time at the fabric store."

No surprise he didn't want to tag along on female errands. Plus, too many people stared at his clunky movements. He hardly left the house. "Enjoy the peace and quiet."

Still seated, Eddie spread his arms wide. "A hug for my girls."

Martha unabashedly threw her arms around his shoulders. Dodie followed suit. He hugged them, tears trailing his cheeks. "I love you, Martha ... I love you, Dodie ..."

"I love you, too, Papa." Dodie kissed his cheek.

"I love you *more*," Martha added before the girls dashed off.

"Must *everything* be a competition?" When Klara bent to kiss him goodbye, his arms fumbled to enclose her. She embraced him. "I love you more than they do."

"And I love you best of all." His tears wet her cheeks. He finally released her.

"Count on a special treat tonight. Something to do with peaches." Grabbing her purse, she took one more look at her dear husband, so forlorn. But she detected a swell of serenity in his eyes. Perhaps he was doing the best he could, making peace with his broken reality.

* * *

After errands, Klara drove home. The girls had chosen peach pie and ice cream for dessert with their papa tonight instead of the ice cream parlor. In the driveway, they fought over who'd carry what until Klara designated bags to each. "Eddie, we're back!"

He was nowhere in the kitchen or parlor. Perhaps he was resting in the bedroom. She shooed the girls outside.

"Let's play dodgeball!" Martha squealed.

"No, hopscotch!" Dodie held a bin of chalk.

Klara sighed and unpacked produce, loaves, jars, and canned goods, looking forward to baking peach pie and making his favorite peach lemonade. She turned on the radio, inviting Pat Boone's mellow voice to fill the room with his newest song, "Love Letters in the Sand."

Five minutes later from the backyard, Dodie screamed. "Papa!"

Klara charged outside, following the yells. She scooted around the side of the house, between the garage and shrubbery. A ladder leaned against the garage. Eddie lay still on the grass. "No!" She swooped over and fell to her knees. "Call an ambulance!" She shouted neighbors' names. "Help!"

Dodie kneeled by his shoulder. "He won't answer, Mama. What's wrong?"

Adrenaline took over. Eddie's face was ashen, skin already taut. "Oh, dear God, no!"

"Papa!" Martha caught Klara's terror and burst into tears. Dodie wailed too.

Klara bent over him, her cheek against his. Cool. Hard.

Even under this warm sun. No breath. No movement. Nothing.

The neighbor, Harriet, appeared and screamed.

Klara glanced up. "Please take the girls and call an ambulance."

Harriet took a girl in each hand.

Dodie pulled back. "No! I wanna stay with Papa."

"Go with Mrs. Johnson," Klara said.

Still wailing, Martha covered her face. "What's wrong with Papa?"

"Come along, girls." Harriet tugged their arms. "Give your mother a few minutes alone." The three disappeared around the corner, cries as forlorn as a train whistle at night.

Klara hovered over Eddie's body. "My dear, dear Eddie ..." Words choked. Salty tears offered hazy vision. "What did you do?" Had he tried to climb the ladder?

Then she saw it. A few feet away in the grass lay the rooster. Had he planned on installing it himself?

She stood and looked up. No cupola. No arrow. No directional signals. What was he thinking? Had he fallen off the ladder just like his father plunged to his death? The death Eddie felt responsible for.

She knelt over him, weeping. "Oh, Eddie ... I love you ..." She laid her head on his chest, arms surrounding him.

Something lumpy under his shirt at the neckline scratched her cheek. Sitting up, she fingered it—a wool scarf, wrapped around his neck several times, ends tucked in his shirt. In July? Shaking, she slowly unwrapped it. The bottom layer was caked with drying blood. Her stomach recoiled. What on earth? Removing the scarf revealed a sharp gash.

She squinted up at the ladder. Something compelled her to climb. She grasped the rails, heart thumping. One step up, two steps ...

At the top, inside the gutter lay a razor blade covered in blood, floating in a red puddle. Bile clogged her throat. Her stomach clenched.

Realization dawned. Her grip tightened as she numbed. He'd taken his own life. He must have slit himself at the top of the ladder, the scarf hiding the wound. He bled out, or almost bled out, and let go. Stepped off the rung to meet the ground. He might have died on the ladder, or shortly after hitting the ground. But she knew one thing for sure. He'd wanted it to look like an accident. Surely for her sake, especially for his daughters' sake.

One thing he hadn't counted on, though, was his daughters finding him first.

Maybe he'd figured she'd look for him after getting home.

Dizzy and shaking, she gripped the ladder as she stepped down each rung. By choosing to die the way his father had, he surely sought absolution.

His Christian roots assured him of God's forgiveness, affirming he could never pay for his own perceived sin. But his distorted mind didn't let him rest in truth. He kept beating himself up.

Back on the grass, she inspected his wrists. Nothing. Only his neck had oozed blood, now drying. Most drained into the scarf. She ran inside, grabbed old rags, wetted them, returned, and wiped blood from his neck. Very little reached his shirt. She threw the scarf into the garage garbage can.

As far as Martha and Dodie were concerned, their papa had a bad accident falling off the ladder. And that was that.

* * *

Trembling, Klara called Fritz and August at the store. She fetched Martha and Dodie from Harriet's and told them their daddy had fallen off the ladder, died, and gone to heaven. The three of them huddled over Eddie and wept.

With tear-stained cheeks, August and Fritz arrived five minutes later, the same moment the ambulance came. Shock and grief permeated as they embraced Klara and wept over their brother's body. Their grief shook Klara to the core.

Medics loaded the body into the ambulance. Wilma and Irma and their children appeared shortly and took Martha and Dodie inside. August followed them to call the two Buckwalter sisters.

Still outside, Klara pointed out the rooster in the grass.

Fritz picked it up, stroked it as if contemplating the last moments his brother held the Buckwalter relic.

"Had Eddie mentioned putting a weathervane on the garage?" Klara asked.

"Never. Why?"

"Today he said he had plans to restore the weathervane and buy a cupola. That you'd help him. Like it was all arranged."

He stared as if realization hit. A cloud of sorrow washed over his face. "Apparently, it *was* all arranged."

"What do you mean?"

"He told you this right before he climbed a ladder with a useless weathervane and no cupola. He did it while he knew you'd be in town awhile."

Klara swallowed hard. "Maybe he just wasn't thinking straight. You know, his memory was disappearing, his coordination lacking."

"Or ... he knew *exactly* what he was doing."

She buried her face in her hands. "I didn't want to say, but at the top of the ladder, in the gutter, is blood and a razor blade. He was wearing a scarf that soaked up most of the blood. Before anybody got here, I wiped it up and threw the scarf away."

"No ..." Fritz shook his head, eyes squeezed shut.

"He'd never want his girls to know it was suicide. He'd never want them to think he left them on purpose. Even if it was to spare them the agony of having him for a papa."

Fritz fisted his hands. "I've never seen a more devoted father."

"I know. But he felt he couldn't do anything for them. He scared them without meaning to. He didn't want them to have such a distorted view of their father."

Fritz clutched her shoulders. "Then nobody must ever know. This can't get into the newspapers."

"The morgue will know. They'll see everything."

"I'll make sure the word doesn't spread. Trust me. We'll go to the funeral home right now, and the only thing we'll say is that he fell off the ladder by accident."

Two days later, that's exactly what the papers reported.

CHAPTER THIRTY-SEVEN

2015

Three days after the steak dinner, Leslie knocked at Greg's office door, aiming for cheerful. Otherwise, she'd whither under newfound knowledge of her grandfather's death. Eddie died the same way Oskar did in the novel. But in the book, it was an accident. "Hello! Anybody home?"

He stood and waved her in. "Let's get it over with."

"Wow, that's quite the greeting."

"I could've pelted you with tomatoes."

She smiled. "And I thought you were actually enjoying your Instagram engagement."

"Fat chance." He pulled a chair over for her.

Seated, she warmed at his proximity. After ten minutes flew by, she said, "You're definitely getting the hang of using hashtags."

"You really know how to warm a guy's heart."

She glanced at the rooster on the wall. "So, did you plan your talk for Avondale Reads?"

He arched a brow. "That's autumn. Figured I'd wait till pumpkins are ripe on the vine."

"Oh, yeah." She gazed at the rooster. "Of course. Never mind."

He lifted his chin. "What's going on? You seem more interested in that rusty ole chicken than planning my schedule seven months in advance."

"May I see it again up close?"

"Certainly." He brought it over.

"May I hold it?"

He grinned. "If you promise not to break it."

She offered a faint smile and took the rooster. She brushed her fingers over tail and wing feathers, caressed its chest. She outlined the comb, beak, and wattle, vaguely aware of Greg's gaze on her. Did he sense the sacredness of the moment?

Her grandfather's last minutes flashed as vividly as when reading the diary. His final weepy goodbyes to Martha, Dodie, and Klara. His final steps up the ladder, rooster in hand. The razor blade, the dripping blood, the fall. The rooster flying from his hand and crashing to the ground with him. Her grandmother's words the night before ... *Whether someone's broken or not, love isn't bound up in the things you can do, whether or not you can fulfill your purpose. Love is about knowing you, all that you were, are, and will be, and still wanting you.*

But that hadn't been enough comfort for him.

"Leslie, are you all right?" Greg gave her a handkerchief. Of course, he'd have a handkerchief, not just tissues like most people. Great-uncle Fritz had hankies. But he was old.

"Thanks." She wiped her cheeks. "I'm sorry. I didn't realize I'd be so emotional." Not a complete lie.

"You're throwing me for a loop here. Crying in my office over a hunk of metal." His tone was tender. "What's wrong, Leslie? What happened?"

"Maybe you can quote Dickens again, about tears and rain on blinding dust."

"Only if it would soothe you." Said as if that's what he wanted most. He set a hand on her shoulder.

She startled at his touch. Actually, hearing his voice quote anything would soothe her. Or throw her into a tizzy. Even if he quoted Popeye. "I should go." She set the rooster down and stood.

"Will you be all right?"

She headed toward the door. "I'll be fine."

"I'm not convinced." He glanced at the clock. "Can I get you a coffee? I have five minutes before class."

"No, thanks."

"Do you need to talk? We can go for dinner at five, if you want."

A sprig of guilt poked her—secrets about Buckwalter family chaos she kept hidden from him. Her identity. Only three weeks before his book would go to press. The official, bona fide Fritz Buckwalter biography.

And he didn't know the half of it.

He must think her crazy for nearly weeping over the rooster.

But she couldn't say anything yet. Definitely not before finishing the diary. Just a few pages to go.

"Thank you, Greg. I'd love to another time. I can't tonight."

* * *

Home after a long day, Leslie ordered pizza for delivery, filled a teakettle, and turned on the stove. Greg's tender response to her melancholy over the rooster still warmed her.

Waiting for pizza, she tidied the apartment, then flipped through the mail. Nothing from Vic, thankfully, though it was his usual time of the month to contact her.

He'd been demanding 300 dollars each time. Or else. But he didn't need it. This was another way to control her even long after she had no obligations to him.

She'd call her lawyer if she could afford the fees. In refusing Greg's help, she only had Max's support. Regardless, there'd be no more kowtowing to Vic.

But could she deal with the fallout? She grabbed the phone and punched Max's number.

Somebody knocked on the door. "Just a minute." That was the fastest pizza delivery ever. Didn't the guy usually buzz from the lobby?

More knocking. "Hold on!" She set the phone on the end table atop a magazine, went to the door, and swung it open. "Vic!"

There he was, slick as ever in black pants, a white collared shirt and tie. Successful looking enough to not need her hard-earned money.

She stifled questions roiling through her mind. "You need to leave." She pushed the door, but his foot blocked it.

He stepped inside as easily as a rat skitters across the floor. "Good to see you, Leslie. Looking fine, as usual." He closed the door.

"How'd you find me? I only gave you a post office box number."

"I have my ways." His eyes roved across the living room. "Nice place you got. Better than I anticipated."

"What're you doing here?"

"Just wanted to check on you. Especially since you

unfriended me and blocked my emails, texts, and every possible social media." He feigned a pout.

"For good reason." She tried to sidestep him to reach the door, but he mirrored her move. "You need to leave."

"Or else what? I'll bet you're wishing you had a restraining order on me right now. But too bad. I never laid a hand on you. Never threatened to, either."

"You're a bully and a blackmailer."

"But not worthy of a restraining order, am I?" He flashed a wicked grin. "Too bad for you. Meanwhile, I'm saving myself an envelope and stamp. I need five hundred bucks this time. Within three days."

"Five hundred!" She reined herself in. She refused to give him the emotional response he craved. She crossed her arms. "My lawyer will contact you."

"Really? If you can afford a lawyer, I'm upping it to a thousand."

"If you don't leave in five seconds, I'm calling the cops." Where had she dropped her phone? Scanning the room revealed nothing.

"To tell the cops what? That I stopped by for money rather than a friendly visit? Your word against mine."

"I have evidence from your other letters." But wait—maybe she should play along. "Look, if you need that much money, I need seven days. Till I get my paycheck."

"Five tops."

She hesitated. "Seven. Till payday." Time for her lawyer to do his part. Better to pay lawyer fees than Vic's increasing demand.

Vic strolled over in a cloud of acrid cologne. He dipped his chin. "Just a friendly reminder. If I don't get my money in seven days, I go to the press. Or Greg Stafford."

Did Vic know she worked at Raymond U with Greg? He'd

found her apartment easily enough. She jerked away. Since a demand would backfire, she wordlessly opened the door.

He sauntered over and saluted. "See you around, Leslie."

Hopefully not. She slammed the door after him, locked and chained it. Through the peephole, she watched him walk away. Why hadn't she checked the peephole before inadvertently letting him in?

She threw her head back and groaned. At her desk, she found Vic's last letter and whipped it away, bringing little satisfaction since it wobbled to the ground. She should make a paper airplane and shoot it across the room.

Instead, she stomped to the couch and pounded a pillow. "Why me?"

Where was her stupid phone? Ah, there it was on the end table, blending in with the magazine. She called Max. "Hey. Got a minute? Are you sitting down?"

"Are you getting married?"

She could almost see his grin. "Shut up, Max. No way, and I'm serious. What would you do if the world knew Edmund Buckwalter was your grandfather, and Fritz your great-uncle?"

"Why? You gonna call the press?"

"No. But Vic might."

"What?"

Agitated, she stalked around the room. "Vic's been blackmailing me."

"What?" Alarm gripped his voice. "Why haven't you told me?"

"I was handling it myself."

"By caving in? Les, you can't let him control you anymore. He's a bygone chapter in your life. A closed book. Out of print, even."

"This is the sequel, unfortunately."

"What's he threatening?"

"To go the press about the family connection. Or to Greg Stafford."

"Unless you do what?"

"Send him money every month."

"What?" he yelled.

She cringed and held the phone away from her ear. "I know, I know. But I don't want him blabbing something that's nobody's business."

"He's got you right where he wants you. How much do you send him?"

"About three hundred monthly. The past six months."

"Oh, my—"

"He's asking for five hundred this month. Actually, a thousand."

"No way! No wonder you can't get out of your dinky apartment."

"I happen to like my apartment, so stop your critique." Well, she hated that her place was the size of a cookie tray. For only six cookies.

"Sorry, I'm just saying."

"Look, I called to tell you I'm not kowtowing to him anymore, threats or not."

"You think he'll follow through?"

"Yes. He always has." Topping off a year of such shenanigans, Vic was first to tell their friends about the divorce, casting all blame on her. Charm was on his side. One by one, they fell away, without ever asking for her side of the story. Only Max held firm.

"Have you talked to your lawyer about this?"

"Then I'd have to move to a dinkier apartment. I can't afford a lawyer *and* pay Vic."

"If you hire the lawyer, you won't have to pay Vic."

"But Vic will find another way to get back at me. He'll probably go to the press anyhow."

"Hey, what's the worst that could happen?"

She stopped at the bookshelf with the picture of her and Great-uncle Fritz. Next to the wedding picture of Edmund and Klara. "Folks would know we're in the Buckwalter line."

"And?"

"We'll get hounded for interviews. People will ask questions about Edmund too."

"You can't just say, 'No, thank you'?"

"Yes, but Oma left us in the dark for good reason." She'd soon have to brief Max on the latest entries.

"But only you, Oma, and I know the dirty laundry. The stuff in the diary. Most folks don't know about the jail time. Besides, that was decades ago. And it's not a reflection of *you*."

"It's not just the jail time. It's the odd behaviors. The schizophrenia. The stigma."

"I thought you were all about fighting stigma, Les."

"I'm working on it."

"So, you're not ready to have the world know the Buckwalter connection?"

"No, but I can't keep giving into Vic. This is getting ridiculous."

"Not to mention your poor bank account."

"Ugh. I know." She sighed. "But how would you feel if people knew?"

"I'd deal with it better than you would. I'd also punch Vic in the nose."

"That really bodes well for me."

"Like I said, talk to your lawyer."

"But the lawyer can't prevent Vic from going to the press, can he?"

"I don't know. Ask him. Either way, you've got to have some recourse and get that jerk out of your life for good."

At least he didn't start spouting alliterative labels like Greg might. "Okay, I'll call the lawyer. Soon. But prepare for the fallout. I'm not sending Vic another penny. I'll tell Greg about the Buckwalter connection myself. He'll hear it from me first. It's time."

Though she dreaded telling him, she had to. Only seven days to hold Vic at bay.

She and Max said their goodbyes. Five minutes later, the phone rang. She jumped, her nerves shot. "Max, what's wrong?"

"I just listened to the long voicemail you left me. You must have called me a few minutes before we actually talked. I heard the entire dialogue between you and Vic."

Her face flushed. "Great."

"He knows where you live. Do you feel safe?"

"He's never hurt me physically."

"But he makes up for it emotionally. I'm keeping that dialogue on my phone as proof."

CHAPTER THIRTY-EIGHT

1958—a year later

Saturday evening, Klara arrived at Fritz's book signing with Martha and Dodie, chagrined to find she'd missed his talk. He'd told her seven p.m., but apparently it started at six. Perhaps it was just as well. Her five- and four-year-old girls would have squirmed the whole time.

But she'd never complain. She was ever grateful for her two daughters, with Eddie's imprint on their mannerisms and winsome personalities.

If Eddie were alive, what harmful impressions of an exorbitant or listless father would have remained with her daughters? One whose memory dissipated. Who scolded them due to his own self-loathing. Who, with unreliable limbs, could barely be trusted to protect his girls from danger. Would the pain they endured have taught them compassion or prevented it?

Only three good years of Eddie coming home happy but tired from work, then catching his second wind upon sight of his girls. They'd race screeching, "Papa!" He'd swoop them up, twirl them around, toss them on the couch for giggles and shouts of "More, more!"

That's the father he'd have continued to be if not crippled by illness and treatment.

But the father her daughters knew turned weary, tormented by anxiety. Then he was gone. Forever. She vowed she'd only speak well of him as the girls grew up. His former demeanor would supplant the girls' negative experiences of his last paltry, dreary, anguished months. She only broached good memories. And his falling off the ladder was merely a tragic accident.

"Uncle Fritz is at the table signing books," Klara said. "We'll have to stand in line."

"That's a long line." Dodie's face acquired the melodrama of a forlorn damsel in distress.

Klara smiled at the girl so much like her father with exaggerated expressiveness. His former self. Qualities that made him the best storyteller. "We'll sit here for now." Though wishing this was Eddie's debut instead, she was happy to support Fritz for his first published novel. Such a landmark after years of striving. He deserved this.

Wilma strolled over with her four children and sat with Klara.

"I'm sorry I missed Fritz's talk," Klara said. "How was it?"

"Long-winded. You know Fritz." Wilma chuckled. "He talked about influences for the story, growing up on the Buckwalter farm." She patted Klara's arm. "We all miss Eddie, dear. I wish he could celebrate this night with Fritz. Eddie would've been published, too, someday. What a talent, according to Fritz."

"You never read his manuscripts?"

"Oh, no. Top secret. Fritz said I'd have to purchase my own copy after publication."

Klara laughed, grateful Fritz honored Eddie's privacy. Eddie's three manuscripts lay in a drawer at home. "When the girls are both in school, I'll try to publish them posthumously. He deserves his own literary legacy."

"Absolutely."

Eventually, Klara went alone to the end of the shortened line. Fritz stood. "Klara, dear. They saved the best for last."

"Congratulations, Fritz. I'm so proud of you." She hugged him. "You finally captured your literary dream for the rest of the world to enjoy."

"Thank you. I'm giddy beyond belief."

"Such a crowd tonight. I would've been here, but you told me seven o'clock."

"Did I? Hmm. You didn't miss anything but claptrap and codswallop, horsefeathers and hogwash." He handed her a book. "Already inscribed, my gift for you."

"Thank you." She traced edges of the illustrated barn and the cock riding atop its roof. *The Broken Weathervane*. With the author's name: Linus Fritz Buckwalter. "Such a lovely cover. You must be pleased."

"The illustrator deserves the finest praise."

She read the inscription:

Dear Klara,
Consider this tale a tribute to Eddie. His story matters.
Ever your loving brother-in-law,
Linus Fritz Buckwalter

Tears edged her eyes. "Oh, Fritz ..."

He pointed out the dedication.

In memory of my dear brother Eddie,
whose story will always live on.

Klara put a hand to her heart. Teary eyes fluttered up to his. She hugged him again. "Thank you ... such a treasure."

* * *

After Klara put the girls to bed, she settled in the parlor with tea and the book. She reread the dedication and sighed. If only Eddie were here to relish this moment. If only the dedication were in honor of, rather than in memory of. If they were reading this story together, they'd pause to ponder Fritz's characters and anecdotes, recall shared experiences he'd put to print, list questions to ask him later.

She started reading. By the time she reached page five, her eyes glazed over from familiar phrases, familiar scenes. *Déjà vu.* Confused, she shook her head. She knew this story.

She got to page ten. No ... this couldn't be. She riffled through pages, stopping at random chapters, reading more. All too familiar. Her nerves buzzed.

This was Eddie's story. The first one he'd written but never titled.

She turned pages till halfway through, searching for her favorite passage. Had Fritz used that too? She found it on page 156. *The boy's stomach clenched as the metal rooster silhouette sharpened against the resplendent sunset of orange, rosy hues. The noble fowl perched on the barn roof, its beak and arrow pointing south as if it had no doubt. How could he have misjudged the situation? How could prevailing meadow winds that promised hope now render as still as doldrums?*

Numbing, Klara willed herself to step from the fog shrouding her, stumbled to the desk, opened the drawer. She pulled out his first manuscript, skimmed the top pages, then sat and read portions throughout, noting added or revised scenes.

Besides those, apart from minor corrections and word swaps, most chapters of *The Broken Weathervane* were verbatim the text of Eddie's manuscript.

Until the end—an add-on chapter. The character Oskar falls off a ladder and dies. It was clearly an accident.

* * *

The next day, Klara called Wilma to say she'd miss family Sunday dinner after church but would drop by afterward. It required every reserve to tame her anger on the phone.

Later, knowing August's family would be gone, she stopped by with the girls. Martha and Dodie romped off with their cousins.

"Too bad you couldn't make it for dinner," Wilma said. "Such a celebration! Fritz sold over two hundred copies last night and had to take orders."

Klara's tongue felt thick. With no appetite, she'd no idea how she would've managed the meal without screaming. "I need to speak to Fritz. Privately."

Wilma seemed flustered. "Well, of course. He's in his study."

Klara inhaled deeply and walked to the study door.

Fritz looked up from his desk and smiled. "Good afternoon, Klara."

Words squeezed through her teeth. "This is *not* a good afternoon and you know why. How *could* you?"

Fritz sighed and closed the door. He motioned to a chair, but she remained standing. "Klara, please understand—"

"Understand what? That the one excellent thing Eddie did

in his brief life was write a novel that you *stole* from him? You think the dedication to him eases your conscience?"

"No—"

"No wonder you told me to come at seven instead of six. So I wouldn't hear you speak about *Eddie's* book."

"Consider that I spared you. Please let me explain." He leaned against his desk. "August and I did everything we could for Eddie. We *wanted* him to succeed." His voice hitched. "Eddie and I always talked about being great authors. You know everything we did together, despite our age difference. The printing press, the newsletters, the chapter installments. I encouraged his writing, and he mine."

He scanned the room, landing on a framed 1930s family photo. "He was always my rascally little brother. I wanted the best for him." He faced her. "You endured much when Eddie was ailing. But I don't think you know the breadth and depth of how it was for *me*, as his brother, to watch him go from hearty and happy to hapless and helpless. From merry and mettlesome to muddled and moody. Numerous times we tried to bring him onboard. I did my best to keep him out of jail, out of the newspapers. For heaven's sake, I even bribed a news reporter, the day of the Grand Opening."

"You did?"

"You can't tell anybody. Even Wilma and August don't know." He shared details, his interactions with reporter Fred Rickert. "I also lied outright to the fire marshal, saying nobody but me was at the store the night of the fire."

"You lied?"

"I couldn't let my brother go to jail or get bad press. For *his* sake, not just the store's. For your sake, too, Klara." He lowered his voice. "I also asked Officer Ron Gresham for a favor."

Klara tensed. "What favor?"

"He facilitated expunging the police record in Lynwood.

Eddie's arrest was due only to the traffic violation and disturbing the peace, in the newspaper *and* the police report. Nothing about aliens and hallucinations. All to preserve Eddie's reputation. I've sworn others to secrecy about Eddie's odd behaviors. Al Dyer, Dennis Newburg. Jerry, Jake, and John Reinhardt. Everywhere Eddie worked or had a run-on."

"How? With more bribery?"

"Yes." His jaw twitched. "I'm telling you, Klara, I put myself in moral dilemmas I never anticipated—all for Eddie's sake." A tear wandered down his cheek. "I'd do it again if I had to."

"I never realized ..." Witnessing his tender heart, Klara's resolve softened, but she must give force to her anger. "So why couldn't you publish his manuscript posthumously, giving him the credit? That's what I planned on doing eventually."

"I considered that, but there's no more benefit for him. We're the only ones who care, because we knew and loved him."

"That gives you the right to steal his manuscript? Baloney! The girls and I would've benefitted. His brilliance would be known and appreciated. You assumed you could commit this treachery and I'd stay silent? I can go to the press! Your reputation would sink forever, in both literature and commerce."

He folded his hands, voice lowering. "Yes, you could."

"And maybe I should."

"You'll do what you deem necessary but consider this. During those years, I tended to Eddie and rebuilt the store from the fire he caused, spending thousands of dollars out of pocket for his sake, including hospital and medical bills. I rarely had time to finish a novel of my own. While I was picking up the pieces of Eddie's disasters, I had no time for my own writing endeavors. When I did send something off, publishers refused it, again and again. I was on a wild goose chase for years, extremely discouraged."

"So, it's Eddie's fault you couldn't get any writing done? He squashed your muse and stole your time and resources?"

"Not intentionally. But when I saw the chance to profit from manuscripts he'd left behind, I viewed it as my own ticket to literary success."

"Because he had all the literary skills you envied! How can you sleep at night, knowing Eddie penned most of your book?"

"I edited and changed certain details. I see this beginning as a way to launch my own writing career. Once I'm established with *The Broken Weathervane* and the next two novels, I'll have time to write my own on the strong foundation I'm laying."

"A foundation of lies and theft."

"A foundation of Eddie's solid writing, from which I will branch out on my own."

"After you publish his next two manuscripts? You made copies of them all?"

"Yes, I mimeographed or retyped everything before giving them back."

"How could you?" Klara covered her face. "You planned this all along."

Fritz balked. "No! Absolutely not. I only made duplicates for safekeeping, in case something happened to the originals. Considering the fire—" He paused. "Considering Eddie's general unreliability."

"You mean in case he tossed another cigarette?"

"Yes. But also, that fire devastated our business more than anything else he did. It took months to rebuild and recuperate. Even with insurance, we paid plenty out of pocket. Then all his medical bills."

Klara knew. Fritz willingly paid for every hospital, doctor, and medication Eddie and Klara couldn't afford. "I'm grateful for all you did to help us. I wish we could've repaid you. But now you've repaid yourself by stealing his novel. You say you've been reduced to moral dilemmas for Eddie's sake, but now you've done the most unsavory thing of all!"

As if deflecting her accusation, he picked up the framed photo of Eddie, August, and Fritz from the desk. The brothers stood in front of the store awning and sign. "During his last four years, I was thrilled he could finally join us working at the store without incident. I'd never seen him happier except the day you two got married. And when your girls were born."

Fritz looked up. "Even so, he lost interest in writing and publishing, as much as I still encouraged him to continue." He set the frame back on the desk, but his hand lingered. "Using his work never crossed my mind until three months after he passed away. So, yes, think of my own publishing venture as Eddie's repayment to me. I never asked anything from him, not for myself personally. I only wanted him to be responsible, to take care of you and the girls. I did everything in my power to put him in a better spot to do so. But there's more."

Klara's glare pierced him. "What then?"

"When we were boys, I envisioned our lives differently. With Eddie's drive, literary prowess, and creativity, I knew he'd be a successful writer someday. Furthermore, August and I wanted him to be equal partners in business. We couldn't have anticipated the bad turns after Papa passed away, how his death ate Eddie up. I couldn't stand thinking of him tortured by hallucinations and delusions, then subject to the whims of lunatics. A part of me died during those months he lived at the mental hospital."

In a rare moment of emotional display, chin quivering, he gazed out the window. "So, I told Eddie's story the way I wanted it to be, the life I wish I could have chosen for him. I'd spent years trying to reset his life course by providing viable career options, keeping him out of trouble, out of negative spotlight. This past year I rewrote novel sections to make the protagonist Oskar the hero of the story. The angst and conflict come more from outside forces that Eddie—Oskar, rather—rises above, rather than from inner turmoil he can't escape. I used his basic story and changed parts to reflect that."

He turned back to Klara. "Eddie saw himself as Oskar, down on his luck, wrestling with guilt over his father's death. I kept that premise, but altered events slightly, to show how Eddie would have coped with tragedy if schizophrenia hadn't claimed him. In the original draft, Oskar dies in an automobile crash. I changed that to falling off a ladder. But it's *not* a suicide in the book." Tears slid down his face. "His suicide plagues me daily."

Klara sniffed and wiped her cheek. "If only rewriting someone's life could make it so." Her intensity sharpened. "But is this really about Eddie? Perhaps you see *yourself* as hero of that story, after all you did for him. By rewriting it, you're changing your own role, too, as the strong, reliable, trustworthy older brother. Living the life you wanted to lead as someone with a stronger influence on his brother's outcome. Someone who was a hero to Eddie."

He blinked as if taking in her words.

"As hurt and angry as I am right now, I would be remiss to not acknowledge this, in case it's the last time we ever speak. You *were* the hero in Eddie's life. He adored you. He wanted to emulate you, to please you, even when he was tormented into doing unthinkable things. But a true hero would never stoop as low as you're doing now."

Fritz opened his mouth, but Klara forged ahead. "Now it seems Eddie owes you his talent and his book. That's why you took the story, right? Because of what he did to *your* life. He owes you."

"Changing things in the story is my way of honoring Eddie's life."

Unbelievable! Klara's blood raced. "It's still wrong. You could've told Eddie's story in your own way, but instead, you *stole* his novel. No matter how you justify it."

"Are you going to report me?"

She stared at him. "How could I? You've got me over a barrel. Nobody would believe Eddie wrote it since the hero falls off a ladder. Another change made to your advantage." Though she still had Eddie's original manuscripts to prove authorship.

He stuffed hands in his pockets, voice calm. "Before you go to the press, please know that I've named you as beneficiary of one hundred percent of royalties for *The Broken Weathervane*."

"What?" Conflicting emotions wrestled within. "What do I say? Thank you, so now I'll have enough to pay you back for medical expenses?"

"You owe me nothing. I don't need or want your money, Klara."

"Of course not. You just want the glory of publishing this book. You already stole the most valuable thing. This *story*, the heart and soul of Eddie. Your payback."

Fritz's jawline tightened before softening. "I'm already under contract for the next two books. I'm giving you one hundred percent of those proceeds too. Since Eddie never had a legal stake at the store, you'll be taken care of through royalties, Klara. No need to work as a single mother."

Silence reverberated between them like an echo.

CHAPTER THIRTY-NINE

2015

L eslie held the diary to her chest. Linus Fritz Buckwalter was a fraud, three times over, usurping his brother's role as author of *The Broken Weathervane*. Then *Small Town, Big Dreams* and *Trouble Triumphs in Trumbull*. Anger and sadness clamped her aching stomach.

No wonder Oma tacked on diary entries at the end, with earlier dates, revealing Fritz's multiple deceptions throughout the years.

Spent after a long cry, Leslie crawled into bed with *The Broken Weathervane*. Her next task was to reread this book with newfound knowledge of its true creator. Then she'd read the next two, her own silent tribute to Eddie, an enigmatic grandfather she never had the honor of knowing. The man her grandma loved fiercely to the very end and beyond.

She couldn't comprehend the ramifications—Fritz sacrificing for Eddie's well-being as his rationale for stealing his brother's manuscripts. Her grandma's silence while benefiting from royalties, allowing Fritz the glory. Wrong as it was, would Leslie have done any different? They'd been through much anguish with Eddie.

Leaning against pillows, she found the dogeared passage Greg shared at the library—her grandmother's favorite. She imagined Greg's mellifluous voice. "'The boy's stomach clenched as the metal rooster silhouette sharpened against the resplendent sunset of orange, rosy hues ... How could prevailing meadow winds that promised hope now render as still as doldrums?'"

Leslie rested the book against her raised thighs. Knowing how her opa died, weathervane in hand, this passage took on new meaning. Her grandmother's words to Eddie returned. *Love isn't bound up in the things you can do, whether or not you can fulfill your purpose. Love is about knowing you, all that you were, are, and will be, and still wanting you ...*

Twenty years ago, she fell in love with this story, its inimitable style. How she wished she'd known then it was her grandfather's writing. Now she wished she'd known *him*.

Mental illness stigma was far worse in the 1950s than today. No wonder Klara felt so alone in Dillard, only confiding in Fritz.

Was understanding better than ignorance? Leslie finally grasped her grandma's silence, her grandfather's pain, her great-uncle's betrayal. A tradeoff for damages, stolen time, and humiliation. All culminating in her mother's disappearance decades later. Was that related? The diary ended in 1958.

Leslie called her cousin. "Hey Max, wanna go to Dillard? It's a matter of family honor."

* * *

335

After Leslie divulged the diary's final content, Max said yes. They chose Monday so they could visit an office northwest of Dillard. She took a personal day and rescheduled appointments.

She needed closure. It was all about revisiting Eddie's world, seeing it through his eyes. Gaining more understanding.

On Monday, midmorning, Leslie and Max stood on the road bordering the former Buckwalter property outside Dillard. They walked along the country lane, musing about their grandfather, his three novels and life parallels, his difficult adult life, misunderstandings and judgment, but also the love from his wife and brothers.

Fertile farmland sprouted wheat and corn. Two cupolas topped the barn roof. One had leftovers of a weathervane, arrow and directionals intact, bringing a lump to Leslie's throat. The other vane sported a jalopy.

The acreage had been sold almost sixty-five years prior. Hoping to see the house and barn interiors, Leslie knocked on the farmhouse door. Nobody was home. Perhaps it was just as well, considering the day's emotional toll.

Ten miles away in downtown Dillard, they strolled Main Street, identifying places referred to—by different names—in *Small Town, Big Dreams.* They pointed out the church steeple, meandered through the bakery, laundromat, bookstore, clothing store, and finally the hardware store—the novel's hub, probably sparked by working at Dyer's Hardware. For lunch, they ate hamburgers and milkshakes at the diner, reminiscent of characters gathering at the Blueberry Cafe.

After lunch, they rambled beyond Main Street, identifying locales from *Trouble Triumphs in Trumbull,* including the park, town square, and library. The story paralleled Dillard politics in the early 1950s, aiming for hilarious social commentary based on clashes of its prominent citizens. What had Fritz changed in that novel?

Four blocks from Main Street, they encountered Buckwalter Brothers Grocery. Three of Fritz's grandchildren ran it. Did her cousins have anything to share about Eddie? Hopefully, the tension hovering at long-ago family reunions had dissipated by now. Feeling brave, curious, and nostalgic, Leslie set a hand on Max's arm. "Let's go in."

"You sure you're ready for the emotional upheaval?"

"No. That's why I brought you." A bell tinkled as she opened the door.

Though fifty-eight years had passed since Eddie worked here, the store exuded a bygone era—blue and white checkerboard tile flooring, the aroma of fresh-baked goods, shelves crammed with everything from pasta to peanut butter to chocolate chips. Colorful endcap displays brought to mind Eddie's enthusiasm for creative advertising. In the soup aisle, she imagined him spotting shoplifters, Fritz cajoling him to the stockroom, Eddie's protests among the bustling crowd ...

Blinking back tears, Leslie grabbed Max's arm.

"May I help you?" A familiar woman close to Leslie's age wore a blue-striped apron.

"I'm Leslie, and this is my cousin Max. Are you Fritz Buckwalter's granddaughter?"

"Sure am. If you're looking for his books, we have a display by the checkout."

"Really? I—" Leslie paused. She hated thinking of Fritz's descendants learning about his fraud. "I'll take a look. But I'm more interested in this building's history. In fact"—dare she admit it?—"I'm Leslie Wickersham. Edmund Buckwalter was my grandfather."

The woman's face lit. "Why, Leslie, I haven't seen you in over a decade. I'm Teresa Monaham, formerly Buckwalter. It's good to see you." She turned to Max. "Are you the kid who went around snitching cookies at family reunions?"

Max grinned. "I can neither confirm nor deny that."

"How's Great-aunt Klara doing?" Frowning, Teresa lowered her voice. "Does she still go by Wickersham instead of Buckwalter?"

Bristling at the judgmental tone, Leslie limited her response to one word. "Yes."

Teresa adjusted cereal boxes. "We've all been sworn to secrecy, especially when reporters drop by. But I never understood the name change. Turning Buckwalter into the B-word, while still benefiting from royalties."

Leslie balked. Oma *still* got royalties? Sounded like sour grapes. She'd ask Oma about it. Meanwhile, she bit back a response that would vindicate her grandmother. "Thanks for respecting her privacy. May we look around? For old time's sake."

Teresa straightened crooked granola packages. "We keep the nostalgia going. I'll give you the tour."

Leslie visualized scenarios from Oma's diary—happy or sad or devastating. She clung to Eddie's good years, when he finally felt like part of the family. The day he handed out cigars to celebrate her mother Dodie's birth.

Teresa paused at the bakery counter. "Edmund worked here, too, but he was never officially part of the business on paper. I wonder why."

"Your grandfather and father never talked about that?"

"No. I'm guessing Edmund was too young when they started the business."

Perhaps Fritz never revealed Eddie's gradual demise. Good. Those incidents were too weighty and fresh for people to speak so casually of them, even decades later.

Teresa ended the tour at the checkout by the book display.

"These three titles are facsimiles of the first printings in 1958, '59, and '60."

Leslie picked them up in turn, thumbing pages, examining covers, willing them to say *Edmund* instead of *Fritz*. Another ripple of melancholy embraced her. But stepping forward with the reality of Fritz's fraud would devastate Teresa and other descendants. Another probable reason Klara didn't want to unmask the truth. Would they even believe her? Did she still have Eddie's original manuscripts as she claimed?

Max gave Leslie a sideways hug. "Come on, cuz. Let me buy you a strawberry lollipop."

Good ole Max, always sensing her gloom. "I'm in."

"My brothers are in the office," Teresa said. "Come on back."

In the stockroom with a lollipop, Leslie gazed at shelves stuffed with boxes. Images flashed—Eddie stocking shelves, arguing with August and Fritz, tossing a smoldering cigarette into the garbage can, fire swallowing the room ...

Teresa gestured to two forty-something men at a corner desk. She introduced them as Wendall and Bart, jolting Leslie back to reality. Wendall offered salutations, but Bart spoke stiff greetings through a toothpick.

A vision crystalized: Oma leaving early from family gatherings—lips pursed, a protesting Leslie in tow. That same uneasiness gripped her now as her cousins' presence crackled the air with tension. She aimed for light-hearted. "With Teresa here, why hasn't the name changed to Buckwalter Siblings?"

Wendall chuckled. Bart remained stoic.

Teresa smirked. "Wanna guess how many times I've suggested that? Ha! But we keep the name intact for old times' sake. *Siblings* doesn't have the same ring to it, you know?"

"No alliteration," Leslie said. "Fritz's trademark."

"Do August's descendants work here?" Max asked.

"Just us three," Wendall replied. "August's kids weren't interested. Our father and uncle took over when Fritz and August retired. We inherited the store from them."

"What do you know about Edmund and his family?" Max asked.

Bart cleared his throat. "They still get Fritz's royalties."

Wendall shot his brother a frown, then stepped closer to Max as if to bridge the family gap. "I doubt we know more than you. Edmund died young, fell off a ladder when his girls were little. Great-aunt Klara moved away and never remarried."

Bart crossed his arms. "Abandoning the Buckwalter name but not the money."

Wendall looked apologetic. "Even Greg Stafford didn't discover the name change. Last time we saw him, he was holding out for an interview with her. Did he have any luck?"

Leslie hesitated. "Uh ... not that I know of. But the biography will be released soon. Supposedly." She didn't want to mention any connection to Greg.

"Did your grandfather ever talk about Edmund?" Max asked.

As Bart busied himself at the desk, Teresa and Wendall shared humorous anecdotes about Edmund and Fritz.

"I heard your opa took the weathervane after Edmund died," Leslie said. "Do you know what happened to it?" Their version of the story could prove interesting.

"Our aunts wanted to donate it to an archives or library," Teresa said. "But Uncle Drake sold it on eBay to make a buck. The aunties weren't too happy."

"Probably brought a chunk of money," Max said. "*That* could make someone happy."

"It made Uncle Drake happy," Wendall said. "Until the aunties said he'd better spread the wealth."

"It was handled fairly," Bart said through the toothpick. "Unlike the royalties."

Cue to leave. Leslie tapped Max's shoulder.

The royalty quandary was suspect enough. If those siblings ever caught wind of Fritz's fraud, Leslie never wanted to see them again. They surely wouldn't want to see her either.

Not to mention, wouldn't Jason demand royalties as Edmund's grandson? That is, if he knew the situation. Fritz's fraud might mean nothing to him if he only cared about money. But so far, he'd only mentioned sharing the glory of the family connection.

Incidentally, what would happen to the royalties when her grandmother died?

This day was wiping her out. But they had one more stop.

An hour away, Leslie and Max parked near the former Carlton Mental Hospital. The main building was refurbished as an office complex. The outbuildings were a series of chic shops, with more stores. A parking lot replaced sidewalks and landscaping. They quietly wandered through shops.

Leslie took Max's arm, needing to feel his presence. "I wonder what this must've been like. It's like a whole era and the people who were affected have been obliterated."

"Yeah. Hard to imagine."

But imagine she did. Her grandma's descriptions of the grounds came alive. But worse, as they entered the office complex, Leslie froze. "I hated reading about this, Max. It was horrible. Oma never even brought our parents here to see their daddy when they were babies. She couldn't stomach the idea of exposing them to such a depressing environment."

"I don't blame her."

What was it like for Eddie to live here three months straight? Twice. Listening to deluded, irrational people yell, howl, and bicker, subject to hallucinations himself, surely wondering if his family had abandoned him, wondering why he was the way he was and having no control over it.

"Leslie, you're zoning out. Are you sure you want to walk through here? It's triggering something. Even though we're smack dab in the twenty-first century and the shops feature cute kids' clothes and high-end handbags."

"Yes, I need to be here." If Eddie could live here three months—twice—she could tolerate vicarious memories for ten minutes.

Soon they found a lawyer's office on the second floor. Possibly the Ward D location? They walked to the front desk.

"Hi, I'm Leslie Wickersham. I called last week about wanting to see old records from Carlton Mental Hospital." She'd learned that a private company had archived the records, making accessible the information on patients who had deceased over fifty years ago.

"Yes, I remember. I'm Rhonda." The nonchalant, middle-aged brunette wore a tidy bun and a gray dress so bland it could have been hand-me-downs from Carlton days. "I pulled records for you. You're lucky we have these. Most old records were destroyed after seven years. But since Carlton was a private entity, the powers that be retained everything." She presented the file as if it were nothing more than an account of car repairs.

For a moment, Leslie hoped Edmund's name wouldn't be found. Then maybe everything she read never happened. But was that a better alternative? That would make her grandma a big, fat liar. Or a victim of her own hallucinations.

Leslie opened the file to reveal a piece of paper listing patients in 1953 and 1957. In business mode, Rhonda pointed out Edmund Buckwalter's name on line five. "These other papers list treatments prescribed, along with dates, doctors' names, anecdotes, and medications."

It listed lithium and CPZ, just as Oma had written. Treatments included hydrotherapy, then electroconvulsive therapy. The beginning of the end. Anecdotal records included the typewriter, the missing manuscript incident, and Edmund's demotion to Ward D.

The treatment paper shook in Leslie's trembling hand until Max took it, scrutinizing.

"May we have a copy?" he asked. "Two, just in case."

"Sure." Rhonda made copies and delivered them. "Any more questions?" Her tone indicated she may as well have been asking about hair dye colors.

Leslie wanted this woman to feel the weight of her opa's disturbing experience in this very building but couldn't think of a word to utter that would do it justice. She left in silence.

On the way home, Max drove, pensive, while Leslie cried.

CHAPTER FORTY

On Friday, Leslie breezed into the English office.
Today she planned to tell Greg about being a
Buckwalter. She tried to slot fifteen minutes, but
could only get five, for an appointment he'd initiated for some
reason.

Vic would receive her refusal-to-succumb-to-more-
blackmail letter today. Unless the postmaster suddenly turned
efficient overachiever. She'd mailed it two days ago.

"Janet, is Greg free yet? I have a three-oh-five with him. For
five minutes."

Janet looked over her glasses. "No. It's only three-oh-four."

Such odd scheduling. "Did he say why he wanted to
meet—"

"No, but he said to go right in at three-oh-five." Janet
pointed to the clock.

Leslie headed down the hallway as a man in black
sauntered out of the professor's office.

"Leslie!" The man's voice epitomized cheer. "Fancy seeing
you here in this ivory tower."

"Vic!" Leslie suddenly felt encased in stone as nerves ricocheted within. "What are you doing here? Did you know I worked here?"

"LinkedIn tells all." He smirked. "I just had an appointment with your esteemed Professor Stafford."

"For what?" A cloudy darkness rolled into her head. Had Vic made good his threats to share family connections by going to the renowned Buckwalter expert?

"For business. *Family* business." He lowered his voice as he swished to a stop. "You should have cooperated. I warned you."

"You said seven days."

Stepping from his office, right behind Vic, Greg held a thick manila envelope. He lifted his hand like an umpire.

Stewing, Leslie could hardly see straight. Her fingers twitched.

"See you around, Les." Vic strode down the hallway. His evil smile seemed to crackle in the air even after he disappeared around the corner.

Almost in tears, she faced Greg. "Why'd you meet with him?" she stammered.

"Come in for your appointment." Solemnly, he nodded toward his doorway.

"But why would you meet with him?" Though she hadn't admitted to being blackmailed, Greg knew Vic was taunting her.

She stomped in, preparing to unleash all her angst. How could Greg betray her this way? Especially after she'd stood up for him to Jason, and he'd promised his protection.

He closed the door.

"How could you let Vic Rinaldi into your office?" she sputtered. "I trusted you. I told you how he tried to ruin my life, yet you—"

"Leslie, please." Greg touched her arm.

She shook him loose. "How dare you! How could you stoop so low? How—"

"Leslie, stop. Listen first."

"Why?" She pointed to the manila envelope. "Now you can be happy, get published, remain the expert."

He set a calming hand on her shoulder. She shook it off again. "Leslie, give me one minute of your time. One minute is all I ask."

Heart throbbing, she sniffed and wiped her wet cheeks. "Okay. One minute. As if it will make a difference."

"Thank you." He lifted the fat envelope and showed her both sides. "He gave this to me. It's still sealed, so rest easy. Number one. Vic contacted me by email on Tuesday—"

"Tuesday?" Well before the seven days were up. That scoundrel!

Greg raised a hand as if to gentle her. "Hold on, I still have fifty seconds. He claimed to have vital information on the Buckwalter family, unknown to the general public. I recognized his name from your reminiscences and immediately suspected foul play. So, I paid attention. If his information was genuine, I didn't want it to fall into anyone else's hands. Especially since I ascertained the degree of varmint he is." He lifted an eyebrow. "Number two. I'm guessing he's been blackmailing you."

She grimaced.

"No surprise there." He waved the envelope. "I insisted that if he had information, it needed to be documented from primary sources. He assured me it was. I also said I didn't want anything sent over the internet, that I would only accept hard copies, exclusive ones, here in my office."

"I'm still waiting for the good news."

"I still have fifteen seconds. I scheduled a five-minute

appointment for him, followed by this appointment with you, so I could deliver this sealed envelope directly into your hands. Vic need never know. I haven't opened it, and don't plan to." He handed her the envelope. "For your eyes only."

"W-what?" She blinked, accepting the heavy envelope. "What do you mean?"

"My minute is up. Do you want me to continue?" He lifted his chin.

"Please do."

He covered her fingers with his own, as if tightening her hold on the envelope. "It should be obvious by now. But to clarify, these documents are yours to do with as you like."

His hand on hers radiated warmth through her arm and beyond. "But you need additional Buckwalter information for your book. You've been waiting a long time."

"I've found something more important than the perfect biography and the praise of colleagues."

She raised an arm in a wide gesture. "What's more important than that?"

"You. And your peace of mind."

His words wrapped around her like a balmy breeze offering respite from the scorching sun. Yet she was shaking.

"I wanted to tell him to bug off but perceived that would harm you, so I gave him the impression I'd put the information to good use." He smiled. "Which I am. Just not in my book." He removed his hand. "Now take it and go. I never need to see it."

She wanted to hug him. His actions touched her core, but at great sacrifice to himself. How could she rejoice in something that must be hugely disappointing to him? Even if he orchestrated it that way.

"I hardly know what to say, just thank you." She shuffled out, clinging to the envelope bound to her chest.

* * *

In her apartment that evening, Leslie held the envelope as if it were glass. Why had Greg given it to her unopened? Why would he forfeit the chance to learn something more about the Buckwalter family to maintain his expert status?

I've found something more important than the perfect biography and the praise of colleagues ... You. And your peace of mind.

That revelation dawned over her the way snowflakes gradually fill a landscape with peace and grandeur. Yet there was nothing cold about it.

Her hands held whatever Vic chose to use against her. But he only knew the Buckwalter ties, nothing about Oma's diaries —the job-hopping, the adultery, the fire, the mental hospital, the stolen manuscripts. Or Fritz's glory as a novelist at his brother's expense. Fritz the fraud. Only she, Max, and Oma knew those secrets. Secrets Greg deserved to know.

Greg would be devastated to find out. His book was going to press next week, right before Tuesday's committee meeting, ensuring his full professorship. Or not. He'd met all criteria, embracing community events and social media, espousing excellent teaching skills and student rapport. But learning Fritz was a fraud could change everything.

In uncovering Fritz, the world would know about Edmund's mental illness, his arson, his time at Carlton Mental Hospital. Wasn't it bad enough the papers reported his jail time? Wasn't it bad enough he was misunderstood, subject to hallucinations, wrestled with rejection, languished at the hospital, was robbed of his personality, creative spark, and hope, then took his own life?

Leslie, too, deserved privacy. What if she woke up one day

to find herself plagued by delusions and hallucinations? Like her grandfather.

Yet revealing Fritz's thievery could vindicate Edmund, who deserved credit for his beautiful novels. But the price was uncovering Fritz as a scoundrel—unless the whole story was told, including Fritz's exasperation after years of helping Eddie. What does one do about a brother set on destruction? One who inadvertently sets fire to the family business? Fritz constantly tried to protect Eddie, his reputation, giving him chance after chance.

Was there a way to vindicate Eddie without dragging his frailty into the limelight?

How would this devastating news impact Fritz's descendants, so proud of their grandfather's accomplishments?

With a shaky hand, she slit the envelope and withdrew papers. She paged through records from her own files: birth records and census records from 1950 to 1990, plus pages of personal research notes in her handwriting, including notes of her visit to Fritz and Wilma. Her fists clenched. Vic must have raided her files and made copies when they lived together, then returned the originals.

Her heart softened toward Greg. Without a clue of the envelope's contents, he'd handed it over to her to dispense with as she pleased. She dropped pages in her lap, leaned back, and sighed.

Greg's protection of her heart meant more to him than his career advancement. Even though he didn't have a clue what he was protecting her from. He willed himself to remain ignorant for her sake. But why'd he make her peace of mind paramount over his ten-year project of analyzing Fritz's novels and interviewing dozens of Dillard townsfolk and Fritz's progeny?

She roamed the apartment, crying salty tears, shaking her fist at Vic's treachery, then weeping from Greg's deference.

She paused at the bookshelf of family pictures. She held the photograph of her with Great-uncle Fritz, wishing it was Eddie, the grandfather she never met.

Greg needed to know about the three stolen novels.

She couldn't let him publish his book with partial information, perpetuating a lie. He'd resigned himself to publishing it without the one interview he lacked. He wouldn't lose his job if new facts emerged later. But her conscience couldn't abide it. Hiding facts would weigh her down, sucking the life out of any future friendship with him. Revealing the truth later would only prove her to be selfish and dishonest. More untrustworthy than she already was.

She hated to shatter his illusions. Yet she must. Now or never. But the second she told him the truth, he'd lose a literary hero. And lose face.

She might lose his friendship and whatever was budding between them.

Plus, could she dare refuse him the right to use the information, despite feeling exposed?

She was suddenly over the Edge of the Wild, as in *The Hobbit*. Where Gandalf cautioned there were no safe paths.

It was no longer safe to hold her secret. Nor was it safe to share.

Yet she knew what she must do. What she wanted to do, without coercion. The thought flickered through her mind numerous times since he'd handed her the envelope. Now it settled in heavily like impenetrable fog.

She texted Greg.

> Can you meet me at
>
> Kipp's Diner in 20 minutes?

A minute later, he replied.

Yes. See you at 7.

Then she called her grandmother.

CHAPTER FORTY-ONE

Greg waited for Leslie at a corner table. A small pot of hot water with a steeping teabag graced her place setting.

He stood and helped with her coat. "I ordered chai tea for you, with fresh, steamed whole milk. I know it's risky business ordering for a lady without her knowledge, but I was fairly certain you'd be satisfied with my choice."

"I am. Thank you." She sat as he hung the coat on the chair back. Surely, he wouldn't be so gentlemanly if he knew her impending revelation. Heat crept over her skin as she anticipated the outcome. "I've come to a decision." She handed him the envelope.

He shook his head. "That's yours."

"I'm sharing it. I want to honor your life's work. You deserve to know."

"I don't want it at your expense."

All the more reason to fall for him, to believe his good intentions. "The reasons to withhold this information are no longer valid. Please open it." She pushed it toward him.

He tentatively picked it up, slowly opened it, and pulled out papers. He scanned the top one—the 1960 census—brow wrinkling.

She pointed to the name Dolores Wickersham. "That's my mother. Living in Crestwood, Wisconsin, age six."

"So, you share her last name, since your father was out of the picture."

"Yes." She pointed out two other lines. "My grandmother and my aunt. Klara Wickersham, Martha Wickersham."

"Klara with a K. Hmm."

Perspiring, she handed him a legal document. "This shows my mom's name change, after moving to Crestwood in 1959."

He squinted at the paper. "Dolores Buckwalter ... becomes Dolores Wickersham." He cocked his head. "Wait. What? Your mother's a Buckwalter?"

"Yes." She let that sink in, then handed him another document. "This is Aunt Martha's name change." He nodded. "And this is my grandmother's." She revealed the third document.

He honed in on the names. "Klara Breslauer Buckwalter changed to Wickersham." He looked up, spearing her with his gaze. "Your grandfather was Edmund Buckwalter?"

"Yes." And there it was. Out in the open. His face expanded. Her muscles tightened.

"Unbelievable." His eyes darted between documents and the census. "I hardly know what to respond to first. The changes, the move, or—" He looked up again, jaw tight. Hurt tinged his voice. "The fact that you're a Buckwalter and never told me."

Leslie winced. "My grandfather had some rough years. After he passed away, my grandma found much-needed anonymity by changing names and moving to Crestwood."

"Which explains why she can't easily be found." His lips pressed into a fine line.

Was he furious with her right now?

He crossed his arms. "I'm sorry to hear about your grandfather's rough years."

Wasn't he going to ask for details? "Everything Vic had in the envelope is still here. Unbeknownst to me, four years ago, during our divorce, he made copies of my family tree files, including my personal research notes. But except for my bloodline, and personal time spent with Fritz and Wilma, this is information you already know from archives and town hall records."

Greg riffled through them, then slid the pages into the envelope. He handed it back, face stoic. "These are yours."

She didn't take it. "I'm giving them to *you* now."

"Why now and not months ago, while I was editing my manuscript?" Seemed his anger and hurt masqueraded as a business tone. She hated it.

"Because I didn't want you to play the nice game with me just because of my family ties. Nor did I want you to wheedle information from me I wasn't ready to share."

He poured cream in his coffee, his manner stiff. "Fair enough."

"I wanted you to respect me, *not* for being a Buckwalter, but for who I am in my role as grants officer. Respecting me for who I am, apart from my name or ancestry."

"Quite a feat, which you aptly accomplished. But would you have held out longer if Vic hadn't been so generous with your findings?"

"I planned on telling you today in your office, until Vic showed up. But first—" She removed the spoon from her tea and fumbled. It clattered on the table. "Aren't you furious with me right now?"

He offered a tired smile. "I'm debating the monumental effort and merit of such anger."

"I know how angry you were at Jason Hendricks when he wrote that despicable article. You were calm and collected on the phone, but behind his back, you were blowing your top. And now you must feel like I've betrayed you by withholding vital information."

"I suspect your not wanting to share stems from some of Edmund's questionable history. His time in jail, specifically."

"That's part of it. Knowing what you think of jailbirds. But I didn't want the world to know the connection, either. Edmund the black sheep and all."

"But that's not who *you* are." His voice generated warmth. Greg well knew how to assess himself differently from his father. "Frankly, I'm concerned about Vic's next steps. Will he leave you alone now that he's passed off this information to me?"

"I hope so."

He swallowed some coffee. "What was he demanding?"

"Money." Something made her plow forward. "Three hundred dollars monthly. That's how he gets his kicks. Last week he demanded more, but I finally refused to cave in. He gave me seven days to pay him but waited only four to contact you."

"I hope you can steer clear of him now. You need a lawyer."

"That's what Max says."

"Max? Ah, yes, your cousin, lover of *hors d'oeuvres* at the library."

"Yup. He watches out for me."

"Good. I expect you to inform me if otherwise."

She tilted her head. "Really?" Why was he so kind and protective instead of pressing her for more information? "Professor—"

"It's Greg."

"Greg. Okay. I'm sorry I waited this long to tell you. I planned to after finishing the diary. Vic made it happen sooner." She stirred her tea. "But he doesn't know the half of it."

"Diary?" He raised his brows and sipped coffee.

Leslie cleared her throat. "I need to share other things."

"No, you don't."

"I want to. And I will. Without regret."

He crossed his arms on the table. "*I* wish to have no regrets, either."

Oh, dear. He'd have plenty of regrets after she dropped the bomb of tightly held family secrets.

"From the look on your face," he said, "good news is doubtful."

She should hand him her grandmother's diary and leave. Let him read the harrowing experiences himself. But no, he didn't have the luxury of time to explore a diary. He had till Monday to submit any revisions. Maybe.

She must do the right thing. "Greg, I have hard things to tell you."

"Don't worry. I won't shoot the messenger." He offered a thin smile.

In minutes, with newfound knowledge, he might change his mind.

"I know it's difficult to share private things about your family. You don't have to tell me anything."

"Yes, I do." She swallowed, then went full force. "In January, my grandmother gave me the diary she kept in the 1950s, during the early years of the Buckwalter Brothers Grocery. I finished reading it several days ago. Some things came to light you should know." She pulled the diary from her purse, set it on the table, and folded her hands over it. "First of all, the grocery store fire was arson."

"Not according to Fritz."

"He lied to you. He lied to protect Edmund."

"Edmund set the fire?"

"Accidentally, after a string of jobs he failed to keep. Eddie had emotional problems. Mental problems, delusions. He was convinced he saw shoplifters and tried to arrest innocent customers. August and Fritz found jobs for him elsewhere, but Eddie kept quitting or getting fired. Though his brothers did everything to help him, he claimed they were conspiring against him, even broadcasting it on the radio. The fire started from a cigarette he tossed in the wastebasket. Fritz didn't want Eddie in jail, so he lied to the fire marshal."

Greg cocked his head, another frown creasing his forehead. "Yet he still did jail time."

"That was later, for a traffic violation and disturbing the peace, as reported in Lynwood newspapers. That incident escalated from his hallucinations. He was certain that Martians spoke to him on the car radio, about impending danger for the town."

"I went to that very police station for the report." Greg fingered a napkin as if restless. "There was nothing about Martians."

Leslie's voice hitched as Eddie's pain spirited through her. "Fritz had an officer friend wipe it from the police record. Eddie's thirty-day jail sentence was shortened to ten because the psychiatrist intervened." She sought compassion in Greg's face and found it. Mixed with confusion and concern.

"So, Fritz was underhanded and Edmund was under psychiatric care?"

"Yes." Leslie sat back, winded, letting Greg soak everything in. Her shaking hands encircled her teacup, nearly spilling. She sipped the warm, milk-spiked tea, but found no solace.

"So, Fritz spared Edmund from a longer stint in jail, bad press, and a worse police record."

"Yes, and spared him from bad press on other occasions. Like when Eddie sabotaged Opening Day. Fritz bribed the reporter."

"Ah, verifying Fred Rickert's testimony."

"Oma mentions Fred in the diary. Though she didn't know about the bribery till later. She wrote more entries after learning everything from Fritz."

Face grim, Greg tore a corner off the paper napkin. "All this lying, bribing, and manipulating make Fritz an unreliable source."

"Right. Remember you promised not to shoot the messenger. He also bought silence from townsfolk who had rough interactions with Eddie, to quell gossip. Al Dyer, and other employers."

Greg's lips twitched, frown deepening. "That explains numerous dead-ends."

She dipped her chin, summoning courage, then looked up. "These events were wake-up calls for Fritz and August. They had to get Eddie help. After the fire, he was so angry, he slit his wrists. He ended up in Carlton Mental Hospital near Madison. The place closed in the 1970s."

He tore off another napkin piece. "I never saw anything documented."

"You had no cause to look up those records. But *I* did. After finishing the diary, I went to Carlton." She pulled out more papers. "Line five. With anecdotal records."

Greg took the sheets. "Paranoid schizophrenia. Wow."

Wow was right. And she hadn't even reached the climax.

"He was diagnosed with manic depression first, now called bipolar disorder. Turned out to be a dual diagnosis."

"Did treatment help? The 1950s was still rife with questionable methods."

"Initially. With medication, he had three good years at home, 1954 to 1957. He and Klara raised their two daughters while Eddie worked at the grocery. But the med's side effects caused permanent neurological damage." She tightened her grasp on the teacup. "Then they tried electroconvulsive therapy." Leslie swallowed. "It changed his personality. He was listless and lost some memory. Permanently."

"A terrible shame."

She nodded. "Yeah. Which makes me concerned for Jason. He could be Edmund's descendent. In 1952, Eddie had a brief affair."

"I'm sorry to hear that, but it proves nothing."

Leslie lowered her voice. "Look, I'm angry about Jason's actions, but when I saw him last time, he said such strange things, I wonder if he suffers from his own delusions."

"What strange things?"

"Promise you won't hit the ceiling, but he was certain you had a secret Flintstones website, written in code, to expose your plot to overthrow the literary world."

Greg guffawed. "At least he didn't put *that* in the article."

"It was more than a weird conspiracy theory. He seemed completely deluded."

"Aren't most folks who fall for conspiracy theories?"

"Maybe. But his allegations and assertions scared me. It reminded me of things I read in my grandma's diary. Besides, schizophrenia has a genetic component. I looked it up."

Greg's face went from consternation to compassion. "Are you afraid for yourself?"

Her lip trembled. "I was. Usually, women get it by their

early thirties. So hopefully I'm past the prime." She twiddled her thumbs. "I'm still concerned for Jason, though."

"Who hasn't bothered with a DNA test."

"Yeah." She swallowed again, words stuck. "And Eddie didn't *just* fall off a ladder."

Greg's eyebrows shot up. "What?"

"The papers reported his death as an accident. But he took his own life. He slit his neck. And at the top of the ladder, he held the rooster. Right before stepping off the rung."

Greg's eyes were riveted to hers. "Thus, the crying in my office. I'm so sorry. That's a horrific thing to discover about your own grandfather."

Her hands shook. "But there's more. From 1952 to 1954, he wrote stories."

"He and Fritz both aspired to write great novels."

"Eddie finally fulfilled that wish." She gulped. "He wrote three."

"Seriously? Do the manuscripts still exist?"

"Um ... yes. The novels were published."

He scooted forward expectantly. "Under a pseudonym, I presume. Which name?"

She took one last look at Greg without him knowing the terrible truth. She lowered her voice as if it would lessen the blow. "Linus Fritz Buckwalter."

A dazed look struck him. His shoulders slacked. "What are you saying?"

"Fritz Buckwalter stole his brother's manuscripts and published them himself."

Greg blinked as if warding off visions of evil spirits. "Which ones?"

"*The Broken Weathervane. Small Town, Big Dreams.* And *Trouble Triumphs in Trumbull.* Fritz's so-called first three novels."

Greg sat back as if stunned.

Now came the time she would sit in the pain of reality with him. "Greg, I'm so sorry." Such feeble words. "I didn't know about the stolen manuscripts until I finished the diary a few days ago. Eddie's sickness was bad enough, but Fritz taking his stories, well, it's deplorable. My grandma called it stealing Eddie's heart and soul."

The silence stretched between them. Greg's expression turned grim.

She pulled out her grandmother's copy of *The Broken Weathervane* and turned to the inscription. "These are Fritz's words to Klara."

Greg fingered the page. *Consider this tale a tribute to Eddie. His story matters.*

"Oma was furious that Fritz took all the glory. But he said it was recompense for damages Eddie caused over the years, including the fire. Fritz paid all the medical bills too. Store duties and Eddie's care robbed Fritz of time for his own writing. So, these novels jump-started his rise into the literary world. He also revised Eddie's life story his own way. The way he wished it had unfolded."

"Did Fritz rewrite Eddie's story? Or *steal* it?"

"Both. He made changes, but it's still Eddie's story." She paused. "Oma received one hundred percent of the royalties from day one."

"A hundred percent?"

"Yes, and she still gets them. It's in Fritz's will." Oma had told her last night. "Prompting more family tension."

Greg spoke as if in a dream. "Nobody knew of this deception besides your grandmother and Fritz?"

"Right. Fritz had his own retyped copy of each manuscript because he helped Eddie with proofreading. I'm positive his descendants don't know. And they have no clue why Klara receives royalties. Especially since she rejected the Buckwalter name."

"Wow." Greg's gaze swept over the restaurant, out the window, back to Leslie. "Didn't she want to see Edmund vindicated? Why didn't she speak up?"

"Speaking up would've put Eddie's problems in the spotlight. After all Fritz did for her and Eddie, she couldn't bring herself to discredit Fritz. And I suspect the royalties played a part. Fritz always took care of family. Financially, she was set for life as a single mom."

"With one last bribe for her silence."

Nodding, Leslie held the diary out to him.

"No, that's yours. Private family information."

"What happened to the king of research? It's a primary source."

"Look, Leslie, I'm reeling from all you've told me. Fritz is a fraud. I'm still digesting everything, but I can't take the diary."

"She gave me permission to share it with you. I called her last night. She knows about Vic's visit to your office, about you giving me the envelope. She said to invite you to Crestwood. For tomorrow."

"Why? She successfully avoided me for years."

"Because you refused to look inside the envelope. Because you gave it to me. And she's tired of carrying her secrets." She pushed the diary his way. "Please take it. Consider it homework for tomorrow."

CHAPTER FORTY-TWO

The drive to Crestwood was quiet, pensive. Leslie was glad Greg insisted on driving since her scattered thoughts drove her to distraction. Last night, she'd asked her grandmother questions on the phone, but Oma insisted on providing answers in person. Leslie had vouched for Greg's good character, but how would this long-avoided meeting go? Was she right to bring him here? She wished Max could have joined them, to lighten things up.

Klara Wickersham sat in the parlor chair, a crocheted afghan in her lap. After hugs, Leslie made introductions.

Greg took Oma's thin, veined hand. "I'm honored and humbled to meet you, Ms. Wickersham. Thank you for your gracious invitation."

Oma waved her free hand. "Bah! In the end, you win."

"This is no competition."

"Not anymore, since I've conceded."

"To be clear, I'm here only as Leslie's friend." He spared Leslie a warm glance. "Not as a researcher."

"Oma, he didn't even bring a pen, notebook, laptop, or

recording device." Leslie eyed his suspicious briefcase, though, resting against a chair leg. He'd assured her earlier the contents had nothing to do with research.

"Then what's the purpose?" Oma shrugged. "After rejecting all your interview requests, I'm ready to talk. Isn't that why you're here? To put it in your book?"

"I'm here only for understanding."

Aunt Martha shooed them to chairs and set a tray of jam-filled Linzer cookies on the coffee table. She filled cups from a pitcher. "This is peach lemonade. I know it's late February, but this was my papa's favorite beverage." Her voice cracked. "We drank it together with these cookies for princess tea parties when I was four."

With a sniffle, she faced Leslie, her expression more careworn than usual. "Your oma told me everything from the diary last night, so talk freely without concern for your ole aunt." Her words reflected her flippant demeanor, but her tone suggested otherwise. It must have been devastating to learn her father had schizophrenia and committed suicide. Not to mention Fritz's betrayal. And Oma's decades-long silence.

Leslie sipped tea. "Oma, I'm so sorry for everything you went through with Opa. I had no idea."

"Nobody did. Those first years of marriage, Eddie's escapades left me friendless. I loved him so much—" her voice tripped. "But the fallout was humiliating. My own family lived out of town. I never confided in them, or they would've whisked me away. August, Fritz, and Wilma were my only confidantes." Her composure dipped to sorrow. "They were always there for us. Until Fritz took Eddie's stories."

"Why didn't you take legal action?" Leslie asked.

"The deed was already done. When I confronted him, I finally realized how difficult Eddie's troubles were for his brothers too. Multiple fiascos chipped away at Fritz's time and opportunities." She tented her fingers. "I was torn. I canceled many lawyer appointments. With Eddie's manuscripts, I could prove Fritz's plagiarism. But I needed that royalty money. And proving his fraud would discredit Fritz in the public eye and shame his family." She shook her head. "I just couldn't do that."

"Fritz shouldn't have perpetuated a lie," Leslie said gently.

"Scolding me won't help, dear. I made my choice. I've had to live with it." She stared at her hands. "I couldn't have sought justice without dragging my dear husband's problems into the spotlight."

Greg leaned forward, elbows on knees. "Ms. Wickersham, did moving to Crestwood and changing your name help you move on with your life after your husband passed?"

Leslie's heart warmed at his sensitive question—asked as a concerned soul.

"It helped me avoid more humiliation and woeful stares from folks who'd witnessed his episodes or saw him go from job to job. Everyone knew me in Dillard. After Fritz's debut novel became a bestseller, I couldn't bear living there. My girls needed to grow up untainted by their papa's reputation, *not* under the shadow of their uncle's success." She sighed. "We'd still visit the Buckwalters periodically, so my girls knew their cousins, aunts, and uncles."

Aunt Martha patted her mother's hand. "It was the right move, Mom. Dodie and I had a good upbringing, surrounded by a loving community here."

"Of course, you say that now," Oma said. "You don't want an old lady going to her grave with more regrets."

"Have I ever said anything just to make you feel better, Mom?" Martha smirked.

"No, frankly. Never too late to start, though." Oma winked at Greg. For heaven's sake, her grandmother winked at Professor Gregory Scott Stafford!

The others chuckled. Leslie fidgeted. "Now I see why those family reunions were so tense. Fritz's kids and grandkids didn't like you receiving royalties they saw as their due."

"Honey, that's exactly why we high-tailed out of those picnics. Along with the beer, out came the rancor. They were doubly offended that I benefited financially even after abandoning the Buckwalter name. Fritz's will stated that I'd keep getting royalties from the first three books. He stipulated that if his progeny leaked to the press or anyone, royalties from books four to twelve would reroute to me instead of them. All for the sake of Eddie, the girls, and my early widowhood. He and August never told anyone about Eddie's mental illnesses."

Oma lived so modestly in this old bungalow, surely her bank account was overflowing. No wonder she had easily paid for Leslie's college education.

"Later on, I donated a chunk of royalties to mental health organizations and subsidized patient fees at therapy centers, in hopes that people like my dear Eddie would find help, and families could be preserved."

"Oh, Oma, that was a lovely thing to do." It captured the heart of everything Leslie aimed to do with mental health awareness.

Oma pointed to a box on the table. "Dr. Stafford, that's for you." Greg took it and waited expectantly. "Go on. Open it."

He removed the cover, revealing three full binders.

"I know this is a huge blow," Oma said. "Fritz's fall from grace. But it's literary history and truth coming to light. Those are Eddie's original manuscripts."

Greg handed the box to Leslie. "You should have the honor."

Leslie fished out the binders. She flipped through the first one—with personal penciled notes by both Fritz and Eddie—and held it to her chest. Her grandfather's work. His first spark of literary genius. His brainchild. "How about a reading right now? In memory of Opa."

Oma smiled. "Yes, please do. I put sticky notes on favorite passages."

Leslie eyed the top page. "Titled Novel Number One." She paged through it, pausing to read paragraphs aloud. The others laughed or sighed, depending on the line. She found the marked paragraph about Oskar contemplating the weathervane. "Would you read it, please, Greg? The way you did at the library."

"Ah, that's a favorite. I'd be honored." He read in an expressive, moving baritone voice. If he was sad about reading them as Eddie's words rather than Fritz's, he gave no indication.

At Leslie's request, he read excerpts from the second and third manuscripts too, eliciting chuckles, gasps, or sniffles in an impromptu ceremony giving Eddie his due.

Afterward, Oma nodded, words choked. "Beautifully done, Leslie, Dr. Stafford. I do wish Eddie could have heard you. His way with words, his ability to draw a smile or a swoon—that's how I want you to remember your grandfather, Leslie. I wish you'd known him."

"Me too."

Greg replaced the binders. "I wonder which Fritz-isms I use are actually Eddie-isms." He listed several, and Klara confirmed the ones original to Eddie. "Good to know. The two about hyperbole and ice cream are my favorites. No more misattribution." He winked at Leslie.

How could he be such a good sport? He must be devastated. "Oma, what do you think of Fritz's changes? He wanted to write Eddie—or Oskar—as the hero, the life he would have chosen for him."

"The end result's a masterpiece, a tale of courage and overcoming, the perfect collaboration. If only Eddie had been credited. He was a creative genius." Oma faced Aunt Martha. "I only spoke well of your father to you and Dodie. I needed to supplant negative images, wanting you to know the real man, and remember him fondly."

"I do, Mom. I always have." Aunt Martha dabbed a tissue on her cheek.

"What do you remember?"

"Bouncing on his knee. Telling stories. Cinderella, Aladdin, Paul Bunyan. He pushed me on the swing, took us to the zoo. We played Candy Land, ate ice cream." She paused. "I vaguely remember him yelling, watching TV for hours on end, and lying in bed for days."

"I hope the former images linger longer than the latter," Oma said.

"They do, but ..." Aunt Martha bit her lip. "Never mind."

But Oma should have told her sooner?

Oma's jaw tightened. "I know. I should have told you long ago instead of keeping it all a big, fat secret."

"I don't want to second guess you, Mom. I haven't walked in your shoes."

"I thank God you didn't have to. Your Russell was the best thing that ever happened to you, may he rest in peace. A wonderful son-in-law too."

"Like a father to me," Leslie added. "Oma, so much was beyond your control. If Opa were diagnosed today instead, it'd be so different. Schizophrenia is very treatable nowadays. People can have normal, productive lives with medication and therapy."

Oma sniffed. "But back then, it was horrible. My biggest concern was the hereditary nature. I prayed till my knees wore out that Martha and Dodie wouldn't develop symptoms." She squeezed her eyes shut, wrinkling her face as if willing not to cry.

Leslie's mind flashed to Jason. What if he was related—and mentally ill? Whether he proved to be a relative or not, Leslie would never tell her grandmother for fear of breaking her heart. Living proof of her husband's infidelity.

Oma formed her fingers into a tent whose pitch kept rising and falling. "Your mother wasn't officially diagnosed, but I'm sure that's what she had."

Leslie numbed. "Oh, my word ..." She looked at her aunt for confirmation.

Aunt Martha nodded. "Your oma and I talked about this last night, in light of everything. In her twenties, your mom had delusions of grandeur, went on rampages, had different boyfriends monthly. Basically, she underwent a sudden personality change."

"Like your grandfather," Oma said. "For three years, I tried to get her to the doctor. She wouldn't go. After she moved out at age twenty-four, I only saw her on holidays, if at all. Her choice, not mine."

Leslie squeezed her hands into fists, stretched her fingers as if to test their existence.

Greg took her hand, his strong grip holding her in place. She was grateful he accompanied her today.

Oma continued. "I believe that's why your mother left you, Leslie. There was something wrong, beyond her reach. She knew she couldn't care for you well. So, she brought you to me."

"She said that?"

"Basically. When you were born, she was still living in the fast lane. And refusing help." Oma sighed. "The last time she came, she said, 'I know you can give her a better upbringing. The one she deserves.' She was weeping when she walked out."

"Do you remember that day, Leslie?" Aunt Martha asked.

All eyes were riveted to Leslie. "Vaguely."

"You were seven and went off playing in the other room," Oma said. "She only said her goodbyes to me. She couldn't bear telling you."

Hot tears filled Leslie's eyes. "Do you know where she is? Or if she's still alive?"

Oma shook her head.

Leslie couldn't imagine watching schizophrenia claim her husband, then a daughter. "Have you ever tried to find her?"

"Many times." Aunt Martha replied. "But it was clear she didn't want to be found. I even searched on Facebook recently. With no luck."

"I prayed you wouldn't get ill yourself, Leslie," Oma said. "Thank God you didn't. Chances are, it would've happened by now."

Being spared didn't compensate for a loved one who wasn't. "Why didn't you tell us any of this before? Especially the schizophrenia. It explains so much about Opa and Mom."

"Darling, maybe I can't justify my silence anymore." Oma turned to Aunt Martha. "But I don't regret not telling you about the suicide. You would've grown up believing your father didn't love you enough to stay alive. It's more complicated than that."

"I know, Mom." Aunt Martha patted Oma's shoulder.

"I hate it that you girls found him lying by the ladder. He said he wanted to perch that rooster on the roof. That weathervane comprised his whole childhood." Oma's voice wavered. "That's why I wanted it back after Fritz passed away. I thought his family would donate it to a museum. That's what I wanted to do eventually. But they said they couldn't find it." She shook her head. "They probably lost or sold it. Angry that I still received royalties."

Greg opened his briefcase. "Ms. Wickersham, I have something for you." He withdrew the metal rooster and carried it over. "I bought this on eBay ten years ago, shortly after Fritz passed away. John Buckwalter, his grandson, assured me it was genuine. His Uncle Drake had posted it. It has graced my office walls, but I had no idea it still meant something to you. I want you to have it." He set it on her lap.

Oma blinked back tears, her fingers roving over the feathers. "Oh, my ..."

Silence fell over the room as Oma traced details of the face, wings, and tail. "The last time I saw this was on the grass, by the ladder ... on that terrible day."

"If you want to donate it to a museum or archives," Greg said, "I can facilitate that."

Back at his chair, Leslie met him with a hug. She tried to offer thanks but couldn't forge any words.

"Thank you." Oma's shaky voice straightened out. "Dr. Stafford, I've given Leslie all power of decision-making regarding anything I've said today, and anything in my diary. If she wants to hide it under a rock or yell it from the mountaintops, it's completely up to her."

"I understand." He took Leslie's hand again and afforded her a glance before riveting his gaze on Oma. "Leslie takes priority over scholarship, if that's your concern."

"That's my *sole* concern. Thank you, Dr. Stafford."

CHAPTER FORTY-THREE

Aunt Martha served a delicious supper of schnitzel, potato dumplings, and Black Forest cake topped with whipped cream, chocolate shavings, and cherries. She brewed a strong pot of coffee. The meal was presented as Eddie's all-time favorite. Leslie had little appetite, but Aunt Martha's labor of love and remembrance had Leslie dabbling in each dish.

Through erratic thoughts and ragged emotions, she relished Greg by her side, sharing these moments with her family. Somehow, he fit in. Kindness infused his speech, but he mostly listened. He was attentive to her, gracious with Oma and Aunty.

Oma sent Greg and Leslie home with Eddie's three manuscripts. In the car, after five minutes of staring out the window into darkness, Leslie said, "I give you permission to use anything in the diary for your manuscript."

Greg gave a low, throaty chuckle. "Oh, no, you don't. This day has run roughshod over you. Better to wait a few months to decide that."

She snapped around to face him. "But *you* don't have a few months. Your biography is going to press next week."

"Even if I integrate new information, three days isn't enough time."

"They'll give you a few weeks, won't they?"

"My meeting with the promotion committee is Tuesday."

"Ask for an extension."

"You make it sound as easy as rescheduling a trip to the grocery store."

"Won't they accommodate you?"

"Leslie." He reached for her hand in the darkness. "This isn't about me and my book. This is about *you*. Your family, your lifeline. Your ancestry. I won't exploit you."

"If I give you permission, that's not exploiting."

"Give it time, Leslie."

"But you need this for your book. Or are you having it published as is?"

He sighed. "No. As a scholar, I can't publish it now, knowing the truth."

"Then what will you do?"

"That's not yours to worry about, Leslie."

How many times had he said her name? She loved how it sounded on his lips. Months ago, she had to bribe him with lattes. "But I *am* worried. I want you to succeed."

"At your expense?"

She bit her lip. Was she being too rash? In a month, would she regret forking over anything she gave him tonight? "Look ... I feel like I've been living under Eddie's shadow of shame my whole life. That's without knowing much. Now I'm under a bigger umbrella of shame. Fritz's fraud." She stared out the window. "You don't need a family tree, do you? I'm not ready to say I'm a Buckwalter, but the truth should be told. Eddie should be vindicated. And Fritz, well ..." She couldn't say it.

"Should be discredited?" There. He'd supplied the words.

"Not completely. But he shouldn't get credit for the first three novels. The thing is, telling only part of the story doesn't cut it. Fritz isn't the devil. Neither is Eddie. Eddie was ill, but Fritz was worn out after doing every earthly thing possible for his brother. He—oh my, I'm rambling." She clamped her mouth shut.

"Ramble on. You're thinking aloud, sorting through everything."

"Okay, Fritz tried to save Eddie's reputation every chance he had. I almost don't blame him for claiming the novels as his own." She quickly added, "I don't condone it. Not in a million years. But I understand it. He'd given up everything. Money, time, goals, emotional energy."

"They were both broken weathervanes."

The realization struck like lightning. Broken, but still pointing to stormy weather. And decades later, to her mother. More winds blew now, with pelting rain, as truth came to light.

The floodgates opened. She wept as Greg drove silently, holding her hand.

* * *

When Greg pulled into her parking lot, Leslie invited him inside for hot chocolate. She wasn't ready to be alone with all her feelings. She wanted to bask in his presence, even in her woeful confusion. Such a far cry from months ago, when he was more bristle than balm, more cynic than comforter, more sarcasm than safety.

He hesitated. "Well, just until *The Odd Couple* starts. That gives me thirty minutes."

"Is that your guilty pleasure? Vintage 1960s, not very highbrow. I never would've guessed. Especially since it's my guilty pleasure too." She chuckled. "I can stream it for you. As many episodes as you want."

"Streaming." He grunted. "That's just excess technology that defeats the purpose of mastering delayed gratification."

"That's exactly what I'd expect you to say." She smiled.

They went up to her third-floor apartment. She winced at scattered piles. "Please, no judgment. I haven't cleaned in a week." She filled her copper kettle with water and lit the stove. "Guess I'm more Oscar than Felix."

"Pristine is overrated."

"Exactly." She pointed out the framed family photos on the bookshelf, the picture of her with Great-uncle Fritz.

"I'm sorry you couldn't have a photo of you and your grandfather."

"Me too. Would you like to see my family album? I've got pages of old Buckwalter pictures." She pulled it off the shelf.

"Not unless you want to. This evening's about you, not me."

Touched by his thoughtfulness, she slid the album back into place.

She prepared hot chocolate. He sat on one end of the couch with his mug, feet on the ottoman. She took the other end, cross-legged, facing him. "I still want you to use the diary as needed."

Greg shifted, angling his legs toward her. "I can't reshape the manuscript with new details unless I have two weeks minimum to indulge myself. It's more than just tacking on a new chapter. The new aspects affect every part of the story."

"How about this? Ask for a two-week extension based on receiving new intel. It's in the committee and Grable Press's best interest. Implement what you want from the diary and Eddie's manuscripts. After two weeks, ask me again, to ease your mind."

"Benevolent dictator, are we now?" He winked.

"Just brainstorming. I'm considering your options. I see my role as masterful, not bossy."

"Well played, Leslie." He chuckled. "But this isn't your problem. Why are you suddenly so concerned about my achieving full professor?"

Because I think I love you. You're good and kind and full of integrity. No, that wouldn't fly. "I'm feeling awful for withholding everything. I was afraid it would change our friendship, for starters."

"You have a lot to soak in right now. So, working with our constraints, I'll follow your dictatorial lead."

"Suggestions only. No dictatorship here."

"Why not? You've had no qualms telling me what to do before."

She tilted her head. "What?"

"Case in point. 'Use this wording on line three.' 'Time for Instagram lessons.' 'Tie this question to your morning latte.'"

The teasing twinkle in his eye was unmistakable, yet she took the defensive. "I don't sound like that."

He laughed. "I'll ask for a two-week extension and get to work. Assuming they agree. Grable Press might cancel my contract if I insist the manuscript can't go to press as is."

"Then what happens to achieving full professor?"

"The committee must agree to the delays too. If Grable Press won't publish it, it'll take time to find another publisher." He frowned. "Worse is Grable Press publishing it as is."

Leslie bit her lip. "What will happen when you reveal Fritz as a fraud?"

"Weeping and gnashing of teeth. Mine already started."

She eyed him closely. "I'm so sorry, Greg. I know this is heartbreaking."

He shook his head as if snapping himself out of it. "It

hasn't sunk in yet. And the fallout? I don't know. If I expose him, I must prove my statements with reliable sources. The diary, the manuscripts, mental hospital records. But it's a blow to every Fritz Buckwalter fan out there."

"Will *you* lose credibility too? You've written so much about him without knowing any of this."

"The publisher might not be happy. They want an official biography that holds Fritz up as a stellar example of a community-minded family man. Not someone who stole from his brother."

"But the context ..."

"The context of Eddie's mental illness, which you may not want to expose."

Leslie warmed her hands on the mug. "Greg, for years, I've encouraged dialogue about mental illness to reduce stigma. Why should I hold out when it's my own family? My mother too." Leslie could hardly grasp the scope of her mother's illness and absence, dealing with these demons. Once again, she wept without restraint.

Greg slid next to her. His arms circled her as she nestled her face into his shoulder. His hands glided across her back, stroking, soothing. His warmth became hers, buoying her up, yet inviting her deeper. His musky cologne soothed.

After several minutes, she quieted and felt the rise and fall of his chest under her hand. She startled. When had her hand moved there? "I'm sorry for crying all over you."

He grasped her head with two strong hands and drew her up to face him. "No apologies."

Old Spice engulfed her, his compassionate eyes alluring. She wanted to touch every endearing whisker and laugh line. His lips twitched, enticing. Was he going to kiss her?

Instead, he slipped her hand into both of his, then pulled

back as if doing the honorable thing to not take advantage of the moment. "I must go, Leslie. Will you be okay?"

No, she wanted to yell. She sniffled, offering a meager smile. "I'll manage."

"I'm only a text away."

Don't leave me! "Time to watch your show? I told you I'd stream it."

"I've no more appetite for *The Odd Couple* tonight." He stood.

She rose too. "Thank you for coming in." She walked him to the door. "If your publisher and the committee both say yes to a two-week extension, will you please text me immediately? I'll bring food over Tuesday evening. You'll be so immersed in your project, I'm afraid you won't eat dinner otherwise."

He grinned. "I'll look forward to that, as long as it's not liver and onions."

CHAPTER FORTY-FOUR

They can't say no. They just can't.

Those words became Leslie's mantra all day Sunday, morphing into a prayer. She hated to think about the consequences of the publisher refusing to accommodate new material or the university committee rejecting delays and refusing full professorship. Greg probably wouldn't give her the play-by-play, since new developments hinged on information she'd refused him earlier—details he might be disinclined to tell the committee, to protect her privacy.

What would Dr. Douglas Stafford think about Greg's hero being exposed as a fraud? Especially since he already took such a dim view of literary pursuits. He'd chalk it up to sloppy scholarship.

Greg was dealing with his career and a fallen hero. A literary fraud. Linus Fritz Buckwalter, an author Greg admired, lied to his face when interviewed.

The Buckwalter Brothers will rise again, Eddie once predicted. Though the store came forth from the ashes and flourished for decades, Fritz and Eddie never rose together from childhood dreams, broken dreams, refashioned dreams. Would Greg rise from this mess?

* * *

All day Monday, Leslie's nerves sizzled, anticipating news from Greg about the publisher's and committee's decisions. Unable to concentrate, she scrolled through Instagram, then checked online for Jason's abominable article. Still gone. Fortunately, it had vanished three weeks ago.

Leslie gazed out the window. What if Jason was a Buckwalter relative? He'd wanted to be acknowledged in Greg's book as Fritz's great-nephew. But would he still want the family connection after learning about Fritz's fraud? Though he'd never mentioned money, once he heard of Eddie's literary prowess, would he seek royalties after Oma's demise?

She sent Jason a text:

> Please get a DNA test to substantiate your claims.

She pored over grant proposals. Finally, at five, a text came from Greg:

> Publisher said 2 weeks is OK. Informed committee. Meeting still at 8 am tomorrow.

She texted back:

> Great! Praying all goes well. Keep me posted.

Tuesday morning at nine-thirty, he texted:

> Got a 2-week extension. No pickleball or any fun in my future.

She wrote back:

> Wonderful! Good, tasty food will compensate
> for no fun. Bringing Chinese at 6 pm. Don't
> waste time dusting or sweeping. Pristine is
> overrated, after all. Your address?

*　*　*

Leslie walked into Greg's condo, a stiff, formal space designed with rectangles and straight lines in every direction, in creams, beiges, and browns. She was tempted to draw flowers on the walls to offset the rigidity. And paint them plum, yellow, and periwinkle blue to compensate for drab. He had impeccable taste, nothing shabby—unlike her apartment, chock full of Goodwill and garage sale specials—but also lacking fluidity. No random piles like his office desk. A knick-knack would have felt ostracized. His furniture would pass the white glove test.

Pristine is overrated, he'd said. No kidding! This lonely place needed help. He was the Felix to her Oscar.

One framed picture over the mantel stood out. An original painting of a farmhouse, field, and barn.

"It's the Buckwalter farm," Greg said.

She set food bags on the table. The picture lured her like a magnet, squeezing out everything in her peripheral vision. Up close, the richness of the brushwork's textures and complex color combinations came to light, along with the rooster weathervane atop the barn. "Where'd you get this?"

"From a local artist in Dillard about five years ago. He improvised the rooster."

"It's exquisite."

He came alongside her. "And holds great meaning."

After a silent moment passed, they went to the table, his laptop and papers shoved to one end. A luxurious burning pine candle blended perfectly with his cologne. Too bad he had a manuscript to write, especially with more pleasurable options. Mainly involving candlelight and the couch.

Stop! Why had her mind gone there? Her face warmed at Saturday night's memory—his face hovering, tempting a kiss. All the better he had pressing deadlines.

"I figured out my two-week plan and daily goals to complete the integration of new material. After completely changing my thesis statement."

She doled out chicken subgum and beef vegetable stir-fry. "I hope it doesn't involve all-nighters."

"Ha! Those days are long gone." He grunted. "I want to show you what I wrote to Grable Press and the committee. So as to be above board, respecting your privacy."

"I trust you, Greg."

"We've come a long way, haven't we?" He chuckled and opened each email in turn.

She read them. "About as vague as oatmeal, but it did the job if everyone agreed to the postponement."

"Matt at the press is intrigued by new material I dangled like a carrot, but he can't promise timely publication if revision takes longer than two weeks. The book must go through multiple edits again. Plus, I dodged the committee's plethora of questions in favor of ambiguity."

Chicken subgum slipped from her chopsticks. "I should have told you things sooner."

"I understand why you didn't. I was a toad."

She smiled. "You have such a way with words. I couldn't have said it better myself."

He harrumphed.

"Reminding me of your eloquence four years ago when I asked you for an interview."

He balked. "What interview?"

"I was Leslie Rinaldi then, my married name. I wanted to interview you about your Buckwalter research for *Inspired*, a women's magazine."

"Ahh, Leslie Rinaldi." He took a bite and chewed as if pressing his memory, then poked at his rice. "What did I say?" He cringed.

"You said, and I quote, 'Why would I interview for a magazine as inconsequential as a dog scratching fleas?'"

He blinked twice, reddening. "Not my best simile."

Mouth agape, Leslie straightened. "You—"

"Just teasing." He held up a hand. "I'm sorry. I was off base completely. Preferring my publications in scholarly journals doesn't excuse my arrogance."

Leslie's heart fluttered, softened by his humility. "You're not the same person I met three months ago, Professor. What changed?"

"Meeting you." He cleared his throat. "You might recall we're on a first-name basis."

She laughed. But what did he mean by *meeting you*?

Apparently, he was quite ready to change the subject. "After church yesterday, I spent the entire day reading the diary."

"Really? I could never read it that fast."

"Of course not. It's your family, your roots. With much at stake and much heaviness."

"There's plenty at stake for you too."

"But I already knew the ending. For you, it was a process of discovery." He finagled more beef onto his chopsticks. "Incidentally, remember Renee Piquette?"

Leslie inadvertently dropped an egg roll on her plate. "Um, yeah."

"She's working on that Buckwalter novel. I should share the new information with her, too, before my biography is published. The changes will impact her story as well."

Leslie's face heated as she twirled her chopstick in the mush on her plate. "She'll definitely need to know. Historical fiction, right?" *Stop it!* Playing dumb would only make things worse. But if privy to her deception, Greg might never trust her again.

"The novel's set in Dillard," he said. "Though some townsfolk are fictional, she wants to be true to Fritz's personal life. That's all I can say without breaching confidence. How do you feel about a stranger writing historical fiction about your great-uncle?"

She shrugged. "Fritz Buckwalter is part of literary culture and in public domain."

"Don't you feel protective of it?"

"Yes, but I can't change anything."

"Renee asks a lot of questions, well beyond the twenty we agreed on. Perhaps she's taking advantage of me."

"Be happy she goes directly to the expert."

He chuckled. "You women sure stick together. I'll tell her my good friend Leslie advocated for her. You ladies always talk in circles around us men, but you understand each other." His eye held a merry glint which would surely disappear the minute she admitted to being Renee. Worse, he'd say deception ran in the family, starting with Fritz.

He cocked his head. "You two could be good friends if you ever met. In fact, I'll arrange it. Then you can share whatever you feel comfortable sharing."

A flush of shame overtook. Nerves prickled. But she must hold his gaze as spoke the truth. "I ... already know her."

His brows raised. "Really? Through that wicked platform of social media? Are you two conspiring against me?" He winked.

She tensed. This wasn't just breaking the merry mood, but his trust. Muddying their friendship. If they had one after this. The room heated.

He babbled on. "We could all meet for coffee at Kipp's—"

"Stop! You're tormenting me." Her hands flew to her cheeks, flaming hot.

"Okay, forget Kipp's. How about Biscotti's?"

"No, just stop. I—"

"All right then, cross off Biscotti's. Ribollita's has a lunch buffet—"

"Stop talking, Greg. This is torture."

"My voice, word choice, or restaurant selection? How about Zorito—"

Her fist pounded the table. "No! *I'm* Renee!" And there it was. She braced herself, then wilted in the chair.

His mouth dropped open, brows shot up. But no words ensued.

"Just say it and get it over with," she snapped, then slithered into the kitchen. "I'm so sorry." She plopped dishes into the sink and ran the water full force.

A strong presence emanating Old Spice overwhelmed her.

He turned off the faucet. His husky chuckle reverberated through her body as his scent filled her. He shifted her shoulders toward him. She trembled at his tender touch. Why wasn't he berating her? But his voice was kind. A sparkle tipped his eye. "I knew it was you."

"What? When? How?"

"Since three weeks ago. Renee knew something she couldn't have known. I had a gut feeling."

So, he knew before she told him about the diary. Yet he still rescued the information from Vic. He still went with her to Oma's. "Why didn't you say anything?"

"I almost did." He smiled. "But it was more fun watching you flounder at the suggestion of us all having coffee together."

She pulled away, but his grasp on her shoulders tightened. His voice soothed. "I really wanted you to come clean on your own."

"I'm so sorry. Why aren't you yelling at me right now?"

"Because I understand. You didn't think you'd get my help otherwise. I was a bully."

"Yes, you were petulant. Persnickety. With every little thing."

"Unfortunately. How can I scold you for posing as Renee when you're ghostwriting for me? And I've not felt one iota of guilt about it."

"It's not the same."

"Close enough. I'm afraid to ask, but what incident prompted Renee to write me?"

"The day I misquoted you in your office."

"Again, I was a toad. Hopefully I've grown up since then." He grinned.

She laughed. "But I still can't justify my ongoing deception."

"Let's call it even steven. I hope I'm more approachable now." He threaded fingers through her hair. His face was mere inches away, his citrusy smell intoxicating, his eyes like pools to swim away in. He closed the gap between them. Her heart nearly flew out of her rib cage.

He kissed her, short and sweet. When she lifted her chin for more, he deepened the kiss, sending tendrils through every limb, inviting, longing, wishing. How was this happening?

He pressed her close, chin and whiskers nuzzling her cheek. "I believe I've just complicated our friendship."

"It's a complication I welcome." Or was she foolishly lured

into the moment's revelry? Tomorrow, would she regret this? She only wanted kisses with commitment.

He cupped her chin. "Do you really welcome it?"

She replied with another kiss that multiplied.

He murmured into her hair. "I couldn't resist you anymore."

"How long were you resisting?"

He put a hand to his heart and quoted, "'I cannot fix on the hour, or the spot, or the look, or the words, which laid the foundation. It is too long ago. I was in the middle before I knew that I had begun.'"

"You're quoting Mr. Darcy to me?"

"I hope it meets your approval."

She smiled. "Now be more specific."

"Since the day you first quoted Mr. Wimpy."

She giggled. "Seriously?"

"Absolutely. I knew then I'd met my match. You pulled me off my high horse, but with finesse, grace, and Mr. Wimpy lines."

"Is that why you asked me to play pickleball as your number fourteen?"

His husky chortle made her want to kiss him again. "I was jealous of your attentions to Jason, and I wanted to ask you out myself. But there were two problems."

Jealous of Jason? "What problems?"

"I didn't want to complicate things at work, and I didn't want to be rejected. So, I acted desperate for a pickleball partner."

"I wasn't really number fourteen?"

"No, you were. I wouldn't lie. But I acted like it didn't matter who filled the spot."

She offered a wry smile. "*Now* who's Mr. Wimpy?"

"Touché." He sighed. "I'm afraid I overstepped. I'm sorry."

Was he reneging? She shouldn't have fallen for this, not when feeling so vulnerable. Not when Greg had so much at stake. "Why? Do you want me to leave?"

"No, but I jumped the gun. I had no intention of kissing you tonight. It feels like I'm taking advantage of you."

She stiffened. "Taking advantage of me assumes you acted without sincerity."

"I assure you that's not true. You've *never* had a more sincere kiss."

She narrowed her eyes. "How can you know that?"

"Because I know my own heart, now that I've admitted the truth. I deeply care for you, Leslie Wickersham. But I should've given you more time before jumping in."

"Perhaps you should let me be the judge of that." To avoid his gaze, she eyed a cabinet doorknob. Were they to return to their previous awkwardness? She blinked away tears.

He gently grasped her arms. "Please forgive me."

She looked up, relishing his closeness. "Are you backtracking because you're afraid I'm not clear-headed? That I only responded to your advances because I'm vulnerable?"

His mouth formed a grim line. *Bull's-eye.*

"I'll get back to you on that." She left.

CHAPTER FORTY-FIVE

L eslie was glad to be busy with meetings and grant proposals, because every spare minute engendered worry over the publisher's and committee's reactions to Greg's manuscript changes. She also daydreamed about his kisses, wanting more of them. More of *him*.

Her longings morphed into fretting over his apology. Why'd he regret kissing her? Was it merely an indiscretion? Did he have no intention of furthering their relationship?

Would they even be allowed to have one, working at the university?

She'd started loving him weeks ago. Despite moodiness, he was a man of substance and integrity. Protective, a man of his word. The kind she yearned for. But her guard went up.

Nightly, she brought takeout for supper. He insisted on paying. She relished their thirty-minute supper break, filled with updates, random news, and comic relief.

He regularly asked her to stay longer to read chapters and offer feedback, dubbing her his sensitivity reader. His writing was as smooth, deft, and as thought-provoking as his lectures.

After two weeks, on Sunday evening, Leslie brought sandwich wraps and chowder. Monitoring his Instagram account while he focused on manuscript revisions, she mentioned several responses to a post.

Greg's arm shot up. "May this social media anomaly be forever known as the Year of the Dying Quail."

She drew back. "What?"

He chortled. "Baseball slang for a fly ball that descends too quickly for the outfielder to catch it, resulting in a single. A blooper. Or call it the Year of the Golden Sombrero."

"What's *that*?"

"A fictitious trophy awarded to batters who strike out four times in one game."

She laughed. "Either one fits *your* purposes."

After eating, he read aloud the final chapter from his laptop. As usual, he'd emailed it to her so she could read along, offer commentary, and make corrections.

"The end." He closed his laptop, leaned back, and crossed his arms. "I'm only submitting this tomorrow if you're still on board one hundred percent."

"You're okay with not including the family tree?" One of his many concessions.

"Yes."

She hesitated. "It'll be noticeably absent."

"The bombshell news might detract from that."

"Right. Um, I'm ..."

He quirked an eyebrow. "What's wrong? Did I not portray your grandfather in a fair, empathetic way?"

"Yes, but ..." She doodled on scrap paper. "I wish we could vindicate Edmund without revealing all his weaknesses."

"'Half the Truth is often a great Lie.' Benjamin Franklin." He leaned forward, quoting from *The Scarlet Letter*. "'To the untrue man, the whole universe is false—it is impalpable—it shrinks to nothing within his grasp. And he himself, in so far as he shows himself in a false light, becomes a shadow, or, indeed, ceases to exist.'"

"My grandfather did become a shadow, a fragment of himself. Not from living a lie, though. It was his illness."

"Exactly. Nobody but Klara and Fritz saw the real Edmund, a good man at the core. They all lived in shadows as things deteriorated, growing more shameful. Tell me, Leslie, what parts are objectionable to you?"

She scrolled through several pages. "The hallucinations, the affair, the fire, the mental hospital. Your beautiful prose brings to life all the stark, torturous reality."

He took her hand. "I see why you'd want to keep your connection to Edmund under wraps, and keep his buffoonery hidden, but there's no vindication without public knowledge of his suffering. There'll be no empathy for Fritz apart from the context of his generosity and patience with Eddie, everything he did for him and your grandmother."

Sighing, she nodded.

"I want to show the whole person. Both Fritz and Eddie. Nobody's merely good or merely bad. Eddie was so much more than his mental illness. Alongside his outbursts were his exuberance and brilliant storytelling. His love for his wife and daughters. And Fritz is more than a liar and thief. He put himself on the line for Eddie, over and over. By sharing this now, you can shine a light on it all."

"That's what *you're* doing." She twiddled with a napkin. "In fact, I was thinking—"

"Always an adventure for you." He winked. "With the rest of us at your mercy."

She withdrew her hand. "What about this? You could share sections of your book at the writers' workshop. Assuming we get the grant. Since students will be interviewing senior citizens about mental health issues, this biography would be a great springboard for discussion about what happens when people aren't diagnosed or receive proper treatment. How people could've responded in more helpful ways so Oma wouldn't have felt so isolated. These folks would be close to Eddie's age now, if he'd lived. In fact, each participant should receive a copy. It could be included in the miscellaneous costs we allowed for the grant."

"Chalk up another grand idea to Leslie." Greg mimicked writing on a chalkboard. "But consider this. In the spirit of open dialogue about mental health—so near and dear to your heart—what if *you* speak on the topic as a Buckwalter heir. Share how Eddie's illness impacted your family. How you're fighting to overcome stigma yourself."

Leslie froze. "But I still don't want to be identified with the Buckwalter family."

"I *know* what you said." He let her chew on the notion.

She stared at the table, avoiding his burrowing eye. Not accusing but challenging her to live by her creed. "I deal with it through my historical fiction."

"Admirable. But incomplete. Think of how you could open dialogue by speaking to audiences. Particularly as you attend book signings, promoting your novel."

"Whoa. That's a long way off. Besides, *you're* the Buckwalter expert."

"But you're family. And you've a passion for people to embrace mental health dialogue."

"That's why I pushed for the writers' workshop."

"Splendid. But promise you'll consider what I've said. You have the gumption for it."

"Thanks for your confidence in me."

"It's not confidence you lack. It's a matter of choosing transparency over the comfort of privacy. But it's your call."

Leslie twirled a pen in her hand. "I'm also concerned about how Fritz's family will respond to the book once it releases. I can't imagine their shock."

"How would you feel about accompanying me to tell them? Face to face. No pressure. I'll be the bearer of bad news alone, if need be. But it's only fair they know before it goes public."

Another reason to admire him. "I'll go with you. Next week."

* * *

The next few days sparked a whirlwind. Leslie barely saw Greg except in passing. Communication reduced to brief texts. On Monday, he submitted his revised manuscript, asking Matt to expedite the process. He needed an answer before reporting to the committee Thursday afternoon.

On Tuesday, he texted:

> How about dinner Thursday after my meeting?

She replied:

> How about a party? I'll plan it.

Greg:

> No. I might be sulking instead of celebrating.
> ☺

Well, that was a first. A smiley face? She didn't know whether to be more shocked by him using emojis or his pessimism regarding full professorship. His potential new role rested on publication. Unable to predict the publisher's response, there was no way to gauge.

But why'd he choose to spend that all-important evening

with *her?* Maybe because she alone knew the stakes. He hadn't shared details of his delays with colleagues, for her sake, to keep her Buckwalter heritage undercover. Except for her, he was alone in his turmoil.

She texted back.

> If you're sulking, I'll pay for dinner as part of my condolences. If we're celebrating, you pay.

His response:

> Deal.

But she had more in mind than that.
One more text arrived:

> Don't think I'm ghosting you if I don't reply the next few days. Tight schedule and all. See you Thursday, 6:30 at Winslow's.

It was just as well. Her schedule got more hectic too. Just that minute, in fact. Self-induced. She started making phone calls.

CHAPTER FORTY-SIX

Thursday evening, Leslie sat in Winslow's corner booth overlooking Pine River. Evening sun spilled through the windowpanes, a fitting close to a beautiful March day—hopefully reflecting Greg's day. Assuming his manuscript had been accepted with its new findings, and that he was welcomed as full professor.

Would dinner be an occasion for joy or sorrow? She had people waiting in the wings.

Greg appeared. She waved him over, trying to discern news from his face or gait. No clue. Was he putting on a brave front or containing his excitement?

She stood as he approached, determined to take her cues from him.

He draped his jacket and scarf over the chair and took her hands. His face lit. "Yes!"

"Oh, Greg, that's wonderful!" She threw her arms around him as his hands slid around her waist. She planted a kiss on his cheek, then pulled back. "Excuse my exuberance." She scanned the restaurant for familiar faces. None, fortunately.

He laughed. "I didn't mind." They sat.

"So, you hit it out of the ballpark?"

"A grand slam." He grinned. "You're the first to know. Everyone else left the office."

"Should I ask the waitress to play 'Jump'? Or 'Celebration'?" She fumbled in her purse for her phone. "I need a tissue." She covertly texted:

HOME RUN

She pulled out a tissue and wiped a tear. "Tell me all about it."

Greg slugged some water. "First of all—"

"Hold on. Sandy!" Leslie flagged the waitress. Greg's brows raised at the intrusion. "Do you have cakes for special occasions?"

Greg put up a hand. "No need." Sharing his good fortune with the waitress apparently wasn't his plan.

Sandy's face expanded as if fully expecting the interlude. "I'll bring dessert menus, but first, I'm sorry I have to move you to another table."

Greg frowned. "You don't take reservations."

"Not usually." Sandy's cheer was contagious. "I'll be right back. Wait here." She left.

Greg shook his head. "What's going on?"

"Yeah, strange, but I'm guessing nothing can dampen your mood tonight." She fired questions about the committee meeting until Sandy reappeared. Leslie and Greg grabbed their coats and trailed her, meandering around diners into the Petunia Room.

"Surprise!" Eight English department colleagues stood near a candlelit table.

Leslie watched Greg's face, hoping he'd be pleased by the

396

little gathering she'd arranged. They'd been on standby, waiting for either *home run* or *strikeout*.

Greg's face brightened. He lifted two thumbs up as they clapped. Each offered hugs and congratulations.

Leslie stood aside, delighted by his happiness. He surely needed his colleagues here, after all he'd gone through.

"Greg, you're at the head of the table." Dr. Lucas gestured to a chair next to him. When Rob Louden pulled out the chair on Greg's right, Greg said, "That seat's taken." He waved Leslie over. Stunned, she sat beside him. Wouldn't the professors think it odd he chose her to sit at his side rather than a long-standing colleague?

Chatter and laughter ensued as a waitress took orders. Another server poured peach lemonade—out of season but requested by Leslie as Edmund Buckwalter's favorite sweet beverage.

Rob Louden offered a toast. "To Greg, rich in scholarship and wit, lifelong learner of all things new, including Instagram, a stickler for Socratic method and anti-formulaic essays." Glasses clinked along with Sheila MacIntyre's earrings. "Let's have it, Greg. Give us the play-by-play."

"What was the holdup these past two weeks?" Norma Tomquist asked in her Southern drawl. "You've been as busy as a cat on a hot tin roof."

"It's a long, woeful story," Greg said. "Way too long for a three-course meal."

"Let's add courses." Sheila MacIntyre lifted a full glass.

As the professors echoed Sheila and continued chatting, Leslie leaned his way, lowering her voice. "Tell them whatever you want. Don't hold back on my account."

Greg eyed her directly. "No."

She kept her voice low. "What do you mean? This is your night, your spotlight."

"Then let me have it my way." His voice dropped, too, as he moved closer, his breath tickling her ear. "I'm saying *no* to sharing your family connection. That's your story to tell, when you're ready. But with your permission, I'll share about Fritz and Edmund."

She nodded and sipped lemonade.

Greg faced the others. "Part of the holdup was some last-minute digging only to discover Fritz Buckwalter was a fraud."

Gasps rippled down the table to choruses of "You've got to be kidding" "What on earth?" "No way."

"I kid you not. I had to let Matt at Grable Press know about Fritz's fall from grace, because that changes the whole course of my book. Fortunately, he still wants to publish it. As the first to have the scoop, of course."

"Where'd you find this new intel?" Rob Louden asked.

"That's the long-story part of the equation. Better saved for another time. Since I had to revamp my manuscript, and Matt needed time to reconsider the change in course, I postponed my committee meeting until today. It all hinged on Matt's agreement to publish. Which I heard about right before my meeting."

"Whew," Norma said. "All this time, I thought you were living in high cotton. Instead, the creek was rising." Leslie smiled at her Southern idioms.

"How is Fritz Buckwalter a fraud?" Rob asked.

Fingering his glass, Greg offered a summary of Edmund's schizophrenia and the fallout, Fritz's overtures to help him, Edmund's death, and the stolen manuscripts launching Fritz's career as compensation for his losses. "The dedication is an ironic tribute to his brother."

Leslie appreciated hearing his faithful rendition of events intoned with respect for the Buckwalter family as if they were his own.

Voices chimed in with questions as if it were a press conference. Greg fielded each one with wit and charm, preserving details for Leslie's privacy. "Edmund left behind two young daughters and a wife, Klara."

"The one who managed to evade you," Rob said.

"Exactly."

"This tips the Richter scale like nothing you've ever done before," Norma said. "I sensed that seismograph moving all month long with your postponed meetings."

"But where'd all this new information come from?" Rob asked. "Did you finally wear Klara Buckwalter down?"

"I can't yet reveal my sources, but primary documents recently surfaced. I met her, but without any formal interview. Believe me, nobody could ever wear down Klara Buckwalter."

* * *

After dessert and discourse, the group dispersed. As Leslie slipped into her coat, its weight mysteriously lightened. She turned around.

Greg held it as she shrugged it on. "How about a riverwalk before heading home?"

"I'd love that." Weariness dissipated as her heart quickened.

He guided her to the river boardwalk, hand on the small of her back. "Have you given thought to speaking at the workshop about your Buckwalter connection?"

She bit her lip. "I'm leaning toward yes. I need to live by my own creed of transparency with mental health issues."

"Good." He relayed more details of Matt's acceptance call, a mixture of condolences for the fraud—the fall of a hero—with jubilation for being the first publication to relay the truth. Greg cited details of the grueling three-hour committee meeting.

After several minutes, he took her hand, his warmth enveloping her. "The dinner party tonight was a fine, fine thing, Leslie. Thank you for that. But truth be told, I would've been content, actually quite happy, spending the evening with only you."

Honestly? Words she'd never dreamed of hearing except in her imagination, considering their rocky start. If he kept watching her face that closely, he was going to stumble into the river for lack of checking his course. "Me too. But I'm glad you had colleagues to celebrate with."

"What would have happened with the party if I hadn't made full professor?"

"They would have stayed. I told them to bring tissues, just in case. I had a surprise myself. I thought you'd want to sit by Dr. Louden."

"I have plenty of opportunities to sit with him." He stopped near the railing. They stood side by side, overlooking the river. The moon lit his face. "You're the one I want by my side, Leslie."

Her heart skipped a beat. "Meaning?"

He faced her, his eyes flickering with affection. "If I have my own way, people will have to get used to seeing us together."

In this surreal moment, his earnest, authentic expression directed at her flooded her heart. His academic demeanor shed, reflecting the man she'd come to know the past few weeks.

"I want to earn your trust, Leslie. I'm not a Vic or a Jason—may curses rain on their hideous heads. I'll be here for you, no matter what." He squeezed her hand—could he feel her throbbing pulse? "Not because you're a Buckwalter either."

Tilting her head, Leslie turned demure, yet hopeful. "Then *despite* my being a Buckwalter?"

"No. You being a Buckwalter has nothing to do with it."

His husky voice hinted at both feigned annoyance and mirth. "Oh, blast it all, you're going to force me to say it, aren't you?" He turned her toward him, his mesmerizing eyes riveted to hers, his rugged face handsome, whiskers endearing. The sweep of his bangs dipped over his forehead, scarf flying behind him. "If I may be so bold as to call upon Keats. "I love you the more in that I believe you have liked me for my own sake and for nothing else.'"

She gulped. "Oh, Greg ..." She squeezed his hands. "That reminds me of my oma's words."

"Of being an emotional meteorologist?"

The journal memory, along with the rusty rooster weathervane, brought a lump to her throat. "No, when she told my opa, 'Love isn't bound up in the things you can do, whether or not you can fulfill your purpose. Love is about knowing you, all that you were, are, and will be, and still wanting you.'"

"And I want *you*." His gaze arrested her, his citrusy musk captivating her.

She lifted her chin. "It was lovely to hear from Keats, but what would Gregory Scott Stafford say in his own words?"

"I want to pay for your steak dinners and tacos. I want you for my number one pickleball partner, not number fourteen. I want you to cancel my Instagram account, and I want to change Monday morning orders from caramel macchiatos to mocha lattes. Oh—and I must report any potential change of status to H.R. It's protocol."

Her eyes widened. "Maybe I'd rather hear more Keats."

He laughed. "I can do better. I hope I don't appear too forward, but the older I get, the less I like to waste time." He cleared his throat dramatically. "You are the bravest, most compassionate woman I know. I want to share your joys and sorrows, protecting you the best I can. Will you give a reformed heckler a chance and say yes to our first official date together next Friday evening?"

Her heart thrilled, but when she opened her mouth, no words came.

He eased into a smile and smoothed her windblown hair. "I daresay I know what Mr. Darcy would say about that."

Leslie found her voice. "I care more about what Elizabeth Bennet would say."

"And what's that?"

"Yes. Pure and simple. Just yes. With all my heart, I will join you for dinner."

Author's Note

Dear Reader,

Thank you for choosing to read *The Broken Weathervane*. I am honored.

This novel grew from a desire to show the impact of mental illness on families, with hopes that more awareness and understanding will spark both empathy and dialog. If this story touched your heart in some way, it has served its purpose. Let me know. I love to hear from readers.

If you or anyone you know struggles with mental illness of any kind, please reach out for help. There are hundreds of viable therapy options in person and online.

Start here:

- top10.com/online-therapy/exact-comparison

This includes BetterHelp (considered one of the best), FaithfulCounseling (geared to Christians), and Calmerry (subscription-based for those without mental health insurance).

Search by location, specialty, and insurance for someone in your area:

- psychologytoday.com/us/therapists/
- goodtherapy.org
- mentalhealthmatch.com

Please check the acknowledgements for other valuable resources on mental health.

I'd be thrilled to visit your book group as a guest author, either in person or via Zoom. Please contact me through my website: lauradenooyer-author.com.

For updates, freebies, giveaways, book recommendations, and a free prequel, join my monthly newsletter StandoutStoriesNewsletter.com.

Warmly,
Laura DeNooyer

P.S. If you enjoyed this story, would you consider leaving a review on Amazon, BookBub, GoodReads, and Barnes & Noble? Thank you so much!

Discussion Questions

1. How did you identify with Leslie, if at all? (Consider her previous teaching career, her mental health struggles and the mental health literature curriculum she implemented, her new job as grants officer, her writers workshop idea, her desire for more family information, her intimidation by ex-husband Vic, and her precarious relationship with Greg.)

2. Do you agree with Leslie's choice to hide her connection to the Buckwalters and/or put up with the blackmail?

3. In what ways did Greg mature throughout the story? Did Leslie's growing attraction to him make sense? Did he prove himself worthy? If so, how?

4. Even with Fritz's support, Klara felt alone in her silence about Eddie's problems and her fear of the townsfolk not understanding. How did you identify with Klara, if at all? What do you wish she would

have done differently in handling the difficult situations with Eddie?

5. Do you agree with how Klara and Fritz helped Eddie? Did they over- or under-compensate for Eddie's failures?

6. Were you surprised to find out about Fritz's betrayal of Eddie at the end? Why or why not?

7. Why do you think Klara kept Fritz's secret all these years?

8. How does the weathervane function as a symbol for the story? Who does it best represent?

9. Mental health issues breed shame when hidden or ignored. Yet transparency, understanding, and open dialogue can defeat shame and invite empathy. How can we encourage more dialogue on mental health?

Acknowledgments and Resources

I don't know what I'd do without my critique partner who painstakingly went through each chapter with me, week by week, for over a year, offering advice and solutions. Laura Dritlein, you're the best! Additionally, Mark Stay, Darla Phillips, and Brooke Cutler gave feedback on early chapters.

Thank you to Dr. Mike Williams (professor of political science and international relations), Dr. Kevin McMahon, and Dr. Charlene McMahon (both chemistry professors) for answering my questions about tenure and/or obtaining grants at the university. Any errors in the story are mine alone.

I'm deeply indebted to my nine beta readers who gave me great feedback for improving the story. Four of these are college professors who were willing to share their knowledge of the college setting, protocols, and faculty/staff dynamics: Dr. Ellyn Lem (English professor), Dr. Nelia Beth Scovill (religious studies), Dr. Charlene McMahon (chemistry professor), and Dr. Erin Taylor (chemistry professor). Other wonderful readers were Mark Stay, Harriet Schlassberger, Jan Hall Glas, Anita Klumpers, and Elizabeth Daghfal. I'm so grateful for all of you with your unique perspectives and an eye for what matters.

Above all, thank you to my husband, Tim, for putting up with me and the writing life! I'm pretty sure he never anticipated that part of the bargain.

The website BPHope.com is a valuable resource on bipolar disorder. I highly recommend this site to anybody who has bipolar disorder or has any family members or friends with this diagnosis.

The National Suicide & Crisis Lifeline is in English and Spanish, 24 hours a day: 9-8-8. For free and confidential support, visit 988lifeline.org.

Helpful websites about schizophrenia symptoms and treatments now and in the 1950s included:

- National Alliance on Mental Illness (NAMI.org)
- WebMD.com
- PsychCentral.com
- PubMedCentral (pmc.ncbi.nlm.nih.gov)
- AMA Journal of Ethics—Illuminating the Art of Medicine (JournalOfEthics.ama-assn.org)
- BioMedCentral Psychiatry (http://bmcpsychiatry. biomedcentral.com/)
- National Institute of Mental Health/National Institute of Health (nimh.nih.gov)
- National Library of Medicine (nlm.nih.gov)

I learned a few things about food and grocery stores in the 1950s from:

- ChainStoreGuide.com
- kenosha.com ("Grocery Stores Galore: The History of Food Shopping in Kenosha"—a SE Wisconsin town)
- ProgressiveGrocer.com
- FoodReference.com.

ABOUT THE AUTHOR

Laura DeNooyer thrives on creativity and encouraging it in others. A Calvin College graduate, she is a teacher, wife, parent of four adult children, and a multi-award-winning author of heart-warming historical and contemporary fiction. She's an active member in her church and American Christian Fiction Writers. When not writing, you'll find her reading, walking, drinking tea with friends, or taking a road trip. For updates, freebies, giveaways, and a free prequel, join Laura's monthly newsletter StandoutStoriesNewsletter.com. Learn more at lauradenooyer-author.com.

A Hundred Magical Reasons

Most fairy tales have happy endings, but is it too late for this one? After all, Mrs. Charlotte Rose Gordon, the disgruntled town recluse, is eighty-eight and has grown weary of fighting the dragons of her past—including the desire to clear her husband's name of a 1918 crime.

Dragons of a different kind pursue Carrie Kruisselbrink. During 1980, the summer of her private rebellion, Carrie defies parental expectations and pursues her café dream. While waiting for funding, she takes a job with Mrs. Gordon.

As Mrs. Gordon unfolds the story of her oppressive childhood and delightful friendship with *The Wonderful Wizard of Oz* author, L. Frank Baum, Carrie never expects to encounter her own fears and soul-searching.

In this modern-day fairy tale that weaves between 1980 and the early

1900s, Mr. Baum's influence impacts each woman's personal quests on a hero's journey neither anticipates. Can Carrie and Mrs. Gordon find common ground in battling their respective dragons?

A Hundred Magical Reasons awards:

- First Place in the StoryTrade Book Awards for Regional fiction: USA Midwest (August 2025)
- Hawthorne Prize Winner for Fiction (American Writing Awards, May 2025)
- First Place in The BookFest for Literary Historical Fiction (April 2025)
- First Place in the Firebird Book Awards for Biographical Fiction (April 2025)
- Bronze Medal for the Illumination Book Awards for General Fiction (February 2025)

Get your copy here:

https://scrivenings.link/ahundredmagicalreasons

Stay up-to-date on your favorite books and authors with our free e-newsletters.

ScriveningsPress.com

Excerpt from A Hundred Magical Reasons
Chapter One

Once upon a time, there lived a girl who didn't know she was a princess, or that three dragons pursued her ...

May 28, 1980

Two weeks after college graduation with no diploma to show for it, Carrie Kruisselbrink stormed from her house like a prairie gale. Mom handed her an overnight bag, but Carrie left with an overstuffed suitcase. She wasn't going back.

The storm started brewing in childhood, but this morning the temperature spiked as she emptied the dishwasher, her mother barking orders. As if Carrie hadn't been responsible while away four years at college.

Mom chose that moment to pounce. She thrust a paper under Carrie's chin. Skimming the list of elementary teacher positions, Carrie resisted the urge to rip it up and cast it to the wind. She had her own career goals.

413

She trudged upstairs to her bedroom and found respite among her overflowing bookshelves. But not for long. The room shrank, the headboard rattled as Mother barged in. Gusting at ninety miles per hour, she tidied Carrie's desk. "Most teachers have contracts already." In the updraft, Mother rearranged pens. "When will you mail more résumés?"

Never. Carrie winced, thoughts spiraling. "Later." Though she'd walked at graduation, she had no diploma, no teaching certificate, and no intention of retaking Philosophy of Education. She fanned her face and opened the window. Three thousand square feet in this house, yet claustrophobia suffocated like pre-storm humidity.

Her mother slammed the window shut. "Your sister had three teaching offers by graduation. What's your plan?"

Swinging open the closet door, Carrie inhaled. Plan B, in effect: *Take charge of my life. Now.* "I'm going to Oma and Opa's." Two hours northwest on Lake Michigan should be far enough away. She'd planned to visit her grandparents anyhow. Why not the whole summer?

"Fine." Mother left and returned with an overnight bag. "Don't forget résumés, envelopes, and postage."

Carrie plopped her suitcase on the bed. She tossed in sundresses and sandals. Home decorator magazines. Colored pencils, sketch pads. Books from Children's Lit class: *Mary Poppins, A Wrinkle in Time,* Chronicles of Narnia.

"Why the kids' books?"

"I like them." Angry retorts galloped through her like gathering winds, but she bit her lip. As usual. She tucked *The Princess and Curdie* in sideways. Too bad her entire classics book collection wouldn't fit.

"What about your date with Brian on Saturday?"

"I'll call him." According to her parents, dating Brian was her crowning achievement. They'd dated six years, now anticipating a summer packed with fancy restaurants and Brian's baseball games. Like Cinderella, she might finally get to the "palace ball." A wedding and a move to Wolcott.

Then, the deluge. "When're you going to do something worthwhile? For two weeks, you've moped around, cluttered my kitchen baking ..." Words whirled and lashed, twisting into a column of anger.

Carrie rummaged through the bookshelf. "Where's *The Tasha Tudor Book of Fairy Tales?*"

"In the garbage downstairs. It's falling apart."

Panic surged like a thunderclap in a squall. Carrie dashed down the steps and dug through trash. She retrieved the book— ripped binding, pages dangling, egg yolk dripping, coffee grounds stuck. In a torrent of tears, she wrapped it in a clean garbage bag and whisked upstairs to her bulging suitcase. Now topped with résumés.

Carrie scattered the papers and replaced them with bagged book remains.

Mother rolled her eyes. "Figures you'd value dilapidated fairy tales over anything practical." She stalked off.

Surely Mother would regret her words in August when Carrie revealed her intentions—one that included fairy tales. Meanwhile, she slipped a manila envelope with her covert business plan into the suitcase and called Rita at the café to say she'd miss work this summer.

* * *

Wolcott, Population 945, the sign announced.

A mile later, on the front porch, Carrie's ginger-haired Dutch oma greeted her with a breathless hug that infused life.

All sweat and axle grease, Opa stepped from the garage and

grinned, then noted the suitcase. "How long're you staying, Carrie Bell?"

Carrie plopped onto the porch swing. "I'll never measure up to their expectations."

Oma sat beside her. "They're just eager for you to follow the family footsteps into your first elementary classroom. We're proud of you, *liefje*."

Carrie grimaced and blew her nose. "Any job openings in Wolcott?"

"Burger Flipper's hiring," Opa said.

"Ed, that's ridiculous." Oma swatted the air. "Arlene would throw a fit."

Carrie sniffed. "Maybe that's *exactly* what I want." Even her grandparents didn't know her alternate career plans, though she'd spent spring break here scouting out the perfect location for her future book café—booths flanked by shelves of books, savored with pastries or tea. After six summers of restaurant work in Barrowdale and making a fifteen-page business plan with her mentor Rita, she was ready to obtain financing. Then she'd tell her parents. They'd watch her succeed following her own dream instead of theirs.

After lunch, Carrie called the bank's loan officer to make an appointment—the culmination of Phase One.

She walked McKinley Street, a stroll through yesteryear: Victorian homes with turrets, wraparound porches, gingerbread trim, and perfectly placed pansies as dainty as ruffles on a lady's dress. But the disastrous year of midnight studies and student teaching still trailed her. Critiques and comparisons. Rough, ineffective classroom management skills. Fighting nausea every time she entered the classroom. Carrie couldn't measure up. Just like at home.

Shaking off memories, she meandered through a park and circled back to a shady street. One dark green house with white shutters and plum-striped awnings sported a picket fence. An invitation rather than a boundary, the fence drew her to peek at the yard's secrets.

Four triangles of spring blooms surrounded a winding brick pathway. Similar colors clumped together. Lilac bushes hovered over purple pansies and early irises. Yellow daffodils and primroses cheered in unison. Rosebushes huddled with fading tulips. Blue splashed over violets and late hyacinths.

"I need help."

Carrie jumped at the unexpected sharp voice.

Wearing a large-brimmed hat and sunglasses, an old woman rocked in the porch's stark shadows. "Would you please water the sunflower seedlings along the fence?"

Curious, Carrie stepped through the gate. Was she arthritic? Or even lucid? "Such a lovely garden."

"I'd expect nothing less. The watering can's full."

Carrie picked up the can and spilled. "You weren't kidding."

"I never kid." She drew out *never* like pulling yarn from a skein, teasing Carrie's memory.

Wincing under the woman's stare, Carrie began watering. "Sunflowers are my favorite, the epitome of summer."

"'Ah, Sunflower, weary of time ...'" The woman recited eight lines of poetry.

Amazing! "William Blake," Carrie said.

"You know something that counts. Did Mr. Blake inspire your love of sunflowers?"

"No." Carrie squinted toward the sun. "No matter where the sun or how weak the light, the sunflower faces it."

"Mature sunflowers always face east," the woman snapped. "But in this poem, a girl rooted to the ground is scorned, doomed to face the sun, far from reach. No optimism here."

Carrie tensed. If she wanted criticism, she'd have stayed in

Barrowdale. "Maybe it's about being trapped on earth while yearning for the divine."

"Hardly. Preoccupation with the divine interferes with worthwhile aspirations."

What was this lady's problem? Anger at God? "Or it's a slighted lover."

"Or any unfulfilled desire. Surely you've heard William Blake was well acquainted with fairies living near his cottage. Muses for his poetry and art. Alas, logic and reason kills them." She quoted:

> "The good are attracted by men's perceptions,
> And think not for themselves;
> Til experience teaches them to catch
> And to cage fairies and elves."

"The end of imagination," Carrie murmured.

"Each flower whimpers when it's picked, he says. The loss hovers like a cloud of incense."

"I love that image."

"Do you now? Quite admirable. Especially considering my flowers' demise in 1969. Remember, Miss Caroline?"

Carrie jolted at her name.

"Kids these days. Off to college and—poof! The elderly are forgotten. Come here." She hobbled into the house as Carrie climbed two daunting porch steps. The woman returned, shaking a sheet of paper.

Carrie read the childish handwriting: "'I, Caroline Kruisselbrink, age eleven, being of sound mind, do solemnly swear to never kick, hit, bat, or roll a ball into Mrs. Gordon's flowerbed or step foot onto said sacred place, as long as I live, so help me God. June 1969.' Oh, my." Carrie looked up as the woman removed her sunglasses.

Mrs. Charlotte Rose Gordon. Nothing like her beautiful name, except for the thorns. Images washed over her: Carrie with Oma's next-door neighbor Jodi kicking to each other down the sidewalk, the ball rolling into the garden, flattening tulips, then old Mrs. Gordon, who'd always been old, shouting from the house. The fence appeared a week later.

That mishap would have brought their childhoods to a screeching halt, if not for the advocacy of Carrie's grandparents. Carrie deemed Mrs. Gordon a witch of the Hansel and Gretel variety, the Victorian home of stained glass and gingerbread trim enticing like candy. Carrie never walked that way again. Fortunately, it was blocks away from her grandparents' house, easy to avoid. Until today.

Here, eleven years later, sat a hunched shadow of the woman who'd stomped around the garden, smacking their ball with a broom. "Mrs. Gordon." Carrie smoothed her rattling voice. "Good to see you."

"Is it now?" Mrs. Gordon slipped her sunglasses back on, peering at her over the top.

"I'm sorry for the trouble." Under Mrs. Gordon's gaze, Carrie shrank to age six.

"I'd appreciate compensation beyond new bulbs. Finish reading."

Carrie clutched the paper. "'P.S. If I fail to keep this oath, I'll make it up to Mrs. Gordon as she sees fit.'"

The woman pointed to Carrie's feet. "You've failed your vow miserably. Today, you stood in my garden."

"You invited me."

"No such stipulations in this contract."

"I was eleven when I wrote that!"

"No statute of limitations, either."

Carrie flicked the paper. "I can't believe you saved this all these years."

"I heard about graduation and figured you'd visit your grandparents soon."

Had she perched on the porch for two weeks watching? Crazy lady. "Shall I plant more perennials? Read poetry?"

Belying her witching powers, the woman patted the wicker settee. "Come."

Carrie gingerly stepped up, the creak in each step like a squeal of derision. She sat.

Mrs. Gordon removed her sunglasses. Bags under her eyes stood out where a map of wrinkles had long ago settled in. "You'll help me clear my husband's name, God rest his soul."

"How?"

"In 1918, he was doomed to prison for a crime he didn't commit. He died of cancer before his trial."

Why was she revealing this? And why'd it matter now? "I don't see how to help."

"I need a scribe, good at research. You just graduated, so perfect timing. My eyes aren't what they used to be."

Oh, yes, they are. Just as beady as before. "Mrs. Gordon, I'm applying for summer jobs."

"I'm saving you from a summer of *fast food.*" With one tongue cluck, she relegated all fast food to the abyss.

"I accidentally trample your flowers, then owe you my entire summer?"

"You're a feisty one."

Carrie crossed her arms. "*I'm* the feisty one?"

"I'll pay you what you're worth."

Carrie shifted forward. "What am I worth to you, Mrs. Gordon?"

"What you don't realize" —her eyes bore into Carrie's— "is what *I'm* worth to *you.*"

"Meaning what?"

"Never mind. It's money that concerns you graduates." The

woman sighed, as if the old days were nothing but cherub children, apple pies, and sunflowers. "I'll pay double minimum wage every Friday for a forty-hour week. *If* I'm satisfied with your efforts."

"How'll you measure that?"

The woman resumed rocking. "One criterion you already meet. Spunk. You don't roll over upon meeting an obstacle."

That obstacle being Mrs. Gordon? She'd surely change her mind if witnessing Carrie's usual demeanor at home.

"Miss Caroline, you're in the right place at the right time."

"That's debatable."

"See? You have spunk. Like me. The only reason the Broderick Resort was so successful."

"That tearoom by the lake?"

"Yes, I take full credit. For what it *used* to be."

No wonder the woman disdained the notion of fast food. Such a fine piece of serendipity! Carrie could pick the woman's brain about best restaurant practices.

"Come at nine tomorrow with notebook and pen."

"I never said yes."

The woman slipped her sunglasses back on, eyes disappearing. "But you cannot say no." Not a command. She spoke as if it were destiny.

www.ingramcontent.com/pod-product-compliance
Lightning Source LLC
Chambersburg PA
CBHW060612100726
47907CB00006B/1588